MICHAEL

a novel of suspense

John Osborn

AuthorHouse™
1663 Liberty Drive, Suite 200
Bloomington, IN 47403
www.authorhouse.com
Phone: 1-800-839-8640

This book is a work of fiction. People, places, events, and situations are the product of the author's imagination. Any resemblance to actual persons, living or dead, or historical events, is purely coincidental.

First published by AuthorHouse 10/6/2008

ISBN: 978-1-4343-9578-8 (sc)

Library of Congress Control Number: 2008907170

Printed in the United States of America
Bloomington, Indiana

This book is printed on acid-free paper.

MICHAEL LORD IS THE SECOND son in a wealthy family where the father believes in primogeniture. Set in 1990 on the Lord family estate in Somerset where the family manages their forests and Brainware, their software development company, the story describes Michael's strategies at age twenty to become the inheritor of the Lord family fortune by his twenty-first birthday.

In a family brought up to ride, to sail and to rock climb Michael manages to demonstrate how he is a survivor and an opportunist where his future is concerned. Michael manages to merge studies, business opportunities, women, drugs, sex, plagiarism and family affairs in a variety of ways to advance his own future. Around this character of Michael, an intelligent but self-centred young man, the story describes the concerns and efforts of Anthony and Sylvia Lord, Michael's parents to understand their son as well as their three other children. The challenge of the second child in the Lord dynasty has been repeated in each previous generation.

Just after Michael's twenty-first birthday, when he partially achieves his annual objective the story concludes with Michael being pressured to find a supposed lost or hidden part of the Lord family inheritance. In his efforts to find this at all costs Michael ends up paying a high price.

Prologue

Michael Lord 1990

Michael Lord opened his eyes. Bright sunlight streamed through the tall windows of Fotheringham Manor. The first day of a new year thought Michael, and this is a special year. The man sprawled in the bed was twenty years young. He was young in years maybe but already bitter, reckless and callous. Born the second son in a wealthy family where his father was a traditionalist, a strong believer in primogeniture. His brother Geoffrey would inherit all of the estate and the software company. To make matters worse Geoffrey already had a son, one-year old Peter Lord.

In the early 1700s a Bristol merchant built Fotheringham Manor as a country estate. The house had been set in 1250 acres of rolling Somerset countryside with a home farm and several acres of woodland. The Lord family had lived on and off the estate through to late Victorian times with the usual rises and falls in fortune of most families. Until along came George Lord, and the family fortunes improved substantially. George Lord refurbished the house and set to work on the estate. Later,

George's son Desmond improved the estate. Desmond also learnt the basics for the company that his own son Anthony started. This was a software development company, and soon to become the property of eldest son Geoffrey. Life was a bitch thought Michael.

This year however thought Michael I will be twenty-one. Maybe that is a good omen. Something has to happen this year. I will make something happen this year said Michael to himself. With this positive thought Michael rolled out of bed and stood up, briefly. His head continued to roll with the after-effects of New Year's revels. The sunlight hurt his eyes - even though it was late afternoon.

'This year will be my year,' Michael prophesied to the mirror. 'By this time next year it will all be mine. I'll beat the lot of them. Nobody will get in my way.'

The gunshot made him jump, hold his head with pain, and involuntarily piss on the carpet. It was not a good start, but what the hell. 'Somebody will pay,' muttered Michael, almost as a New Year's resolution.

The House of Lord

Earlier that same morning, at the start of 1990, Sir Anthony Lord was sitting in his study and contemplating his future. Perhaps New Year's morning he mused was a good time for looking back and then looking forward. At that very moment Sir Anthony was a very successful man. In fact, the House of Lord had improved over the last three generations. So, thought Anthony, let's think back to Grandfather George because that is when the family really started to develop into today's world.

The Lord household had become landed gentry and established the estate on the Mendip Hills in Somerset back in the early 1700s. Over the next two hundred years the family fortunes had waxed and waned according to the character of the head of the family. Early in the 1900s George Lord substantially advanced the finances of the family.

George Lord, the eldest boy in the family, was born in 1880 in the heyday of Queen Victoria's reign. Following in the tradition of all the males in the Lord family George attended Bristol House at the age of seven. Bristol House was a very English Public School that had been established in 1793 by the merchants of Bristol as a preparatory and boarding school for sons of gentlemen.

At the age of eighteen George Lord joined the army as an artillery officer. Very soon George was off with the regiment to South Africa to fight the Boer. Whilst in South Africa George saw a lot of the countryside and learnt a lot about guerrilla fighting. In the rugged terrain George thought that method of fighting made a lot of sense, even though it was not the proper British way. Even in those rather traditional times thought Anthony grandfather was prepared to think and perceive smarter ways of doing things. But then he engineered a fortunate series of events for the Lord family.

George became fascinated with the country of South Africa and managed to stay on after the war. Through some hard work and lots of luck he made a small fortune in the diamond business. In 1905, with the untimely death of his father, George Lord returned home to the estate in Somerset as a very rich man. He became a partner in Lloyds, which seemed a sensible and secure place to invest his considerable fortune.

Although he hadn't been a dashing cavalryman he still commanded enough panache to sweep Virginia Milne off her feet. Virginia was the only daughter of Lord and Lady Exmoor who were minor gentry in the West Country. As a debutante, Virginia had come out at age 21 in 1904, and then had traveled extensively with her parents. She had done the Grand Tour of Europe and had visited India for two seasons. Whilst in India Virginia had visited the Imperial Forestry School at Dehra Dun in Uttar Pradesh and been shown many of the teak plantations. The practice of mixing farm crops into forestry plantations stayed in Virginia's mind as something that could be done back home on her father's estates. However, back home Virginia wasn't prepared to sit and just be a pretty lady for she persuaded her parents to let her go to Europe, where, unlike many young ladies of her time, Virginia spent two seasons mountaineering in Switzerland. This very modern and well-traveled young lady fascinated George Lord. He married Virginia Milne in 1908.

Anthony looked out of the study window. It wasn't the view he was contemplating but the world of his grandfather. Speaking to himself, but actually out loud to no one in particular, Anthony muttered, 'so Grandfather George made an impressive start to the Lord family fortune in the early 1900s. But after that he didn't sit on his hands. He put his money and his wife to work.' Anthony smiled to himself trying to picture anybody putting his Grandmother Virginia to work.

After seeing the Drakensburgs in South Africa George Lord himself had become fascinated by mountains. Coming from the relatively rolling countryside of Somerset the world of mountains opened up a new and fascinating vista. With his wife as an enthusiastic alpinist George and Virginia climbed and skied in Europe every year from 1909 until 1913. During this time Virginia managed to fit in having children and George managed to fit in building Fotheringham Manor on his estate.

Virginia gave birth to Desmond in 1910, to Harriet in 1912, to Veronica in 1913 and to Matthew in 1914. Fortunately Fotheringham Manor was built in the years 1908 to 1910 before the family expanded. Perhaps this was the "work" grandmother did in the early years thought Anthony as he imagined what their life must have been like. 'But just think,' Anthony said to the room, 'this happy and exciting world of family and pleasure came to a temporary halt in late 1914. Everyone in England thought the war would be over by Christmas and Grandfather George patriotically re-enlisted in 1914 as an artillery officer.'

Anthony recalled what he had heard from his father, his grandfather and his grandmother. His Grandfather George had died when Anthony was only six and so he couldn't really remember much about his grandfather's early years. It was Grandmother Virginia who had recounted much of this early family history to Anthony. Grandmother had told him that at the age of thirty-four, and having been out of the army for ten years, George spent the first part of the war in training. In 1915 High Command posted his regiment to France. After some time experiencing the horrors and stupidity of the western front George and his regiment were posted to fight with the Italians in the Dolomite Alps against the Austrians. Because George could ski and climb, as well as having artillery experience, he spent some time in the front lines with the Italian alpine troops. In the various skirmishes he got to know the Dolomites area and found he worked well with Italians. George was impressed with the mountaineering skill of the Italian alpine corps plus their courage.

Back in England from 1914 to 1918 Grandmother Virginia herself had taken over the running of the Lord estate. Having seen some of the forestry work done in India Virginia decided to expand that part of the estate. The Templeton family had been gamekeepers on the Lord estate since the beginnings of time. Although Albert Templeton was out fighting with her husband in Italy, Virginia spent long hours working with other members of the family to bring a traditional gentlemen's shooting estate into a more modern forest estate. Again, based on what she had seen in India Virginia thought the woodlands could combine hunting with products for the farm, and possibly even commercial timber.

Grandmother had mentioned that the children were growing up. My Dad Desmond was packed away to Bristol House School in 1917 but young Miss Harriet was proving a handful. Aunt Veronica and Uncle Matthew were still children during the Great War.

Grandfather George and Albert Templeton returned to Fotheringham Manor in 1919 to a different world. Virginia had continued to make changes to the estate. Although George was a strong traditionalist he was also open-minded and could see what his wife had planned. Virginia had even written something like a Management Plan for the forest, which was another idea she had seen in India. Albert Templeton had left the Lord estate as a huntsman's gamekeeper. Albert knew pheasants, trapping vermin, fox hunting and maybe openings in the forest for deer hunting. Now her ladyship had fences, tree nurseries, new kinds of trees and talk of a sawmill. It took Alfred a while to get used to the new world. It also took Albert a while to get used to his son Edward, who had been born in 1914.

His grandfather had had a very interesting young life thought Sir Anthony. Great changes were going on in England, in Europe, in fact in the whole world. Our family came through these formative years safely. It certainly put everything on a good footing for later events. Strong people.

However, in the 1920s and 1930s the Lord family went through some highs and lows. One of the highs came from my Dad Desmond. From Bristol House Desmond went to St. Johns College Oxford to study forestry and mathematics. Somewhat amazingly Desmond did well and graduated with a second in 1932. What was surprising, thought Anthony, was that Desmond survived College at all. Most of his spare time he spent in, on and up in flying machines. Although he only crashed twice he had to write his final exams with his left hand as his right arm was in a sling. After Desmond graduated he went to work officially for his father managing the estate, but in reality Desmond spent as much time as possible learning to fly. By 1939 he was a very competent pilot. Again, Anthony spun round in his chair and gazed out of the window, but this time he was seeing his dad as a dashing young pilot. Dashing like grandfather but driving flying machines rather than manipulating howitzers and field guns. Plenty of guts and drive in the family so far thought Anthony, but the family had its sad moments as well.

The New World of the 1920s was a tempestuous time for Aunt Harriet. Virginia could never understand her eldest daughter, and Harriet was already set in her ways when Grandfather George returned from the war. Like many young people in the 1920s, especially the girls with so few eligible men around, Harriet partied too hard and burnt herself out. To the sorrow of the family Harriet died in 1933 at age twenty-one from an overdose. George particularly took this death to heart. Having seen so many young people die this seemed such a senseless loss.

Veronica Lord followed in her mother's footsteps. Perhaps because of the death of Harriet in 1933 the Lord family went to holiday in Switzerland in 1934 and 1935. Desmond, Veronica and Matthew all learned to ski and climb, although Desmond would sooner have been flying off the peaks. Veronica became a proficient skier and she went to Cortina, Italy in 1936, 1937 and 1938. After one season of climbing with Italian guides Desmond cried off with work and flying and Matthew had now got his head buried in books or radio valves. With the family seemingly happily bonded together George and Virginia were really shocked in early 1939. At the age of twenty-six, after seven years in a shipping company in Bristol, Veronica Lord joined the W.R.N.S. 'She has never looked back,' said Anthony, 'and she has proved such a pillar of strength to the family later on.'

George and Virginia's youngest child, my Uncle Matthew, turned out to be the real brains in the family thought Anthony. Born at the start of World War I young Matthew was already a very inquisitive and dexterous child when his father returned home from Italy. Following in his brother's and father's footsteps Matthew went to Bristol House but was bright enough to skip one year and entered Cambridge University in 1931 at age seventeen. Matthew had enrolled to study science but quickly narrowed his field of learning down to physics, electronics and sound. When he graduated in 1937, complete with a PhD he was already quite an expert in radio, sound waves and communications technology.

So we came through the thirties thought Sir Anthony with mixed emotions. The house and the estate were in good hands. Grandmother, the Templetons and finally dad had brought both the farm and the forest to a productive state. Virginia's ideas and work had born fruit and already some of the early thinnings were helping with farm fencing, wagon repairs, as well as the usual sheep hurdles and pheasant coops. The Lloyds investments were paying well and the house was in good repair, but then came another wave of uncertainly for the family and the country. But before that all happened thought Anthony, dad found mum.

In 1938, when he is twenty-eight, Desmond could see World War II looming on the horizon. As a pilot Desmond predicted a different kind of war to the one in which his father fought. After some lengthy discussions with both his parents about family traditions and responsibilities Desmond speeded up his wooing. Anthony laughed to himself. With his head so much up in the clouds flying it is a wonder dad ever had time for any wooing. If he wasn't looping through the clouds he was talking to the trees on the estate. It's a wonder of all time that he found mum at all. Just think about it, Anthony asked himself.

Rosamund DeWinter was a beautiful and exotic young lady. She was also very very intelligent and dad was in awe of her. He was also head over heels in love with her but had been a little frightened to "pop the question". But then anyone would have been in awe of mum. She must have been a most enchanting lady.

Rosamund DeWinter was born in 1912 of French parents. She had come into the world in England but had been brought up in both England and France. Coming from intellectual parents Rosamund was fluently bilingual and highly educated in mathematics and statistics. She reveled in numerical puzzles and codes. She was a very studious young lady but a hopeless romantic about men in flying machines. In the end Desmond doesn't have to "pop the question" and he and Rosamund got married in 1938. Maybe I should have asked thought Sir Anthony who asked who? In a way they both had their heads up in the clouds.

In September 1939 when WWII broke out Desmond enlisted as a RAF pilot. Despite being twenty-nine he became a fighter pilot in the Battle of Britain. Late in 1940, very near the end of that nightmare threat, Desmond was shot down and severely broke a leg in the process. More serious for a pilot however, was the loss of the right arm and hand. Somewhat intelligently for the armed forces the RAF promptly redeployed Desmond in logistics, with his background in mathematics and forest management. Instead of managing blocks of forest Desmond managed blocks of stores, ammunition, airplanes and tried to have them moved efficiently from A to B. Towards the end of the war this process becomes quite sophisticated with the early days of Operations Research mathematical techniques.

While Desmond was active in the RAF sister Veronica was working at the Admiralty. Matthew worked as a boffin (lovely word thought Sir Anthony) in World War II and was very involved with radio communications and the early days of radar. Most intriguing of all was what mum did, and perhaps that is what upset her.

Very quietly Rosamund DeWinter was summoned to Bletchley. With her background in mathematics and statistics, and especially her ability with puzzles Rosamund becomes a natural talent with codes. Being completely bilingual also was a great asset. After the war Rosamund wouldn't talk about her work, perhaps because she knew the sad story behind so many brave people who died.

And just to add to the excitement thought Anthony I came along. Probably find old Granddad George insisted dad have a son and heir before he was allowed to fly. So I get born in 1940 while dad is up there trying to shoot down Germans. Mum is sending coded messages to places unknown in France. They still have time to produce brother Charles in 1941 and sister Stephanie in 1942 and the entire family survived the war. In fact by 1945 the Lord family was perhaps even better off. Dad has learned the basics behind my business and Uncle Matthew was into computers before anybody knew what they were. Matthew in fact had gone to the United States soon after the war ended to learn about something called ENIAC. Auntie Veronica, married to a Rear Admiral had some good contacts in the navy. Still, thought Anthony it took its toll on mum in the end.

During the 1940s, as the parents were busy, their grandparents George and Virginia had brought up all three Lord children. Rosamund's parents were both dead in France. Anthony particularly learnt a lot from his grandfather up to age six when George died in 1946. His Grandmother Virginia continued to strongly influence his life. Anthony went to prep and boarding Bristol House from 1947 to 1958 with his brother Charles following one year later.

Desmond and Rosamund supported both boys, and daughter Stephanie going to the Italian and French Alps in 1955, 1956 and 1957. With his injuries from the war Desmond could no longer climb but his mother Virginia went out to the Alps again, partly acting as a chaperone for young Stephanie. Anthony finished Public School with four 'A' levels and two 'S' levels in pure and applied mathematics. After some discussions with Uncle Matthew about computer developments in the United States Anthony went to Imperial College London to study mathematics and computer science from 1958-1962. Hard work and good fun thought Sir Anthony. London was a humming place in those days.

Dad had come back from the war very tired. He reverted back to his old profession as a Forester and continued to oversee his father's estate. His father, Grandfather George died in 1946 and that was quite a blow for dad. Life in the 1950s for Desmond and Rosamund was fairly quiet with the children at school. Grandmother Virginia remained a driving force in the family, which was just as well as Rosamund was becoming more and more eccentric.

Whereas I grew up successfully in the 1950s along conventional lines remembered Anthony, brother Charles took a different route looking for fame. Throughout their history the second child in the Lord family seems to resent being second. The family had been traditionally minded through the ages and the eldest and heir certainly came first and foremost in the minds of the parents. Just as Harriet Lord had struggled so did Charles. Having been conceived during the uncertainty of the Battle of Britain Charles grew up as a problem child. From his early days Charles demonstrated the Latin temperament he inherited from Rosamund, his mother. Expulsion from Bristol House was only prevented after lengthy pleas from Desmond. However, things came to a head in 1958. Charles had gone with his brother Anthony and sister Stephanie to the Alps in 1955, 1956, and 1957. Whilst in the Alps Charles had become an avid and brilliant climber. In 1958, in his last year of school at age 17 Charles went alone to the French Alps for some big climbs in Chamonix. There Charles met a soul mate in Helene Forcier. Although she was only eighteen Helene was also a brilliant climber. So when I went to London University brother Charles kept very quiet during that last year planning what he would do. He did finish school but he went straight to France, partly to avoid the draft in England, but more to climb. Charles and Helene did some big climbs and celebrated by getting Helene pregnant. So, while I was starting to grind my way through University thought Anthony my brother Charles is living in a different world. Unfortunately Helene miscarried in 1959 but she and Charles produced a baby son Marcel in 1960. Despite pleas from his family, including a determined visit from his sister Stephanie, Charles stayed in France climbing. While still actively climbing at a very high level another son Henri is born 1961 and a daughter Giselle in 1962.

Poor mum though, thought Anthony. I was doing well at school. In fact, after graduating from London University I went and did a crash

PhD at Berkley, California from 1963-1964 in computer science and that thought Anthony was bloody hard work and not fun. Everyone may rave about being at Berkley in the '60s and tuning out but I slogged my bloody brains out. Worth it though he thought. Meanwhile mum was still suffering from both the war and the tantrums of Charles. Fortunately Stephanie was more or less at home and could help. Stephanie Lord had grown up close to her brother Charles and really loved him despite his tantrums. After finishing High School Stephanie enrolled at Bristol University, just down the road so to speak, and studied Veterinary Science from 1961-1964 intending to be a country vet. And then I come home to stir things up again with Sylvia and the roof falls in thought Anthony.

Anthony remembered how he had come back from the States in 1964 full of ideas, enthusiasm and American go-go-go. Perhaps as a contrast to the longhaired blond chicks of the West Coast Anthony found the soft voice and dark curls of Sylvia Trelawney irresistible. Anthony thought back. While at Imperial College he had climbed on several weekends up in North Wales. There he had met Sylvia but she was just one of a bunch of young University students up there climbing and drinking. However, when he met her in 1964 when he was down climbing in Cornwall it was a different matter. Sylvia came from a family who had been in the china clay business in Cornwall for a long time. She had gone from High School in St. Austell to the London School of Economics where she studied from 1960 to 1964. The meeting on the cliffs at Bosigran was a meeting of minds. There followed a whirlwind of meetings, romance and marriage with Anthony Lord and Sylvia Trelawney in late 1964. And then what did we do, so young and hopelessly naïve? We charged into the establishment of Brainware Pty Co. to produce software solutions for small business. Perhaps we did get in at the right time as the business gradually expanded into several different specialties, including security, communications, and encryption following in the steps of my father and mother, and abetted by Uncle Matthew. And, thought Anthony, we have continued to manage the company through 1990 very successfully.

Yes, thinking back, 1964 was a good year. Sylvia got on well with Grandmother Virginia but she found Rosamund a little strange. She also got on well with dad while he was still alive. The brief time she met him she had no time for Charles. Not surprisingly, thought Sir Anthony, she got on well with sister-in-law Stephanie, but then everyone gets on well with Steph.

Stephanie Lord had graduated from College in 1964. Still very much attached to both her dad and mum she went into practice locally and didn't marry. In 1965 Stephanie went out to Chamonix to see Charles and Helene. Although unsuccessful in pleading with her brother to come home Stephanie did meet Marcel, Henri and Giselle.

The good news of 1964 was followed by some better news in 1965. Sylvia gave birth to Geoffrey, another male in the line of the House of Lord. All of the family seemed to be doing well until that fateful year of 1966.

Having seen the family safely into the next generation Grandmother Virginia decided she had done enough and quietly died in 1966 at the grand old age of eighty-three. All of the family was there except Charles. Two days before Virginia died the family heard that Charles and Helene had been killed in a tragic climbing accident in the French Alps. This news hit the family hard and Desmond had a stroke from which he never really recovered. He died two years later in 1968 at age of fifty-eight.

In 1966, when Charles and Helene were killed, Stephanie took on the adoption of Marcel, aged six, Henri, aged five and Giselle at four. With the death of Charles, who was perhaps most like his mother, Rosamund didn't die but her mind became further deranged. She was in no fit state to take over looking after Charles's children. Anthony remembered how he and Sylvia had been very supportive of Stephanie's action in this binding together of the family.

This series of setbacks led into the relative stability of the 1970s thought Anthony. Now this is where Sylvia and I made some real progress. Uncle Matthew was really supportive and very knowledgeable in where the computer industry may go. Matthew's own company was primarily involved in the production of computer hardware, which included mainframes and minicomputers. However, Matthew foresaw the development of personal computers and a real change into hands-on development. Inevitably this led to the need for systems maintenance, better security and the gradual development of distributed systems. Anthony and Sylvia listened to Matthew, plus landing some naval contracts through Aunt Veronica, and Brainware did very well expanding in the '70s. In addition, as computers entered more and more into the life of many institutions, people started to pay attention to information security and this led to encryption. Not quite back to the days of mum and dad thought Anthony although the concepts were the same, but now the systems of security were digital.

In addition to expanding the company in the 1970s Anthony and Sylvia also expanded the family. We had four children thought Anthony; Geoffrey, Michael, Samantha, and Daniel.

Geoffrey Lord, the eldest son, went to Bristol House from 1972 up to 1983. Anthony remembered working hard with Sylvia during the rest of the sixties and Michael wasn't born until 1969. As soon as he was seven Michael was sent away to Bristol House too. With two older brothers Samantha Lord, who was born in 1972, grew up to be a tomboy, even though her mother tried to have her grow up as a lady. Samantha was always competitive thought Anthony; she always wanted to be first. And then there was Daniel, who was Sylvia's pride and joy. Sylvia sort of gave up on Samantha mused Anthony, perhaps because her daughter was too much like her mother. Daniel grew up as the baby in the family and Sylvia must have made her mind up that Daniel was to be the last, and hers.

Well, thought Anthony, we introduced the children into most pursuits, at least the athletic ones. None of the family had ever been artistic, or even scholarly and outdoor pursuits came easier to the Lord family. From the earliest age all four of them learnt to ride. Sylvia took them down to her parents in Cornwall and they all went sailing. Anthony managed a week away down in Cornwall too and he and Sylvia relived some earlier times teaching the children to rock climb on the rough granite of Cornwall's sea cliffs. However, after the tragedies of Charles Anthony didn't pursue this too hard. Daniel was only five when they first went climbing in Cornwall and was not keen at all. Geoffrey, as a serious teenager, climbed conservatively and was ultra cautious. Michael at age nine was his typical reckless self. Samantha took to it like a natural and both Sylvia and Anthony watched carefully.

Soon after the events of 1966 Auntie Veronica re-asserted herself. At the end of the war Veronica had married an older Rear Admiral. Reginald Bassett died early in the sixties leaving Veronica a very rich fifty-year old widow. Veronica came down from London and invested part of her fortune in Brainware Pty Co., and in addition she bought a cottage on the Dart estuary. Reginald Bassett had gone to Dartmouth College like most English naval officers and both he and Veronica had spent many happy days on the river Dart.

Aunt Veronica's cottage on the river Dart was unimaginatively called 'Riverside', but it did come with an anchorage and a yacht. Stephanie had always enjoyed sailing and she took Marcel, Henri and little Giselle down to Riverside soon after the events of 1966. Marcel was just six years old. His earlier uncertain upbringing caused him to resent his parents and he wanted to be as different as possible. Life down with Auntie Veronica was really different and Marcel took to sailing like a duck to water. Although trying to be different from his parents Marcel retained a strong Gallic streak in being highly competitive. Over time Anthony reminded himself young Marcel became a highly successful competitive yachtsman.

Whereas Marcel spent as much time as he could down in Devon his brother Henri stayed happily with his sister and Aunt Stephanie around Bristol. It was only when he became a teenager that Henri started to stray thought Anthony, but then most teenagers struggle to find themselves. Young Giselle didn't really remember her parents and grew up as a youngster close and safe with Auntie Stephanie and her menagerie of veterinary friends.

And over the past ten years thought Anthony the kids have grown up and have changed. Perhaps we all have changed he thought. Some of the old folks are gone. Mum had died just three years ago in 1987 at age 75 but she hadn't really been with us for some time. Auntie Veronica is seventy-seven and still pottering around at Riverside. Uncle Matthew sold his company and retired but his brain still keeps producing new ideas. I really should put him on some sort of retainer though Anthony but he would be offended.

Charles and Helene's three children were just that much older than Sylvia's and mine. The older three exhibited both a Gallic and competitive streak from their parents. His sister Stephanie hadn't been able to keep up with the whirlwind of Marcel. Not only did Marcel give up on school and become a competitive sailor but he also met and married Marie Dauphin in 1980. In short order Marie gave birth to Jean Lord in 1981 and Philippe in 1982. Marcel and Marie settled in Dartmouth where Marie tried to baby the two boys but they both rebelled. It didn't help, thought Anthony, that brother-in-law Henri spent too much time with Marie while Marcel was away sailing. To escape Uncle Henri Jean desperately wanted to emulate his father as a sailor but inside he was afraid. With Jean escaping to the river as often as possible Henri takes out his bullying on poor Philippe. And it is somewhat surprising thinks Anthony that it is Michael who acts as a protector for Philippe.

Living in Bristol as a teenager Henri Lord escaped the confines of Aunt Stephanie by scrambling off to the cliffs of Cheddar Gorge. Henri inherited the talents of his parents and became a bold climber. The rather loose and vegetated rocks became a happy playground for him. In the late eighties Henri took off with a group of fellow climbers for some serious artificial climbing in the Dolomites. Within the Lord family what goes around comes around thought Anthony. Family members are back playing where grandfather was in his youth.

And what of my own children thought Anthony that New Year's morning? Geoffrey seems a steady sort of chap. Traditionally he had gone to Bristol House from 1972 to 1983, but after that Geoffrey had gone to Oxford University. However, unlike his Grandfather Desmond Geoffrey had graduated in 1987 with a MBA. Perhaps not quite as dynamic as Desmond or even myself he thought, and certainly not as intellectual as Uncle Matthew but son Geoffrey is okay. Anthony employed Geoffrey on his graduation in the business end of the company. With new rules and regulations coming out of Europe the business end needed to be up to date. It could be useful that Geoffrey married a European, because in 1988 Geoffrey married Christina DeLucci, from an Italian family in the import/export business. In keeping with the Lord family tradition Geoffrey and Christina produced a son Peter, who was born in 1989.

Sylvia walked into the study and smiled at her husband. 'Early in the year for such a gloomy face,' she said, and she walked behind Anthony and rubbed the back of his neck and shoulders.

'That's good,' he said, 'please don't stop.'

'So why the serious face on this bright sunny morning?'

'I was going back over the history of the family to determine where we are.'

'And it was that frightening a history that you had to wear that face?'

'No,' laughed Anthony, 'it has been a very successful history to tell you the truth. The House of Lord is a family of substance.'

'Well, it certainly improved its fortunes when it joined up with the older, better-established House of Trelawney,' said Sylvia.

'Come here you and learn to speak better to your elders.'

'Oh, going to come the older statesman are we? Actually love, you're right we have done well and the future looks bright.'

'Yes, but the reason for the "face" as you put it was I had reached Michael.'

'Well, I'm glad you can because I sure can't. That lad has some serious problems and I can't seem to talk with him.'

'Nor me, and that is part of my gloomy face. I almost feel we are back to the unfortunate tradition of the Lord family. Through the generations the second child has been a problem.'

'Can't Michael accept the fact that Geoffrey is his older brother? It is a fact and nothing can change it.'

'Yes, I thought he understood that. Back four years ago when Geoffrey turned twenty-one we held that family party and by tradition we pledged the future of the House of Lord to the heir, the oldest son in the family.'

'Yes, Michael was there. He was sixteen and he certainly understood what the event was all about.'

'He certainly didn't seem too pleased though. He thought all this tradition was a load of outdated cock. He mentioned to Samantha that he thought the family estate should be divided up more equitably. He challenged her to stand up for her share.'

'I didn't hear that,' said Sylvia.

'No, neither did I directly,' said Anthony looking up into his wife's face. 'Actually I overheard it from Daniel. He was talking with Stephanie.'

'And so we have a challenge with Michael?'

'Yes my love and that is why I had a gloomy face when you walked in. I had come quite happily through from 1900 to 1988 and then stumbled.'

Michael Lord was born in 1969 and went to Bristol House until 1988. Just as his dad had done Michael went to London University (and to Imperial College like his father) to study mathematics and electronics. In many ways Michael echoed the youth of his father, and like Anthony Michael is both intelligent and gifted. But Michael also has a touch of his Grandfather Desmond in him, and perhaps even his Great Grandfather George. He is reckless, and often thoughtless. Like all the four Lord children Michael can sail and rock climb. While at London University Michael sailed at Burnham on Crouch in Essex. He competed in University races there. Perhaps because of the memory of brother Charles, Anthony and Sylvia had always been conservative in their teaching the kids to climb. So, on the rock Michael was only a moderate rock climber but he had strength and good endurance. However, he was still reckless. When Cousin Henri climbed with Anthony's children Henri isn't impressed with the slow, methodical Geoffrey or the erratic nature of Michael. Henri tried to get Daniel to understand climbing and warned him of Michael's recklessness.

'The gloom over Michael is really one of a lack of communication,' said Anthony.

'That is also something of a problem with Samantha,' said Sylvia.

'Yes, but at the moment she is being taught by someone else at the Lycee in Switzerland.'

'Too true, and at our expense.'

'Yes my love, but we have been through that before. We both agreed that Samantha would develop better away from the pressures of this household.'

'Anthony, you thought so. Samantha tends to twist you around her little finger. Samantha thought it would be a great idea to be away from her mother, and rules.'

'Sylvia, how can you say that? We both agreed.'

'Darling, I agreed when I saw there was no point in arguing. Once Samantha told you what she was going to do you caved in and I couldn't, or wouldn't fight you both.'

'Sylvia, you're so practical. Where would I be without you?'

'Anthony, you may be the smart and innovative one in the family but I'm the one from L.S.E. with both feet on the ground dealing with the realities of life. My family was in china clay remember; muck from the ground, practical, real.'

'I give in,' laughed Anthony. 'So, what are your thoughts on young master Daniel?'

'He struggles Anthony. All three of his older brothers and sisters seem so much older than him. Like Jean, Daniel is a little afraid of the ocean and rock climbing worries him. Geoffrey tends to ignore him as just a kid and Michael bullies him. Samantha has no time for people who won't compete against her so poor Daniel is a bit of a loner.'

'Well, let's not turn him into a mummy's boy,' said Anthony.

'Heh buster, watch your language. I can still outsail you and outclimb you so watch who you're calling a mummy's boy.'

'Peace, peace,' said Anthony holding up his arms in surrender. 'I stand corrected, my Lord.'

'No Anthony, you're my Lord,' said Sylvia, and she came around the chair and sat in Anthony's lap. 'Happy New Year love.'

'Mmm, yes, Happy New Year, and the next question is will it be?'

'As you said before, 'said Sylvia,' I don't see why not? Take stock. The house is in good condition. We modernized the kitchen, we resealed the roof, and you had all the windows checked last year. The farm is going really well and the work that Stephanie does on genetics with the sheep has proven very valuable. As long as we keep abreast of any new genetic breeding regulations that part of the family should be making money for years to come. The forest is finally coming into some really good production.'

'Yes, but we need to watch the staff there,' warned Anthony. 'Norton Ferris isn't the most reliable of people and he is in charge now after Ronald O'Rourke got killed.'

'Yes, but you brought in Jeffers as a professional forester.'

'Only as a consultant and as a professional to author the Forest Management Plan.'

'Perhaps you should hire another professional forester?'

'No, Geoffrey is supposed to oversee the entire estate and he hasn't suggested it. I'll let him decide what should be done. He has to learn how to manage people as well as businesses.'

'But the sawmill is doing well?'

'Yes, we installed that new machinery two years ago when there was a lot of timber on the market. With a narrower saw kerf the lumber yield is better, and we have upgraded the kilns.'

'So, that just leaves the Company, and that couldn't be better. We have four new contracts taking us into 1990 and that new work from Luke is supposed to be state of the art. What was it he called it?'

'It is called Distributed Processing. It's like, well sort of like doing lots of things in multiples of parallel. You remember your basic understanding of serial processing and parallel processing?'

'Yes Anthony. In fact our sawmill is serial processing with the logs going through one at a time up the green chain.'

'Right, good example, and then they found certain things could be done in parallel in computers.'

'Yes, Uncle Matthew explained how his company made array processors.'

'Yes, well multiply that thought in a way and imagine a whole multitude of very small, low-level processors all working away at the same time.'

'Like an army of monkeys typing Shakespeare?'

'No,' Anthony laughed, 'not quite, but a good effort. In techie terms imagine you divide the work up among several processors, in fact among a network of virtual agents you created within the computer. The individual agents don't have to be big or very clever individually but altogether they produce something valuable.'

'You mean like an army of ants in the forest. Each of them is small, not exceptionally clever, but all combined they are one of the most important processes in the forest and very effectively break down complex tissue into smaller parts.'

'Actually, that is a very good analogy. More importantly Luke tells me this form of processing is likely to be a major building block in neural networks and artificial life as in robotics.'

'Some time ago I thought you said that Artificial Intelligence was dead. What was the headline, "the Eighties saw the death of A.I"?'

'Right, but that was A.I., and I am talking about Artificial Life. Rules, so many rules killed A.I. and the computer programmes bogged down in millions of lines of code. They literally tied themselves in knots, or loops from which they couldn't get out, but this is different. Luke explained that this new programming is designed or written for the smallest elements, those at the bottom of the hierarchy. So you tell the individual agents at the bottom level how to behave but you never tell, or program the entire system. Because the system as a whole is never defined you can get surprising results. Sometimes these results are not what you expected, which is why they appear "lifelike".'

'So my little ants in the forest all know individually what to do but no-one ever wrote the specs for an anthill.'

'Hey, that's good. You're good.'

'Lover boy, I've always told you I'm good. Now you tell me my little old ants in the forest are so smart that one day I will get ant-hills looking like skyscrapers because no- one told them to build them flat.'

'Enough, enough of the ants; I'm just telling you that Luke wants to use this technology on the new contract for the robotics controllers.'

'And what about us, you and me Anthony; how will we fare in 1990?' Sylvia wrapped her arms around her husband's neck and kissed him gently on the lips.

Anthony looked up into the smiling face of his wife and whispered, 'Lord knows.'

2

Broken Hearts

'I'll be there, I'll be there,' said Michael into the telephone, 'trust me, I'll find you.'

A long flurry of excited female vocals whistled down the telephone wires and Michael held the handle at arms length for a moment until the pace slowed a little and the volume scaled down.

'Yes, yes, I'm coming with Veronica. It's her friends who invited us.'

Another verbal barrage filled Michael's ears before he could get a word in.

'It will be a big party and people will be all over the house so we'll meet somewhere.'

Finally, after another lengthy listening session Michael managed to ring off. He looked around the room of his flat and relaxed back into the armchair. 'Christ, women,' he muttered, 'as the cliché goes you can't live with them and you can't live without them.' However, having a fiancée, a mistress, and a very loving friend can be a little stressful he thought.

For a bachelor Michael's flat was exceptionally neat and tidy, but that was in keeping with Michael's character. He liked to keep both objects and people in their correct places and mix and match as he pleased.

While studying mathematics and electronics at London University Michael liked to spend his spare time mixing and matching, especially with women. And, as he was very intelligent Michael found he had quite a lot of spare time.

That morning Michael had driven up from the family home in Somerset and organized his next couple of months at Uni. The timetable for coursework and practicals was already set from his registration in September and so most of the organization dealt with how to best use the spare time. As Michael had made a very ambitious New Year's Resolution there was a fair amount of strategic planning to consider: making it "all mine" required some careful thought and even more careful action.

'And tonight,' Michael said to his room, 'tonight will be a start, or really a continuation of financial strategy number one – namely how to marry into money.' Although Michael's family was very well off it was Lord family money and not under Michael's control and that was what Michael needed. 'I think that Veronica Matheson will be a very welcome contributor to the Michael Lord benevolent fund,' he told the wall. 'Maybe tonight we will stir up the jealous juices a little and persuade young Veronica that I will be a real trophy for her and she will prove to be everlastingly grateful.'

With this thought in mind Michael padded around the flat slowly getting ready for this night's party. Michael decided that he didn't need anything chemical to stimulate or sustain him that evening as he might need to keep his wits about him. With three of his women all in the same house it may be wise to be very aware and quick to move.

Outside, rather typically for a January evening in London, it rained. Cold rain and orange fluorescent streetlights cast a surreal vista along the little canyons of the city. Pedestrians hurried along trying to avoid being splashed. Motorists aggressively carved their ways through a network of wet roads. Everyone was engrossed in their own space.

Alan Matheson drove his Jaguar swiftly and surely into the spacious garage beside his house. He was a vigorous fit man who prided himself on getting things done. As a skilled refrigeration engineer Alan was the works manager for Matheson Storage. He was also the owner, a self-made man. Alan parked his car neatly alongside the compact silver BMW. Passing by it to enter the house he ran his hand smoothly over the bright bonnet and smiled as he thought of its owner.

Inside the house, Veronica his daughter, and the owner of the BMW, put the final touches to the table silverware. When Veronica's mother ran off ten years ago Veronica had become the mistress of the house. At twenty-two Veronica was an athletic young woman. She had inherited her father's drive but her mother's emotions. Maria Matheson had been a hopeless romantic and had run off with her dancing teacher. Alan had spent a fortune, and a large amount of time trying to find them and bring Maria home, but to no avail. The thrill and romance of the tango had overwhelmed the efficiency of automatic defrosting devices. Perhaps telling Maria that the tango was a whore's dance from Argentina didn't make much impression on Maria's decision. Maria in turn just told him that he was as square and as cold as his bloody refrigerators and that ended any further discussion. Alan now turned his personal love and protection full force onto his daughter.

'Dinner in half an hour; shall I fix you a drink?'

'Thanks Veronica. I'll have a large whiskey please. Just let me wash up and I'll be right there.'

'No rush Daddy, everything's under control. I'm not going out until much later.'

Water ran in the washbasin as Alan washed off some of the grime of London. Taking a quick glance in the mirror he smoothed his hair and straightened his tie. Even though he was a hands-on manager Alan

Matheson prided himself on his professional appearance. Just because you got your hands dirty didn't mean you couldn't look neat and tidy.

Entering the dining room Alan gave his daughter a full-hearted hug. Holding her at arms length he looked at the young woman. Veronica looked her father up and down and got her gibe in first.

'Heh, what's this all about? You look very smart for a freezer fixer.'

'No cheek from you young lady. Freezer fixer is not quite the right description for the owner of one of the largest refrigeration manufacturers in the business. But, how about you then? What's the special occasion for you look really lovely tonight?'

'I'm taking Michael to a party at Lord Dampier's house in Chelsea.'

'You mean the Lord Dampier?'

'Yes and no Daddy. The party's at his house but I believe the Lord Dampier is elsewhere. His son Charles organized the party. We met Charles last summer at Chamonix, don't you remember?'

'Yes I remember young Charles Dampier. He wasn't much of a climber was he?'

'No, but then this isn't an Alpine meet Daddy, it's a house party.'

'Whilst his Lordship is away I presume?'

'Of course. I don't think Lord and Lady Dampier would like the music.'

'I don't think Lord and Lady Dampier would like anything else about the party but then it's not my house.'

'Don't be such a fuddy duddy Daddy. Drink your whiskey and relax before dinner.'

Alan sat down and relaxed as instructed. He took a swallow of his whiskey and looked again at his daughter. 'You really are quite a remarkable young lady Veronica. Michael Lord is a very lucky young man. You make your father very happy. Where would I be without you?'

Veronica pondered. Where would she be? Where could she be? Veronica was engaged to Michael Lord, the son of Sir Anthony Lord. The wedding was scheduled for December, right after Michael's twenty-first birthday. Michael was young, restless and full of spirit. He was just the kind of white knight that Veronica desired. The pair rode together, climbed together, and sailed together. Veronica had learnt to rock climb from her father. Alan was an enthusiastic mountaineer as well as a spelunker. He had taken Veronica several times to the Alps and to most of the major climbing centres in England. Michael had whirled Veronica off to the cliff, to bed, to the cliff, and back to bed again in an explosion of energy. It was wild and Veronica couldn't get enough of Michael Lord. Daddy was okay but a bit too possessive for a father. What Veronica did not know was that Michael could also be quite possessive.

Michael Lord in the meantime couldn't get enough of Danielle Made. With her mother Danielle had escaped from the horrors of Mozambique three years ago. Before she left Mozambique, however, Danielle had learned a lot about life, especially life for a young sensual black woman. Danielle had brought these experiences to England and Michael Lord was eager to learn. Danielle had thought she could snare Michael by having a child. In many ways she was successful. She had a son by Michael and little Anthony was now four months old. What Danielle did not realize was that Michael would never marry her. The colour was wrong. However, Michael was not going to let any marriage interfere with his sex life, and Danielle was slotted to stay the exotic mistress, at least in Michael's mind. Danielle had other ideas, but she had learnt to be patient. She would bide her time and carefully plan an appropriate future for young Michael and her son Tony.

And then, whirling along on the sidelines there was Melanie Rogers, an American party girl. Bella Turner joined Melanie Rogers on a crash course from the sophistication of coastal California to the wilds of the West End. Much of the crash came from drugs. Raised on their parent's tales of Timothy Leary both girls lived much of their lives in the kaleidoscope world of chemicals. Michael's interest in colours was more specific. He liked black, as in Danielle. He also liked green, as in money. The interest in Melanie Rogers was distinctly green. Melanie Rogers' father was CEO of Future Graphics, one of the largest and richest computer graphics companies in Silicon Valley. Melanie was rich, and Michael was in need of the green.

Michael's strategy was fairly comprehensive and he liked to hedge his bets over the money side. Originally, and still basically, Veronica Matheson with her doting rich father was a very good objective. Michael thought that this objective was very straightforward with the union of two well-established, rich English companies. He had met with Alan Matheson on several occasions and shown that he had the dash, flair, and skills to meet Alan's expectations for his daughter's beau. Both families had met and there seemed to be a mutual admiration or at least respect for each other's successes. Michael felt he was nearly home and dry with this objective. But, just in case something went wrong, Michael was keeping Melanie Rogers definitely in his sights. It had been a rather high Melanie that Michael had been talking to on the telephone earlier.

While Veronica was efficiently serving dinner for her father and herself Michael was admiring his own reflection in the mirror. It's all a matter of timing, he said to his image. You have to programme events in a neat sequence with ad hoc actions to hand if events screw up. If I learnt anything in electronics it is that random events can cause some disturbing ripples in the current. But, Michael said, as he leaned forward and contemplated the colour of his tongue, I have also learnt how to charge up the situation or dampen it down, so I'm still the controller. Satisfied that he looked a desirable party animal and that his brain was completely in gear Michael put on his coat and left his flat.

Because Veronica was driving that evening Michael took the tube over to her father's house. The rain continued to fall and dampen everyone's mood but Michael was feeling exceptionally light-hearted as he rang the bell. The challenge of this evening's juggling act stimulated Michael's sense of adventure. It was like being on a rock climb and facing a whole series of difficult moves. You had to look and think through how you were going to carry on, and that challenge caused an adrenaline rush to course through Michael's veins.

'Good evening Mr. Matheson. It's good to see you again sir.'

'Hello Michael, Happy New Year to you. I hope the trip down home was successful?'

'Really good actually Mr. Matheson. The whole family was down at Fotheringham and dad and mum had had a good year so they were in a very happy mood.'

'Was Samantha there too?' asked Veronica. 'I seem to remember her having a falling out with your mother especially.'

'No, your right Veronica, my rebellious sister was skiing on her school team in Switzerland and decided that she needn't come home for Christmas. Mum was a little worried and dad was quite concerned but then Samantha does as Samantha pleases. She did send the family a Christmas card to say she was thinking of us all but Samantha loves to compete.'

'And to win,' said Alan Matheson.

'Yes,' said Michael, 'that tends to run in the family or parts of it at least. Mum is far more aggressive than dad and Samantha picked that trait up and ran with it.'

'You told me she used to beat you Michael,' said Veronica with a twinkle in her eye.

'I never did,' said Michael, but he smiled as he turned towards Veronica. 'I told you she could give me a good run for my money but she never beat me.'

'Even in the slalom?' asked Veronica, still smiling as she twisted the knife a little.

'Heh young lady, you're in a very combative mood tonight,' said Michael lightly. 'Mr. Matheson, is there a reason for this aggressive behaviour from your daughter tonight? She seems to want to joust, or spar at least.'

Alan Matheson smiled as he watched the two young people try and score points off each other. He liked Michael. He knew that Michael liked to compete as much as his sister Samantha did, and that Michael liked to win too. But Michael hadn't blown his own trumpet about that, merely gently sparred with Veronica. And he also knew that Veronica really loved Michael and wouldn't have been so challenging if she had felt otherwise. They make a great couple he thought, even if Veronica is my only family left. I will have to think how events will unfold he thought to himself, but then any wedding is a year away.

Veronica eased the silver BMW out of the basement garage and slowly drove down the road. Streetlights continued to glisten in the pools of water over the surface. 'Today or tomorrow?' asked Michael.

'What, what did you say?' asked Veronica.

'I said, today or tomorrow,' replied Michael, 'and I was alluding to the party.'

'Michael, if you haven't noticed the streets are wet and with the temperature running around freezing there are patches of ice. So, so we get there in one piece I'm being rather careful, capicse?'

'Sure, sure, but I do want to get there. Do you want me to drive?'

'Get stuffed Michael. I'm quite capable to getting you there tonight, before you turn into a fairy or whatever. Anyway, what's the rush?

The house won't go away and the party will probably last well into tomorrow.'

The party was in Chelsea. Lord Dampier's son had taken over his father's house while his parents were cruising in the Caribbean. A little bash for his friends seemed in order. It was a chance to lighten the January gray of London. Over a hundred young people talked, smoked, drank, snorted, and puked throughout Lord Dampier's house. Set behind high brick walls the party community was a little island of its own. The throbbing music stayed inside the walls and the copulating couples stayed inside the beds, for the most part.

Michael had lost Veronica early on in the evening. It was that kind of party.

'Michael,' breathed a valley voice. 'Where have you been?'

Melanie. You're just the person I've been looking for.'

'Well Michael, I hope I look as beautiful as you do. You're all swirly blue and orange stripes, like a marmalade cat swimming in an ultramarine pool. Do you purr and lick, or lash your tail and show claws?'

'Come with me Melanie and we'll find out whether I can do both.'

Her silent laughter rippled through her body under the sheath dress and Michael moved closer.

'Willingly,' Melanie murmured as the acid raced around her head and a menage of cats writhed behind her eyes.

Lord Dampier's House was a large four-storey townhouse and so it was a while before Veronica found Michael. He was flat on his back, naked. Straddled over him was a demanding Melanie, alternately purring and howling.

'Michael. Michael!'

Veronica's voice went up in decibels.

'Michael,' she shrieked.

Melanie screeched in concert, but certainly not in harmony.

'Go away, he's mine,' the cat murmured. To prove it the cat lady gyrated her hips, which caused Michael to react. 'All mine.' Melanie purred contentedly.

Veronica swung a fist. It never landed. Sitting bolt-upright Michael's hand seized the wrist. Without losing Melanie off his lap Michael cruelly twisted Veronica's wrist.

'Piss off. Go find your own trip.'

'You bastard; you outright fucking bastard.'

Veronica grabbed Melanie's hair with her free hand and jerked. The cat lady howled. Erotic pain was displaced by electric shocks. It was becoming a bum trip.

'Bugger off Veronica. You're not wanted here. You're not wanted anywhere. Just piss off home to Daddy.' Michael's hand came up fast and pushed Veronica violently away. Melanie slithered backwards and ended up rubbing her tongue over Michael's chest, purring again.

Veronica screamed and staggered backwards.

'No, no, no,' she sobbed, and rushed from the room.

Michael smiled and stroked the cat lady's hair. Very slowly, with a lot of hand movements, the two of them resumed their original positions.

In Chelsea a slammed BMW door disturbed no one. The squealing tyres were not uncommon either. The accelerated engine did echo down the empty wet street but didn't waken anybody. The crash at the T-junction and the ensuing fiery explosion did. Response and rescue however, came too late. Veronica Matheson was pronounced dead at the scene of the accident. The officer-in-charge later called Alan Matheson and asked him to come and identify the charred remains of his beloved daughter.

Michael ran his fingernails down Melanie's back, moved his hips, and thought of Danielle. About three hours later Michael's thoughts and actions were rudely disturbed.

Alan Matheson came out of the morgue with very mixed feelings. He carried an enormous sorrow for the abrupt loss of his beloved and delightful daughter. Perhaps even more than the loss of his wife, the death of Veronica hit him hard in the heart. When Maria ran off Alan's pride was hurt as well as his heart. After the long but futile efforts to persuade his wife to return Alan realized that his pride could be salvaged in both success in the business and in the championing of his daughter. He put his heart aside and channeled his love towards his daughter as a proud and supportive parent. And now, thought Alan, the life of this precious child has been extinguished. What I can't understand he thought was how the accident happened. According to the police no other vehicles were involved; there were no hazards Veronica swerved to avoid; and a preliminary examination indicated alcohol was not a cause. So how or perhaps why did this all happen? Alan knew that Veronica was normally a very safe and competent driver. He wouldn't have bought her such a powerful car if he didn't know so. Why was she driving so fast on such an icy and slippery road? The officer-in-charge at the scene wouldn't give him any details but Alan overheard a comment about there being no skid marks. It sounded as if Veronica just drove straight through the T-junction deliberately, and that Alan could not understand. Perhaps Michael might know something thought Alan.

Alan stood outside the doors to Lord Dampier's House. He was about to knock when the doors were flung open and a couple came rushing out in a flurry of arms, legs, and semi-detached clothing. Alan stepped aside quickly before he was engulfed in the melee. 'Quite obviously Lord and Lady Dampier are not at home,' muttered Alan to himself, 'or maybe the butler has found a new way of helping people leave.' Inside the house Alan found several repeats of the incident at the doorway but after a few moments he caught sight of Charles Dampier's distinctive blond curls.

'Charles, Charles,' called Alan, 'do you have a moment? It's something rather serious.'

Charles elbowed his bulky frame through parts of the throng and towered over Alan.

'Hello sir. Good to see you again. Where was it we met? Chamonix wasn't it? Yes, now I remember. You're Veronica's dad. How is she by the way? Haven't seen much of her tonight? Thought she was here though. Can I do.....'

'Charles, just hold on a minute,' said Alan, trying to get a word in. 'Yes we met in Chamonix and yes Veronica was here earlier tonight.'

'Well then she'll be fine. Grand party. Lots of fun people. Everyone having a good time. Can I get you anything?'

'Charles, can we go somewhere a little quieter and a little less crowded? This is serious and private.'

'Sure, why didn't you say. Serious eh? Well, I hope that nothing puts a damper on the party. Going really well. Music's good. Lots to drink. Sure I can't get you anything?'

'Charles, some quiet!'

'Oh, yes, sure, come this way.'

Charles powered his way through a knot of people and opened a side door. 'Come in here. Should be quiet.'

As Charles had prophesied the library was quiet and empty. Alan sat down feeling emotionally wrung out and not quite sure how he was going to explain why he was here.

'Now it's nothing about pops or mumsie is it?' asked Charles a little nervously. 'I'm not really in the right frame of mind for some bad news from them.'

'No Charles, this is to do with Veronica. There's no easy way to say this so I'll come right out and tell you. Veronica is dead.'

'No, no,' said Charles. The smile disappeared and his face paled. Rather heavily Charles dropped his lanky frame into a fortunately placed armchair. 'But she was here tonight,' you said, 'so where did this happen? It can't be in this house can it? Heaven forbid it happened here and I didn't know. Mr. Matheson I'd never forgive myself. Tell me it isn't true?'

'Charles it didn't happen here although what did happen here may have been why it happened.'

'What do you mean? Something happened here and now Veronica is dead? I don't understand.'

'Neither do I Charles,' said Alan, 'neither do I, but Veronica died just down at the end of your street in a horrific car crash.'

'It was some accident? Was anyone else hurt? Who caused it?'

'Charles slow down. I don't know half the answers to your questions. I've just been woken up and asked to come down to the morgue to identify my daughter. I'm all torn up....' Alan hung his head for a moment but just as quickly he shook himself and looked Charles straight in the face. 'Charles, I'm sure that something happened in this house to precipitate this accident. No one else on the street seemed to cause Veronica to crash the way she did. It almost looks like she did it on purpose, although I can't believe that. I can't believe Veronica would want to do that, unless,' and Alan paused as several thoughts whirled around in his head, 'unless something really traumatic happened here. That's one reason why I am here.'

'But Mr. Matheson nothing has happened here. As I said the party has been awesome and everyone is having a great time.'

Alan sat back in the chair and thought for a moment. Shifting his head out of an emotional state into a logical state let him consider how best to get Charles to understand.

'Charles, do you know all the people here tonight?'

'Yes, well I think so,' said Charles. 'Of course I don't know all of them equally well.'

'Do you know who Veronica came with tonight?'

'Sure, she came with that young Michael Lord from London Uni. He's a mathematician or something equally obscure, but then isn't he engaged to Veronica?'

'Yes Charles, he is. And was Michael with Veronica here or did Michael meet someone else?'

'Well, I suppose I don't really know Mr. Matheson. It's a big house as you know and everyone mingled. It's that kind of party. Why don't we find Michael and ask? Oh. No, he'll not know what has happened. He'll be devastated. He and Veronica were all over each other when we were all together in Chamonix. I can't tell him Mr. Matheson. I couldn't bear it. Can you ....'

Alan held up his hands. 'Charles, Charles, it's okay. I'm not asking you to explain things to Michael. I'll take care of that but I will take you up on your suggestion of asking Michael what happened tonight. So, let's discreetly go and find him shall we?'

As Charles and Alan stood up in the library and looked at each other each had a head full of confusing thoughts and emotions. Charles was still white and a little wobbly on his feet. The full impact of Veronica being dead hadn't yet hit but he was already into a serious guilt trip over something happening in the house. Something he may have caused. Oh no, he thought, it's really too much. Everyone has been having such a good time.

Alan's thoughts were a little more pragmatic. He had had time to bottle up the emotional loss of his daughter and now he was in an engineering mode looking for answers. Veronica wasn't prone to suicide. Something really serious must have happened to provoke such an action. Increasingly Alan was looking for that something.

Charles led the way through the suite of rooms on the ground floor. Music flowed, people danced and talked and as Charles had said "everyone was having a good time". Charles asked a couple of people whether they had seen Michael but no one had. The search continued upstairs where the music was faint and the dancing was primarily horizontal. Alan found this somewhat disconcerting and tried to keep reminding himself that he was young once. Charles was quite discreet how he invaded people's privacy but still no Michael.

The corridor on the top floor gave access to the maid's quarters. The shrieks and laughter pulsed down this spartan floor as Charles and Alan slowly climbed the last set of stairs. All of the noise appeared to be coming from the end room where the door was shut and a crude notice was pinned to the door. Charles's face reddened and he slowed down as he walked along the corridor to the door at the end. Alan in turn was becoming more and more disturbed. All of the other rooms off the corridor were empty and Alan finally strode up to the last door and read the note. It said "Melanie Maids Service Room".

Charles pushed past Alan as he was reading the notice and softly knocked on the door. Before he had time to say anything a male voice cried out, 'Veronica if that's you again, get lost. Go and diddle Daddy.'

A burst of girlish laughter followed this pronouncement. 'This maid is servicing Michael.'

Alan thrust open the door. Several voices spoke at once. 'Oh no,' came from Charles as he captured the scene. 'Who's the old guy?' said Melanie, wearing a maid's pinafore rather loosely and nothing else, except she was brandishing a feather duster. All Michael could say was, 'Mr. Matheson.' Strapped naked spread-eagled to the bed frame it was a wonder that Michael could say anything.

Alan Matheson stood and his expression hardened as he looked into the room. 'A word Michael, if you please,' he said, and he slammed the door shut pushing Charles outside.

'Michael, this little man doesn't look cool,' said Melanie. 'Perhaps we should dress him up as the butler and I can teach him how to polish the silver or something. I'm very good with my bush, brush.' Melanie looked up at Alan Matheson from her kneeling position on the bed. 'Don't you think my brush looks good little man?'

'I'll be outside Michael, when you're quite ready.'

The door opened and slammed shut as Alan marched out into the corridor. 'Okay Charles, I'll take it from here,' said Alan. 'Thanks for finding Michael for me. I'm sorry I had to bring you such sad news to a memorable party. Michael and I will find our own way out thanks. We'll be quiet about it.'

Charles was about to speak but Alan held his hand up. 'Don't say anything. This doesn't concern you and I'll sort it out with Michael away from the house.' Charles straightened up a little and looked Mr. Matheson in the eye. He offered his hand and Alan shook it without a word being spoken. Charles quietly retreated down the staircase. 'Yes, everyone was having such fun,' he muttered to himself, 'great party and now Veronica is dead.' Charles quietly found his way back to the library. There he raided his father's best whisky and drank until he passed out.

Some two hours later as a grey light gradually seeped over the sprawling city Michael lay on his back on his bed and gazed up at the dusty ceiling. He thought back over "the word" with Alan Matheson. Actually he thought back over the several words of Alan Matheson. It had not been a comfortable listening. Alan had told Michael about the death of Veronica but instead of commiseration about the loss Alan had launched into a rather brutal interrogation of Michael's activities that evening at the party. Before Michael had time to get over any shock or even any grief Alan Matheson was firing quick sharp questions at him.

'Did you and Veronica have words Michael?

Were you together at the party?

How come I found you where I did?

Who was that maid?

What could possibly have made Veronica so upset?

Obviously it was something really serious or really disturbing?

What did you say Michael?'

Michael weakly held up his arms in defense to stall for time while his mind churned over possible answers.

'Hold it, hold it right there Mr. Matheson. I'm trying to take all this in. You say Veronica is dead, well pardon me if I do a little grieving before I have you badgering me.'

Alan Matheson changed his tone. 'Michael, I'm not badgering you, and I suppose at the moment I have bottled my grief until I have resolved why this happened. Veronica was my life and joy as well you know but I can't really grieve until I have sorted out why. That's just the way I am and you were the last person she was with. So, despite your comments, what happened for God's sake?'

By this time Alan Matheson's voice had risen an octave and he moved towards Michael to shake him into an answer.

'Back off. Veronica took off somewhere. After the first few minutes I hardly saw her. I met a few friends, had a few drinks, and so on. I was having a good time until suddenly you come storming in. Hell, I was your daughter's fiancée but not her keeper. I don't know who she saw or what she did at the party. It's a big house. There were lots of people. Go ask Charles or whoever and get off my case. I need to find a stiff drink and curl up in a ball somewhere. I sure don't need this fifth degree.'

'Michael, something happened.'

'So you say but I don't know what. You've never told me how or where Veronica died so how the hell should I know what happened. We went to the party together – end of story.'

'No Michael, it's not the end of the story. Something upset Veronica, really upset her, and she died in a car crash at the end of the street.'

'Jesus, but how?'

'It looks like she skidded straight through the junction at the end of the street into a lamp standard and somehow the car rolled over and caught fire. She died in the car.'

'Christ, how could she do that? She was so careful driving. I had even joshed her a little about that on the way to the party about how careful she was. She must have been really traveling.'

'Yes Michael, but why? As I keep saying, something upset her, something distracted her, or perhaps someone upset her? Answer that can you?'

Alan looked straight at Michael with a very determined look on his face and Michael felt the inference vibrating towards him. Michael gritted his teeth and glared back.

'Mr. Matheson, as I said before, this is neither the time nor the place. I'm out of here before you say things you'll regret.' Michael remembered how he opened Alan Matheson's Jaguar's door and strode off down the street without looking back.

'Michael, something happened at that party. Something you know about and I'll find out,' the voice shouted up the street after Michael. 'I'll not let this go. I'll pursue you........', and the voice died away Michael remembered as he turned the corner.

Lying on the bed in his flat Michael went back over that hour. He had turned the corner of the street and sort of collapsed onto the wall of the first house. 'What a mess, what a bloody cock-up,' he muttered. After a moment's deep breathing Michael grabbed a hold of himself and found a quiet way home musing on the past events. Back in the flat he poured himself a stiff drink and collapsed onto the bed.

'So much for the strategy of stirring up jealous juices,' Michael said to the ceiling. 'Christ, you never know with women what they will do next. All I was looking for was a little competition; a little challenge to get Veronica firmly chasing me and she bloody well goes off the deep end. Now she was a lovely lady. To sink into the vernacular she was "a bit of a goer, know what I mean, nudge, nudge, wink, wink". Jesus Veronica, you were supposed to fight not flee, and now look what's happened.'

Michael rolled over onto his side and put the whisky glass down on the bedside table. His eye caught the photograph of him and Veronica taken in France last year. They had been so good together. Rolling back to study the ceiling Michael left the past behind and concentrated on the future. He thought back for a moment on his New Year's Resolution and set this objective firmly in his sights as he worked on a more productive strategy.

True to his word Alan Matheson did not let this go. After Michael leapt out of his car outside the Dampier House Alan drove back to the police station to find out more about the accident. They still wouldn't give him any details "until our investigation, analysis and reporting is complete sir" but he did manage to find out the name and rank of the officer in charge of the accident. He also managed to harangue the desk sergeant long enough about something happening at the party to cause the sergeant to get a constable to help Mr. Matheson leave the station. 'At least that might stick in the thick plod's mind,' muttered Alan as he shook off the constable's arm. 'Okay constable I'm leaving but remember something happened at the party. Go and talk to some people.'

'Yes sir. We understand you're upset sir. We'll find out what happened sir. You go home now sir and leave it to us.'

But leaving things to others wasn't how Alan Matheson lived and became successful. Very carefully he drove his Jaguar back to Lord

Dampier's House in Chelsea and went to find Charles again. It's time somebody started to ask penetrating questions thought Alan as he looked around for Charles. Opening the library door Alan found a sprawled out snoring Charles still clasping the whisky bottle. Okay thought Alan, time for some answers, and he left the library to start a personal investigation of the party people.

A little after eight o'clock that morning after the party Michael had decided on a plan of action and come to some noteworthy conclusions.

1. Veronica Matheson was dead.
2. Alan Matheson thought Michael partly (or more) responsible.
3. Alan Matheson would be a future threat to Michael.
4. I need to tell Dad quickly what has happened before Matheson does.
5. I need to tell Melanie Rogers what has happened, and to keep her mouth shut.
6. I need to appear grief-stricken for a while.
7. I need to keep a low profile for a week or so.
8. I need to cultivate Melanie Rogers.

Michael filed the first three conclusions safely away in his head and promptly telephoned down to Fotheringham Manor. In a soft and emotional voice Michael explained as much as he knew. He also added that Alan Matheson would probably be phoning to tell them much the same thing but not to worry as the police were investigating the accident. Michael said that he didn't need to come down to Fotheringham and thought that studies would help him work through his grief. It was a busy time of the year and he didn't want to fall behind in his classes. Michael knew that such an attitude would satisfy both his parents and this helped with some of Michael's other planned actions.

Veronica had told Michael that Matheson Storage was a sufficiently up-to-date company to have electronic mail facilities. Michael sat down at his computer and composed a short but sincere note of grief to Alan Matheson, adding that he would do anything he could to help Mr. Matheson.

Finally, Michael telephoned Melanie Rogers. Not surprisingly all Michael heard was a recorded message saying that Ms. Rogers was not available and could you leave a message after the beep. Given the state of mind Melanie was in when he left her Michael reckoned it would be a while before Ms. Rogers answered the telephone in person. Michael left his name after the beep. She had his number. 'And I have yours,' said Michael to the telephone, 'Yes Melanie Rogers, I have your number.' Having set the desired actions in motion Michael busied himself for morning lectures at the University.

'Ever onwards and upwards,' Michael told the mirror as he chased the whisky out of his mouth with toothpaste. 'The future is yours if you're prepared to work at it, and work I bloody well will.'

Flying Lessons

3

Alan Matheson had to wait for over a week before the police released his daughter's body. He organized the funeral two days after this and Michael's parents came up from Somerset and attended with Michael. It was all very calm and civilized but Michael could detect an undercurrent of mistrust every time his eyes met those of Alan Matheson. Apart from attending the funeral Michael continued with his plan of keeping a low profile and studying hard. Understandably Michael's mother was very upset about the accident and the death of Veronica. Sylvia Lord had got on well with Veronica and was looking forward to the wedding and a possible calming influence, or perhaps some influence on Michael.

While she was at the funeral reception Sylvia managed to catch Michael by himself. Holding Michael's arm and looking seriously at her son Sylvia asked, 'what really happened that night Michael? However could Veronica have driven so fast? From what little I knew of her she seemed a very sensible girl. I know you and she did some scary things climbing together but I never thought of her as reckless.'

'Mother, I really don't know,' said Michael in an exasperated voice. 'She seemed fine on the way to the party. After we had briefly talked to

Charles we sort of lost sight of each other. You know what those kinds of parties were like; you and dad went to similar things when you were young.'

'Careful Michael,' said Sylvia as she lightly punched Michael's arm. 'It's not that long ago we don't remember how those things went. Still, something must have happened. You didn't see her again? Come on Michael, it wasn't that big a house unless you or she was hiding out somewhere. Who did she know there she might have spoken to, or danced with, or whatever?'

Michael disentangled his mother's arm and stood back at arms length. Looking around to make sure no one was particularly listening or paying attention Michael said, 'now look here Mum, you sound just like Mr. Matheson on one of his interrogation sessions. He came and gave me the third degree almost in the same breath as he told me Veronica was dead. I had just about taken in what he had said before I'm being grilled, and now you sound just like him.'

'Michael, Michael, I'm sorry. I know you and Veronica loved each other and that this tragedy is very painful but you must admit the accident seems a little unexpected. Given that the police concluded no one else was involved, no other vehicles, no other pedestrians, and that Veronica wasn't drunk then something else triggered this accident.'

'It was slippery Mum. The roads were wet and icy. Even going to the party the driving was tricky. Veronica must have slipped her wet shoes off the brake pedal onto the accelerator by mistake. It was a very responsive car and you had to pay attention. It was late at night. Perhaps Veronica was over-tired. Hell, I don't know Mum. Let it go.' Michael swiftly but quietly slid out of the reception room. This was all too much, too bloody much.

Anthony was about to chase after his son when Sylvia caught him by the arm. 'Let him go Anthony love. He's still all very emotional and upset in his own way. Michael never likes a situation where he doesn't feel in control and at the moment that isn't the case.'

Anthony grunted. 'Hmm, not sure about that Sylvia: Michael is always pretty adept about keeping his emotions well in check and thinking things through so that they come out best for himself. I've just been talking with Alan. He's convinced that Michael knows something, or did something. He's not sure but right now he's a volatile mixture of profound grief over the loss of his only daughter and rage over someone being the cause. From what he has managed to find out from people at the party there was quite a scene sometime during the evening between Michael and Veronica. Alan couldn't find out the details but he's sure that something Michael did caused Veronica to react. He's still pursuing it so I was going to tell Michael to keep a low profile.'

Away from the funeral Michael thought back over the past events. He had noticed that his father had spent some time talking with Alan Matheson at the reception afterwards and several times Michael felt his father's eyes flash over in his direction. Michael thought he had done the right thing in phoning his parents so quickly after the party and getting his story in first. He still wasn't sure exactly what Alan Matheson planned to do, or what stories he had heard. He also was quite shaken about the doggedness of his mother's questions. It was time to disappear for a while.

After a week of studying hard and "disappearing" Michael found it was doing his head in. He felt that he needed some other diversion, some other form of release. He also felt that perhaps it was time to move forward. Flipping back over his plan of action Michael thought it would be a profitable idea to renew his cultivation of Melanie Rogers. Sitting in his flat Michael made several phone calls to ensure the "cultivation" would be more successful than his last move.

Ever since he had met her a couple of months ago Michael had considered Melanie Rogers a worthwhile investment. Her money would help Michael succeed. It would help overcome the second son handicap. With the sad demise of his fiancee in January Michael set about the capture of Ms. Rogers and her inheritance.

Melanie and Bella Turner were a dyad - a partnership of two where one complements the services of the other. So, when Michael invited Melanie down to Fotheringham Manor Bella was part of the package. Michael accepted the situation but privately decided that he would help Bella "fly away" chemically during the time at Fotheringham. He needed some private time to ensnare Melanie.

Michael had arranged a weekend at the Manor when none of the rest of the family would be there. The two girls had fussed and fretted in their London flat trying to decide what to take. Anybody would think they were going away for a month instead of a weekend. It had taken Michael most of the morning to get them to the front door of their flat let alone down to the Manor.

Eventually, sometime after lunch on a sharp frosty day in February, Michael drove the two girls from London down to the Manor. Most of the scenery was stark black and white. Leafless black hardwood trees were coated with white branches born out of an ice storm. It was like going to see an old time movie. Soon after Bristol Michael branched off the Motorway onto the minor roads leading to the house. The two girls gasped as Michael turned the car through the entrance gatehouse of the long drive to the Manor. Fotheringham Manor was built of a soft creamy limestone with a copper green roof. With the fading reddish evening sunshine glistening on the frost the entire house looked like a fairy castle.

'Wow. Far out,' exclaimed Bella. 'It looks like something out of Tolkien.'

'Where are the hobbits Michael?' asked Melanie.

'Yes, where's Frodo?' squealed Bella.

'Wait until we get there girls,' said Michael, 'and I'll show you a land of wizardry and dreams like you've never seen before.'

'Did you get the stuff Michael?' asked Bella. 'Did you? Did you?'

'Sure,' said Michael, 'I got it from Freddie who just came in from L.A. two days ago. He says it is top quality; just the thing to put you into orbit.'

'Now Michael. I want it now.' Bella bounced up and down in the car with excitement. 'I want to be the princess and spread my protection over the hobbits. I want to swoop around my castle casting mystical spells. Can we dress up Michael? Do you have some people who could be orcs? Can we banish them to the cellars in perpetual darkness?' Bella's voice dropped to a whisper as her mind took over and a swirl of images revolved around her head.

Michael looked at Melanie and smiled. He took her warm hand in his and stroked the inside of the wrist gently. 'And what will we do?' he asked, as he ran his fingers smoothly across the palm of her hand.

'Perhaps we should be Romeo and Juliet, or better still Anthony and Cleopatra with their unbridled passions?' Michael mused softly. 'Two turtle doves billing and cooing.'

'Don't be sick Michael,' said Bella. 'You're so conventional at times.'

Melanie shuddered as ghosts walked over her grave, but she took Michael's slender fingers and sucked them powerfully in her mouth.

'I think we should enjoy a roaring log fire, mulled wine and let the sizzling juices of tender meat dribble over our bodies,' she said with her eyes closed and her limbs trembling.

'I have just the tiger skin for the cat lady to sprawl on,' suggested Michael.

As dusk fell Michael guided Melanie and Bella around the large house. Before it got completely dark Michael led the two girls out onto the roof. The view was magnificent along the edge of the Mendip Hills. The attic access onto this uppermost part of the Manor opened close to the ridge of the roof besides the main chimneys. The smooth copper green roof ran the length of the building with a low castellated parapet over the front of the house. It was a dramatic location.

'Great Grandfather George rebuilt and refurbished it in 1908 to celebrate his win over the Boers, or to protect his wife from the dreaded Hun, or something,' explained Michael.

'It's certainly a dramatic house Michael. Does Geoffrey live here, with, who is it, Clotilde or somebody?'

'No,' said Michael through clenched teeth. 'My brother Geoffrey and his beloved wife Christina live in the Home Farm, along with little Peter.'

'But they will live here won't they? You said Geoffrey gets it all didn't you? You were very pissed that night and growling. I remember you gnashing your teeth and looking quite scary. Actually I was quite frightened that night Michael.'

'Yes, yes, and yes again. All of this bloody great estate belongs to precious elder brother Geoffrey and his Italian Countess. To hell with him.'

'Lighten up Michael,' said Bella. 'Look at it this way. You're far brighter than he is; you're far more adventurous than he is; and you've got us. What else could anybody wish for?'

Michael looked around and laughed. 'You're right Bella. The night is far too precious to waste wishing for things we can't have. Let's go and get some things we can have.'

'Whoopee Michael, now you're talking. Let's find Freddie's powder.'

'Michael, I'm famished. Can we eat first? I almost feel dizzy up here. We haven't eaten since breakfast and my tummy is grumbling.'

'Sure ladies. I am forgetting myself. Let's find your rooms, some dinner and some fun.'

Back inside Michael showed the girls their own rooms. These were in the front of the house overlooking the driveway with its magnificent avenue of trees. Michael had made sure that Bella's contained a massive high four-poster bed. It seemed to fit with her fairy princess fantasy. Melanie's room was far more suitable for romance, and that was really what Michael had in mind.

Meredith, the butler, served dinner. The three young people clustered around one end of the gleaming dining room table. A couple of magnificent candelabras graced their end of the table. The soft candlelight reflected delicately off the golden faces of both Melanie and Bella. Meredith looked beyond the faces and winced. Melanie's tie-dye muumuu hung like a sack. As she moved the colours whirled around in a heady profusion. Not quite "dressing for dinner" thought Meredith. Bella was still in her fairy princess fantasy. A series of gauzy streamers appeared to be pinned to her halter-top. These streamers were made of some wispy material in pastel colours. They sort of fell from her bodice in an uncontrolled series of petals.

'Can we ride tomorrow?' asked Melanie.

'We'll be in no condition to ride tomorrow if we ride all night,' giggled Bella.

'Michael, you do have horses don't you?' continued Melanie. 'Daddy has a whole stable of polo ponies in the Valley and I ride every day.'

Michael looked up and smiled slowly at the two ladies.

'Yes, my sweet. We have horses. As Bella suggests we'll ride on flying horses tonight and fleeing horses tomorrow.'

'Fleeing from what Michael?'

'From the terrifying colours in your dress Bella.'

'Then I won't wear it tomorrow. I'll change from being a fairy princess to lady Godiva.'

Bella popped a pill and let the cool Riesling sweep it down her throat. She shuddered and the petals whispered. Michael watched in fascination as the chemicals raced around Bella's body. His hand gently stroked Melanie's knee.

'Will that be all Mr. Michael?' inquired Meredith. Michael snapped out of his mental fantasy.

'Yes Meredith. We will have coffee in the drawing room. There's a good fire there and the ladies are cold in this chilly room.'

Michael was right. The dining room was cold and the girls had shivered off and on throughout the meal. Soon we will all be nice and warm mused Michael.

'Candy time boys and girls,' whispered Michael when they were all in the warm room, 'come and see what the candy man has brought.'

'Michael is it good? I must be a fairy princess tonight in this magnificent castle. It's a night for spells and riding flying horses.'

'You'll fly all right pretty lady.'

The three of them sprawled on the thick carpeting in front of a glimmering fire. Brandy washed the acid down three slender throats. Flickering flames threw transitory shadows around the room. Jim Morrison and the Doors extolled the virtues of the L.A. woman. Michael thought it was funny in a way that the music of his dad's time still seemed to be relevant. I should ask dad sometime what it was like to be in Haight Ashbury during the early sixties he thought.

Bella's body could not keep still. With the warmth of the room and the messages from the drugs Bella proceeded to glide around - sometimes in harmony with Morrison and sometimes in her own orbit. Michael and Melanie also moved into another world.

'It's fall, it's fall,' cried Bella and her petals started to fall one by one. She continued to pirouette around the room slowing shedding the wisps of her dress. Michael watched Bella with lazy eyes as he slowly pushed Melanie's muumuu up and up and up.

Bella's whirling became more frenetic. The light behind her eyes rolled through a kaleidoscope of colours as the firelight flickered off the furnishings in the room. The halter fell away with the last petal. A completely naked and panting Bella pushed her face close to Michael and said: 'the princess needs more magic.'

Michael reached out slowly with his hand and stroked the tender quivering neck. He slid a pill onto his tongue and offered it to the trembling nymph. Bella leaned forwards and opened her mouth to receive her gift. Michael slid his hand between Bella's thighs as he slid his tongue deep into her mouth. Bella started as she felt herself being penetrated and she writhed with the touch.

Very languidly Michael slipped his fingers from Bella and licked the juices off into Melanie's mouth. Michael moved his fingertips over the hard erect nipples under Melanie's muumuu while the other hand slipped back into Bella. Slowly Michael eased the muumuu off Melanie until she too was dressed like Bella. Bella couldn't keep still. The heat from the fire and the arousal from Michael's fingers were too much. Slowly Bella stretched out beside Melanie. She let her hair sweep over the Melanie's thighs. Michael's tongue gently explored Melanie's mouth and Bella moved her tongue to taste between Melanie's other lips.

Michael sat back and watched as Bella straddled Melanie. Bella's lips and tongue were demanding between Melanie's thighs. Slowly she lowered her own excited clitoris onto Melanie's tongue. It didn't take the two girls long before their two bodies were in motion.

As the fire died down the shadows lengthened in the room. Michael was warmly lying between the two girls feeling relaxed and content. He popped another pill on his tongue and playfully passed it to Bella, tasting Melanie inside Bella's mouth. She giggled and slowly rose from the floor.

Michael rolled over and looked at a dreamy Melanie.

'Did it work for you?' he asked.

Melanie replied by kissing him and sliding a smooth thigh over his stomach. Michael slid his hand over a firm white buttock and squeezing gently. Melanie's lips covered his and he felt her juices trickle down his stomach.

'Yes Michael. It worked for me, but it seems to have taken its toll on you,' Melanie whispered with her tongue in his ear. 'You seem to have expired - well part of you,' she chuckled quietly as her fingers got no reaction from Michael's manhood.

Jim Morrison was trying to "Break on through to the other side" when Bella came to life with a series of swoops from the sofa. Michael and Melanie rolled across the floor to avoid a suddenly on-high visit from Bella. The threesome came to life and the party entered another round.

'Stay here; I've got just what we need.'

Michael walked quickly out of the drawing room to get what they all needed.

Bella switched Jim Morrison to Country Joe and the Fish but the anti-Vietnam sentiments didn't fit. The Grateful Dead's rendition of Viola Lee Blues electrified Bella and she glided around the room to the distinctive rhythms. She popped another pill.

Michael returned with three fur coats, three sets of woolly hats and gloves, and three sets of down booties. In minutes the three of them were outside and shrieking down the smooth frost-covered lawns. Down booties make responsive short skis and the two girls were excellent skiers.

'Michael, this is too easy. We need a steep slope.' Bella pranced away to find another challenge.

Melanie continued her slalom around the decorative conifers dotting the sloping lawns.

'Found it,' shrieked Bella.

Michael and Melanie looked up. Bella had climbed up through the barn onto its roof. This sloped steeply down to the piles of hay that had been brought in that summer. With a scream of delight Bella launched herself down the steep roof. Her fur coat flapped behind her like a train and her white body stood out clearly in the moonlight. She flew down the roof and ended up deep in the pile of hay.

'Fab, fab, fabulous,' Bella squealed as she threw hay everywhere.

Melanie and Michael watched as Bella staggered out of the hay pile and danced around them.

'Come on my darlings. Come and play the flying beauty.'

Melanie shuddered as the ghost walked over her grave again. She clutched Michael's arm.

'Let's go to bed. I'm getting cold.'

'Bella, let's go,' called Michael. 'We can ride tomorrow and fly then.'

'I need a bigger roof Michael - one with a longer jump.'

'Bella, enough, let's call it a day.'

'Shit Michael, what a party pooper. I'll look for my own roof another time.'

The colours whirled in Bella's head as the three of them glided over the lawn back to the house.

The clock in the village church struck two. Gleaming coals still glowed in the drawing room fire.

'One for the road,' said Bella and quickly downed a brandy. A convulsive shudder ran through her body as the alcohol flushed the heat into her extremities.

'Bedtime ladies. Horseback riding in the morning, well midday anyway.'

Bella continued to swirl and prance across the hall floor to the main staircase. She swung her fur coat from her hands, narrowly missing upsetting the suits of armour placed around the floor. Michael slid his arm around Melanie's waist as they slowly moved up the staircase.

The scream seemed to go on and on. It ran around and around in Michael's head. It was so close but it wasn't a dream. Sunlight streamed into the room although Michael could remember drawing the curtains before he tumbled Melanie into her big embracing bed. Still the scream filled the room as Michael opened his eyes.

Melanie was at the window: her whole naked body shivering convulsively and her mouth wide open with terror. Again the scream tore through Michael's drugged brain and he realized that it was Melanie who was screaming.

Melanie's body seemed to sag with exhausted emotion. The tension just streamed out.

'She wanted to fly Michael,' sobbed Melanie. 'She was a fairy princess who wanted to fly and do good.'

'Eh,' grunted Michael, still trying to focus on the world. 'What are you on about? Come back to bed. It's cold out there.'

'She'll never be cold again Michael. She just wanted to fly.'

Bella it seems had found a new roof to try, one with a bigger jump. Her white body was smashed on the forecourt, just wearing a pair of down booties. Later it was discovered that she had found her way onto the main roof of the house. Although the frost had long gone from the roof the police found several tracks with scraps of down showing Bella's slalom runs around the chimneys and out over the parapet.

Walter Turner and his wife came over from L.A. to take their daughter's body back to the States. Stanley Rogers, Melanie's father also came across. The parents spent a lot of time with Melanie trying to learn and understand the circumstances. Somerset police investigated the accident and it was concluded that it was "death through misadventure" and no crime had been committed. Neither Melanie nor Michael were tested for drugs and it appeared that Bella had taken the drugs herself, unbeknown to the other two people. It took a while for the police to release Bella's body to her parents. This proved to be ever-increasingly stressful for the Turners. Eventually they managed to fly Bella back home. Soon after the funeral Mrs. Turner had a mental breakdown. During the long wait to release Bella's body Melanie got to think about the whole incident and she talked at length with her father. The police never determined the source of the drugs. Michael was obvious by his absence.

Although, Michael said to himself, that is not quite true. We all did stay down at Fotheringham for the inquest and we did make a statement for the police. I did offer to drive Melanie back up to London but the Turners insisted she go with them. So, I really wasn't absent. I even went to the airport to see Melanie off back to the States. The only way I was absent was when I didn't stay long at Fotheringham because mum was giving me such a hard time, but then I told her there was pressure from work. I had to study for exams, but I don't think she was convinced the investigation really found out the whole truth.

Working with the truth was never a high priority on Michael's agenda and he realized that he needed to find another way to cultivate Melanie Rogers. If it wasn't directly through Melanie herself then perhaps I should try and impress Stanley Rogers. Michael remembered Melanie telling him that her dad was a fan of English pomp and tradition. Well, thought Michael, there is something I might be able to do about that but I need to do a little planning before Melanie and her dad return from the States. Just let me remember a little bit of recent history before we set wheels in motion. I think the answer may be back at my old school.

The Bully Boy

4

A prosperous Bristol merchant, Sir Rupert Denvers, had built Bristol House in early Georgian times as the main house on his country estate. Italian-inspired Palladianism dominated the architecture of the house. There was an imposing gentle staircase at the front of the property ornamented with classical statues. The doorways were high and massive and tall "Venetian" style windows allowed light to stream into the rooms. Profits from the increasingly lucrative slave trade were invested in expansions to the house and property. However, the fortunes of the business were offset by the misfortunes of the merchant's family. All of Rupert's offspring, and his wife, died before the old gentleman finally gave up the ghost. In an effort to reclaim his soul from damnation Sir Rupert established an educational Trust for the sons of gentlemen, and bequeathed the property to the Trust as a school.

Bristol House gradually expanded from the late Georgian times and by the turn of the twentieth century had both a Prep school and a main Boarding school. Boys entered Prep school at age seven and continued through usually up to sixteen or older. From Bristol House they typically went to University, into the Armed Forces, or into the Church. The school had developed over the years as a conventional English Public School. Education was a hit or miss affair depending mostly on the character of the headmaster. Food was atrocious. Discipline was harsh. Life was cruel. Charles Darwin need not have gone to the Galapagos Islands as he could have observed "survival of the fittest" at this typical English Public School. Attending such a Prep school and Boarding school had influenced Michael Lord's character. A strong hierarchical structure dominated this boy's only world of Bristol House. After being a fag for some loutish teen-ager Michael nurtured the idea of getting his own back when he was a senior. As a result, life became hell for young Aubrey Worthing.

Aubrey Worthing was a young gentleman and heir to the large north of England estates of his father's family. His father was a competent contributor in the House of Lords, as well as the owner of a very successful security devices company, Worthing Securities. His mother was a dragon. Lady Diana Worthing came from a family of power since early Elizabethan times. As a girl she had toured the cultured sights of Europe in a luxurious style. However, she had also been on several rugged archaeological expeditions in the caves of the Middle East. The dangers from fortune-hunting males in Europe she had dismissed easily. Shooting and killing local bandits in Syria and Turkey had taught Lady Diana something else. She liked to kill. The fear, the adrenalin-rush and the whole experience brought her alive. Lady Diana, as was her mythological namesake, was a huntress. In due course Lady Diana passed this character trait on to her daughter Vanessa. Unfortunately this trait missed Vanessa's younger brother Aubrey.

'Tea fag, with toasted crumpets,' bawled Michael, as he loafed in the prefect's room.

Young Worthing scurried around the room looking for the ingredients.

'There's no tea in the caddy' he muttered.

Michael's shoe redirected Worthing's attention to the other side of the room.

'Look you little pip-squeak, you lordly lump of shortsighted humanity. Look. Up on the shelf, in a tin labelled tea.'

'But that belongs to……Agh!'

Again Michael's shoe found Worthing's anatomy.

'Use it,' yelled Michael, 'before I become annoyed. And when you've managed that minor task blanco my cricket shoes and pads: I need them for this evening's practice.'

'But I've got prep to do; an essay and a translation,' wailed Worthing.

'You fag for me and I come first. Don't you ever forget that Worthing. You're nothing, you hear me. All your life you will be nothing. Every time I speak you jump.'

Michael's last year at Bristol House was a curious mixture of success and nearly fatal disaster. Inherently Michael was an extremely intelligent young man and did well scholastically without any particular effort. As a result he did well in his final exams and was set to go to London University. However, at the same time Michael lived on the edge, especially in the outdoors world. On several weekends the entire Lord family went down to Aunt Veronica's at Dartmouth. Cousin Marcel, Charles's son had taken Michael out sailing on several occasions on the Dart and taught Michael some of the rudiments. Now Michael thought he knew it all.

'Ready about; lee oh,' called Michael as he put down the helm. The little dinghy turned in a gentle arc up into the wind and the sails and sheets flapped. 'Let go the bloody jibsheet Daniel or she'll never turn.'

Daniel blushed and let go the rope he was holding. As the boom swung over Michael took in the mainsheet and the dinghy leapt forwards on a new port tack.

'Now take in the starboard jibsheet Daniel.'

'Sorry Michael. I was looking at those cormorants.'

'You're supposed to be learning to sail young'un, not looking at bloody birds. Let the sail stay full. Don't pull the sheet so tight that you flatten the sail. And don't leave the sheet in the jamcleats. Christ, will you never learn?'

'Do it one thing at a time Michael. You try to tell me too many things all at once.'

'Well smarten up you little wimp. Wash you're ears out. We'll go about again okay? Wait 'til I get past this cruiser. Ready about; lee oh.'

Once again Michael smoothly eased off the mainsheet a little as he pushed the tiller away. Watching the bow of the dinghy he eased his body around the tiller and sat down on the new windward side of the boat. As the head eased off to port and the mainsail filled Michael trimmed the mainsheet. 'See, you got it right that time,' said Michael, as Daniel had released the starboard jibsheet and taken in the port one. 'See how smooth we can make the turn with minimum turbulence astern and little loss of way.'

'Watch out Michael,' yelled Daniel, 'a powerboat.'

Michael had been so engrossed in congratulating himself on the neat turn that he hadn't seen the motor cruiser bearing down on him.

'Sod him. Power gives way to sail,' muttered Michael.

'Yes Michael, but not in a restricted channel like here in the anchorage.'

The cruiser hooted loudly and veered off. The wash rocked the little dinghy and Michael and Daniel were shaken off the thwarts into the bottom of the boat. Passengers on the cruiser peered down into the little dinghy as they passed.

'Need to keep a better lookout young man,' bawled the naval man at the helm of the cruiser. 'Next time we'll board you and make you walk the plank.' The other people in the cruiser laughed. 'Keep the natives in their place Bertie,' someone piped up.

'Arseholes,' muttered Michael, settling himself back in the stern. 'Keep those sheets trimmed Daniel for Christ's sake and let's get out of here.'

Michael spent the next hour tacking downstream towards the ocean making sure that Daniel knew enough about that process. The wind had picked up a little and down near the mouth of the estuary there was quite a swell coming in from the English Channel.

'Michael, I'm wet and cold. Can we go back home? I've had enough for today.'

'Bloody wimp you are Daniel. You're even more of a wimp than Lord Geoffrey.'

'Don't you mean Geoffrey Lord?' laughed Daniel.

'Don't take the piss or I'll stay out here for hours you little weasel.'

'Sorry Michael, I do want to go back. I'm freezing.'

'I'm going to gybe and run back home,' Michael said. 'You need to learn how to run and trim the sails to prevent yawing.'

'What's gybe Michael?'

'I'll turn downwind and let the wind move the boom over from starboard to port from astern. The boom will go over quickly so keep you're bloody head down or you'll be knocked over the side.'

'What about the jibsheets?'

'Just do what I tell you when I tell you.'

Michael eased the dinghy off from the wind from a tack into a broad reach. The speed increased slightly and the dinghy rolled as it was going straight across the estuary now and the swells swung it from side to side. Michael told Daniel to slacken off the jibsheets some more as he in turn paid out the mainsheet. Easing the helm off even more Michael turned the bow of the dinghy slowly back up the estuary and the boom stood far out on the starboard side.

'Michael, just look at those two yachts further out. They're lying virtually flat on the water.'

'No time for sightseeing now Daniel. Just pay attention to this boat.'

What Michael hadn't realised, partly because he just wasn't skilled enough, was that a front had come through with an abrupt change of wind direction plus a little squall.

'Stand by to gybe,' said Michael, almost to himself, and he eased out the sheet some more. The next thing Michael knew was that he was choking with salt water. Kicking his feet and looking around Michael saw the dinghy flat on its side and Daniel was nowhere to be seen. The squall had come through with a ninety-degree change in wind direction. This had lifted Michael's boom, slammed the sail over in a violent gybe and knocked the dinghy flat. To add to the disaster the jibsheets had been left in the jamcleats and when the dinghy gybed the tight jib had pulled the little craft round another ninety degrees and it tried to become a submarine.

'Daniel,' called Michael. 'Daniel, where the fuck are you you stupid little git?'

'Michael, I'm here,' piped back a frightened little voice. Daniel's head and very white face appeared above the gunwale.

'Just hang on there. You can't drown: you've got your lifejacket on. Just hang on and I'll sort this bloody mess out.'

Michael knew enough to catch the end of the mainsheet and haul himself up to the stern of the capsized dinghy. He checked that the rudder and tiller were still safely attached and set about righting the ship. With a little effort Michael managed to get the dinghy head to wind.

'Find the bailer Daniel. It's tied to the thwart so it won't have floated away.'

'Got it,' came back a whisper.

'Now, I'm going to stand on the centreboard and pull her upright. You need to bail as fast as you can. She won't sink because of the floatation so we're okay. Got that? Bail like crazy when I've got her upright.'

'Yes Michael.'

Michael managed to right the dinghy and there was enough floatation to let Daniel bail. As soon as he could Michael hauled himself in over the stern and helped bail. Once there was enough freeboard Michael gently steered the dinghy into a gentle reach. The automatic draincocks in the stern started to work and the amount of the water sloshing about in the bottom of the boat went down considerably.

'Right, now why are both of us cold and wet?'

'We capsized Michael.'

'Wrong answer Daniel. First, I wasn't cold and wet to begin with. Second, we never capsized. A bloody great cruiser who didn't know his rules of the road swamped us.'

'But Michael we......'

'Shut up and listen. Dad'll accept us getting swamped by a cruiser. You know how he hates the bloody tin cans with engines. He's a sailor and he'll understand getting swamped. So that's the story. Got it?'

'Yes Michael, but let's get home, please.'

Back at Riverside cottage Michael's story was accepted without question. As Michael suggested Anthony railed against the stupidity and ignorance of cruiser helmsmen. Later however, Henri who was more sensitive to Daniel's body language quietly talked with his cousin. Daniel confessed that Michael had really capsized way out near the mouth of the estuary.

'Watch out for your brother Daniel. He may be clever and bold, but he is too reckless. He looks after himself so be very careful when you are out with him.'

'I will Henri. He frightens me on occasions.'

'Yes, Michael tends to frighten people, and he doesn't really care what happens to them. Marcel warned me that Michael was a "know it all" as a sailor. Trouble is Michael is the same when he climbs.

Too true, Michael exhibited the same reckless approach when climbing. His brain told him he could do anything, even when the rest of his body knew it couldn't. It was as if Michael lived in two different worlds where part of him said yes and the other part said no. In high-risk adventures this proves very dangerous. It happened later in Michael's final year at Bristol House when his mother took him up a steep cliff climb in Cornwall. Sylvia Lord was still a very compact and competent climber, even at forty-six years old. When she led young Michael up a particularly tricky and exposed climb she thought she might teach Michael some humility. Her idea was to teach Michael that some things were beyond him. In a way Sylvia was successful because Michael found the climb very difficult and needed a tight rope on two occasions.

'On belay, climb when ready,' called down Sylvia. 'Take your time and look first Michael.'

'Of course, of course,' muttered Michael. 'Take in. Climbing.'

Michael reached upwards and pulled.

'Remember to use your feet or you'll wear your arms out.'

'Okay, okay. I know. Let me climb will you. I waltzed up the first three pitches. Piece of cake really.' Michael moved his feet up and looked up at the next few feet. The rope snaked upwards above him to the next runner. The sea crashed on the cliffs well below his feet.

'So what's so hard about this climb that you took so long Mum? Seems straightforward to me. Can't see why the grade is so high.'

'Just look and think before you move up Michael. Nice and smooth, just as Henri told you.'

'And what does precious Henri know about it? Trying to be like his dad, and Uncle Charles died doing it so what's Henri think he knows?'

'Michael, concentrate on what you are doing.'

At this point Michael's left foot slipped off the little ledge and his body weight swayed left. His right hand gripped tighter as his left hand also slipped a little in the jamcrack. Michael felt his arms feel heavier and the forearms starting to burn.

'Try and keep the weight evenly distributed, and use your feet.'

'Jesus Mum, just what do you think I'm doing down here. I'm fine. Lighten up and let me climb.'

Michael rushed at the next section and with some strenuous arm pulling up the rough granite he reached a good wide ledge where he could rest.

'I'm at your first runner,' he called.

'Good, but now it gets a little tricky. You have to move left out onto the very edge of the rib before you come up.'

Michael looked up again and the rope went straight up to the next runner, up a very smooth wall. Looking over to his left Michael could see a possible line of holds but there didn't seem to be anything at the very edge of the rib, only a lot of space.

'Don't go too far around the rib Michael or you'll end up on the big overhanging zawn.'

Sod that thought Michael. 'Climbing,' he yelled. There didn't seem to be any handholds on the traverse going left and so Michael decided to climb straight up. He reached up for a couple of handholds and pulled. He was half successful but there was nothing for his feet. His arms tired and he lunged upwards for a good ledge, only it wasn't. Michael peeled.

Sylvia looked backwards for a moment and checked her belay was secure. She knew that this was a serious pitch and that Michael might want some help. That was why she had chosen this route. She gripped the rope firmly in the glove of her belay hand and made sure it ran smoothly through her belay plate. The anchor was bombproof. Everything was fine. Suddenly the rope went tight and pulling downwards.

'You off? You okay Michael?' she called down, and peered over the edge of the cliff. Sylvia could only see the top of Michael's helmet but she could hear a fair amount of scrambling and subdued muttering.

'I'm fine. Slack a little,' came the shout up the cliff.

Down below Michael was swearing fluently under his breath. He had tried to climb straight up to the runner but he was not good enough with his feet and his arms had blown out on him.

'Follow the line of footholds left Michael. Just move sideways delicately with your feet and balance with the hands until you reach the good holds by the rib. This bit's in your head.' Sylvia took in the rope a little tighter so there was no slack down to Michael.

'Don't pull me off,' cried Michael. 'Slack a little for God's sake. And what do you do with your hands on this next bit?'

'Balance.'

The rope went tight again but Sylvia could see Michael's head had now moved to the rib. Presumably Michael had just grabbed the rope and swung across.

'Slowly, delicately up the rib. It's quite exposed so look carefully for each hold.'

In a series of grabs, pulls, and lunges Michael managed to shimmy up the ridge with a tight rope looking nothing like a climber. When he reached the top of the climb he continued on, up past his mother's belay without saying a word.

'You safe?' asked Sylvia.

'Yeah, yeah, off belay,' said Michael, and he untied and walked away. Sylvia undid her belay and walked up to coil up the rope.

'It's tough that,' she said.

Michael didn't say anything then, and he didn't say much the rest of the weekend. Perhaps he had learnt his lesson thought Sylvia. Maybe now he will realize that there are some things at the moment he can not do, or can not do easily. Unfortunately Sylvia hadn't quite read Michael's mind the right way. Michael was storing the experience up to bully his brother.

Two weekends later Michael enticed Geoffrey to do the same climb, claiming that he had done it with mum and that all was fine. 'Mum sailed up it,' said Michael. 'It's really not as hard as the guidebook says. The only really tricky bit is the top pitch.'

'Did you lead through?' asked Geoffrey.

'No, I let Mum lead all of it. She hadn't climbed in a while and wanted to lead it. I told her I didn't mind if she wanted to lead all of it.'

'But the guidebook says the grade is far harder than anything you have ever done before Michael.'

'So, I got up it easily. It really is a neat climb.'

Geoffrey led the first three pitches fairly well, with a bit of a struggle to finish the third pitch. The belay ledge for the last pitch was two hundred feet above the foaming ocean. Already the sound of the splash of the waves was muted. It was an exposed position.

'Okay, so the next pitch gets interesting. Straight up for twenty feet and you can place a runner. Then it goes left out onto the rib and follows the rib to the summit,' explained Michael.

'Good protection?' asked Geoffrey, looking with some concern at the exposure and the drop off the belay ledge.

'I've got a good belay here. Place a runner as soon as you can if you're frightened.'

'Michael, I'm not frightened I'm just safe. If I fall off here it will be a free fall and you're going to have a strong pull on your hands and the belay.'

'Well don't fall off then. Remember what Dad used to say. What was it? "The leader never falls".'

'You on belay?'

'On belay, climb when ready.'

Geoffrey looked up the cliff and sorted out his first few moves. At twenty-three Geoffrey Lord was a cautious and somewhat conservative individual. He climbed surely but not forcefully. This fourth pitch was the crux of the climb and was distinctly harder than any part below. Geoffrey moved carefully up and placed a runner as soon as he could. He knew that a fall on this pitch without a runner could result in a serious strain on Michael and his belay. Once he had placed the first runner Geoffrey moved easier up the rest of the first twenty-feet and placed a second runner where Michael had said.

'Now you move left to the rib,' said Michael.

Geoffrey looked left and didn't like what he saw. A line of sketchy footholds showed a few scuff marks from previous feet. There was very little for the hands on this smoother granite face. After a few tentative attempts to go left Geoffrey knew that he couldn't lead this.

'Michael, this is too hard. I'm going to come down. Watch the rope.'

'Geoffrey, don't be a wimp. I did this two weeks ago with Mum. Just go for the rib man.'

'Michael, watch the rope. I'm coming down.'

'Well leave the bloody runners in then and I'll do it.'

Geoffrey downclimbed back to the belay ledge besides Michael.

'You think you can lead that?' he asked.

'Bloody right I can. I did it two weeks ago didn't I?'

'Maybe, I suppose so, but I thought Mum mentioned you had to have a tight rope a couple of times?'

'No, she's pulling your leg Geoffrey. It's a bit hairy you know but I got up before.'

The two brothers changed positions on the belay ledge and Michael organised the slings and stoppers on his harness. 'On belay, climb when ready,' said Geoffrey, and he carefully took in the rope as Michael climbed up to the first runner. Michael reached the traverse by the second runner and looked again to the left. From up here it looked even more difficult than it did two weeks ago. Nothing ventured nothing-gained thought Michael to himself. I only fell off because I tried to go straight up. He managed to forget he fell off on both the traverse and on the rib above. In fact, he had been lucky he didn't fall over the edge of the rib into the zawn.

It took all of Geoffrey's strength and skill to lower Michael down from that belay ledge. Needless to say Michael fell off on the traverse and pendulumed across the cliff with the rope held at the second runner. He didn't break anything but suffered severe bruising and scraping where his body had bounced and brushed itself across the rough granite. Geoffrey's second runner was sound and Michael ended up about ten feet below Geoffrey. Slowly Geoffrey lowered Michael down to the next belay ledge and made sure he was safely belayed. Leaving the runner Geoffrey rapelled down and lowered his brother two more times to the foot of the cliff. Michael's body was somewhat battered but his mouth was going a mile a minute. As usual somebody else was at fault. As usual someone else would pay for Michael's cock-up.

Back at Bristol House it was the unfortunate Aubrey Worthing who was to suffer from Michael's battered dignity. Michael returned to school with his hand bandaged and the other arm in a sling. He made out he was an immobile invalid and ordered Worthing about for everything.

'You fag for me and I come first. Don't you ever forget that Worthing. You're nothing, you hear me. All your life you will be nothing. Every time I speak you jump.'

A couple of months went by and it was the end of term. Michael graduated from Bristol House and went up to London University, but young Aubrey Worthing did not breathe any sighs of relief. Life at home was almost as bad as at school. His mother Diana insisted that he learn to ride and shoot. 'You need to be a gentleman Aubrey. Every gentleman can ride. Sit up straight and ease off on the reins. You'll strangle the bloody horse. Use your legs to guide the poor animal or he won't know what you want to do. Here, watch Vanessa; see how she uses her thighs.'

Yes thought Aubrey. I've seen her using her thighs, mostly on the lads in the stable rather than the horses.

'Pay attention boy. You're wandering again. Let the horse know who's in charge. Gently with the hands.'

Gently with the hands was what Aubrey was good at. His father took a different approach with young Aubrey. As Diana had taken over Vanessa and turned her into a tomboy so Lord Worthing decided to teach Aubrey the intricacies of locks. Lord Worthing's great grandfather had developed a passion for watches and locks, but only as a Victorian hobby. However, a setback in the family fortunes led to his grandfather turning the hobby into a business. Although "being in trade" was frowned upon in the aristocracy the grandfather Worthing developed a useful business in locks and safes. Lord Worthing's own father had refined the business and changed it to concentrate on locks and security systems. It had moved from the purely mechanical into electrical and ultimately digital.

Aubrey's gentle hands moved slowly and smoothly over the mechanism. 'Feel the inside Aubrey,' said his father. 'See the mechanism in your mind. You've seen what it looks like in pieces and how the parts work together. Now, imagine how they can be undone.'

Aubrey listened, focussed his mind, moved his delicate tools, and 'click' opened the lock.

'There's a clever lad. Now try this one.'

To escape from his mother and her passion for shooting and riding young Aubrey grew up over the next couple of years learning from his father. It wasn't long before Aubrey was a very adept locksman. This helped Aubrey rebuild his self-confidence. However, just when life started to become a little more pleasant for Aubrey, Michael Lord came back into his life.

Michael had remembered young Aubrey Worthing, and how he could bully him into doing anything. He had also remembered the skills that Aubrey possessed. Now there was a worthwhile object in the school that Aubrey could get for him, and that would surely impress Stanley Rogers, and Melanie too come to that. After a couple of weeks Michael heard from Melanie that she and daddy were coming back to England. So, thought Michael, time to set some plans into motion.

'You're nothing remember,' whispered Michael. 'I've told you over and over that when I speak you do.'

On a cold sharp March evening Michael and young Worthing were crouched in the shadows of the school quadrangle.

'You're mad,' muttered Aubrey. 'You've come back here to steal the "Sword of Honour".'

'Not steal you gibbering idiot, replace. I've got a replica. No one will know the swap has happened.'

'Why?' persisted Aubrey, while thinking of the dangers of reaching the "Sword of Honour".

'Shut up,' snarled Michael. 'That's not your concern. Just take this copy and swap them.'

Michael thrust the wrapped package into Aubrey's hands. 'Now, get on with it.'

Michael had left the school some two years before. During the time of his last year as a prefect Michael had discovered that his young fag, Aubrey Worthing, had a developed a useful skill - lock-picking. Young Aubrey was going to get the school's Sword of Honour for Michael because Michael needed it for a scam. Michael thought it was important to impress Mr. Rogers that Michael was a man of character and achievements, and worthy of marriage to his daughter Melanie. The Sword of Honour, after being suitably engraved with Michael's name as the student of his graduating year, was to be photographed. Michael pictured the scene with Melanie and himself holding the sword as a happy competent couple. Such a picture and such an award from a prestigious English Public School were just the sort of thing to impress an American, particularly an American with ideas about English character.

Aubrey crept away from Michael in the quadrangle and made his way to the Great Hall. Several things had changed at the school since Michael had left and Michael needed Aubrey's knowledge and expertise to obtain the sword. The sword itself was valuable as an antique, coming from the seventeenth century. The long tradition with the school as a Sword of Honour added value, and uniqueness to the item.

For many years the sword had been kept in a glass case at the end of the Great Hall. This case was under the various plaques listing headmasters, head boys, and the memorial tablets of old pupils killed in the wars. Numerous silver cups and chalices of sporting events won over the years were also exhibited in this area. Several thefts from the school had resulted in some changes to this arrangement. After some consultation the school authorities decided to remount the sword in a special case with high technology locks. The locks came from Worthing Securities and young Aubrey knew how they operated.

The Great Hall was large, cavernous in fact, and dark. The wood-panelled walls dulled the little moonlight that drifted in from the long slender windows. Aubrey had no difficulty with the simple locks on the main doors. He paused and looked at the case containing the sword. As a minor inconvenience the case had been moved from a table on the floor to be mounted higher up on the wall.

Aubrey moved to the panel controlling the various security devices. Lock-picking for him was easy and not at all frightening. So why were his fingers sweaty? Why was he shaking? Why was he frightened? Michael Lord, Michael Lord frightened him. In fact Michael Lord terrified him.

'Fail me fag and I'll let it be known that you stole the examination papers in my last year. I'll quietly inform the Head that you were responsible for the ammunition theft out of the armory. Remember how puzzled they all were that the locks did not appear to have been touched. I know you, and I know what you can do. Fail me and I'll break you.'

Standing shuddering in the gloom of the Great Hall Aubrey cringed into a little ball. He curled up with the fear and embarrassment of what Michael Lord could do. The school would expel him. His father would disown him. His mother would tear him to shreds and his sister would scorn him. His life would stop.

'Remember you are nothing. All your life you will be nothing.' Michael's words rolled around inside Aubrey's head to torment his frightened body.

With an effort that wrenched at his heart and soul Aubrey looked back at the control panel. Deftly he moved switches, entered key codes in the numeric pad, and turned off the various safety devices. He did this in a dream with the fear pushing him into automatic mode. The case could be opened and the sword removed.

In his fear-filled body Aubrey moved across the Hall to the array of exhibits. To reach the sword case he had to balance up on the various shelves holding the cups. Slowly Aubrey moved up the wall towards the case. He stopped.

'Now what?' whispered Michael in a threatening tone. 'Why have you stopped?'

'I can't do this,' whimpered Aubrey. 'I think I'm going to fall.'

'Get back up there you useless arsehole or do I have to do everything myself?'

'No Michael, you wouldn't know how to open the case.'

'Well then. Now that we've settled that obvious problem get the hell up there and get that sword.'

Aubrey shuddered and looked back up the wall to the sword case. He balanced his way precariously back up towards the shelf. Michael watched in the shadows of the wall. Aubrey reached the right height and looked across at the case.

'Is it there? Can you see it?'

'Yes Michael. It's here. It's really here.'

'Well get it out slow-poke and hand it down. I'll give you the replica to put back in its place.'

'Michael, I need a spare hand to hold on with while I open the last lock.'

'I thought you said the controls were all down here on the floor?'

'Yes, they are.'

'Well then, what are you babbling on about? Get it open and hand it down.'

At the case itself Aubrey paused to check the status of the various security device lights. All green, all safe. He opened the lid and reached down for the sword. As he touched it a violent shock ran up his arm and through his body. With a sob of anguish that he had forgotten one of the devices, and with a scream of pain from the shock, Aubrey fell slowly backwards to the floor of the Hall. He landed on his right leg that folded unnaturally under him, breaking in the process. His shoulders crashed onto the floor and his head thumped on the boards. His physical pain was overwhelmed with the fear of the inevitable outcome of his failure. In his mind Aubrey went mad.

Contrary to Aubrey's suppositions his father didn't disown him, even though the school did expel him. Moreover his mother did not tear him to shreds. With his sister Vanessa his mother visited Aubrey in the nursing home many many times. After a series of slow and painful conversations Lady Diana started to gain an inkling of Aubrey's life and Aubrey's state of mind. As these histories gradually evolved the huntress in Lady Diana slowly resurfaced. Also, somewhat belatedly, the mother instinct returned. No one had the right to harm the Worthing offspring. No one!

5 Daredevil

'Get a move on kid,' grumbled Michael. 'I haven't got all day.'

'I'm coming as fast as I can Michael,' panted Jean as he struggled to fit his Laser onto the boat trolley.

'Here,' said Chuck, 'I'll help you Jean.'

Chuck rested his dinghy trailer on the ground and offered a hand to Jean. Michael's nephew, really a second cousin, Jean was only nine, and slight for his age. Trying to lift the bow and slide the trolley underneath at the same time was awkward for the youngster. He had only been sailing for one season but he had developed a passion for the thrill of letting his Laser skim over the water. He had been pestering his Uncle Michael to go sailing for weeks. Marcel, Michael's cousin was an international yachtsman and his son Jean wanted to be like his father. Unfortunately Marcel was away racing most of the time somewhere around the world and had little time for his two boys. Marcel's brother Henri pestered Marie, Marcel's wife, and bullied the two boys Jean and Philippe. To escape Uncle Henri Jean had latched onto Michael as a sailing instructor.

Michael raced with the University of London's sailing team and they kept some boats at Burnham-on-Crouch in Essex. After some persuasion Marcel had bought a laser for his son and also stored it in the trailer park at Burnham. Jean kept pestering Michael and eventually Michael agreed, but for a fee. Chuck was a school prefect at Jean's school and Jean fagged for him. Like many prefect and fag relationships at Public Schools this was beneficial to both boys. Chuck acted as a mentor for young Jean. Part of the fee that Michael had exacted for this day's sailing was a series of introductions and invitations to Chuck's family's country house.

Master Chuck Faxon was the eldest son of Foster Faxon, who ran a software communications business but also had interests in the media of radio and television. Although Foster ran his business out of Atlanta Georgia he wanted all his children educated in England. Chuck was the eldest, and he had pioneered the way at one of England's better Public Schools. To bridge the Atlantic Foster Faxon rented a spacious country house in the broker belt south of London. Invitations to Mr. Faxon's house were a useful entree into parts of the software world. They also provided opportunities to meet some of the eccentrics of the media crowd, especially those of the female gender. Michael had demanded a high price for his company as a sailing instructor. After his failure with the "Sword of Honour" Michael was in need of some other way to influence Melanie Rogers and her father. Going for a day's sailing might be a cheap price to pay for some useful contacts and impressive acquaintances.

Jean was a slight slip of a lad and so pulling his dinghy was tough sledding. By contrast, Chuck Faxon was built like a tank. He rowed for the school and made a devastating wing three-quarter in rugby.

'Just watch the stern Jean as we go up the ramp,' said Chuck, as he easily pulled Jean's trolley up the riverbank. 'I'll spin it round on top of the bank and you can hold it while I get my boat up here.'

'Okay Chuck, I can hold it once it is on top.'

'God you two take forever,' muttered Michael as he impatiently waited on the ramp.

With the sails all rigged, the battens in their slots, and the sheets ready to tighten, it was easy to reverse the trolleys down the ramp to the river and be off. Michael quickly eased his dinghy "Raider" into the water and just dropped the trolley on the ramp. Fitting the rudder onto the pintles went smoothly. Michael skipped lightly over the gunwales and settled amidships. With a deft backing of the jib and a quick tightening of the sheets Michael slipped easily off the ramp - leaving his trolley for someone else to worry about.

Chuck's hackles rose as he watched Michael take off without another thought.

'He's an arrogant bastard,' grunted Chuck. 'All for one and screw the rest of the world. Let this be a lesson to you guy,' stated Chuck, pointing at Michael's actions. 'Don't ever give him any opportunities or tempt fate with your precious Uncle Michael. He'll walk all over anybody.'

Jean watched. Chuck might be his mentor but Uncle Michael was Jean's hero. Jean wanted to be able to do what Michael could do, and then maybe he could do what his father did. Michael had already won several yacht races, including some in "Raider". Michael sailed hard and competitively. He pushed the rules as hard as he could with shouts of 'right of way'. As a well-coordinated youth, Michael could be quite acrobatic when the conditions were windy and he took on any challenge.

The three dinghies responded to the gusting April breeze and tacked downstream. A brisk easterly wind blew over the Essex marshes and funneled up the river between the mud banks. Although it was springtime it was still chilly on the East Coast. The tide was ebbing and more and more of the grey ooze that made up the land of this part of England appeared. It was an open and exposed countryside and the breeze blew straight in from the cold North Sea.

Sailing close-hauled with their centreboards lowered the dinghies flew over the water. As the wind continued to freshen the dinghies heeled over further and further. Jean was sailing in "Scud" and he had to let the bow come up into the wind on several occasions as the gusts swept down on the trio. Each time that he did this he would lose some momentum and drop back.

'Keep it upright and keep it moving,' shouted Michael. 'You've got to keep the mast upright and maintain momentum. Just ease the sheets a little rather than luff, but you've got to learn to keep the hull driving.'

'It's blowing a bit hard Michael,' observed Chuck. 'Shouldn't we reef?'

'What!' exclaimed Michael. 'You don't reef in Lasers - you bloody sail them through anything and make them fly.'

'Well then, let's turn around and head back upstream,' said Chuck. 'It'll be more sheltered up the river.'

'You bloody Confederate wimp,' yelled Michael. 'This isn't a placid rowing event Chuck; this is just the right element for these Lasers. If Jean's going to learn to race dinghies he needs to know how to handle them in all conditions.'

They had tacked for a couple of hours downstream and the river had widened as it approached the North Sea. Already there was a swell coming in from the open sea that was making the ebb tide choppy. Combining this with the force four winds made for some vicious whitecaps.

'Michael, we'd better turn back,' repeated Chuck. 'This is getting pretty hairy out here. I have no desire to check how bloody cold the water is if I capsize.'

'You won't capsize dumbo,' said Michael. 'Anyway I was planning on turning after the next couple of tacks. We can reach across the river mouth and gybe by the channel buoy. With this wind the reaching should be really fast.'

I might not capsize thought Chuck but Jean could. He is a lot lighter and the swells will make him roll. Chuck glanced over at Jean. The kid's face was pale and strained. The wind had been finicky. To ensure that he was ready with a quick response Jean had not let his sheets go into the jamcleats. This meant he had been gripping the jib sheets, the mainsheet and the tiller now for nearly three hours - he was tiring. It was a strain.

'We'll race around that channel buoy and head upstream,' called Michael.

'Michael, with this ebb tide that's going to be very shallow around that buoy,' observed Chuck.

'Yes, well, just be prepared to raise your centreboard quickly as you go round the buoy. You'll want it raised anyway for the run back up the river. I'll teach you to sail goose-winged. That way the boat can plane and really pick up speed. You just have to keep watching you don't yaw and gybe.'

Jean listened to this exchange and shuddered. He was cold. The spray from beating into the wind for three hours had soaked through most of his clothing, even though he was wearing a life jacket. The water that came on-board emptied itself through the self-draining cockpit but still his feet were soaked. He pulled himself closer into his damp clothes. The thrill had long gone. Survival was the order of the day but he daren't let Michael see his misery.

As he eased off the sheets onto the reach the dinghy picked up speed. Now they were sailing across the mouth of the river and the swells rolling in from the east made the little yachts heel over sharply and then spring back up again. Concentrate, concentrate, concentrate Jean told himself. Watch the waves, the wind, the tell-tales, the sheets, and the tiller. A large wave suddenly broke viciously over the port bow and green water was flung all over Jean. He started to lose some feeling in his hands as they tightly held the sheets.

'Remember,' yelled Michael, 'let her head fall off the wind and monitor the sheets to stop the boom sweeping you overboard. Do this slowly but positively. Once you are running then worry about the centreboard. I'll go first to show you what to do. Let Chuck come after you.'

Jean nodded that he had heard, even if the instructions had not all gone in. The wind whipped the tops off the waves and salt splashed into his eyes. Dam, that stung.

Michael expertly sped across to the channel buoy. He rounded it very tightly with a beautiful controlled gybe and the sails filled immediately. A quick body movement and he had the centreboard up and Raider was planing fast upriver.

Chuck and Jean were both reaching across the river with the wind abeam. To let Jean go next Chuck went about and headed northwards away from the buoy. Michael was already moving rapidly upstream with a following wind. Jean flinched as another large wave broke over the port side. At least I won't be getting wet when we are running thought Jean.

Suddenly, faster than he expected he was near the big black channel buoy. These buoys marked the deep-water channel. There was too much to do all at the same time. Jean pulled the tiller up into himself and eased the bow away from the wind. The bow wouldn't turn quickly enough and Jean continued way past the buoy. He dropped the jib sheets and nearly let go of the mainsheet. Quickly he tried to haul in the mainsheet to control the boom. A sudden gust made the boat heel over and tried to pull the head up into the wind. I can't turn downwind sobbed Jean. Desperately now he jumped over to the other side of the stern and forced the tiller up into the wind.

'Turn, turn, please turn,' cried Jean. The wind squalled and the boom lifted threateningly. The mudflats under the shallow water grabbed at the centreboard and the dinghy stopped almost dead in the water. The fore and aft line of the boat pivoted and suddenly the boom crashed over and the dinghy was laid flat on its port side. Water poured over the port gunwale. The mainsail thrashed with its loose sheets and the jib flogged itself around the forestay.

Jean panicked. He released all the sheets. He let go of the useless tiller. Sobbing distractedly he pulled the centreboard up. The dinghy floated free and immediately ran before the wind. Jean grabbed the tiller and steered back towards the channel. With no centreboard down the dinghy crabbed sideways. Gradually things returned to normal. Jean fielded the mainsheet and helped trim the mainsail so that the dinghy had steerageway. He managed to temporarily lash the sheet so that he could go forward and reach the crazy jib sheets. Eventually things were back to normal.

Chuck hadn't seen the start of Jean's adventure. He had sailed across the river mouth on his reach. He had just gone about when he saw that Jean had sailed far past the buoy and was in trouble. By the time that Chuck had eased off the sheets and sped across to Jean the situation was under control.

Chuck gybed slowly and carefully and sailed alongside Jean. He saw the cold blue face with the white claw like hands strangling the sheets.

'Are you okay Jean?' asked Chuck. 'What happened back there?'

'I went too far past the buoy and ran aground,' whispered Jean. 'It's all a blur. Everything went too fast. I think I let go of everything. I'll never be a sailor,' he sobbed.

'Don't worry,' said Chuck. 'You're in one piece. You're upright, and you're sailing. You did okay.'

'What the hell's going on?' bellowed Michael. 'Can't you do something as simple as rounding a buoy without turning it into a bloody circus? Hell, I told you what to do. I even showed you what to do. You know the river is shallow outside the markers at the bottom of the ebb. You dam nearly ended up being a houseboat.'

'Leave off Michael,' growled Chuck. 'You push too hard. There was too much wind and the swells made it hard to steer.'

'The kid's got to learn sometime,' said Michael. 'That is a simple routine. Just think what it is like doing that in a real wind when there are a dozen other skippers anxious to get round the marker at the same time.'

'Okay, okay, but it's not a racing environment and you are supposed to be teaching not terrifying.'

Chuck's attitude was wasted on Michael and Jean was somewhat oblivious to the entire exchange. Jean retreated further into his shell - disillusioned at appearing a failure in front of his hero. Actually, Michael hadn't even seen what Jean had done. Michael had come back downstream because the other two had taken so long.

'When you two are quite ready then we'll continue the lessons. Are you ready for the next simple exercise Jean?' asked Michael. 'This is one procedure where you really have to keep your wits about you, otherwise you might get wet.'

'I'm fine Michael,' said Jean. Michael was oblivious to the white pasty face and the slumped shoulders. He was also unaware of the cold, wet shivering going on in Jean's boat.

Michael turned Raider upstream and let the easterly wind fill the mainsail with the boom well out to port. Gradually turning directly downwind he reached the point where he could draw the jibsheets smoothly and let the wind fill the jib on the starboard side. Watching carefully for any severe rollers coming upstream Michael neatly let his dinghy glide goose-winged.

'There Jean, see how he gently did that?' said Chuck. 'He went smoothly from a conventional run into directly downwind and eased the jib across to starboard. Just do it slowly and if anything happens slide back into a conventional run.'

Chuck made it sound easy but Jean was already shell-shocked and not hearing everything. Effects of hypothermia were starting to invade his body. Already he wasn't completely focussed. The wind from the east picked itself up in spiteful gusts and created short sharp swells on the ebbing tide.

Jean slowly eased his dinghy into a more downwind mode playing out the mainsheet carefully. The swells rocked the little boat with its light ballast and the boom rose and fell alarmingly. As instructed Jean gently pulled the jib sheets to feed the wind into the jib so that filled to starboard.

'I've done it,' he cried. ' I'm sailing goose-winged. I'm really flying.' And indeed he was. The little dinghy planed up and sped upstream chasing Michael. Chuck watched carefully. The spiteful gusts increased.

Without warning the wind suddenly bounced round to the southeast and caught Jean's mainsail. The boom lifted violently and the sail slammed across the boat to the starboard side with lightening speed. Fortunately Jean was short and the boom didn't behead him. The dinghy spilled violently to the right as both sails pulled the little boat onto its starboard side. Without any warning Jean was flung bodily out of the stern into the mainsail lying flat on the water. Catching his toe on the gunwale stopped his flight but caused his head to smash into the boom. The dinghy half lifted up before another gust flattened it again but this time Jean was now under the mainsail with his feet tangled up in the mainsheet.

Impervious to any of this drama Michael was far upstream. Chuck however was closer to hand and he saw Jean's dinghy capsize. As quickly as he could Chuck sailed past Jean's boat and turned to come back upwind. He laid his own dinghy neatly alongside Jean's hull. Just as he did this Jean's dinghy turned turtle completely. Chuck grabbed his painter, dropped his sails anywhichway and jumped into the river alongside Jean's boat. Frantically he searched for the jib jamcleats to attach his painter and keep the two yachts together. All this took time.

'Jean!' Chuck yelled. 'Jean!' Chuck tried to stay calm and organised but panic was starting to set in. He too was cold and wet. Systematically Chuck traversed the hull of Jean's dinghy but Jean wasn't there. It took precious seconds for Chuck to realise that he couldn't dive under the boat still wearing his life jacket. He quickly shed it and lashed it to the painter. Taking a deep breath he dove under Jean's upturned boat. Chuck never stopped to think how dangerous this might be. With both sails still up and the sheets floating anywhere Chuck could easily become entangled underwater.

Chuck was virtually sightless in the gray cold muddy water. You could only find anything by feel. Drawing breath on the upturned hull Chuck decided to try and right Jean's dinghy. Lasers are fairly light and by twisting at the stern Chuck was able to roll the boat at least halfway. Jean's body had now rolled up in the mainsheet and foot of the mainsail. Wearing his life jacket helped keep him buoyant in that position. Chuck fought his way through the cold water to Jean's white face. Instinctively Chuck held Jean's head back while supporting the neck and tried to check his breathing. Feeling nothing he pinched Jean's nostrils and clamped his cold mouth on Jean's to breathe warm air into the cold body.

'Breathe dam you,' said Chuck. 'Come on, breathe for god's sake,' he thought as he pushed his air into Jean's mouth. The response was nil. Nothing stirred in the limp cold body. Chuck didn't know CPR and there really was no hard surface to press against anyway. He grabbed Jean and spun his back to his own chest. With his hands clasped tightly together under Jean's heart he tightened his arms one, two, three, four. Again, one, two, three, four. Nothing stirred. There was no coughing up of river water. There was no audible inhale of breath. There was no gasping.

Nothing changed. Again Chuck spun the body round and performed mouth to mouth. Still no response. There was never any response.

Four gulls wheeled over the river and called. It was a long mournful shriek. It was also a long struggle for Chuck to eventually hoist young Jean's body over his stern. Righting Jean's laser wasn't too hard and Chuck downed the sails. Very slowly he managed to get his own dinghy under way and despite a gusting easterly wind driving him upriver he gradually sailed back to the marina.

ဆ

Marcel, who had been racing down in Australia flew back for the inquest. Marie was inconsolable over the loss of her firstborn. She berated Marcel for sailing. She berated Henri for driving Jean to Michael. She berated Michael for letting Jean drown. All of the Lord family was at the inquest, which came in with a decision of "death by drowning through misadventure". Chuck Faxon was obviously a key witness at the inquest. He answered all of the coroner's questions in a very subdued quiet manner. The accident had deeply disturbed Chuck, and Cousin Henri sitting in the courtroom detected some things unsaid. After the case was over Henri spent some time talking with Chuck, trying to find out a little more of the events of that day.

Henri then compared what he learnt from Chuck with the testimony or answers of Michael. There were several things that didn't quite add up here. Henri talked things over with his brother but Marcel was anxious to be off back to his races. 'What's done is done brother. Talking any of this over won't bring Jean back and that is the only thing that will help Marie. Leave it and let Marie grieve.' Henri remembered the similar incident with Daniel down at Riverside on the river Dart. As soon as he could Henri got Chuck Faxon and Daniel together and the three of them went over the evidence again and again. Somehow, this wasn't quite so simple an accident. It needn't have happened.

Although troubled by the accident Michael didn't let Chuck Faxon renege on his promise of an invitation to his father's house. Foster Faxon's back garden looked like a cross between a Hollywood film set and part of the Science Museum. Several types in suits were debating the intricacies of a fascinating array of media technical equipment. Wandering between the suits was another set of people with loud shirts, pastel shorts and ponytails. Decorative ladies hung on arms.

'You've got a nerve being here Michael. I thought you'd been banished from civilized society.'

Alan Matheson was always to the point. He jabbed his stubby finger into Michael's chest to emphasise his comment.

'Heh, back off,' cried Michael. 'I'm here at the express invitation of Foster Faxon, our host. My Dad's company has been doing business with Mr. Faxon and I'm here to go over some details.'

'I'm surprised your Dad trusts you to be out of the house let alone handle any business details.'

'Problems Michael?' asked Stanley Rogers, Melanie's father.

'No Mr. Rogers, I'm just getting the third degree from Mr. Matheson here. He is nursing a grudge from earlier in the year and this is the first time he has seen me.'

'Hi, I'm Stanley Rogers of Future Graphics in California. I do business with Foster Faxon back in the States. And you are?'

'Alan Matheson. You know this reprobate?'

'Certainly do. Michael is engaged to my daughter Melanie. We know the Lord family fairly well, Anthony, Sylvia and their kids.'

'Well Mr. Rogers, a word of warning. Michael was engaged to my daughter earlier in the year, my precious Veronica, and that ended in disaster – for Veronica.'

'Yes, but that wasn't my fault,' interjected Michael. 'It was Veronica who crashed her car. Sure, it was a rotten night with the road like glass but I wasn't driving. I wasn't even there with her.'

'No, you weren't, but you were supposed to be weren't you? You should have been looking after her. You took her to the party and you should have looked after her, but no, you had to be womanizing with some floozie.'

'Enough,' cried Michael. 'I don't need this. I'm sorry for your loss Mr. Matheson but Veronica caused the accident and I had nothing to do with it.'

Michael walked away leaving an angry Alan Matheson and a puzzled Stanley Rogers.

'Be warned Mr. Rogers, that lad is dangerous. Despite what he says he caused my daughter's death. I know it.'

'Well now, I am concerned at what you are saying,' said Stanley Rogers. 'Michael has known Melanie for some six months and they seem an excellent couple. My daughter loves Michael and his life style, plus I know he is intelligent and quite successful at University. The family is strong and supportive. In fact I get on very well with Anthony Lord, Michael's father.'

'You're right. Anthony Lord is a good man. I have climbed in the mountains with him a few times. A very sound straight arrow but the family has a history.'

'What history?' asked Rogers.

'Get Michael to explain some day the history of the second child in the Lord family in each generation. They are always a problem. Traditionally they have been wild, eccentric, and dangerous to those around them, and Michael is the second child. Haven't you noticed anything unruly about Michael?'

'Well, yes. He is self-centred and was involved in a tragic accident earlier this year.'

'Sounds like Michael,' said Alan.

'It was kind of strange because Michael was helping a friend of my daughters. One of Melanie's friends had come over from California and didn't know many people here in London. Michael took Melanie and her friend Bella down to the Lord's Fotheringham Manor in Somerset in the winter. Melanie said the house was marvellous and the grounds beautiful in the snow and frost.'

'Yes, Michael with more than one woman again.'

'No, nothing like that. Bella was gay. It was just a chance for her to see some other parts of England before she returned to California.'

'But she didn't return to California?'

'No, well yes, but not the way she intended. She tried to ski off the roof in the nighttime and killed herself. Her parents came over and they took her back to be buried in California.'

'And Michael was nowhere to be found I suppose?'

'No, Michael was in the house with Melanie, but the accident had happened in the middle of the night.'

'And I'll bet the coroner's verdict was "death through misadventure",' said Alan Matheson. 'Just another example of how Michael and mishap seem to go together. As I said Mr. Rogers, be very aware of young Michael Lord. There is a zone around him, around his very self-centred core.'

Foster Faxon had drifted over to the two men at the tail end of the conversation. He touched glasses with Alan and Stanley. 'Hear you two talking about a black sheep?'

'I'm not sure he is a black sheep in the eyes of his family,' said Alan, 'but he doesn't get my award for "Man of the Year".'

'Well my son Chuck has just been telling me about his last little escapade with Michael up on a river on the East coast. This didn't involve any daughters, just a second cousin, a young lad, Jean Lord.'

'And the lad survived?' asked Stanley.

'No, unfortunately not. Chuck was involved in trying to rescue and resuscitate young Jean but he died. It was a traumatic experience for Chuck as this was his first encounter with a dead body.' Foster briefly described the series of events leading to the death of young Jean. 'Caused some strife in the Lord family I can tell you. But, they have had a history of personal tragedies. Anthony can get quite philosophical about it after a couple of drinks. Calls it the "survival of the fittest", but I'm not quite sure it is the fittest that actually survive. Anyway, you two come and meet some happy people. I've some guys from Atlanta Stanley who need some special video equipment for small-scale modeling, for children's TV programming. For you Alan we have a challenge on how to freeze some plastics without them becoming excessively brittle. Your expertise would really help. I'll refill your glasses and move you into a more positive frame of mind.'

The three men wandered back to the main throng of people and the conversations turned to technicalities of machines rather than the shortcomings of humans. Michael circulated, but kept a wary eye out on who was who. Perhaps the young lady over there twirling her champagne glass would be glad of his company.

Through the Looking Glass

6

'Party-time, party-time,' purred Melanie down the telephone. 'Michael, can you hear me? I said it's party-time.'

'Yes, sure darling,' muttered Michael as he fondled Danielle. 'I'll be there.'

'Michael, I said we would take Maureen and David. They're staying with me. They want to meet some real people for a change. Do you hear me Michael?'

'Yes, sure darling,' said Michael as he tucked the telephone under his chin and tucked Danielle under his thighs. Danielle chuckled deep down in her throat and bit Michael's nipple. Michael reacted viciously by pinching and twisting Danielle's nipples. She squirmed and squealed.

'Michael, what are you doing?' demanded Melanie down the telephone.

'Balling my black cat,' replied Michael, 'and it's tight.'

'Michael, your horrid sometimes,' wailed Melanie. 'Pick us up at nine tomorrow evening.'

The telephone slammed down. Michael slammed Danielle down and finished what he started.

After Bella's death Melanie Rogers had calmed down a little. However, that was three months ago and some new friends from California had come to stay with Melanie. Maureen and David Frinton had fronted a rock group from Berkley for the past nine months. It had been a frantic series of gigs up and down the Californian coast. There had been a revival of the music and dancing of the sixties without the drug scene. In fact most of today's kids seemed more hooked on alcohol and binge drinking was far more the in thing.

David Frinton was tall and muscular. He had the power in his arms gained mostly from wielding a hammer and chisel in his sculpting. His commanding presence and forceful voice had captured the heart and soul of Maureen O'Donnell. David was already a force at Berkley in his mid twenties. His art was hard and spectacular. As a native of Mutare in Zimbabwe David had inherited his mother's love and understanding of artistry in stone. David's Shona grandfather had been a native artist although at a time in Southern Rhodesia when such art was not appreciated. The stark juxtaposition of black and white in the statues and the strong stripes that looked like a lion had carved them with his claws caught the eye. It was powerful emotional art from a strong man.

Maureen had arrived at College to study voice and drama and she was soon very involved in the music scene. She was emotional, passionate about music, and had all the laughter and sorrow of her Irish ancestry. It had been Maureen, who was the lead singer for the folk/rock group called the Night People who had enticed David into the group. Now the pair of them fronted the band.

Michael had finally disentangled himself from Danielle's arms, legs and lips. The sensual black cat stirred in her half-sleep.

'You're leaving,' she purred, and rolled over provocatively.

'Got to go lover.'

'I suppose you're going to see that fat cat Melanie, the one who whores in green.'

'She's not fat so pull your claws in. And yes, green is a very desirable colour.'

'So is black,' said Danielle, and she rolled over and over on the bed.

'Well, just to please you Danielle I will see someone black tonight. I going to see and hear David Frinton.'

'He's not black. He's, how do you say it in England, he's a coconut, a Hershey bar, all brown on the outside and white inside.'

'Whatever. Keep the sheets warm.'

'Fuck you Michael. Maybe I'll crash this artsy-fartsy party and see whether black and black goes well together.'

The door crashed as Michael left. Christ, I need a drink he thought. It didn't take Michael long to find a pub and drown part of his annoyance in best bitter. Better thought Michael. Just one for the road and then home to get organised for tonight. I hear the lovely Maureen with the flaming red hair is a passionate lady. Maybe she will sing for me tonight.

'Melanie, I hear that your brother Rodney is coming over here from California?'

'Yes. Daddy wants him to go to an English Public School like Michael did before he goes to College.'

'You mean a private school don't you?' asked Maureen.

'No love, she means a Public School,' said David. 'The English take a delight in confusing anyone not English with their unusual use of common words. It seems to make them feel superior when they think you don't understand the simple Queen's English.'

'And they do love to feel superior,' added Maureen. 'The history and much of the music of my people's country relate to the sorrow caused by the superiority of the English.'

'That's where I have an advantage,' laughed David. 'I inherited the strength and attitudes of my father complimented by the emotions and artistry of my mother. I am a man of tomorrow.'

'Well go and be a man elsewhere,' said Melanie. 'Us ladies are getting dressed.'

'Not nervous are you Maureen?' asked Melanie. Maureen flushed as she put down the bottle.

'No, not really. David often does this to me. He is so powerful and his voice is so good. I sometimes wonder whether I fail him; whether I let him down.'

'Nonsense,' said Melanie. 'You know you sing wonderfully and powerfully together. Your voices blend and harmonize beautifully.'

'I suppose,' whispered Maureen. 'It's just every now and then I find I need to feel better about myself.'

'But David's nuts about you. You saw the last piece of work he did. He dedicated it to you and it was a masterpiece. All the critics loved it. Even David himself thought it was good.'

'It's true to be sure, but, always but, I'm not so sure of myself. This is especially when we go on stage. He's such a big man. You don't realise how that makes you feel when you're up there on the stage. I almost feel lost and insignificant.' Maureen had wound herself up into needing another swallow.

'Courage mon brave,' laughed Melanie, trying to lighten the mood.

'Ladies, the evening draws closer,' came the voice from offstage.

'Okay David: we've got our glad rags on and all we need now is the driver of the chariot.'

The "driver of Melanie's chariot" had managed two or three for the road before roaring home in a better frame of mind. Michael parked his sports car and navigated his way upstairs to get organised for the evening. In a hot bath Michael relaxed and contemplated the possibilities of the forthcoming evening. Melanie had described Maureen to Michael. True it had been a rather careful and guarded description, as Melanie did not want Michael straying too far. She had mentioned David in passing. Then, thought Michael there was always the possibility that Danielle would make a surprise appearance. Now that could really stir things up. A kaleidoscope of black, white, green and Maureen's swirling red hair flickered around Michael's mind as he snorted and breathed in heavily.

'Dam,' said Michael, as he nicked himself with the razor. Having a head full of coke and a gut full of beer didn't quite lead to steady hands whilst shaving. He staunched the trickle of blood and wandered downstairs to find a whiskey. He sat naked at the foot of the grand staircase and supped gently on the whiskey glass. He was sitting there musing when there was a knock at the door. Michael dropped the glass and unsteadily rushed upstairs as the butler came into the hall to answer the door.

Posing in front of the mirror Michael said, 'gorgeous; a work of art.' He swivelled round in a pirouette and succeeded in crashing down onto the softness of his bed rather than the floor. 'Balls to that,' said Michael as he closed his eyes and nearly fell asleep.

'Balls, and Prince Charming, and Lords on White Chargers.' The words spun around the bedroom as Michael went into overdrive with socks, shirt, pants, trousers, and shoes being tried, rejected, retried, laced, buttoned, and finally, perfected. The Lord, Michael Lord, paraded in his finery in front of the mirror again and looked the part. Michael walked elegantly slowly down the grand staircase as if making a celebrated entrance. Much to his chagrin no one was home and so the effort was wasted. However, a couple of drinks and he felt quite the man of the moment again.

Dam, fuck, and dam again,' exclaimed Michael. His father's Jaguar was gone from the garage. This was to have been the chariot for the night.

His mother's car had gone too. Perhaps that was what the knock at the door was all about. Well, looks like it's all aboard the Mighty Mouse. Michael's sport scar was flash, fast, luxurious, but only a two-seater. It could roar like a mouse, based on the film that Michael had always liked. However, seating four was tight.

'Michael, we can't possibly fit into Mighty Mouse.' Melanie was quiet upset. She had been telling Maureen some fine tales about Michael and the Lord family. Now, the tales looked rather deceiving as Michael roared up in his sports car.

'Princess, your chariot awaits. It is a magic carriage. What you see as having two seats actually has four. When David and I sit in the two seats we create two more seats for you two ladies.'

'When David and you sit in the two seats there isn't any room for anything let alone two ladies,' wailed Melanie.

'Christ, stop weeping woman. A couple of drinks and we'll all be fine.'

'I need a drink if we're to fit in there,' said Maureen. She and Michael reached for the bottle and their fingers touched. 'Nice,' said Michael. 'Fiery and soft all at the same time.' Maureen snatched her hand away and David moved his weight a little closer.

'Michael,' he said somewhat ponderously, 'let's see whether we can get ourselves calmly organised and down to this gig.' Michael downed his drink and grinned maliciously. 'Sure bwana, I'll clear the mombes out of the road.'

David didn't rise to this jibe but went out to the car and opened the doors. 'Okay ladies, let's see how we can do this as best we can. Michael, do the seats move back at all?'

'Sure, leastways the passenger seat can. I can't move the driver's seat any further backwards or I won't be able to reach the pedals.'

'Well, let's move them back as far as possible, shall we?' said David.

'What are mombes David? Do they jump on the road or block it?' asked Maureen.

'They're bloody great cows lady, with big humps, just like Melanie here,' muttered Michael, 'but you'll only find them in Shonaland.'

'David, what is he talking about? Melanie, has Michael had too much to drink?'

'Don't mind Michael Maureen, he's just showing off that he knows where David comes from. What were we talking about earlier concerning the supposed superiority of the English? Why don't you two sing some "Freedom" songs tonight and make Michael realise the English have lost the Empire.'

'Don't you believe it kiddo. We may not fly the flag over half the countries in the world but we still rule in language and communications. If you don't speak English no one will understand you, apart from a few froggie people.'

'Michael, you're positively loco, but we do need to get to the gig.'

With the seats moved back they found that they could comfortably sit Maureen on David's lap. However, it soon was obvious that Melanie could not sit on Michael's lap. There just wasn't room.

'Switch ladies,' said Michael. 'Melanie's bigger than Maureen and.... ouch.'

'Pig,' said Melanie, and she slapped Michael again.

'I just meant it would be easier if you sat on David's lap and Maureen, being smaller, could fit on mine.'

'Sure, sure,' said Melanie. Maureen giggled but David only glowered.

They found that the most practical solution was a compromise. Melanie could fit on David's lap and the easiest way for Maureen was in-between Michael and David. She slid a leg down each side of the crankshaft and rested her buttocks on the edge of the seats.

'Just be very careful how you change gears Michael,' she giggled.

'All aboard,' yelled Michael and the car jumped forwards leaving behind a spray of gravel. Maureen fell half backwards and her knees flew up. Her skirt rode up to her waist and Michael nearly drove off the road. Fortunately David couldn't see where Michael was looking.

Michael changed gears, letting his fingers slide up the soft thigh each time. Maureen tried to press her legs together and bite her lip. Michael watched the effect of his hand on the thigh. He wondered whether Danielle would be at the party.

The Arts Department of the local College had staged the whole event. They had erected a couple of enormous marquees on the sports field with one for the band and a second as a beer tent. By the time that Michael and the Mighty Mouse arrived the place was jumping. Maureen extricated herself from the gear lever and Melanie peeled herself off of David's lap. David got out without a word to Michael but the body language said a lot.

'So what's the agenda? Actually, I could do with a drink,' and Michael set off to the beer tent.

'Let him go for the moment Melanie,' said David. 'He really is a rather uncouth Englishman.'

'Too handy by far,' added Maureen.

'Maybe,' said Melanie wistfully, 'but I like him whatever you say. He really can be so exciting. He's so full of life.'

'He's so full of himself,' said David, 'but, come on Maureen we've work to do. We'd better find the rest of the musicians and see what's lined up for tonight. Melanie, you going to come with us to find out?'

'Yes, I'll come along with you for starters and then find Michael after he's had his drink.'

The threesome set off to the main tent where they could already hear someone strumming on a guitar. Most of the tent was filled with folding seats but there was a cleared area in front of the stage for people to dance. The Arts Department had collected several large photographs of David's sculptures and arranged these around the walls of the tent.

'Well, you didn't expect them to get the sculptures themselves did you?' asked Maureen when David said he was surprised to see the photos.

'No, I'm just surprised that they got them at all,' he said.

'They are an Arts Department David. Perhaps some of the people here think your art is worthy of display. You should be flattered.'

'True, true, I am, although I sometimes wonder whether the folk here really understand what is in the sculptures. Can they feel the message?'

'Probably not David,' said Melanie, 'but that doesn't mean they don't enjoy them, for the artistry in itself. It's like some of the music that Maureen sings. Many of us don't know the history behind the words and don't know the pain behind the emotion but we can still enjoy the beauty of Maureen's voice. Even without understanding the message we can still appreciate the skill of the messenger.'

'Hi, I'm Pat, the so-called stage manager for tonight. You look like Maureen O'Donnell and David Frinton. Am I right?'

'That's us,' said Maureen. 'What's the set-up? Do you have some musicians, singers, dancers, or whatever? We're prepared to sing most things, well, aren't we David?' and Maureen turned to look up at the big man.

'Sure Maureen, we're here to help however we can.'

'Great, well you know tonight's really a Charity do, with the money going to UNICEF, so we thought we'd try and plug the children's issues as much as we can. Can you put together some numbers that have children somehow in the themes; failing that, some words about family values? Maureen, the Irish are full of family issues.'

'And don't I know it,' answered Maureen.

'We've got a drummer, a bass guitarist, and a girl with a heart-rending violin. Actually Maureen, Maeve Finnegan is also Irish, but then what would you expect with a name like that? She's from near Newry.'

'Which side of the border?' asked Maureen.

'I'm from south of the border my love, don't you worry. I'm a strong Republican and an ardent supporter of the Sinn Fein.'

'You support the I.R.A.?' asked Melanie forcefully.

'If they help the cause darling I do. I'll support anyone who can help the cause.'

'But they're terrorists. They throw bombs.'

'Not quite love. They don't tend to throw anything, except a few sticks and stones at the Provos on March Day. But, you're right, they're not averse to a little attention getting. Just make sure the dear old English realise they're on the way out.'

'Whist Maeve; we're here to sing tonight not go on any political march. David, let's get together with the group and sort out a couple of sets. Melanie, we're fine. Why don't you go and find Michael before he consumes too much of the beer tent?'

'Fine, as long as you lot don't start an anti-British revolution just outside London. I'll go and get myself a drink. I'll see you all later.'

While Maureen, David, and Maeve joined up with the other musicians Melanie walked over to the beer tent. The place was crowded with lots of young people drinking and joshing each other. There was a background of piped music but the noise from the chatter drowned out most of the melody. It didn't take Melanie long to find Michael. He was propping up a large keg on the plank bench chatting to two ladies who didn't look old enough to drink.

'Michael, there you are. Can I have one of those?'

'Which one would you like love? This one is Susie and this one is Teena. They both swing both ways so it doesn't really matter which one you choose.'

'Michael, I want a bloody drink. I'll have a pint of bitter.'

'Well why didn't you say so? Excuse me ladies whilst I seek refreshment for the princess here.'

Melanie linked her arm through Michael's and dragged him off the keg. This happened so quickly that Michael stumbled and dropped his tankard on the floor. The two girls giggled.

'Christ woman. Now look what you've made me do. I've spilt beer on the dresses of these two lovely ladies.' Michael picked himself up and started pawing the front of Susie's dress.

'Michael, put a sock in it. You really are a clown at times.' Melanie laughed in spite of herself.

'Jesus, don't laugh at me woman. I'm just being the perfect gentleman.'

'In your dreams maybe. Come on, get me a drink and then let's go and hear David and Maureen.'

'Coming ladies?' asked Michael over his shoulder as Melanie started to drag Michael away. Susie and Teena continued to giggle as Michael appeared to be reluctant to leave.

'Beer Michael! Beer, now!'

'Sure, sure, can't a chap have a few words with some friends? Okay, so what'll it be? Can't seem to remember what you asked for. I think I'll have a beer, how about you?'

Melanie managed to guide Michael over to the counter and ordered two beers. She took a sip out of one of them and Michael watched. 'And mine?' he asked. 'Where's mine?' Melanie picked up the other glass and slowly poured it over Michael's head. He spluttered and shook himself.

'You silly bitch. Now look what you've done. What a waste of a perfectly good pint.'

Turning round Melanie ordered another pint and gave this to Michael. 'Here, you silly Lord, drink this and come and hear the music.' Melanie leant over and licked the dripping beer off Michael's face and kissed him. 'Come on lover, let's go and hear Maureen.'

The pair wandered back to the stage tent. On the stage a pair of young girls in spangled tights was juggling. They combined their routine of passing coloured balls with lots of rolling and other acrobatic moves. Before long there were five balls in the air and the two girls appeared to have non-stop movement.

'There Michael, there's a new challenge for you.'

'What, keeping my balls in the air?'

'No Michael, writhing on the floor in star-spangled tights.'

'Heh, I can do a really good writhing on the floor as you well know.'

'Too true Michael,' said Melanie rubbing up against Michael, 'but I seem to remember you couldn't keep your balls in the air at the same time.'

'No, but I kept something else up in the air.'

'Yes, but not for long if I remember correctly. I don't think your routine was as long as the two girls on the stage.'

'It's quality that counts lady, not quantity. I don't remember there being any disappointments from the audience about quality. Quite the contrary, I remember the audience shouting for an encore.'

There was an explosion of clapping as the two girls ended their routine with a dramatic finale. 'See,' said Michael, 'even the audience here agrees with my recall.'

'That's not for you bighead. The girls have finished, just as you were that night. Anyway, Maureen and David are on next so let's listen to some real talent.' Melanie lightly punched Michael's shoulder and holding his hand she led him to the rows of seats.

Pat walked to centre stage and held up his hands. The din in the tent diminished a little to a low buzz.

'Okay folks. You've just seen the Lazlo sisters from Hungary. They were great weren't they?' The crowd responded with a loud burst of applause and clapping.

'Now, remember this evening is a UNICEF Charity event so please give what you can. There are donation boxes around the tent and over in the beer tent. As a special surprise this evening we managed to persuade David Frinton to come here. Those of you in the Art world have seen David's dramatic sculptures. For those of you who haven't we have several pictures around the walls of his art. In addition David is a singer with a group in California. He will sing for us tonight along with his co-singer, Maureen O'Donnell from the group called Night People. Let's give a big hand for David and Maureen.'

A wild and loud burst of cheering thundered around the tent. Pat stayed on the stage and held up his arms again as the noise dropped. 'One final thing I forgot. The group playing with David and Maureen is of course our own trio of Maeve, Donny and Mike on drums. So, let's all have a great time and don't forget to make those donations.'

As Pat left the stage Mike sounded out a formidable series of drum rolls and the trio settled into a strong rhythmic beat. David walked onto the stage from the left side and lifted the microphone off the stand. The music pulsated strongly behind him and flooded the tent. On queue David's voice soared into a passionate tale of the yesterday's children growing up into the world of today; the world of today that our parents created. It fitted right in with the age group in the tent. They could all relate to the lyrics of the song.

As the applause died down at the end of the first number David looked across to the other side of the stage and smiled. 'And now,' he said, 'from Galway Bay, via Candlestick Park; from the green of Eire via the sunshine of San Francisco, I bring you the lovely voice of Maureen O'Donnell. Listen to her words and weep. Feel the power and the passion that comes from this little colleen.' Maureen walked in quietly from the right side of the stage and stood alongside the massive frame of David. She looked up at him and smiled. She turned to face the audience. She felt the ripple of amazement rather than heard the gasp from the crowd after she had sung her first few notes. The power of her voice from such a diminutive frame was truly awesome. As David said she sang with a passion about the sorrow of her people struggling with oppression. Again, the words were easily heard by the youth in the audience. Any "protest" song tends to be well received by the youth of every era.

'I need a drink. All this listening makes me thirsty.'

'Well, go then Michael. I want to listen to Maureen. Come back and find me here.'

'I won't be long. I need a piss too.'

'Shush, let me listen. She has such a wonderful voice. She sings so well with David. They make a great couple.'

'I've gone.'

'Well go then but be quiet about it.'

Michael took off and succeeded in reaching a quiet corner of the outside of the tent before he pissed himself. Shaking the drips off he was about to pull up his fly when a quiet sultry voice whispered, 'I can help you with that kind sir.'

'Danielle, what are you doing here?'

'Helping undo your fly Michael and stroking your penis, don't you think?'

'Heh, cut it out.'

'Why, don't you like me stroking my little friend here?'

'It's not your little friend, it's...'

'No Michael, you're right, it's not my friend when it's little is it? It's only my friend when it is big and strong, and it's getting bigger and stronger Michael.'

'Danielle, let's go somewhere quieter? This isn't the right place.'

'True, but I'm off to see some other friends Michael, see you.'

Leaving Michael with his penis semi-erect and sticking out of his pants made Danielle giggle as she looked back. 'You must be in mourning Michael with you're flag at half mast.' Laughing to herself Danielle wandered away into the stage tent. Michael stuffed his penis back in his pants and zipped up his fly. He was too vicious and the zip caught and wouldn't do up. 'Shit, shit,' said Michael. 'Christ, a guy can't take a piss in peace nowadays.' Two girls came by and stopped to watch Michael jumping up and down tugging at his fly. 'Can we help?' asked Teena. 'Oh look Susie, see who it is? It's our Lord.'

'We're real good with zippers,' said Susie. 'We'll soon have your pants off.'

'Bugger off girls. I've just got it stuck.'

'We've heard that before. Playing the one-handed flute were you? Got caught in the act? Bloody pervert, can't even give a girl a thrill.' Susie and Teena stomped away in their thigh-high white boots. Michael was getting really wound up by this time but eventually he managed to sort out his pants and find his way to the counter of the beer tent.

'Two pints please.'

'Coming up. That'll be ten quid.'

'Ten quid? I want a beer not liquid gold.'

'This is a Charity event mate. You're here to give.'

'Bloody right I'm giving.' Michael downed the first pint without the beer touching the side of his throat. 'Jesus, that feels better.' He worked his way steadily through the second pint.

'And again mate. It's been a trying night and I'm trying to forget most of it.'

'And another fiver then.'

Michael peeled off the five pound note and sat down on one of the benches. There were still lots of people hanging around in the beer tent. The amplifiers were good enough to send the music over and the noise level in the beer tent had diminished from earlier.

'Got a match dearie?'

'Don't smoke.'

'How about a drink then? Not good to drink on your own.'

Michael looked up at the pair of deep brown eyes broadly set in the smooth face. Wavy brown hair covered the top of the head and as Michael panned downwards a pair of moist lips pursed themselves.

'You look like you should certainly buy me a drink love. Mind if I perch?'

Michael slowly let his eyes focus on the rest of the body. A shirt undone to the waist showed a hairless chest leading to a cinched waist and a tight pair of Levis. 'Like the view sweetheart?' The arms moved and a heady fragrance rolled across the space between Michael and the questioner. Michael took a sip of his beer and looked back up at the face coming closer to him.

Once again beer flew through the air. 'You bloody poofter,' shouted Michael. 'Get your bleeding face out of mine you bloody cocksucker.' Michael threw what was left of his pint upwards at the pouting face.

'You animal you. You've ruined my shirt.'

'I'll ruin more than that if you hang around here any longer. Get your fruity body out of here.'

'Heh, enough of that. Let's calm down can we?'

'I'm quite calm,' said Michael. 'This animal was just leaving. He didn't like the beer but I'll have another one.'

'Well, try drinking this one then rather than throwing it all around the place.'

'No problem,' said Michael.

'Michael.'

'Oh God, more trouble,' said Michael to his pint.

'Michael, we need to go back to the stage and pick up David and Maureen. The shows over, or didn't you hear any of it?'

'The show was over here love, and now it's over too. Let's have one last drink and we'll go back to my place for coffee or whatever.'

'One last drink Michael and then we're off. I told Maureen we'd be about ten minutes.'

'Bartender, two more pints if you please for my lady and I.'

Melanie managed to pry Michael away from the bar after the one last pint and half-carried him back to the stage. David and Maureen were saying thanks and goodbye to the three musicians. Obviously it had been a successful gig.

'Back on the road said Mr. Toad,' cried Michael as he wandered back to Mighty Mouse.

'Michael, you okay to drive?' asked Melanie.

'Cos I am love. Can drive in my sleep.'

'Yes, that's what I'm afraid of; you falling asleep.'

'No problem. Look, we got here alright. The show was a gas. We'll all trundle home and it will have been a great time. David, you've had a good time haven't you? Beats hammering and chiselling surely? You just stand up there and sing; piece of cake.'

'Yes Michael, it's been a piece of cake but Maureen is tired and we would like to get home to Melanie's.'

'Yes Michael. It's been a grand evening but singing can be quite demanding and I am tired as David says.'

'Right folks, then let's sort ourselves out and load up the Mouse.'

Once again David slid his solid frame into the passenger seat.

'Can't I sit on David's lap this time Michael?' asked Maureen.

'Yes Michael, it might help you keep both hands on the wheel if Maureen sits on David's lap. I noticed you changing gears too often.'

'Won't work love. Maureen's just that much smaller. You'd never get your legs down alongside the crankshaft.'

'Well okay but keep both hands on the bloody wheel and I'll change gears when you need to,' muttered Melanie.

'Whatever you say love. Anything to keep the peace.'

'Come on then Michael, let's all go home.'

Melanie slid into the passenger seat onto David's lap. Michael went round to the front of the car and fell over. 'Michael, Michael, are you okay?'

'Yes, I'm fine. Must have been something I ate earlier.' Sliding his hand along the top of the bonnet Michael managed to reach the drivers-side door.

'All aboard,' cried Michael, and slipped and slid himself down into the bucket seat. 'Hop in gorgeous,' he said to Maureen. Maureen carefully climbed over Melanie and David and organised herself between them and Michael. She was feeling tired.

'Home James, or whoever,' cried Michael and let out the clutch. 'Change Melanie,' he called. 'Up into second. Now third.' The engine speeded up. 'Now fourth, and home free,' cried Michael. The car sped along the dark country lanes.

'Heh kids, see the moon? Looks like a giant lantern up there. Look, coming out again behind those trees.'

'Michael, watch the road not the moon,' said Melanie.

'Give over. Talk to David or something and let me drive.' Michael accelerated. Melanie was half-turned and talking to David but the wind whipped past the windscreen in the open-topped car and carried most of the words away. David concentrated on trying to hear what Melanie was saying. Only Maureen saw the lorry. Everyone else was looking elsewhere.

Too slowly, much too slowly, Michael's foot stabbed for the brake but his foot couldn't reach. His slow-reacting body twisted to reach the brake but the seat belt constrained his extension. There was a sudden tilt as the back wheels lifted and a piercing scream, which cut off immediately.

'Lucky you had your seat belt on mate. 'Ere, sit quietly. Keep yourself wrapped up. The ambulance will be back in a while. It's just rushed yer mates to the Hospital. Feeling okay are you? You've no broken bones and no bleeding the doc said. Bloody lucky you were.'

Michael's head swam round and round in a semi-concussed fog. Over by the lorry he could see what was left of a redesigned Mighty Mouse. The front end had ploughed into the side of the lorry but fortunately almost head on into the back wheels. This had prevented the car from sliding right under the lorry and decapitating everyone.

Melanie had a broken arm and broken nose from the windscreen. David had thoughtfully drawn the seat belt around Melanie and himself and this had prevented both of them from being thrown forwards. By instinct Michael had belted himself in. Maureen had been found the other side of the lorry. As the back wheels lifted she had been thrown headfirst against the side of the lorry. Her scream had been cut short on impact and the momentum had tumbled her inert body forwards.

'Here comes the ambulance sir. We'll have you looked after straightaway. Not to worry eh?'

7 Broken Backs

THE NIGHT OF THE GIG had passed without undue incident. Michael had gone to hospital in the ambulance but only to be checked over in the Outpatients. He had several bruises but nothing broken. The police were a little slow in following up on the incident and so the alcohol test was taken well after the accident. As David and Melanie were buckled up the police presumed the same was true for Michael, just that Maureen was so small she slipped out of the belt when the car stood on its nose. True, Michael was charged with drunkenness and speeding, based on the damage at impact, but then the lorry had no lights and was not roadworthy, so much of the investigation concentrated on the vehicles rather than the people. Michael didn't see David after that evening at the hospital but Melanie said he was absolutely furious over Michael's actions. Michael managed to drop off the radar for a while into the library stacks of London University. Days passed.

Examination time had come and gone. After two years at London University Michael still managed to do well academically. Without any real effort at studying Michael could easily put pen to paper. He could sit through the stuffiness of large rooms with many students shuffling papers, books, and parts of their brains and read and answer the questions without too much stress. It was the "after exam" events that stressed Michael. There were parties, and parties, and then more pressure. Within a week, by mid June, Michael was stressed out and felt he needed to clear his head. He also realised it was now nearly mid year and he hadn't done much about his New Year's resolution. He telephoned Geoffrey with a plan.

'Say brother, what about a weekend in the hills? I need to get out of London and clear my head. Let's the three of us have a family weekend away somewhere?'

'Michael, I can't just down work and flit off somewhere because you're bored.'

'No Geoffrey, no, not at all. I thought it would be cool for you, Daniel and me to get together. We haven't seen much of each other for a couple of months. I know Daniel can get away from school for a weekend. Why don't you pick him up, pick me up and we'll go for an excursion up in North Wales?'

Geoffrey held the telephone away from his ear for a moment and thought about it. The last escapade of Michael's had really shaken him. The police had investigated the accident and the results were not pretty. Michael was found to be drunk, and so was Melanie but she wasn't driving. The police had taken away Michael's driving licence and it was a wonder that there weren't further charges. Michael had come back from that accident to the last week of lectures and then the exams. All in all Michael had been through a rough patch. Geoffrey could understand that Michael might want some supportive activity. Perhaps a weekend for the three brothers would help.

'Michael, let me think this over. I'll need to talk to Christina and explain the need, and I'll talk to Dad.'

'Geoffrey, who runs your life? This is a brotherly thing. Christina's Italian, she'll just get told it is a macho event that happens regularly. The boys need to get together.'

'Okay Michael, keep your shirt on. I was just thinking out loud about how to sort things out my end.'

'Well brother, just remember that you're in charge, head of the family like before anyone gets any false ideas. You'll call Daniel? My name isn't really respected at Bristol House these days remember after the little fracas and rumours about Aubrey Worthing.'

'Michael let me organise things down here. I'll pick up Daniel on Friday evening and drive up to Bangor overnight. We'll all meet up in Bangor.'

'You're not going to come to London to pick me up? The police have taken away my licence you know, and the Mighty Mouse is hors de combat so to speak.'

'No Michael. I will not drive up to London just to pick you up. You're perfectly capable of catching a train up to Bangor. That's by far the most efficient way to get us all there. Just bring some hiking gear and we'll meet up at Bangor station.'

'Christ Geoffrey, London's not much out of your way. Just pop up the M4.'

'No Michael, I'm going to pick up Daniel and pop up the M5 and meet you in Bangor. Now, which weekend?'

Michael sat on his bed swinging his legs and kicked clothes around the floor. Which weekend? Well it didn't bloody matter did it? It was Thursday, and Michael was seeing Danielle tomorrow, and Melanie had talked about a party on Saturday.

'Geoffrey, let's go for this weekend. Tomorrow evening.'

'Michael, that's impossible, it's too short notice. I'll never get my work organised for this weekend. It's not the office that's the problem it's the estate. I've a sheep breeder coming to see me Saturday and the sawmill manager wanted me to go with him on Sunday to look at a new kind of gang saw.'

'Well if you're not going to make the effort, why are we bothering?'

'No Michael, we'll do it but let's make it the following weekend. As I said, I'll bring Daniel up with a load of gear in the car. Actually, I'll probably bring up one of the estate Landrovers. Daniel can sleep in the back on the trip up so he won't be too tired. I can carry lots of gear and the rover will go on any rough roads further than the car.'

'Fine Geoffrey, I don't need a detailed itinerary of your planning. Agreed, next weekend and you'll pick me up at Bangor Station first thing in the morning. I think the overnight train gets in about five. See you then.'

Michael dropped the telephone on the cradle and lay back on the bed. Hell, he'd have to find another way to unwind for a week. The flat was driving him crazy. Other people's books lay scattered around and CDs splayed over much of the floor. Posters advertising various concerts hung sloppily from the walls. Hiking and climbing gear was conspicuous by its absence, but there Michael was neat and tidy. Such items saved your life and Michael was very careful with such equipment. Borrowing other people's books and music was okay but you looked after the personal "life preservers".

Wandering over to his cupboard Michael opened the door to do some stocktaking. He took everything out and carefully laid the array of equipment on the bed. He picked over the various gaiters, gloves, helmets, ropes, harness, slings and nuts. Carefully he checked the condition of the soles of climbing slippers. He tested, and tightened where necessary the knots on the runners. The climbing ropes he uncoiled slowly and ran his fingers along the length of the kernmantel sheath as he re-coiled the ropes. He stowed the gear back into his climbing sack and hung it back in the cupboard. The climbing gear looked good and the hiking gear was always in good shape. Just missing my hiking boots noticed Michael. I'll sort out the clothes later. Still, it all depends on what Geoffrey brings he mused and I'd better tell him to bring my boots.

Down in Somerset Geoffrey mulled over the conversation. Sounded like a good idea. Actually, he thought a weekend away from Christina and a teething son Peter might be a very good idea. He might get some peace and quiet. Geoffrey picked up the telephone and spoke to the Head Master's office at Bristol House. It wasn't too difficult to arrange for Daniel to be away with his brothers for the following weekend and Geoffrey promised he would have Daniel back at school by Sunday evening. The Head Master's Secretary agreed that Daniel having a weekend away with his brothers was probably an excellent idea. However, on the home front Geoffrey experienced a different reaction.

'Geoffrey darling, you can't be away for a whole weekend. Peter needs you now. He needs his father to be with him. Remember you said it was never too early to start grooming him to be the next heir. You and your father told me very early on that you were so proud of your family traditions. That always impressed my papa.'

'Christina, this is a Lord family thing. The family has always supported each other. Look how Stephanie went over to France to try and persuade Charles to come home. Hell, even Dad went over. And then Stephanie adopted Charles and Helene's three children after the accident.'

'Si amore, I understand, but a whole weekend. What will we do?'

'Christina, don't get so dramatic. Let's sit down and have a glass of wine and we'll sort out what you can do while I am away with Daniel and Michael.'

'And you will be so far away darling. You will call every night? You will call and speak to Peter?'

'Christina, calm down. Dad and Mum will be here, or perhaps you would like to go to Stephanie's?'

'No Michael, there is too much pain in that household after Jean was drowned. Marcel is gone and Henri keeps pestering around Marie who spends her days crying over Jean. That house is too sad.'

'Well, just stay here with my parents. They'd love to see more of Peter. Remember, he is their only grandson. Dad thinks the world of him.'

'Maybe you're right Geoffrey. I get too excited. I should, how do you say, develop the stiff upper lip.'

'I don't know about that but just spend a quiet weekend with my folks. I'll phone every night, unless we're camped somewhere up in the hills.'

'No Geoffrey,' wailed Christina. 'Stay somewhere civilised. Why do you have to be off in the wilds? It is dangerous. All sorts of things could happen to you. There are wild people out there.'

'Christina, this is Wales, not the hills of Sicily. We do not have bandits or any such folk roaming Snowdonia. It is quite civilised. We're more likely to have our tents invaded by sheep than partisans.'

'Geoffrey don't joke about it. It's not funny. I just get worried about you. A husband's place is by his wife's side. You should look after me. Papa would expect it.'

Geoffrey's patience was wearing a little thin from this dialogue and he thought back over one of Michael's comments. Who really wore the pants in the household? Would his mother ever have spoken to dad in this way? No, mum was much more subtle. She never nagged, but she did keep score and had her share of success with dad. They were a good couple. Actually a weekend for Christina with mum and dad would probably be a good thing; she might learn a thing or two. Come to think of it Christina and I haven't been apart since we were married. Perhaps it is time for a little "absence makes the heart grow fonder" cliché thought Geoffrey.

'Mum was just saying the other day how much she would like some time with you Christina. You know that the pair of you have never really had a good girl to girl session. Mum would love that and Dad could spend most of the weekend showing Peter all the various parts of the estate. He's never been up to the top plantations that Great Grandmother Virginia started. Dad might take him to meet Antonio and Enrico, our two Italian workers from way back. So, that's settled then. Mum gets to tell you all the family secrets and how to control the Lord men and Dad gets to spend the weekend with Peter. What do you say?'

'Oh Geoffrey, you really can be so clever and forceful. It's a lovely idea.'

Over the weekend Geoffrey organised what had to be done on the estate while he was away. The sheep breeder was very happy with what he saw of the programme on the farm here. He planned to return later in the season after talking with Stephanie. The sawmill manager was content that Geoffrey saw the new saws but there really didn't seem to be any reason to change the ones they had at present. Geoffrey also made sure that Norton Ferris, the forester had his operations under control. Still, you never really knew with Norton. He was a shifty character. Maybe I should think of hiring a professional forester thought Geoffrey, the way we used to have. It could wait though thought Geoffrey and he forgot it quickly as other events crowded his mind.

The following week Michael kicked his heels around London. The round of parties continued even though many of his fellow students had left to work for the summer. Daniel's week at Bristol House was more stressful. Michael might well have finished his exams but Daniel's were due to start in early July. Daniel worried far more about such things and the idea of being away for a weekend just added to his overwhelming woes. Geoffrey had an uneventful week at work but he saw his dad on Tuesday and mentioned what the three brothers were doing over the weekend.

'Great idea Geoffrey. There is nothing special happening here in the Company that needs your attention over the weekend. You finished up the business contracts for Cecils. There are some new regulations coming down about Exports but they can wait until you return. The three of you should have a ball. Any ideas what you're going to do?'

'Not really Dad. None of us are very fit at the moment. I really haven't done anything this year. I've hiked around the estate a bit but haven't done any climbing. Actually, I was a bit put off after that last accident Michael had down in Cornwall a year or so back. Hope that calmed him down a bit.'

'Well that was Michael now wasn't it Geoffrey? Still, you did really well in bringing him down. Good job you kept a level head. Michael always was a little too bold.'

'Maybe we'll just go hiking this time. I know Daniel's not too keen on climbing. I think Henri helped put him straight about his brother.'

'Yes, Henri's a fairly level-headed young man. After watching him I think he is quite a good climber too. He may have helped Daniel overcome some of Daniel's fears. You need to climb though Geoffrey. It does one good to push occasionally, know where the limits are. Helps you later in life and in the business world too. I've learnt a lot from climbing, about myself mostly. I know your mother feels the same way. That's why she took Michael on that climb in Cornwall two years ago, to try and teach him when to say no. Trouble is Michael never listens. Still, I think it's good. Anyway, whatever you decide to do, have fun son.'

'Sure Dad. Oh, by the way, I've told Christina that I will be away for the weekend and she was a bit upset about it.'

'Silly girl. She should know better. The men have to spend time together.'

'No Dad, not about that, but I persuaded her that Mum wanted to spend some time with her. I told her that Mum wanted to have a girl to girl talk and let on about the secrets of controlling Lord men.'

'That's dangerous Geoffrey. You never know what your mother might tell her. Your mother can have a very vivid imagination when the mood strikes her. On your head be it.'

'Well Dad, I had to say something. And, I told her that you would be delighted to take Peter around the hidden corners of the estate. So he can grow up and know the full scope of his future heritage.'

'Thanks a bundle Geoffrey. Actually though, that's not so bad. I like little Peter and I haven't spent a lot of time with him. Maybe that was a good idea.'

'So, it's this coming weekend Dad. I've arranged with Daniel's school that I will pick him up on Friday evening and drive up to Bangor.'

'How's Michael getting there?'

'I told him to catch the train. I wasn't going to go up to London and then to North Wales.'

'Makes sense, although Michael won't think so.'

'No, he didn't but I told him that's how it was. Perhaps it'll teach him not to drink and drive. I'm going to take the estate Landrover so that Daniel can sleep more easily in the back and it'll carry more gear.'

'That's fine Geoffrey. No problem. Have a good weekend and your mother and I will look after Christina and Peter.'

'Thanks Dad.'

While Michael kicked up his heels in London, and Geoffrey organised his world in Fotheringham Manor, Daniel was struggling with being a teenager at school.

'So I hear you are off gallivanting with your two brothers this weekend young Lord?'

'Yes sir,' answered Daniel.

'Well it should be a good chance to clear all of the cobwebs out of your head so you can get ready for the exams,' said Daniel's Housemaster, Dr. Carruthers.

'Well sir, I hope that I can remember enough from now until July. This year seems to have been particularly difficult.'

'Being in the Fifth Form is always hard,' said the Housemaster kindly. 'This is the last year when you have to carry so many subjects. After this year you can concentrate on those things that really interest you, when you go up into the Sixth. Have you thought what you will do in the Sixth?'

'Not really sir. It probably depends how well I do in this year's exams.'

'What would you like to do? Do you have any preferences? I seem to remember your father and your brothers concentrated on mathematics and sciences. Is that what you want to do?'

'I'm not sure sir. I'm not very good in math but I do like biology. Perhaps I could do biology and maybe geography in the Sixth. My Aunt Stephanie is a vet and she did biology.'

'Well, that's good thinking. You need to think where you want to go when you leave Bristol House; whether you want to go to College, or straight into work, or perhaps even travel. Doesn't your Uncle Marcel travel a lot?'

'Yes sir, but he does it to go racing. He's a professional yachtsman.'

'Well, whatever you decide to do young Lord make sure that you give it your best shot. Your brother Michael always wanted to be out front, although sometimes a little too boldly. Perhaps a better role model would be your brother Geoffrey, although he was rather too conservative. But, most importantly, you should be yourself. What do they say, look after number one. Off you go then and get into prep. There's still two more days before the weekend and you've studies to do.'

Daniel took off with his books and entered the prep room. Forty other boys were already there supposedly doing their homework, although the concentration levels varied.

'Where have you been Lord? Late again I see,' said the Prefect in charge of the prep room. 'Care to explain to everyone why you are late, or by just being a Lord does everyone know what a crazy family you come from?'

'Dr. Carruthers stopped me and asked me some questions.'

'Dr. Carruthers stopped me and asked me some questions sir!' said the Prefect loudly. 'Just remember, when I'm in charge here it is just like a master being here. Is that clear?'

'Yes sir.'

'Good, and what did Dr. Carruthers, your friendly old Housemaster ask you Lord, or is that a secret?'

'He asked me what I was going to do in the Sixth sir.'

'And did Dr. Carruthers explain that you have to pass exams before you get into the Sixth Lord, or did you just take it for granted that you would get into the Sixth?'

'No sir. No sir.'

'Well Lord, if you don't sit down and do your prep, and get it right, you will probably never see the Sixth. Now sit down and get on with your work, and that means all of you lazy jackasses out there,' he said as he looked over the rest of the boys in the room.

The room settled down again. For a couple of hours heads and shoulders of forty boys hunched over desks and pens scribbled across paper. There was the usual scratching of heads, whispers, books dropped, and the occasional note circulating but for the most part all was quiet. At nine o'clock the Prefect told all of them to finish and collecting their books the boys filed out.

'Daniel, Daniel, what did old Carruthers really want?'

'Actually, he was asking me about this coming weekend but I wasn't going to tell Vincent that. Vincent would have lauded it over me and forced me to explain, and then tried to ground me and not let me go.'

'He wouldn't dare. You could explain that it was a request from your dad, perhaps even an order.'

'Vincent wouldn't care. He's just a bully. He really gave young Didcot a hard time yesterday.'

'You mean his fag? What did he do?'

'Well first of all he had him clean up all of his cricket gear ready for the weekend. You know, blanco the boots, the pads, wash the gloves.'

'That's normal. Every fag expects jobs like that.'

'True, but Vincent has to go over the top and make Didcot do it for all the Prefects.'

'But Didcot didn't have to because he only fags for Vincent.'

'That didn't stop Vincent trying it on though did it? Young Didcot was partway through the third set of gear before Bessemer caught it and asked him what he was doing.'

'What did Didcot say?'

'Well the poor kid was terrified because Bessemer's such a big chap. He thought Bessemer was going to beat him for going through his gear. It took a while for Bessemer to understand what was going on.'

'And what happened to Didcot?'

'Vincent was furious when he heard what had happened but Bessemer told him to back off and not be such a bully. Give the kid a chance he told Vincent.'

'Wouldn't like to be in Didcot's shoes for a while.'

'Lord, come here, now!' Daniel looked over his shoulder at the source of the demanding voice. Vincent was standing in the corridor looking straight at him.

'Yes Vincent,' said Daniel as he came up and stood in front of the Prefect.

'Did I hear you speak my name?'

'No Vincent.'

'And what did Carruthers really want to see you about? Don't tell me about the Sixth. You just made that up on the spur of the moment. Carruthers couldn't care less about you going into the Sixth. Well, what was it?'

'Nothing Vincent, really.'

'Lord, you're a pitiful liar and when I discover just what it was I will come and find you. Now off, lights out in half an hour.'

Daniel backed off and spun away off to the dormitory. 'Christ, I hope he doesn't find out what old Carruthers was really asking me. Perhaps I had better have a word with Dr. Carruthers and warn him that Vincent is trying to ground me.'

'Bit dangerous that. If Vincent finds out that you've gone to see Carruthers later he will be twice as pissed off. He'll probably try and ground you for the rest of the term.'

'I'll just have to keep my head down and not give Vincent any excuse to harass me. Anyway, we'd better get washed up and ready for bed or we'll miss lights out and I'll be in trouble again.'

Daniel went through Thursday and Friday in a sweat. He tried to be as invisible as possible and any time he saw Vincent he hid. By the time that Friday arrived young Daniel was exhausted just trying to keep out of trouble. He couldn't wait for Friday night when Geoffrey was due to collect him.

Friday turned out to be a busier day for Geoffrey than was planned. The lawyers of the subcontractor suddenly challenged one of their ongoing contracts. There was a difference of opinion about delivery dates and penalty clauses. As a result Geoffrey spent a rather frustrating day dealing with lawyers and word by word interpretations. Soon after six o'clock an exasperated Geoffrey escaped his office and drove home to get organised for the weekend.

'Geoffrey, are you sure you want to go tonight? You're tired and it's a long drive all through the night. Why don't you wait until tomorrow?'

'Christina love, it's all set up this way. I arranged to meet Michael at Bangor early tomorrow morning. He'll be waiting there.'

'Yes, but he won't have left yet. Phone him up and get him to take a later train.'

'Christina, there isn't a later train that will get there before midday Saturday and that'll shoot all of Saturday. We've got to come home on Sunday. Besides, I have to pick up Daniel tonight.'

'You can still pick up Daniel tonight and drive up tomorrow morning.'

'Christina sweetheart, I'm not going to change everything now. Michael will have conniptions and Daniel will be disappointed. No, I'll pack now and drive up tonight. I'll drive slowly and if I feel tired I'll pull over and have a nap. Good, that's settled. Now, I need to pack so if you don't mind let me get on.'

Christina pouted and looked hurt: men, so stubborn on occasions. Geoffrey really looked tired and now he had to drive all night. Why were they so obstinate?

Somewhat surprisingly Geoffrey hadn't got himself organised earlier in the week. He had meant to but other things kept getting in the way. He rummaged through the basement picking various bits of gear up and thinking things over. They really hadn't decided what they were going to do. So, I need to take a little of everything Geoffrey thought to himself. Also, I need gear for Daniel and I'm not sure what Michael has got.

Geoffrey sorted through camping gear, tents, sleeping bags, stoves and then came to the climbing gear. Dad said we hadn't done anything for a while so maybe we won't need this. Maybe we'll just hike. Geoffrey continued with his sorting, picking up boots, breeches, compass, maps, and whistles. The pile in the middle of the floor grew. He bundled most of it up into three rucsacks and stacked them by the stairs. Oh, I nearly forgot the headlamps he muttered, and the billies. I need to scrounge around the kitchen for some food too. Doubt if Christina had any idea to make sandwiches for Daniel and me.

Gradually Geoffrey brought some order to the initial chaos and asked Christina to sort out some food.

'Can you pack a thermos too love? Your coffee is so much better than the coffee at truck stops.'

'Do you want cheese or ham in the sandwiches?'

'Cheese please, some of that old cheddar, and can you pack a jar of marmite? Daniel loves that and I bet he doesn't get any at school.'

'Geoffrey that stuff's awful. It tastes like cow shit, and it looks like it too.'

'Christina, just pack it please. It's an acquired taste, and it's good for you too.'

'Nothing tasting like that can be good for you.'

'Darling it is, and Peter already likes it.'

'What, you gave some to little Peter?'

'No, I didn't, Mum did. Peter thought it was scrumptious.'

'I think I will have to talk to your mother about feeding little Peter.'

'Talk to Dad too, he was giving Peter Guinness after lunch the other day.'

'Geoffrey! What is it with your family? They want to poison the child?'

Down in the basement Geoffrey laughed and continued with his packing. After a few more moments he decided that he ought to take some climbing gear because you never know what they might decide on.

He picked up a climbing sack and stuffed a couple of ropes in. Sorting through the gear he packed some slings, karabiners, a few nuts, and three harnesses. The hiking boots they all had were good enough for simple climbing. If they did anything it was more likely to be an old-fashioned mountaineering type route in North Wales rather than a technical rock climb. They just needed a few slings for protection.

Geoffrey loaded the three general rucsacks into the Landrover and put a foamie down in the back for Daniel. He laid one of the sleeping bags out on the foamie. The climbing sack he put up on the front seat, along with the sandwiches and flask from Christina.

'How about a bite to eat? Did you have lunch today?'

'Yes please, and no I didn't. It turned into a typical mad Friday. I'm not quite sure why Friday often ends up being a day of chaos and crisis. Everything seems to come to a vital need of resolution on Friday afternoon.'

'We never have that problem in Italy Geoffrey. Life is more simple.'

'And how my love do you manage to avoid the fracas of Friday?'

'Easy, we all go to the villa on Friday. Nobody goes to work. We all take off early before the fracas happens.'

'Charming. That's a real Latin answer to the challenge. If you are not there it can't happen.'

'See Geoffrey, life is so much easier without these problems no?'

'Yes my love, life is much easier without these problems. I agree wholeheartedly. Remind me to move to Italy after the weekend. The lifestyle sounds appealing.'

'Geoffrey can we?' asked Christina with real excitement in her voice. 'Do you mean it? Papa would love it. You could work in the estate there. You could look after the vineyards. You could....'

'Whoa, hold it. The question was not for real my love. With or without Fridays our life is here. Dad needs me here, both in the Company and on the estate.'

'Yes,' said Christina dejectedly. 'I know. The House of Lord needs a Lord in charge, and a Lord in waiting.'

'And a Lord in waiting once removed,' added Geoffrey. 'Peter's life is set here too.'

After a quick and rather quiet meal Geoffrey went to find his son. Peter was quietly tucked up in his bed, sucking his thumb and cuddling his teddy bear. He looked so sweet and peaceful with no cares in the world. Geoffrey leant over him and gently kissed his forehead.

'Take care little man. Look after your mother for me. Remember, you're the man of the house while I'm away.' Geoffrey straightened up and went to find Christina.

'I've told Mum and Dad to expect you tomorrow. Mum can't wait to take you into her confidence and Dad is really worried what Mum will say. Dad's all set up to take Peter around the estate. I think he has some surprises or treats for Peter. It should be a lovely weekend.'

'Yes Geoffrey. Thanks for all you have done. It will be a lovely weekend. Peter and I will have a good time and we hope that you do too. Be careful my love. Ti amo Geoffrey.'

Christina threw her arms around Geoffrey's neck and gave him a heartfelt kiss. She held on a long time and Geoffrey had to gently disengage her arms and hold her hands. He looked at Christina.

'Arrevederci darling. I'll be back before you know it.' Geoffrey jumped down the steps of the house to the driveway and opened the Landrover's door. Slowly he eased the car out along the driveway to the gates of the estate. The headlights cut a straight swath through the night sky. He turned the car towards Bristol House and went to pick up Daniel.

At Bristol House it took Geoffrey a while to find Daniel. When he did find him Daniel scurried out and into the Landrover like a rabbit scooting down its burrow. He dived into the passenger seat and said, 'come on Geoffrey, let's go.'

'Okay, okay, but what's the rush? It took a while to find you. No-one seemed to know where you were. As soon as I did find you you took off like a rocket and dived into the car. Is there a problem?'

'No, no, well yes, yes there is. That rotter Vincent is trying to have an excuse to ground me. He's been harassing me all week and I've been avoiding him. Just because of some old feud with Michael Vincent has been trying to get his own back on me.'

'Well you're fine now and we'll be off right away. I've seen Dr. Carruthers your Housemaster and told him I'll bring you back safe and sound on Sunday evening. That's all taken care of. Have you had any dinner or do you want some sandwiches? Christina made some for me.'

'No thanks Geoffrey. I had dinner but let's go, please.'

'Fine. Do you want to sit up front to start with? I've organised one of the foamies and a sleeping bag in the back for later if you want to sleep comfortably.'

'Thanks. I'll start up front until I get sleepy and then I might go into the back. Thanks for fixing everything. I'll be so glad to get away for a weekend.'

'Yes, it was a good idea of Michael's. We all should have a great time.'

Geoffrey eased the loaded Landrover away from the school and set off to find the Motorway leading north. There was no real hurry because Michael's train wouldn't arrive in Bangor until early tomorrow morning so Geoffrey intended to drive steadily and possibly catnap somewhere en route. The drive was fairly easy to start with but after he left the Motorway he would have to pay more attention on the twists and turns of the A5. Daniel snuggled down comfortably in the passenger seat and looked across at his older brother. Yes thought Daniel, we all should have a great time.

Later that evening Michael caught the overnight train north from Euston station. Rather wisely Michael had booked a reserved seat for the first leg of the trip. This was the good news and Michael was pleased with himself as he found his seat and threw his rucsack up on the luggage rack. The train already seemed very crowded and Michael was glad that he had had the foresight to make a reservation. He stretched out for a moment but was almost immediately invaded by the other passengers who had reserved the seats around him. A crowd of young very noisy Chinese students descended on the seats and took over the area.

Normally, when travelling on a British train, where no one speaks to their fellow passengers for the first one hundred miles there is a chance to sleep. However, instead of the relative peace and quiet Michael had expected there was a non-stop hubbub of Chinese chatter, shelling of nuts, hawking on the floor, and clouds of smoke despite the prominent no-smoking signs. Apart from the occasional walk up and down the corridor there was not much Michael could do about it. The train was completely full.

Unlike most people Michael was glad to get off the train at Crewe. Now most people do not enjoy walking up and down the platform at Crewe Junction in the middle of the night but Michael was relieved. It was a quiet and mild night and it was a relief to be out of the alien atmosphere of the Euston train. Michael strolled up the deserted platform waiting for the connecting train to North Wales. He wondered what the hundreds of other passengers had been thinking about while waiting for connections at Crewe in the middle of the night.

Geoffrey drove up the Motorway without incident. He stopped halfway up to munch on Christina's sandwiches and keep himself awake with the coffee. Daniel had moved himself into the back of the Landrover and was dozing. Every so often he would fall asleep only to wake up again in a violent thrashing of arms and legs as he came out of some nightmare. 'You okay back there?' Geoffrey asked when he stopped.

'Yes, I'm fine. Just trying to get comfortable.'

'There's a lot of arm and leg thrashing going on when you seem to doze off.'

'Had a nightmare, well I think so.'

'About school, or something else?' asked Geoffrey.

'Dunno really. Can't seem to be able to see the details. Someone chasing me, or perhaps looking for me. I'm not sure but it feels frightening somehow and then I wake up.'

'Maybe this weekend will be a chance to clear away some of the cobwebs. You've never been to North Wales and it will be some new country to see. They're much bigger mountains than the hills back home.'

'What'll we do Geoffrey?'

'I haven't decided yet. We'll talk things over with Michael when we get there. Dad gave me a couple of good ideas.'

'There's nothing too difficult is there?' asked Daniel.

'No, don't worry about that,' said Geoffrey. 'We're just going for a get-together and do a little hiking. It will give you a taste of bigger hills. We might scramble a little on some of the hikes. Just depends where we go but we won't do anything like some of the cliff climbs you have done in Cornwall. So close your eyes and try and get some more sleep. We've still a ways to go yet.'

'Good, sure,' said Daniel and wriggled more comfortably around on the foamie. He drifted off to sleep but it was still shallow and fitful. Geoffrey looked back at his younger brother. The troubles of a teenager's life he thought. Trying to fit into two different worlds, plus trying to be a young Lord in a world where that name caused a variety of reactions. Well, thought Geoffrey. If you survive being a teenager you should be set for life.

He eased the clutch in and steered the Landrover back onto the road. Hi Ho for the hills he thought. Actually it will be nice to be back in Snowdonia again. Looks like being a good weekend for weather and the three of us should have a chance to talk some things over.

Running late Michael's train slowly pulled into Crewe station. Michael easily found a seat as this train was nearly empty. He slung his gear around him to claim some space and lay down on the seat to try and catch some sleep. Gently the train clicked its way out of the station and headed west towards the hills of North Wales. Michael dozed on and off but he couldn't really get comfortable with the seats. The train stopped at a variety of stations, many of which had names that most Englishmen found difficult to pronounce, like Rhyll, Llandudno, and then Penmaenmawr. At least I can get my mind around Conway thought Michael. Finally the train dived into a tunnel and emerged in the narrow valley containing Bangor station. Michael stumbled off the train with his rucsack slung over one shoulder. It was already dawn but the weak sunlight didn't lighten the foreground of dark gray slate roofs. Just as well it isn't raining thought Michael and then it would look really dismal. As Michael slowly walked to the station buildings the train rolled onwards through another tunnel and on to Holyhead and the guiness-flavoured crossing of the Irish Sea.

The station forecourt was deserted when Michael emerged from the station buildings. Michael sat on the steps and looked down the valley towards the sea. A vista of gray roofs greeted him accompanied by the occasional squawk of the seagulls perched on the gables. Wonder where dearly beloved Geoffrey is thought Michael? Let's hope he hasn't forgotten or something. Be just like Christina to say no and Geoffrey kowtow. Michael took a swig of water from his flask and thought on the coming weekend. Could be interesting he thought. We could show young Daniel a thing or two. Geoffrey said Daniel had never been up here in

Snowdonia. Could do the Horseshoe, or walk the Glyders? How about a scramble over Tryfan, that would be a good introduction? Yes, lots to do thought Michael.

Geoffrey crossed the border into Wales somewhere near Chirk. From here the A5 took on the characteristics of a snake. It was a good road when clear but frustrating on a hot summer's afternoon when you're stuck behind three cars towing caravans. At that time in the morning the road was clear and Geoffrey made good time heading west. Crossing over the Conway River at Betws-y-coed the Landrover climbed between the plantations of Douglas fir. These trees' parents or grandparents had started life in British Columbia, Canada, but they were doing well in Wales. Wonder whether they would do well back home in Somerset thought Geoffrey? I'd heard that it was good timber. Beyond the Forestry Commission plantations Geoffrey drove past a local tourist spot, the Swallow Falls. Geoffrey smiled to himself. A couple of weeks back he was entertaining two Canadian clients at the office. Before they came to Geoffrey the two had spent a weekend with their wives touring in North Wales. As Geoffrey knew the area they had spent a little time chatting about the experience. The two Canadians were quite surprised at how well the trees grew. They were also surprised about the amount of open hillsides. 'You could walk all over,' said one of them. 'It's not like back on the coast where the trees force you back onto the trail all the time.'

'It's a little different,' said Geoffrey. 'First of all the sheep will eat the trees unless you fence the area. Secondly, the wind will break the tops off if you try and plant them too far up the hillside.'

'But you're down almost at sea level,' said one of the Canadians.

'I'd heard my grandfather say that the highest you can grow trees on the west coast of the U.K. is about 250 metres. Above that they just get windblown.'

'What's that in feet?' asked one of the Canadians.

'About 800 feet or so,' said Geoffrey.

'The wives made us go to this big attraction called Swallow Falls.'

Geoffrey smiled, almost knowing what was going to come next.

'And did your wife like Swallow Falls?' asked Geoffrey. 'It really is one of the local highlights: such a dramatic cascade of water. Aren't there three falls if I remember correctly?'

'Son, you could put all three falls and lose them almost anywhere on the West Coast. To top it off we had to pay to see these falls.'

'Well,' said Geoffrey, 'I suppose it is all relative. Actually though, I do believe we grow your Douglas fir up there faster than you do in Canada. So perhaps things aren't quite so small up in Snowdonia after all?'

At Capel Curig Geoffrey called back over his shoulder,' if you look up there Daniel you may be able to see Snowdon.' Daniel's response was a gentle snoring. After tossing and turning for a while Daniel had eventually fallen into deeper sleep. 'Well never mind,' said Geoffrey. 'You can see it on the drive home.' Geoffrey continued driving until the Landrover crested the height of land before the run down to Ogwen. 'Time to get rid of some of Christina's coffee,' he said. 'It was really good at keeping me awake but now it is keeping me tense. I'm just going to stop for a piss Daniel.' Daniel sort of grunted as he rolled over on the floor of the Landrover. Geoffrey pulled off onto the side of the road and stopped. He got out and relieved himself up against the slate walls that bounded the road.

'Where are we? Hey, that's looks neat.' Daniel crawled out of the Landrover and joined his brother pissing up against the wall. 'Real mountains, and what's the lake?'

'The mountain young man is Tryfan, one of the fourteen peaks higher than three thousand feet,' answered Geoffrey. 'There's some good climbing up on the face that we are looking at. That's the East face. And the lake, as you so ignorantly put it, is Llyn Ogwen. Actually, not so long ago, it was the Yellow River.'

'The Yellow River. You're pulling my leg surely?'

'No, Dad told me. Sometime back in the sixties I think they made a film here. It was called "Inn of the Sixth Happiness" I believe. Anyway, the story was set in China about some teacher or missionary who walked some children through the mountains to escape soldiers. They made some of the film here, although it stretches the imagination to think of Welsh people dressed up like Chinese peasants. Still, Dad said there are still parts of the walls and other parts of some of the scenes scattered around up here. When he told me this story he laughed and said if you look closely in certain scenes you can see climbers on the cliffs behind the actors. You have to know where to look though as they are in the background.'

'So, what about the Yellow River?'

'Oh yes, well the llyn in front of you became one of the objectives of this band of children. They had to reach the Yellow River and in some scene near the end of the film they come over a ridge and see the Yellow River, which is really a clever view of Llyn Ogwen.'

'Geoffrey, you're having me on. This is all so much bullshit.'

'No, straight up. Ask Dad when you get home. He'll tell you. He was climbing in this area about the time the film was made.'

'Well I don't think your and my piss will colour a lot of the lake so let's continue?'

'Hop in then. We're nearly there. It's all downhill from here. We'll turn the end of the Llyn at Ogwen and then go down the Nant Ffrancon to Bethesda and on to Bangor. Michael should be waiting for us at Bangor railway station.'

The two brothers got back into the Landrover and Geoffrey drove back onto the road and under the northern end of Tryfan. 'See the big clean white-looking buttress up there at the bottom end of Tryfan's north ridge? That's called Milestone Buttress and many many people have started their climbing careers there.'

'What's on the other side of the lake, or llyn?'

'Over the north side of the llyn are the Carnedds, or the Carneddau to be more accurate. Actually there are two peaks called Carnedd, which means cairn or heap of stones. There are Carnedd Dafydd and Carnedd Llywelyn, plus four other peaks in that range. It's good hiking country once you get up on the tops.'

'And beyond Tryfan is it, there are other mountains? What are they?'

'Linked to the south end of Tryfan is Glyder Fach and next to that is Gylder Fawr.'

'I'll never remember all these names.'

'You don't have to as they are all neatly written down on the map. It's easy. You don't even have to remember what the names mean either, just climb them. There won't be a test at the end of the weekend,' joked Geoffrey.

The Landrover turned the corner at Ogwen and started descending Nant Ffrancon. 'This is neat,' said Daniel. 'I've never seen a valley quite like this. It's steep-sided with a big flat U-shape in the bottom. Lots of sort-of truncated ribs high up on the hillsides too.'

'Well, educated one, give me an idea how this came about. What do you think caused this?'

Daniel looked about him. A little stream ran down from Ogwen and meandered across the valley floor. The lush green grass and even some reeds supported several grazing cattle. A rough track ran along the foot of the valley on the other side. Their road twisted and turned around the several spurs that descended from the ridge on the right. There were no trees in this end of the valley. Daniel pondered. 'It's too big a valley for such a little stream,' he finally said. 'I don't see how water could have carved this kind of valley. It's also fairly short and the existing stream wanders all over the valley floor.'

'So it was wind then that carved it out?' asked Geoffrey.

'Not likely,' said Daniel.

'Well, it was a major geologic event, an earthquake, a volcano, a rift valley?'

'Geoffrey, give over.'

'Think what it might have looked like fifty thousand years ago. That'll give you a clue. It wasn't so sunny and warm in those days remember.'

'No Geoffrey, I don't remember, but I think you're talking about the Ice Age.'

'Good stuff. So, what happened here then?'

'How about a bloody great glacier came trotting down the valley and ground it out?'

'Right, which explains the truncated high-up ridges and the flat valley bottom. Top of the class.'

By now the Landrover had come to the outskirts of Bethesda. Suddenly there were a few trees, although rather stunted and scraggly. However, what caught Daniel's eye was something he hadn't seen before. Away to the left, above the village of Bethesda, were several enormous scars in the hillside with giant terraces. 'What's that? Who has been carving into the hillsides, and for what?'

'Slate Daniel. Lots and lots of slate, although sad to say there's no call for it now. This used to be one of the largest slate quarries in the world. There was a large one here called Penrhyn, and others on the other side of the ridge around by Nant Peris, plus the quarries at Blaenau. In fact the local large landowner made a fortune here. The quarry used to be work for lots and lots of men, which is why the village exists. But, just like the tin mines in Cornwall some one found a cheaper way to mine it or something else to replace it. Now we have tiles on our roofs rather than slates.'

The road narrowed through the village and twisted and curved its way down the terraced street. Beyond Bethesda the countryside became a little greener and less harsh than the upper part of the Nant Ffrancon. 'Changes quickly doesn't it Daniel?' Geoffrey asked.

'Yes, now it's quite like home whereas up above it was austere, more like Cornwall.'

The sides of the valley flattened out as the A5 came to the outskirts of Bangor. Geoffrey followed the road down to the station and they saw Michael sprawled out on a bench in the station yard. 'Michael, good to see you,' cried Daniel as he bounded out of the Landrover. He half fell over his brother's reclining body as he tried to give him a hug. 'Hold on there Daniel. Give a chap a chance to get up on his feet. I was just having a nice doze. Still, it's good to see you too. Hi Geoffrey, good trip?'

'So so Michael, although I'm a little stiff and cramped right now. How was the train?'

'Don't ask, and don't ask me to do that again. It was a pain. I had to endure China taking over the world for the first few hours. Christ those people are like pigs and they are going to rule the world? Heaven help us. And the chatter: I couldn't get a wink of sleep, but I'm here.'

'Well, we probably didn't do a lot better although Daniel may have slept a little. We should go and see whether we can find breakfast anywhere.'

'Fat chance of that in this town. They probably won't wake up until gone nine. Still, the idea is good. Any thoughts where the idea might bear fruit?'

'How about the Castle Hotel?' said Geoffrey. 'I believe it's a residential Hotel and so they must have a dining room. It's worth a try.'

'Could always go up to the refectory in Top College and claim to be students,' said Michael.

'Michael, forget it. Only you have a Student Card and we don't need to be so cheap.'

'Twas only an idea Geoffrey. We'll let you foot the bill as you are the only one of us working. Perhaps Dad will let you write it off as a business expense. Couldn't we be out-of-town clients or something? I'm sure Dad's accountant can be very creative when he has to be.'

'Michael, Dad's bookkeeper is a lady, and no she doesn't need to be creative because Dad runs a tight ship with regards to finance. He does everything by the book.'

'I'm hungry,' said Daniel. 'When you two have finished arguing the toss can we go and eat?'

The brothers were lucky in their decision and all three felt a lot better after a good breakfast. Sitting in the Landrover in the Hotel parking lot it came time to think on a plan of action. As Daniel was new to the area this turned into a discussion between Geoffrey and Michael. Daniel was quite amazed, for he expected a long drawn out argument between Geoffrey and Michael but the two of them quickly came to an agreement. 'A walk over the Carnedds is just the thing to start young Daniel in this area. He will get to see much of the northern end of Snowdonia and on a good day like today will get views over much of the rest of it. It is easy walking.'

'Daniel, you came past the end of the Carnedds this morning. Do you remember where we stopped?'

'Yes, near the Yellow River.'

'What's he talking about Geoffrey?' asked Michael. 'There's no Yellow River.' Geoffrey smiled and said 'this is Daniel's little secret that he'll tell you sometime but he's right. Good Daniel, you were awake at the time. Still, we'll not go in from that end but make a loop from this end of the range.'

'Yes, we could drive back up to Bethesda, up to the top end of Gerlan and leave the Landrover there. We could make a big loop up to the tops, around in an arc and down back to the car.'

'The easiest way would be to walk up besides the Afon Caseg and scramble up somewhere near Yr Elen. Once up on the ridge we could decide what to do next depending on time and weather. If there is time we could walk over to Carnedd Dafydd and come down its northern ridge back to the car.'

'Sounds like a plan to me Geoffrey. Let's get the gear organised.'

It was a dry clear morning so they turfed most of the gear out of the Landrover onto the car park floor. There they sorted out what was needed. The camping gear was packed away. 'What about climbing gear?' asked Michael. 'Unlikely to need it,' said Geoffrey. 'It's only a walk along the tops.'

'Well I'll take some anyway,' said Michael. 'We might get some scrambling in getting up the side of Yr Elen. We'll be on the safe side if we take it. I'll pack the two ropes and chuck in a couple of slings and karabiners. They won't weigh very much and you and Daniel can take some food and water.'

'What about spare clothing?' asked Daniel.

'Good idea brother. And we'd better remember whistles and first-aid kit.'

'And map and compass,' added Daniel. 'Dad always said make sure you've got a map and compass, even on a short walk.'

'Smart man our Dad,' said Michael. 'Always well prepared. Did you bring my boots Geoffrey because I've only got sneakers?'

'Yes Michael. I brought all our boots. They'll be fine for hiking although a little bendy if we climb.'

The three brothers sorted through the array of gear and packed away what was needed for the day's outing into their three rucsacks. Geoffrey made sure that he and Michael both had a compass. He had the map. All three brothers had their own supply of food and water. Daniel stuffed a spare pair of socks into the corner of his sack.

'Thinking of sleeping out Daniel?' asked Michael, noticing the spare socks.

'No Michael. I'm still growing and I'm not sure my boots still fit properly. I want to make sure I can change into thinner socks if these are too tight.'

'Good idea Daniel. If you get too warm up there your feet will swell anyway and that will pinch your feet too if you're not careful. You all got bogroll?'

'Always Geoffrey. I wouldn't go anywhere without it. Beats using Kleenex any day.'

'Michael, you're gross,' said Daniel laughing. 'Yes Geoffrey. Same as Michael, I've always got some because everyone swipes it at school.'

'There Daniel, see what you learn by going to such an elite and sophisticated school. You've quickly picked up some of the essentials of life. Bristol House is certainly an establishment for the education of gentlemen. Even Geoffrey learnt something while he was there.'

The three brothers laughed and piled into the Landrover. Geoffrey drove back onto the A5 and steered the car up and around the twists and bends leading back to the village of Bethesda.

'Know what's special about this village?' asked Geoffrey. Both Michael and Daniel looked at each other but neither of them answered. 'Dad told me and once you've seen it it becomes obvious. Look, it's still quite early and so I'll drive completely up through the village and see whether you can spot it. Actually, Michael is more likely to notice it than you Daniel but you could spot it too.' Geoffrey drove slowly up the main street and let Daniel and Michael watch the houses and the streets. At the top of the village by Ogwen Bank he stopped. 'Well, did anyone notice anything?'

'No gaps between the houses.'

'Post Office looks funny.'

'Some houses are painted the same colours.'

'Shops all over.'

'None of the above,' said Geoffrey. 'I'll drive back down again and this time it may be easier to see what is special. Look what's there and what's not there. Actually, you're comment about the Post Office is good. Dad told me they built it backwards. He thinks the backside is the side facing the street, but that's not what is so very different. We'll go back down.' There was no traffic coming down the long straight stretch into the village and so Geoffrey did a neat three-point turn and drove back down again. At the end of the houses he pulled over and stopped again.

'There's no railway station.'

There's a bus station.'

'The names are all in Welsh.'

'Michael, what do you usually do on a Saturday night?' asked Geoffrey.

'Go to the pub,' answered Michael, 'where else?'

'And,' said Geoffrey, 'where would you go in Bethesda on a Saturday night?'

'To the pub,' said Daniel, 'but what's so special about the pubs here?'

'One more time,' said Geoffrey, 'and then we'll head off up the hill.'

Once again Geoffrey slowly drove the Landrover up the main street of the village. Again, at the top he stopped. 'And the answer is?'

'There are seventeen pubs. Leastways, I think I counted seventeen. Are there more pubs than chapels or something? Twice as many pubs as chapels, three times as many?'

'You're on the right track, but where are the pubs?' asked Geoffrey.

'They're all on the same side of the street,' said Daniel. 'They're all on the west side of the street.'

'Right,' said Geoffrey.

'But why? Why are the pubs only on one side of the street?'

'I bet because whoever owns one side of the street doesn't own the other,' said Michael as the light slowly dawned. 'Someone is a teetotal, or was a teetotal.'

'Right,' said Geoffrey again. 'Sometime in the past, in the history of the landowner on the east side of the street a family member died of the drink, or did something terrible while under the influence. I don't remember all of the details but the family decreed that there would never be a public house or anywhere to buy drink on their property. So, on their property there are no pubs. But, they don't own all of the village, and someone else owns the west side and so all of the pubs are on one side of the street here.'

'Geoffrey, you are a mine of trivia,' said Michael, 'time to head for the hills.'

Geoffrey found the turning off the main road that led up through narrow slate-lined walls to the upper village of Gerlan. He followed the road to the end and found a verge where he could pull off and still leave room for cars to pass. The road continued a little further to a couple of farms.

'This is the place on the map,' said Geoffrey. 'The path starts somewhere here.' The three brothers unloaded their gear from the back of the Landrover and got organised for the hike. Climbing over the gate they started up the path. Geoffrey walked in the front while Daniel followed. Michael acted as the sweeper making sure that no one got left behind. Without any conversation they trudged on for fifteen minutes crossing another slate wall in the process.

'Say Geoffrey. I was reading one of the old Guidebooks to Snowdonia the other day and I came across this neat mountaineering route. It was in the guide to the Carnedds.'

'Was this an Abraham Guide?' asked Geoffrey.

'No, not that far back. They climbed at the turn of the century didn't they? This was more modern than that. I think A.J. Moulam was the author. It was a Climbers Club Guide.'

'So what was this famous route?' asked Daniel.

'Well, it was an old-fashioned route, quite long, but the magic of it was that it led to the Carnedd's ridge. If I remember correctly it would save us slogging up some horrendous talus slope to reach the tops. It would be a neat way for young Daniel here to experience a mountaineering-style route as opposed to the usual cliff climbing he has been doing. Plus, I'd sooner not clamber up a pile of loose scree Geoffrey.'

'Sounds like a reasonable idea Michael but we're not really equipped for a serious climb, and you've not got the guidebook with you,' said Geoffrey, ever cautious.

'Geoffrey, it was a gully climb, so finding it won't be difficult. The guidebook more or less said it went straight up. I told you it was done a long time ago when all they ever did was climb gullies.'

'Was it difficult Michael?' asked Daniel, who was always a bit suspicious of Michael's ideas.

'No Daniel, it wasn't. If I remember correctly it was graded Difficult, or maybe Very Difficult. Remember Daniel there are six grades of climbs here in Wales. They are: Easy, Difficult, Very Difficult, Severe, Very Severe, and XS, although they started to split XS into Extremely Severe and Exceptionally Severe later on. Fortunately they changed the system before people climbed even more difficult routes or we would have had Texas-style grading with Super Gross Extra Large XS. Anyway, this climb was rated in the lower end of the scale. Also, the grade used to be applied to the hardest move on the climb. Even if it was Very Difficult the rest of the climb would be much easier than some of the routes you have done down in Cornwall. We will probably be able to solo up parts of it and then move together like an alpine route on other parts. Should be a good experience for you.'

'Sounds like an idea Michael. Even I don't really fancy slogging up a long scree slope,' said Geoffrey, who was gradually warming to the suggestion. 'Where was the climb Michael? Was it in this valley?'

'No, not quite Geoffrey. The climb was on a cliff called Ysgolion Duon, or Black staircase or something.'

'You mean Black Ladders Michael,' said Geoffrey. 'That's the next valley over, Cwm Llafar, running up the other side of Yr Elen. Anyway, what was the climb's name?'

'Very imaginatively it was called Western Gully,' said Michael, 'and you're right, the cliff is round in the next valley. Let's look at the map just to make sure we've got this right.'

'Where are we now?' asked Daniel.

'Okay Daniel. Find Gerlan and show me where you think we left the Landrover.' Daniel peered over the map and traced the road down from Bangor to Bethesda and quickly found Gerlan. 'So, we came up this narrow minor road and probably left the Landrover about here,' he said, and placed his finger on the map.

'Good, well done Daniel. You're spot on. Then we walked up the start of Cwm Caseg and we're now about here. Michael's cliff is over here,' and Geoffrey traced the location of Black Ladders.

Michael looked at the map and said, 'we'll have to cross the river and then contour across the ridge so as to not lose too much height. Looks fairly straightforward with no obvious cliffs in the way. What do you think Geoffrey?'

'Looks good to me Michael but before we really decide let's do a quick check on what gear we've got. Michael, you brought some climbing gear. What do we have?'

Michael dumped the contents of his rucsack on the path and spread it out a little. 'Don't step on the rope Daniel with your big feet.'

'Michael I know I know. I've climbed before. I'm not a complete novice,' said Daniel hotly.

'Fine, so we've two full weight ropes. That's enough rope for sure. As it is fairly easy we don't need harnesses. We can tie in directly with bowlines, the old-fashioned way.'

'What have we got for slings Michael?' asked Geoffrey. 'Even on an old route we'll need some protection and certainly some belays.'

'I bet most of the anchors are jammed boulders in the gully,' said Michael, 'especially if it is a really old route.'

'We can do a little better than that,' said Geoffrey, and he counted out five slings with five karabiners plus a couple of wired nuts. 'As long as it is only VDiff.,' he said, 'we should be fine. We'll just have to be a little careful about using rope for belays and keeping the slings for protection. Do you understand all this Daniel?'

'Yes Geoffrey. We'll let the leader use all of the slings and karabiners and the others will use classic rope handling techniques,' said Daniel.

'Heh, the kid's good,' said Michael. 'You're right on little brother. This should be fun and a great experience. I'll pack the gear back into the sack and we'll be off. Right Geoffrey?'

'Sure, I think we're set.'

The enthusiasm generated by this idea of Michael's masked the fact that the three of them had had a rather tiring week and subsequent journey. With the excitement of a new more specific objective the three brothers set off to cross Afon Caseg. The valley bottom was open grassland and so it was fairly easy to find a place to cross without getting wet feet. Once over the stream they contoured around the ridge to reach Cwm Llafar. It didn't take long to hike around the ridge and over into the next valley bottom. Coming over the ridge they could see a path on the far side of Afon Llafar. Once over another easy stream crossing they were on a well-marked path leading up into an impressive cwm.

An oppressive heat beat down on the three brothers as they climbed slowly up Cwm Llafar. The clear June morning gradually clouded over as Geoffrey, Michael and Daniel hiked up towards the great cliff under the north face of Carnedd Dafydd. They walked rhythmically up the path as the black and vegetated cliffs of Llech Ddu closed in on the west side and the shoulder of Yr Elen bounded them on the east. The broad face under Carnedd Dafydd rose nine hundred feet up from the valley floor to the ridge above. Splitting the face was a very obvious substantial gully. This had to be Western Gully - a classic V.Diff. Very slowly the three brothers trudged up the path until it lost itself in the scree and outcrop lower slopes of the cliff. At the foot of the climb they paused and looked up the route. Geoffrey unpacked the climbing sack and divided up the gear, slinging one of the coils of rope over his shoulder.

The three young men scrambled unroped up the first easy pitches. The rock was good sound dolerite although parts of the route were quite vegetated. After two hundred feet Geoffrey decided they ought to rope up and belay each other.

'It's a long way to roll if any of us fall off from here.'

'Yes, but this is still easy Geoffrey for God's sake.'

'Those clouds are starting to roll in Geoffrey. Let's keep some speed up.'

Geoffrey was unhappy but his two younger brothers were pushing.

'Okay - we'll continue, but any hesitation and we rope up.'

After another hundred feet the gully narrowed and steepened. Michael found a very old rusty piton drooping out of a crack a little way off to the right. Geoffrey dropped the coil of rope and his rucksack. 'Let's look what's above us? This is starting to get more serious.' Michael and Daniel stopped and looked upwards at the gully walls.

'Look for an anchor Michael,' said Geoffrey. 'We rope up from here. I don't recommend that piton as a safe anchor by the way.'

Daniel started to uncoil one of the ropes as Michael took some slings and organized an anchor around a large jammed chockstone. Geoffrey carefully uncoiled the other rope to lead. Once he was sure there were no knots or kinks in the rope he bent one end around his body and tied a bowline. He tightened the rope around his waist and cinched the knot up tight. As an extra precaution he tied two stoppers knots with the short end of the rope. Once Michael had arranged the anchor Geoffrey pulled the other slings, karabiners, nuts and stoppers out of the rucsack. The sky continued to cloud over and a slight breeze disturbed the sullen air in the valley. The valley looked north and the sky that way was overcast but there was no black base on any of the clouds. Further to the west, and hidden from the climbers by the long northern ridge of Carnedd Dafydd the clouds were blacker.

Geoffrey was now tied on to one end of the rope sure that he had unraveled any kinks all the way to Michael's end. Michael tied into the other end and belayed himself to the anchor he had prepared. Daniel tied one end of his rope into Michael's bowline and tied a bowline for himself in the other end. Geoffrey organized his runners and clipped the other hardware onto his waist. There was no talk - it was a well-known routine. The sun went in.

'On belay. Climb when you're ready,' intoned Michael. In his hands he held Geoffrey's rope. Michael had safely passed the climbing rope around his waist and twisted it once around his right arm. The rope to Geoffrey he held in his left hand. Geoffrey looked back at Michael's anchor, his stance, and how he was belaying the climbing rope.

'Good stuff Michael. See Daniel, Michael has a classic old-fashioned belay position. The anchor can take a pull either way. The rope is tight between Michael and the anchor, and Michael has got the rope secured around his waist and right arm. Just watch how he pays it out to me and never lets go of the rope with his right hand. Any fall and Michael wraps his right arm across the body and the friction helps hold any fall. Looks good to me.' Satisfied with the work of his rope partner Geoffrey looked upwards at the immediate walls of the gully and worked out where he was going.

'Climbing,' said Geoffrey, and he wedged his boot in a crack in the right hand wall of the gully. His hands found ledges around waist height to keep him in balance. After a quick look around Geoffrey moved his other foot up onto a sloping ledge. Slowly and smoothly Geoffrey climbed one or other of the walls of the chimney.

Four short pitches later the three were another two hundred feet up the cliff. The gully had narrowed considerably and the inside of it was dripping wet.

'A true Victorian classic,' murmured Daniel, 'thrashing around in the wet murky depths of a gully. Why did the early climbers have to bury themselves inside the bloody cliff?'

'With the equipment they had, especially the ropes, it was a lot easier and safer to arrange belays in the gully than out on exposed faces.'

'Well today, I would sooner be climbing out on the face,' said Daniel. 'I know we are only beginners but I am starting to get claustrophobia from belaying in these mossy caves. It's like being locked inside a green tomb.'

'I believe the crux comes out onto some slabs besides the gully,' said Michael, trying to remember what he had read in the guidebook. 'You'll have your chance to see whether you can stand the exposure or want to scuttle back inside the comfort of the gully.'

A brisk swirl of wind rushed up from the valley floor. A skein of rain fell and then stopped. Temperatures dropped. Geoffrey shuddered.

'Swans,' exclaimed Michael. 'How bizarre'. Six mute swans purposefully beat their way westwards over Yr Elen towards the cliffs of Llech Ddu and over the northern ridge of Carnedd Dafydd.

Just over half way up the cliff the route became more serious. The three brothers had not really been climbing for very long in their lives. The level of difficulty of this climb, a Very Difficult, was close to the limits of their capabilities, especially for Daniel. As the eldest, Geoffrey was well aware of his responsibilities and carefully watched his younger brother climb up the pitch. Daniel was not finding it easy in his hiking boots. Being shorter in the legs he couldn't straddle some of the damp parts like his two brothers and so he had to try and wedge himself into the wetter corners of the gully.

'Is this too much?' asked Geoffrey to Michael and Daniel. 'Perhaps we should retreat?'

'Come on,' said Michael. 'If you can't make it I'll lead. We'll go a lot faster I can tell you. Actually, we'd better hurry if we are going to beat that weather.'

'No,' exclaimed Geoffrey. 'I will lead, and I will decide if we continue or not.'

'Pompous ass,' said Michael. Daniel looked apprehensively at his two brothers.

'Climbing,' said Geoffrey very emphatically, and moved rapidly up the slabs to the right of the gully.

'Hang on,' said Michael, 'You're not even on belay yet.'

Geoffrey didn't appear to hear Michael's comment and he rushed up the next ten feet. A sudden gust of wind hit Geoffrey just as he delicately mantleshelved up a tricky move. He swayed, slipped, slithered down the slab for a moment and then as his foot snagged on a ledge he cartwheeled over the edge of the gully wall. The coils of rope at Michael's feet whistled over the edge after Geoffrey.

'Michael, hold him,' shrieked Daniel.

Michael was too slow, just too shocked by the events. Daniel jumped past him and grabbed at the slithering rope. He screamed as the fast-moving nylon burned into his hands. Sobbing in agony Daniel hung onto the rope until it stopped. He collapsed with bloody hands and tears pouring down his face.

Michael took the rope from Daniel's shredded hands and tied it off onto the anchor.

'Christ, what a bloody mess,' said Michael.

'What's happened to Geoffrey?' sobbed Daniel.

'We'll sort that out in a minute,' said Michael. 'Let's do something for you first.' Delving through the rucsack Michael came up with some bandages and padding and he bound up the bloody strips of Daniel's hands.

'Don't leave me Michael,' begged Daniel. 'Let's find Geoffrey and sort things out. He'll know what to do.'

'Sure, sure,' said Michael. 'Always Geoffrey will know what to do. Well just think Daniel, maybe Geoffrey will be in no state to know what to do. Just think on that will you.'

Michael slowly lowered a scrambling whimpering Daniel down the cliff through an improvised karabiner brake bar. Daniel called up when he was near the end of the rope.

'I'm at Geoffrey Michael. He's badly hurt. He's not moving. He's not conscious.' The voice climbed hysterically with each sentence.

'Sure, sure,' muttered Michael to himself.

'Tie yourself off Daniel,' shouted Michael. 'Tie Geoffrey off as well to a decent anchor. I'm going to need both ropes to abseil down.'

A whimpering 'okay' floated up the cliff. Michael organized a safe anchor and arranged the ropes to abseil down to Daniel and Geoffrey. He did this very carefully and methodically. Michael wasn't going to get hurt in this bloody charade. The rain turned colder and more persistent as Michael carefully slid down the doubled ropes to Daniel and Geoffrey. With a murmur of a prayer Michael separated the doubled ropes and pulled gently. He had remembered where the knot was and the two ropes fell neatly down beside him.

Geoffrey was unconscious, sprawled awkwardly on a pile of boulders in the bed of the gully.

'He's still breathing,' whispered Daniel. 'Michael, I don't know what to do. I'm frightened.'

'Shut up you baby,' answered Michael. 'I'm going to have to go for help. Let's check you are all safe here for a while. How are your hands?'

'Burning like hell,' moaned Daniel, and he shivered as the wind whistled more forcefully up the gully. Along with the gusts of wind came stinging pellets of rain. The skies were now very gray overhead. The morning's sunshine and light-heartedness had gone.

'I'll check what's wrong with Geoffrey. Then I'll abseil down the cliff until I can scramble to the valley floor. Down in Bethesda I'll telephone for the mountain rescue.'

Michael briefly ran his hands down Geoffrey's body from his head down to his feet. He looked at his eyes - the pupils were dilated. Initially Geoffrey had stopped with his head below his feet and Michael thought this would be dangerous, as the blood would run to his head. He swung Geoffrey's body around and leant his head back against the slabs. The hands were torn from slithering down the slab above. When Michael moved one of Geoffrey's legs a deep shudder of pain ran through the body, and then went dead. There was no obvious bleeding.

'Jesus, I don't know what's wrong. I think he's got concussion and possibly a broken back. Anyway, I've got to go and get help. Let's cover him with whatever spare clothes we've got. You'd better put a sweater on too Daniel - we are all in shock.'

Shock had already set in with Daniel and he crouched in the gully bed whimpering. He held his hands in front of his face and moaned softly. Geoffrey lay motionless. Another rain squall swept up the valley.

Michael arranged the ropes for another abseil. 'I'm off. I've left all the rucksacks, food, spare clothes. I've just got the climbing gear to continue abseiling. I'll be back as fast as possible. I've got the car keys from Geoffrey's rucksack. Keep as warm as you can.'

'Geoffrey, Geoffrey,' whimpered Daniel rocking on his heels.

Michael slid down the ropes as the rain started in earnest. Three abseils and Michael felt he could scramble down. Carefully he coiled the ropes and slung them over his shoulders. Hunching his shoulders against the steady rain Michael started the slog down to Bethesda. The valley seemed to go on forever as Michael plodded north.

'Christ, I could do with a drink,' muttered Michael. He scurried on down to the narrow slate-lined street of Gerlan and the Landrover, and then drove down to the main road of Bethesda. As Geoffrey had previously explained all the pubs were on the west side of the street, a teetotal idiosyncrasy of the Penrhyn Estate which owned the east side of the street. Michael staggered into the first one he could find and ordered a pint. The locals looked askance at his appearance but muttered in Welsh amongst themselves. Climbers were not the most welcome people in the pubs in Bethesda.

Michael remembered why he was there. 'Have you a telephone? I need to call for a rescue.'

'A rescue is it?' asked the landlord. 'You don't seem in any great hurry. And you'll be wanting change I suppose?'

Michael fumbled with his purse and scattered coins over the counter. The landlord scooped up the money for the drink and pointed down the corridor.

'Down the 'all bach,' he said. 'Mountain Rescue's number is on the card.'

Michael made the call and explained where he was. The Team arranged to meet him as fast as they could get there. Back in the bar

Michael continued with his pint. He was safe, warm, bloody tired but unscathed. He smiled to himself.

Michael refused to go back to the cliff with the Rescue Team. He claimed he was too shattered, too exhausted. He would only slow them down, get in their way. The two people on the cliff would be easy to find. The Team didn't have time to argue. They knew the cliff and the climb so it wouldn't be hard to find the other two.

Soon after the Team left Michael walked back to where he had parked the Landrover. Without much thought he packed his gear away and drove back to London. It had been a tiring day.

Michael never knew the state of his two brothers when the Rescue Team finally climbed up the gully to Daniel and Geoffrey. Geoffrey had broken his back. Michael's moving of his legs had turned him into a paraplegic. While still unconscious Geoffrey had vomited. With his head fallen backwards the vomit had choked him and Geoffrey died. The Team lowered Geoffrey's body down on a stretcher. Huddled in the bed of the gully the Team found Daniel still crouched up in a foetal position whimpering with his bloody hands. They treated his hands and after some soft coaxing the Rescue Team persuaded Daniel to lie on the second stretcher. He lost consciousness as the Team expertly lowered him down to the valley floor. After reading some I.D. on Daniel the Leader of the Mountain Rescue Team telephoned Geoffrey's father when they all returned to Bethesda.

'I regret to inform you that your son Geoffrey Lord is dead sir. Your son Daniel is in Bangor hospital with lacerated hands and in deep shock. Your son Michael called us to the rescue but left before we returned and we're not sure where he is.'

Drunk Dive

8

The tragedy in North Wales struck the Lord family hard. Anthony and Sylvia went up to Bangor to see Daniel in hospital. They also had to deal with Geoffrey's body in the morgue. An inquest was held in Bangor and the decision was death through misadventure.

Back at Fotheringham Manor Anthony Lord sat down slowly. Having got over the initial shock and gone through several activities in automatic mode the realization that Geoffrey was dead started to make a painful impact on Anthony Lord. Loss of a first-born strikes strongly at a traditionalist, and Anthony Lord was a traditionalist. The house of Lord was in disarray. Sylvia Lord was even more distraught. As a mother she mourned over her first-born but she also grieved over her living, yet unliving "baby".

'Daniel, oh Daniel, whatever shall we do?' she cried. For Daniel may have survived the fatal fall of Geoffrey rock climbing in Wales but the events of that day had cast a pall of horror and shame over young Daniel. With careful doctoring they had saved Daniel's hands. Drugs kept some of the pain at bay. The hands would heal but Sylvia worried whether anything would heal Daniel's mind.

To try and ease the locked-up nightmare Sylvia softly explored the series of events. 'Tell me what happened up there Daniel. Take me through the whole events of that day, right from the beginning. Lead me up to the climb and then go through the climb from the bottom. Who suggested you climb Western Gully in the first place?'

'It was a good day to start with. Geoffrey drove carefully through the night and I even slept in the back of the Landrover. When I woke up we were in the mountains. It was marvelous Mum, breathtaking. Mountains surrounded us and there was the Yellow River.'

'What Yellow River Daniel? That name doesn't sound very Welsh.'

'No well, that wasn't the Welsh name. It was lin something, Ogbert, Owen, ...'

'Probably Llyn Ogwen,' suggested Sylvia quietly.

'Yes Mum, that's right, but Geoffrey explained it had been used as the Yellow River in some picture. Dad had told the story to Geoffrey sometime and Geoffrey told me.'

'So, here you were by the Yellow River and then what did you do?' asked Sylvia.

'We drove on down to the station and met Michael. We all felt so happy and excited to be together again. Even Geoffrey was laughing and joking with Michael.'

'Yes,' mused Sylvia, 'and Geoffrey didn't do that very often. And after that?'

'Well, we went and found some breakfast.'

'So Geoffrey decided what to do over breakfast?'

'We all sort of did,' said Daniel. 'There wasn't really any decision. We were just going to go hiking. Remember, this was my first time in Snowdonia so it was all new to me. Geoffrey and Michael agreed that a walk on the Cernetts would be a good introduction.'

'You mean the Carnedds,' said Sylvia.

'Yes, that's it,' said Daniel. 'I can't remember all the Welsh names.'

'So you packed the gear for a hike in the Carnedds?'

'Yes,' said Daniel, 'but Michael did throw in some climbing gear just in case we did some scrambling on the way up to the tops.'

'And off you went?'

Daniel thought for a moment. 'It was all a mutual decision. Geoffrey thought it was a good idea to take a little gear. He knew we were all wearing hiking boots. Geoffrey talked of doing some horseshoe.'

'You mean the Snowdon Horseshoe?' asked Sylvia.

'No Mum, that was a couple of valleys over. This was a horseshoe around the tops of the Carnedds. Coming down off Carnedd Dafydd I think.'

'So you were going to climb up the side of Yr Elen?'

'I think so Mum, but I'm not really sure. I know that soon after we started Michael mentioned reading an old guidebook. Geoffrey was joshing him about how old this guidebook was but Michael said it was done in Dad's time.'

'And after this decision what did you all do?' asked Sylvia.

'We drove off back to the village.'

'You mean Bethesda?'

'Yes, Bethesda, and Geoffrey drove up and down the village trying to get us to see what was special.'

'Special?'

'Yes, special. Geoffrey laughed and told us that Dad had shown him how the village had an unusual arrangement of buildings. He tried to get us to work out what was different.'

'And did you?' asked Sylvia gently, still trying to keep the conversation low key and let Daniel unravel the story in his own words.

'Eventually, after about three times up and down the main street. It was obvious once you knew what to look for.'

'Clever boy. You always do keep your eyes open.'

Sylvia placed her arm gently around Daniel's shoulders and hugged him.

'From Bethesda Geoffrey drove up the hillside through another village where we parked.'

'That was probably Gerlan.'

'Yes, that's right Mum. It was Gerlan. You remember things well.'

Sylvia smiled and tousled Daniel's hair. 'Yes Daniel, I do remember things well. You mentioned Michael had talked about a guidebook. What did Michael say about this guidebook Daniel? Did Michael suggest a climb?'

'Well sort of. He mentioned that he was reading this Climbing Guidebook for the Carnedds. He remembered a rock climb that was like a mountaineering classic. Michael said it was an old route and close to where we were going. He talked it over with Geoffrey and they both agreed that it would be a good introduction for me, an introduction to alpine style climbing you know; moving roped together.'

'But you weren't moving roped together, were you?'

'No, but before we got to the climb we had to change valleys. Geoffrey and Michael agreed that going up the climb would be a lot more enjoyable than slogging up some loose scree slope.'

'So Michael suggested it and Geoffrey agreed? Is that right?' asked Sylvia.

'I suppose so but we were all involved in the discussion Mum. I know I was keen to go up a climb rather than slogging up screes.'

'What did you do next, after you changed your minds?'

'Well Geoffrey got the map out and he worked out the best way to change valleys without losing any height. He was very good at finding an easy way. We crossed a stream and over a ridge into the next valley.'

'The Llafar?'

'I don't remember the name but there was a good path and it led straight up towards the cliffs at the end. We hiked up the valley and

Western Gully was the best climb on the cliff at our level according to Michael. It's a sort of traditional classic.'

'Yes, but did Geoffrey suggest it? He knew best how well each of you could climb. He would know not to try something too difficult for you Daniel.'

Daniel dropped his head into his bandaged hands and shuddered. 'I grabbed the rope Mum. Honest, I did. I tried to save him.'

'I know my love. Nobody is blaming anybody. I am trying to let you relive the events to undo the trauma.'

'Mum, I can't relive that again. He died in front of me Mum, and I didn't see it. If I hadn't been so frightened I would have seen he was choking. I could have kept his head forward. I could have helped. I could have........' and the words slipped into sobs.

'Rest now Daniel. We will gently relive it together and together we will fight our way through this. We are Lords remember.' Sylvia quietly withdrew from Daniel's room and walked down to the drawing room. Ancestors of the Lord family gazed down silently as Sylvia slowly descended the great staircase. She lifted up her face proudly and defiantly proclaimed, 'We are Lords, my Lords.'

In the drawing room Sylvia went straight to Anthony and hugged him fiercely. 'Together we will fight our way through this,' she repeated. Anthony gently kissed his wife on her lips and his eyes searched hers. 'Aye, my love. Together we will find tomorrow and the day after tomorrow. One of the obvious questions now, however, is Michael.'

'And Daniel, Anthony,' said Sylvia vehemently, 'and Daniel.'

'Yes Sylvia, and Daniel, and Samantha too,' said Anthony, almost as an afterthought. I'll have to tell Samantha. Perhaps I should go over to Switzerland and bring her back for the funeral. She'll be devastated as she always loved to compete with her brothers. Sylvia, what do I tell her?' asked Anthony.

'Anthony, I will go over to Switzerland and talk with Samantha. You'll get too emotional with her. She's quite the young lady now and a woman to woman explanation is needed. You and I can sort out the funeral arrangements and then I will go and get Samantha.'

However, the question of Michael had hung over the whole Lord household for sometime. Anthony had travelled up to North Wales as soon as he had heard from the Mountain Rescue Team. Geoffrey's body had been taken to the morgue at Bangor Hospital. Daniel was sedated in one of the wards. Michael was nowhere to be found at that time.

Because of the nature of the accident there was a coroner's inquest. This turned out to be a rather routine event. Daniel was still in deep shock and under sedation and so was not called as a witness. The Mountain Rescue Team leader described what the Team had heard, found and done. That part was straightforward. Then there was the doctor who examined Geoffrey's body after the Team brought it down to Bethesda. He explained that he listed the death as asphyxia caused by vomit. After several telephone calls Sir Anthony had located Michael and told him that the inquest needed him as a witness. Michael came back up to Bangor and was called as a witness. Michael left no doubt in his description of events that Geoffrey climbed off without any proper belay and that he was his own worst enemy.

'He just took off. I told him he wasn't on belay. He fell. I lowered Daniel down to him and then I abseiled down as fast as I could. He was unconscious but breathing and I checked for any bleeding. There wasn't any bleeding. I checked that Daniel was okay and told Daniel to cover Geoffrey up as he would be in shock. As fast as I could I ran for help. What else could I do?'

Given this sequence of events there was little else Michael could do. You needed a stretcher with a broken back and the Mountain Rescue Team had the stretcher, as well the required expertise to bring someone down. The coroner accepted this at face value. Climbing accidents weren't rare in his area and leaders do fall. The climb wasn't beyond the climbing capabilities of the party. The weather hadn't made the climb any harder at the time of the accident. The climbers had the right equipment. There really weren't any clear errors. There really weren't any recommendations for the future to try and prevent such things happening again. Death through misadventure – case closed.

And still the question of Michael.

After the immediate sequence of events Anthony and Sylvia had to deal with the real long-term stress in the family. Geoffrey was dead. Daniel's hands slowly healed but he stayed in shock or denial for quite some time. Michael appeared quixotic. He had obviously been in shock right after the accident and the fact that he drove straight back to London while still under suspension was a clear indication that he wasn't thinking properly. Although this fact came up at the coroner's inquest the police didn't follow up on this error. Michael's explanation of events at the time of the accident appeared to be valid but still Anthony nursed some suspicions about what really happened. Sylvia was distraught over the whole sequence of events.

Anthony and Sylvia thought it would be best if they had Michael close to home and under some form of supervision. Both parents thought that the lad was too headstrong, too eclectic in his thoughts and actions. In addition, Anthony and Sylvia had to spend some time thinking and discussing the future of the Lord family. With Geoffrey dead and Peter still a baby Michael was the next choice for overall manager. Anthony had to think long and carefully how he would replace Geoffrey, both in his expertise within the software company and his role as Estate Manager. Michael wasn't groomed for either of these roles, nor did he have the background. Anthony thought they might have to bring in one or two more people, as the two jobs that Geoffrey had done were quite different. Lots to think about mused Anthony.

It was decided that for the University holidays at least Michael should come down from London to work for his father. With his knowledge of mathematics Michael could help with some of the software development plus some logistics analysis. Like his Grandfather Desmond, Michael had become interested and quite adept at some of the techniques in Operations Research. Michael had learnt how to do Linear Programming, Non-Linear Programming and even Dynamic programming. These mathematical techniques could be used to optimise, or determine the best combination of raw materials to make a finished product. They could also be used to determine where to place your distribution centres, or list the best sequence of actions for a manufacturing company. These were quite powerful tools and Anthony's Company had clients who could benefit from these analyses. Michael could be gainfully employed.

After some discussion with Sylvia, Anthony decided not to re-question Michael about the accident. Sad though it was it now was a fact of life and nothing would bring Geoffrey back. The hardest part of the whole affair had been telling Christina. Fortunately, young Peter Lord, Geoffrey's son had been too young to realise what had taken place, but Christina was inconsolable.

Having Michael back at Fotheringham Manor made sense to Anthony and Sylvia but Christina couldn't stand it. As soon as Michael appeared Christina attacked, 'You killed him Michael. If it wasn't for you my darling Geoffrey would still be here. You talked him into that weekend. You talked him into that climb. You forced him to lead. You Michael, you!'

'Hang on Christina. Geoffrey started.....'

'No Michael. He was tired. He'd driven up there all night. He'd had an exhausting week.'

'Well I didn't force him to do anything. We just went for a walk with......'

'But you didn't walk did you? You had to climb. You had to show off. You had to show Daniel, and look at him too Michael. What have you done to Daniel?'

'Heh, what is this, a witchhunt? It was an accident.'

'Yes, how convenient Michael, but we all really know what happened, don't we?'

'Are you accusing me of causing this accident?'

'Yes, I am. I'm accusing you of killing Geoffrey.'

'Christina, that's going too far,' said Anthony. 'I know you're hurting. We all are, but you can't accuse Michael like that.'

'Why not? Look at him. Did he get hurt? He even ran away, didn't you Michael?'

'I've had enough of this,' said Michael. 'I don't have to listen to this. You're deranged lady. You should go somewhere and have a rest, a long rest.'

'Not until I've had revenge Michael. I won't let this go.'

'Christina, we really can't have this kind of conversation,' said Anthony.

'Well, if you can't stand it father-in-law I will go home and talk it over with my father. Maybe there I'll be clearly heard. Obviously here you all band together. I'll leave in the morning.'

'Christina you can't mean that? Talk it over with Sylvia. Let it all calm down a little. Don't be too hasty.'

'Just like the English isn't it? What do you all say, "stiff upper lip", or "have a cup of tea", well I'm Italian and we Italians let our emotions show and talk for us. No more calm down. I go see my father.'

Christina stormed out of the room and left Michael and Anthony shaking their heads. Back in her own home Christina telephoned her father in Italy and explained what she was planning to do. Not surprisingly he completely agreed with her actions and told her that her mother and he would welcome her back with open arms. Next morning, taking Peter with her, Christina left and flew to Italy.

'Anthony, why didn't you stop her?' cried Sylvia. 'Not only has Christina gone but she has taken Peter with her too. He's our grandson, our only grandson may I remind you.'

'Sylvia I couldn't talk her out of it. She was accusing Michael of all sorts of things. There was no way she was going to live in the same house as Michael.'

'Well she wouldn't be in the same house Anthony. She has her own house. She needn't see Michael. He's here in the Manor.'

'That didn't seem to matter to Christina. She wasn't going to tolerate any forgiveness on our part.'

There seemed to be no suitable answer to this situation. Anthony still felt that having Michael at home was the best thing to do. No doubt Christina would calm down when she was away in Italy and had had a chance to talk things over with her father. Anthony promised Sylvia he would telephone Christina's father in the evening and talk things over with him. In the meantime Anthony decided to keep Michael hard at work. The household atmosphere was a little tense for a week or so.

While he was working in his father's company Michael met Ted Crichton and Lester Donald. Ted and Lester were both students at Bristol University who were working for his dad during the summer holidays. Through Ted and Lester Michael met up with other students at Bristol and started to hang out with them. As Melanie was back in America for a while with her folks Michael decided there was a need for another woman in his life. What the hell Michael thought, I'm only young once.

'Michael, you know this part of the world pretty well. Where's a good place to go swimming without getting salt in your mouth? I grew up in the middle of a large continent and the water tasted fine, but every time I go swimming here I end up needing to drink to excess.'

'Ted, I can't see anything wrong with wanting to drink to excess,' said Michael.

'True, but that's not really my question,' said Ted. 'A group of us were looking for somewhere to hang out where we can drink and swim without the swimming forcing us to drink. Know what I mean?'

'Fine, I understand. Well, the hills around here have some caves and some of the caves have collapsed into things called sinkholes. Don't you have some limestone country over in Canada? I thought you had all sorts of limestone areas?'

'We do. We also have hot springs and they can be really a great place to hang out.'

'I don't think we have any of those around here,' said Michael, 'but we do have these sinkholes. Why don't I show you some time this weekend? Grab a couple of the group who are interested and we'll go for a shuftie.'

'And what the hell is a shuftie when it's at home?' asked Ted.

'A look-see, an exploration to achieve the objective of the strategy, a show and tell. You know.'

'Sure Michael sounds good, although I'm not sure I'll ever understand English. I'll arrange for a couple of the guys to come with us on Saturday.'

Back in Bristol Ted Crichton called up some of his friends. Several people had been interested and Ted went through quite a list before he found two who could come this Saturday at such short notice. Jeremy Montgomery was studying geology. He had hiked a lot over various parts of England in his studies but Ted also knew that Jeremy was a caver. Ted thought this might be helpful in assessing some of Michael's suggestions. Working at Brainware Ted had already been advised about Michael's character and the need to be aware. The other guy that Ted managed to book for the Saturday exploration was Barry Hart. Officially Barry was studying Physical Education at Loughborough up in the Midlands but for the moment he was down at Bristol for some special summer-school wrestling training.

Originally Michael was all set to drive the three lads around in one of the Landrovers from Fotheringham Manor until his father pointed out that Michael had lost his licence for the moment. No way was Anthony going to let Michael drive so the group had to resort to Plan B. Fortunately Ted had a motorbike and Jeremy was the proud owner of a rather old and battered Triumph sports car. Plan B might not be quite as comfortable and convenient as having the four of them in the Landrover but at least it was legal.

Jeremy led the way with Michael as a rather frustrated passenger. Ted chugged along behind with Barry muttering Australian oaths at every bump and bend. 'Make sure you Colonials keep up,' chortled Jeremy. 'We Brits will lead the way as usual.'

'Just you watch it sport,' retorted Barry. 'It had better not rain or you're lovely English motor will quit. English electronics never did like water did they?'

Jeremy wasn't going to take that slur against his beloved car so he looked at the pair of them very carefully before hurling his next barb. 'How will you two know which side of the road to drive on? Ted will want to be on the right and you Barry will insist he drive on the left.'

'That's easy Jeremy. We'll just drive right down the middle as if we own the road. Hopefully everything will have already swerved aside to let you through. Anyway, lead on Michael, let's have a shuftie and go and see some sinkholes.'

The four young men spent the day driving and walking over several parts of the Somerset countryside looking at rivers, pools and some sinkholes. For Ted, coming from the plains of western Canada it was an eye-opener. There was so much fitted into such a little space. Everything appeared to be done in miniature. There were little roads, little houses, little fields, but lots of traffic. 'You get a lot done in this little island Michael,' said Ted. 'It's like a little dynamic machine.'

'Come off it Ted,' said Barry. 'What else have they got to do with their time? They don't have to travel for miles and miles like you and me. It's all next door. And as there is no surf you don't expect to find any of them down on the beach.'

'And you're just seeing what's taking place on top,' added Jeremy. 'There's just as many people busily working away under the ground.'

'Pull the other one Jeremy, this one's got bells on,' said Barry. 'Michael, isn't there a pub somewhere round here? I'm dying for a tinny, a cold one.'

True to form Michael easily found a village pub and the four of them soon got stuck into pints and shepherds pie. On the menu there were the usual offerings of pub fare and Barry wanted Steak and Kidney pie, but hold the kidneys. 'Barry, you can't separate the kidneys from the steak.'

'Well you don't expect me to eat dog food do you?' asked Barry. 'We eat meat in Australia, and that doesn't include anything weird like kidneys.'

'What about heart, or liver, or tripe?' asked Jeremy grinning.

'In your dreams mate,' said Barry. 'If they can't take the kidneys out I'd better have this shepherd's pie, as long as it isn't sheep.'

'What about fish and chips?' asked Michael, who was quite amazed at Barry's reactions to the menu.

'Chips are okay, but fish? No, swim around it, even catch it, but nobody in their right mind eats it. All we eat is meat, red meat. Got to be beef too. We don't eat sheep.'

'Well you're in luck then because the shepherd's pie here is beef along with potatoes.'

'No other veggies I hope,' said Barry suspiciously. 'Aussies don't eat veggies either you know.'

Michael placed his arm around Barry's shoulders, trying not to laugh too hard. 'Barry,' he said, 'rest assured you will get meat and potatoes and that's all. Now stop wingeing and drink you're pint. It's your shout mate.'

The other two laughed and even Barry could see that they all meant well. Well into his next pint Barry decided to try and turn the tables. 'So what do you eat Ted?' he asked. 'You must have bear and wolf and that funny-looking animal called, what is it, a mouse?'

'No a moose, and it can be pretty tasty. But, just to let you know we don't eat wolf and rarely do we eat bear, but we do have venison. There's some nice deer about and after a good hunt you can fill the freezer to last over winter. Also, while you're on the subject we catch fish and eat them. Salmon and trout taste pretty good. Why, we even put them on the barbie, just like Crocodile Dundee!'

The good-natured joshing went on through the meal and they all walked out laughing into the sunlight. Michael explained that they had seen most of the variety in the area and asked whether any one of the sites caught their fancy. Jeremy thought that Flett's Hole was a good location. The water was clear and looked deep. There were some good clean rocks to sit and dry out on and a little beach area for a campfire. It was a good hike off the road and so they wouldn't disturb anybody. They agreed that they would meet up soon with a bigger group and give it a try.

Although Michael appeared to be light-hearted his mother still had to work hard with Daniel. It was hot that July in Somerset. Sylvia had spent most of it with Daniel. It was the summer holidays but for Daniel the days stretched and became tiresome. He was still mentally troubled by the accident and his hands took longer than expected to heal. It had been later in the month that Enrico made a positive suggestion that might help lift Daniel's spirits.

'Lady Sylvia, take him to Italy and talk to Christina. Let Daniel see young Peter. Daniel can be a tutor for his nephew. If the little one stays in Italy he will not remember any of his English. I know you want your grandchild here with you and Christina has had long enough to grieve.'

'Enrico, you're brilliant,' said Sylvia. 'I have been on the telephone every week with her and her father and she is gradually listening, but it would be good for both of them if Daniel goes over to Italy. Perhaps they can all bond together over a mutual loss.'

Sir Anthony thought the idea was really good and took time out to thank Enrico and Antonio for the suggestion.

'Family is important Signore Lord, always family should come first. Look at us. We stay together but we also stay here because your grandfather made us part of your family. So, we too are troubled by Christina going home to Italy and the boy Peter being away from his family here. Also, we worry about young Daniel. He was always such a cheerful lad and enjoyed coming to see us.'

'He liked coming to see you because you spoiled him,' laughed Sylvia, 'you were always making him toys. Remember how he loved that fort you made, and all the soldiers and animals.'

'Si, si, but now he is a young man, and he must feel inside he is able to be strong, to fight his own battles and not those of the toys. Take him to Italy. Signore DeLucci has not seen Daniel for a while. I'm sure it would do all of you good.'

Sylvia's trip to Italy was as successful as Enrico predicted. Christina had had a chance to grieve over Geoffrey and had been consoled by her father. Signore DeLucci also understood family and he thought it was time that Christina returned to England. As Enrico and Antonio thought Daniel really enjoyed the change of pace and change of place. He spent many hours with little Peter and the two of them developed a special secret vocabulary of English and Italian baby words. It became a bond between them. Within the week Sylvia brought all of them home and Fotheringham Manor was a happier place for a while.

Christina had recovered well enough to go through the challenging task of handling Geoffrey's things. Somewhat to Sylvia's surprise, because she was going to offer to help, Daniel persuaded Christina that he would help. After a brief discussion with Anthony, Sylvia decided that she needn't be involved. It appeared that Daniel and Christina could sort through the clothes, the books, the papers, the equipment, and all the other "things" that go with someone when they are alive.

'Looks like a kind of therapy for them both,' said Sylvia to Anthony. 'Perhaps by doing something they both find closure. The physical doing rather than just thinking and remembering appears to make them realize it is real and not some horrid dream.'

'I hope so my love,' said Anthony, 'I have been worried about both of them ever since the accident and I know you have spent many hours trying to get them past the tragedy. I know it's trite but time is a great healer, and, there is the added bonus of Daniel getting on so well with young Peter. He never had much time for him before but now those two are almost inseparable.'

'Yes, and that's going to create another problem at the end of the holidays when Daniel goes back to school and Peter will want to go too.'

'Too true,' Anthony laughed, 'you can't win in this life.'

Back in Bristol University someone else was trying out the water. It was rather salty even though it was an indoor pool. Within the steamy confines of the aquatic Training Centre Jean Deville was training Nicole Masters.

'Ten laps to slowly warm up before you practice your routines,' said Jean. Nicole dove cleanly into the water and leisurely crawled the length of pool. With a neat roll she turned in the shallow end and slowly swam her way back.

Jean Deville, a French diving coach was over in England for a sabbatical at the University. As well as expanding his experience in aquatic training Jean was trying to improve his English. Nicole Masters, a young girl from southern Dorset wanted a Physical Education degree, and her passion was diving. She continued to rhythmically plough up the pool letting her muscles stretch and contract.

'Keep it neat,' muttered Jean, half to himself. 'Keep it precise and tidy in all the things you do.'

Nicole somersaulted over for her last two laps. Bloody easy for him to say thought Nicole. She almost missed touching the far end wall. This disoriented her for a moment and she lost the timing of her breathing. Spluttering, Nicole rolled onto her back.

Hell, thought Jean. Nicole has lost her concentration again. Jean crouched down at the end of the pool as Nicole swam the last few feet.

'Nicole, you have to concentrate. You 'ave to let your mind flow into the rhythm of the moment. It must all be a flowing reflex action, a symbiosis of body and soul.'

'Yes, well you're not working off last night's beer are you?'

Jean rocked back on his heels. He ran his hand through his en brosse haircut and sighed.

'Nicole, Nicole, this is work. Now is the time to work, to work hard. You dive well. You dive very well and will win the meet at the end of the month. But, ma petite, it will help if you dedicate yourself. Hanging out in the Students Union is not the kind of dedication I recommend.'

Nicole listened. She wanted to do well. Her parents had helped her finance her University education. She knew she had talent and had won at many junior diving meets. It was all there for her; her choice. Yes, but, and Nicole smiled to herself.

Jean watched Nicole go through her exercises. She dived well. Nicole had excellent timing. Jean knew that Nicole had the right drive; that she wanted to improve. Jean was impressed how well Nicole listened and could interpret the coach's suggestions. Both of them realised that they were a good team. The future looked good.

After the training session Nicole slowly pedalled her bicycle down to her digs and hung up her costume and towel to dry. She ticked off the schedule of her training sessions. Nibbling a piece of toast she repacked her sports bag for the day's series of land exercises in the gym. Nicole thought back over the morning session and evaluated what had happened, what had been said; good positive thoughts. She smiled as she looked at her personal objectives pinned to the kitchen wall: "Onwards and upwards".

The harsh demanding ring of the telephone stopped her thoughts in their tracks.

'Hi Nicole, want to go on a picnic?' Ted Crichton's voice boomed down the telephone line.

'What, right now? I've got classes.'

'So what, you're a mature adult with freedom of choice. A crowd of us is off to Flett's Hole. It'll be a blast.'

'But I've got training sessions.'

'You can run, stretch, do flips, whatever where we're going. Hell, you can even do dives into the Hole.'

'Ted, I can't just skip out on my routine. There is a major meet at the end of the month.'

'Yea I know that. So come and show us your routine. We'll take cards and hold up our impressions at the end of each dive for you.'

'You can't be serious? Anyway, a lot you all know about diving evaluation.'

'Two of the guys from Phys.Ed. are coming, plus a guy who thinks you're pretty cool.'

'Ted, nobody thinks I'm pretty cool to use your words.'

'I'll pick you up in half an hour. Michael is coming.'

The telephone went dead in her hand. She almost dropped the receiver as her heart jumped. Michael is coming.

Ted picked Nicole up in the prescribed thirty minutes. The powerful motorcycle revved indecently as Nicole came out of her digs. 'Looking cool kid; I've got a helmet for you.' She hopped onto the pillion seat and Ted raced away.

Flett's Hole was the result of a collapsed cavern in the limestone hills. Part of the walls and the roof of the cavern had collapsed so you could scramble down to the water. The hole was not very deep and sunlight reached down to the rocky end. Already there was quite a crowd sprawled over the warm limestone slabs. The entire crowd was Uni students and beer bottles were in a constant flow amongst the group.

'What ho.'

"What ho yourself Cyril. Who do you think you are today? Lord Chomley or his elegant cousin Sir Nigel Frogspawn? You should take the plum out of your mouth and speak like a proper Englishman.'

'Alright mate. Got a fag me old bleeder.'

'Take care Jeremy. You'll spill the bloody beer.'

The conversations batted around the group. The men did the usual peacock spread to impress the girls. A couple of the youths were wrestling in the pool with water splashing everywhere. Trying to look decorous a couple of the girls were stretched out on the limestone slabs near the cliff end.

'Ted. About time you arrived. Who have you got in tow?'

'Meet Nicole Masters, Miss Diving Universe of 1991.'

'Hi Nicole,' came several calls. 'Come and grab a beer. Nice legs'

'Ted, pass the bottle. It's nice and cool from the pool.'

Ted swigged and passed the bottle on to Nicole. Wanting to be one of the group Nicole swigged too. It was cool and she had got quite hot sweating up the hill from the motorbike. She took another swig.

'Go easy girl. We've got all day for the picnic.' Water splashed over most of the group as the two wrestlers finally gave up on sparring and kicked water everywhere as they came out of the pool.

'These are the two Phys Ed guys I mentioned,' said Ted to Nicole. 'Nicole, meet Barry and Leo.'

'Greetings Nicole from down under,' came back the response with a pronounced Australian drawl. 'Good on you sport. I'm Barry the brawler. As you can see I wrestle. My mate here, young Leo, is just a hanger on. Doesn't know hold from hurl yet.'

'Alright, alright. This ain't no gobfest. Pleased to meet you luv. Don't mind mouthy here.' Leo punched Nicole playfully on the arm and grinned.

Nicole smiled and shook hands with the two young Australians.

'I heard you boys don't go much on Sheilas,' she said. 'I thought you preferred your mates, or a beer, or both?'

'Don't believe everything you read about Aussies luv. Some of us are quite housebroken. Actually, we hear that you dive.'

'Too true,' said Jeremy, 'a real goer for our Olympic Team is Nicole. Maybe she can teach you Aussies a thing or two.'

'Careful you pommie bastard; them's fighting words. What you'd say Barry? Think she's dinkum?'

Barry looked at Leo and smiled. Australians always like some sort of competition, especially if its sport related. 'Maybe we should have some sort of trial. See if she's any good before we place bets.'

Ted said, 'go in and show 'em Nicole. There are a series of ledge at the cliff end, almost like a series of highdiving boards. Go and show them a couple of moves.'

'How deep is it by the cliff end?' asked Nicole. 'The water is in shadow at that end and it is hard to see the depth.'

'Send Jeremy in and get him to dive down and find the bottom. He's a geologist and a spelunker and so he is used to messing about in caves and rocks and whatever.'

'Oy, Jeremy. Make yourself useful you lazy sod and test the depth of the pool for our champion here.'

'Yes sir, no sir, three bags full sir,' came the retort, but Jeremy did stagger into the pool and swim over to the cliff end. He upended, kicked his legs in the air and disappeared. The group watched with amusement. Jeremy wasn't usually so responsive.

'Must be a reaction to the totty.'

'Where's he got to?'

'Maybe he's found a cave down there.'

'Perhaps he's found a mermaid holding gems of unfathomable value.'

'Or he's got stuck.'

Suddenly the group went quiet.

'Heh. What's up? Why all the dark faces? Where's the beer?' Michael's series of questions refocussed the group's interest as he came bounding down the slopes kicking up limestone pebbles.

'Michael, have a care with kicking all that shit down. Just cool it man. We've lost Jeremy. Silly little sod's got stuck somewhere underwater in the pool.'

'No he hasn't,' said Michael. 'He's laughing at you all looking so concerned. He's tucked over there behind that large slab. Looks like Golem with his white ugly body. Perhaps he put the "Precious" on his finger and disappeared for a moment.

'Jeremy you unthinking sod. You had us all worried.' Several boulders lobbed in Jeremy's direction accompanied these comments. 'After all that how deep is it?'

'I went down about twenty feet and found a ledge and over the edge of the ledge it went down deeper. Is that deep enough for our highdiver?'

'Say, is Nicole here?' asked Michael, who had not noticed her on his erratic entrance.

'I'm here Michael,' said Nicole blushing.

'Cool kid. Good to see you again.'

A warm glow spun itself all over Nicole. She smiled inwardly and remembered the last time she had been with Michael. It had been at a Uni dance and Michael had spent a lot of time with her. He had made her feel special and all grown up. After her very quiet country village youth the experiences at University had opened up a new world for Nicole. True, she had competed at dive meets in larger towns and even cities, but she had never really experienced life outside the village. Michael had made her feel like a princess, particularly when Michael chose her over the other two girls who came barging in. Who were they? Two Americans if she remembered right. Overdressed, or underdressed really, and loud. Michael had protected her from the onslaughts and been her champion. She looked happily at Michael.

Barry's command jerked Nicole out of her reverie. 'Let's see you dive then luv.'

'Yes Nicole, we'd all like to see your routines. Ted was telling us you said you couldn't come because you were supposed to be training. Well show us some of the training exercises.'

Nicole looked at the group. Her face came round to Michael and her eyes posed the question. Did he want her to dive? 'Sure Nicole. Go for it. Show them how good you are. Knock their eyes out.'

Feeling good with the group's support Nicole swam over to the cliff and ascended a sloping ramp leading to one of the ledges. The ledge ran round further into the main part of the cliff and over the deep water that Jeremy had probed. There wasn't any room for movement and the site was like a very cramped high board. Think the dive through and see it in your head. Concentrate and bring the feet together with arms at the sides. Last complete think and away.

The entry was neat with minimal splash and Nicole arced through the pool to the surface. A loud clapping and cheering greeted her as she surfaced. There were catcalls, whistles, and cried of encouragement. The group called for more, at least one more. Nicole could hear the voices, including the drawl of Barry and Leo, the plum tones of Cyril, and the support from Michael. In the end Nicole did four more dives from the ledge finishing with an inwards somersault. On the way underwater her fingers brushed part of the wall of the cavern, scraping the skin, and she emerged to loud cheers but with bloody fingers. As she climbed out over the rocks to the group she left occasional spatters of blood.

'Far out Nicole. That last dive was fabulous.'

'What have you done to your hands? Is that blood?'

'Yes. I just brushed against the wall underwater on the last dive. I'll put some bandaids over my fingers. It's just a scrape.'

Michael came down and rummaging through his rucsack he quickly found several bandaids and tape. It didn't take him long to dry and wrap Nicole's fingers. He lifted the undamaged hand to his lips and gently kissed them.

'There,' he said. 'That should work for the moment.'

Nicole looked at him gratefully. 'Thanks Michael. You are so kind and thoughtful. You even come prepared for any emergency.'

'Lunch kids. Time for lunch. I'm starving, and thirsty.'

'You're always thirsty. Pass the cooler.'

'The beers in the pool not in the cooler.'

'I'm after some food ahole, not more booze.'

The banter light-heartedly rolled around the pool. Folks delved into coolers, rucsacks, opened packets, tins, and squeezed tubes of jam and peanut butter. Conversations rose and fell as the group munched in the warm sunlight. Nicole hadn't brought any food in the rush to come out. She felt a little embarrassed as she was new to the group.

'Ow about a meat pie Nicole?' asked Leo. 'You ain't eating anything. You want some tucker?'

'No thanks Leo. I'm supposed to be in training and I don't think meat pies quite fit into my diet.'

'Ave a beer then kiddo. That can't do any harm. Eh, Barry mate, pass up a tinny.'

Nicole listened to this abuse of the English language and her mind was wrapped up in the words. She took the cold beer without really thinking and gulped it down. It was good and cold from the pool.

Over lunch Ted had been busy. He had collected some cardboard from the lunch material and pencilled on each sheet a number. He distributed one set of the numbers to Cyril, Barry and Susan.

'Now Nicole,' he said. 'I promised Jean, your coach, that you wouldn't be allowed to waste today. Cyril, our language expert knows nothing about diving, but he is fair. He is our neutral representative. Barry, who has already given you a hard time just by being Australian is our Phys Ed expert and very critical. Susan is in drama. She is looking for flair, and being a lady should be on your side.'

'And if you believe that you will believe anything,' said Michael. 'I'm not sure that women ever support other women, especially if things get competitive.' Nicole thought again how Michael seems to appear on his white charger at just the right time.

'So,' said Ted. 'We've got our panel of judges. We've got a very supportive and partisan crowd.'

'That's all you know mate,' drawled Leo. 'I don't see no Southern Cross on that cossie.'

'As I was saying,' repeated Ted. 'We have a very, very partisan crowd. Cheer you English buggers. So, Nicole, we propose to see you at your best.'

'How can you cheer Ted with that lot? You're a Redcoat Canadian, a Royal Mounted Beaver or something. You can't cheer with this bunch of Mother Country buggers. Let Susan, Tony, David, Jeremy and Cecil cheer for the home crowd but don't get too chummy Ted. You only got your constitution back a few years ago.'

'Barry, you can be very lucid and intelligent for an ex-convict. You're right about the constitution but at least we recognised our First Nations people as people early on. Didn't you recently realise legally in Australia that the aboriginals are real people?'

'Oy, Colonials, put a sock in it. We're here to recognise talent.' Michael stood up and made to bang Ted and Barry's heads together. Cecil and Tony both cheered at Michael's actions.

Nicole stood up quickly and swayed a little. The heat had reflected back from the white limestone rocks while they had all been sitting down for lunch. She was hot. The beer on her empty stomach lurched around. Michael came over to her and held his arm around her.

'Take it slowly Nicole. This is your show. You are the star here. Let them be dazzled.'

Nicole swam across the pool to the ramp. She slowly climbed across to the ledge. Her balance wasn't quite so sure and her foot slipped off the ledge. She grabbed the wall above the ledge and continued on. Nobody saw the slip. Cyril was telling a joke in his plummy voice. Barry and Leo were interrupting with comments on Cyril's voice and the whole group was listening to the play on words.

'Fanfare,' called Michael. 'Nicole Masters will now perform her first dive. This ladies and gentlemen will be a forward pike with a half twist. The dive has a difficulty of.... Hell, I don't know, but it will be bloody difficult.' The group laughed and applauded Michael's introduction.

'Judges, cards at the ready please.'

Nicole dived. Clean, neat, concentrated and came up to two signs saying "9" and one saying "7".

'Only nine! Hell, that was brilliant. I think the judges are biased; definitely a fix, especially that seven. Probably the bloody colonials trying to get their own back on the Mother country.'

'Give it another go Nicole. That was good. Jean would be pleased.'

Nicole smiled to herself. Yes, Ted's last comments were right. That was good and Jean would be pleased. What was it Jean had said? 'A symbiosis of body and soul.' She stroked back to the ramp again and walked up along the ledge. Again her wet foot slipped on a part of the ramp.

'Fanfare,' rang out Michael's voice again. 'Nicole Masters, leader after the first dive, will now perform a two turn somersault in the tuck position with a reverse twist. This dive has a difficulty of "harder than the previous dive".'

'Michael, you're not helping the judges. They've only one set of numbers. You're also making the dives harder and harder for Nicole. You're upping the ante.'

'You've got to compete with the best,' said Michael. 'You've got to strive to push to the limit. You've got to beat out all the others, including these Aussie interlopers.'

The Aussie interlopers growled and opened another beer. The group jostled around good-naturedly.

'You show 'em Nicole. Put England back on the podium for us.'

Nicole's second dive didn't quite go right. Her right foot slipped a little on a smooth part of the ledge and this threw her balance off. The tucks were tight but her body was not in the line of the dive and her reverse twist spun her further off balance. The entry was clumsy with the legs coming late into the water creating quite a splash. Zooming to the surface Nicole was mad at herself. The three cards showed two "7"s and a "6" and the group were a little more subdued.

'Heh little one. What about a big finish for me? Really go for the big one and forget about the last dive. Pretend it's the ten-metre board. There's a higher ledge and that will make for a more sensational dive.'

'Michael, do you think I can?'

'Sure kid. Look at me. I know you can do it. It really will show this group how good you are.'

'But Michael, I don't normally dive off the ten metre board.'

'You've got to try once girl. It's a real high.'

Nicole's mind was churning up inside. The heat, the lack of food, the beers, and now Michael's insistence all added to the conflict in her head. Think Nicole she said to herself. Concentrate. You can do this. What was it Jean said? Put any mistakes behind you and do it right now, this time. Get your mind into the present, the here and now, this instant.

Unfortunately the thought of "do it for Michael" was swamping many of the other thoughts. Nicole's brain was a mess of many thoughts as she swam across the pool. She climbed up onto the ramp and started out across the ledge again.

'Up one more ledge Nicole,' shouted Michael across the pool. 'Like a real ten metre board.'

'Michael, that's too dangerous,' said Ted.

'You've got to challenge yourself,' said Michael to Ted. 'If you're going to win anything you've got to push to the limit.'

Nicole started to climb up from the lower ledge to the higher one. With her wet feet the limestone felt a little soapy underfoot.

The group was listening to the dialogue between Ted and Michael when a loud crunch startled everyone. Nicole wasn't on the ledge, either ledge. In fact Nicole wasn't on the cliff.

'No, God no,' screamed Jeremy. He had seen her close to where he had hidden from the group in his depth test. Barry and Leo plunged into the pool almost simultaneously and sped across to the large fallen block.

'Is she alive?' cried Susan. 'Is she breathing?'

'She's alive,' came the answer across the pool, 'but she's badly hurt. We'll need to get some stretcher or something. She's unconscious and her legs are bent at a weird angle.'

The good news and the bad news brought the group together and Ted took charge. 'David and Cyril, off to the cars and get help. Tony, Michael, swim across to Barry and Leo and see whether they need help. If you can move Nicole safely try and tow her back to this side of the pool. The ambulance guys won't be able to take any stretcher over that side by the cliff. The rest of us can gather clothes to reduce any shock and make sure the pathway up to the top of the Hole is easy for carrying her out.'

Ted brought some order into the shocked group. It helped that they all had something positive to do. Michael didn't react kindly to this tone of Ted's but he didn't say anything. With Tony, Michael swam over to where Nicole's body was half lying in the water and half on a rock ledge.

'Spin her round and we'll float her over to the other side,' said Michael, feeling he was in charge again.

Barry jumped up. 'No Michael. Let her be. She might have broken her back and moving her could damage her spine.'

'What do you know about it? Been helping skippy have you?'

'Up yours Michael. I was a lifesaver on Bondi beach for a couple of summers. You need to be very careful with backs. Anyway, you've already done enough damage forcing her to such a dive.'

'Fuck you Leo. It was her call. Thought she could dive. I didn't force anybody. Come on Tony, hold her head while I pull her leg off the ledge. We can easily tow her across while these two Aussies yip and yap.'

'Michael, just cool it. This is serious man. She needs to be looked after carefully.' Leo was getting more and more concerned that Michael would do more harm than good.

'And you think you're going to do that eh? You think you're the man to be the big hero rescuer? Not likely mate. She's my girl.'

Michael lifted Nicole's heel and swung the one leg that was over the rock into the water alongside the other leg. Without anybody bracing the head and the spine Michael immediately rendered Nicole a paraplegic, although nobody knew at the time. With Tony holding Nicole's head above water and Michael towing by pulling on the ankles they moved Nicole's body across the pool. Fortunately the ambulance staff had arrived, complete with a backboard, and Nicole was spared any further disaster. As they lifted her out of the water Nicole opened her eyes to see Michael looking down on her. She smiled. My saviour.

Forestry at Fotheringham Manor

The atmosphere back in the office was tense. Ted had already told Lester what had happened at Flett's Hole. Anthony Lord had heard about the incident and decided to try and put an end to the bad vibes. He certainly wasn't going to get any productivity out of the three of them unless he tried to clear the air.

'Dad, I did my best. I helped get Nicole across the pool to the stretchers, and carried her up to the ambulance, and....'

'After having turned her into a paraplegic you arsehole,' shouted Ted. 'You could have listened to Barry; you could have thought a little before playing Sir Galahad.'

'Okay Ted, that's enough,' said Anthony. 'I'm sure you all acted for the best. I hear everyone pulled their weight and tried to help as best they could.'

'Yes sir, but young Michael here has to pull someone with a broken back and that did more damage than was necessary.'

'And what did you do but stand on the side of the pool and shout instructions Ted. This wasn't some programme you could dictate. Someone had to get in there and do something rather than talk about it.'

'Michael, please,' said Anthony, 'let's all back off shouting at each other. There was an accident where the girl slipped. I understand she hadn't had any lunch and was drinking too.'

'But that's not the beef Mr. Lord,' said Ted. 'The accident was one thing, although perhaps that needn't have happened if we'd all been a little more thoughtful but the later injury was completely unnecessary.'

'And you think I wanted that to happen?' demanded Michael. 'You think I deliberately pulled her legs?'

'No Michael, I don't. All I am saying is that if you had listened to Barry and Leo for a moment, and they have seen accidents like this before we might not be having this conversation.'

'Well Michael, what do you say to that?' asked Anthony Lord. 'Did this Barry or Leo ask you to stop and consider before you moved her?'

'Yes Dad, but somebody had to act quickly. We had to get her off the rocks and across the pool.'

'But what was the rush? No ambulance had arrived. There was no professional help across the other side of the pool. She wasn't drowning in the water and I understand she wasn't bleeding. Why the rather mad panic?'

'Shit, I don't know. She was my girl, I had to do something.'

'Seems like a time when a little forethought might have been better than rushing in with all guns blazing.'

Anthony turned to Ted and Lester. 'Thanks Ted for bringing this to my attention and helping me understand the events. If you and Lester can get back to work now I will have a talk with my son here. Michael, let's go to my office and see whether we can better resolve this situation. We all need the work to go on and I need some productivity from all three of you. Michael, with me.'

Anthony strode away to his office expecting Michael to follow. Michael looked at Ted and Lester. It wasn't a friendly look, but then he spun on his heel and strode after his father. Ted looked at Lester and shrugged his shoulders. 'Sorry to drag you into that but I felt it should be out in the open and that his dad should know.'

'No sweat man. Young Mr. Michael has a lot to learn about life and he ain't exactly making friends while he learns. He's just too uptight man; always trying to prove he's cock of the roost.'

'Yeah, well, he's knocked off the previous cock and he still looks like he's unsure of himself. Let's hope that his dad can knock some sense into him. This is a good Company with good products.'

Down the corridor Anthony walked into his office and sat on the corner of his desk. Michael followed and flopped himself into a chair.

'Before you get comfortable Michael shut the door please,' said Anthony.

Michael sort of sat there.

'Now Michael, shut the door now, before all the office can hear us.'

The tone in his father's voice registered with Michael and he started up quickly and shut the door, quietly.

'Fine, thanks and now sit down.'

Michael sat back more formally in the chair opposite his father. Anthony leaned forwards, looming large sitting on the edge of his desk. He brought his face close to Michaels.

'Son, we need to talk. We need to talk rather seriously about your future and we need to talk now before anymore shit hits the fan!!' Anthony's voice had steadily gone up the fortissimo scale as he spoke and the volume of sound could have easily spun the blades of any fan. Michael blanched.

'So Michael, what's to do? The Lord family has a Company and an Estate. Geoffrey brought expertise for both but now he is gone. So where do we go from here? Where do you go from here? I know the last month has been the aftermath of a tragedy, a prolonged shock, but we have to look forwards. Where do you want to go from here?'

'Dad, I don't really know,' said Michael. 'You're right, it has been a prolonged shock, and this recent accident hasn't helped. I thought I could get my head around things with working for you down here and it was going well. Having to think about logistical problems and do the analysis was helping keep me sane. I really thank you and Mum for making that decision. Working with Ted and Lester has been positive. They are great guys and I've learnt a lot as well as being able to offer something myself.'

'True Michael, this past month the three of you have done some excellent work. However, that is only a short-term challenge. My question also includes what happens long-term. I need to make some decisions pretty soon about personnel and responsibilities, and you certainly need to make some decisions about responsibilities.'

Michael thought this over slowly nodding his head. 'Dad I don't have the same expertise as Geoffrey. I know nothing about the business administration end or the Common Market technicalities that Geoffrey worked on.'

'True Michael, I've already been looking for someone with that background. I'll probably to have to hire someone for the Company for that role, but what about the Estate?'

'I know the area Dad. I know what we do and to some extent I know how we do it but I've no expertise in farming or forestry. I'm an analytical mathematician and problem solver Dad, not a bloody cowboy or a lumberjack.'

Anthony laughed. 'You've been talking with Ted too much about his work experience in Canada, but you're right, that isn't your background. I'll probably have to hire another professional forester, or perhaps an estate manager with forestry experience. Still, how about you? Do you want to stay on at University, always assuming you've passed your exams?'

'That's a certainty,' bragged Michael. 'That kind of work I can do easily. In fact, that is probably where I should continue. Perhaps we should talk about where the Company is trying to go and what I should study to advance that.'

'Good idea Michael, a positive thought. Look, go back and try and pick up the pieces with Ted and Lester. Let your ruffled feathers lie back for a while and get your head into some real work.'

'I'll try Dad. When I can I'll keep an eye on the Estate, although I hear the farm side is well under control. Aunt Stephanie seems to make sure everything runs well while still doing her research with genetics.'

Anthony eased back off the side of his desk and sat back in his office chair. He looked at Michael across the desk. 'Yes Michael, for the moment you carry on working here with Ted and Lester. You're right, Stephanie has enough control over the farm. However, until I've hired a new forester you and I had better keep an eye on Norton Ferris. After O'Rourke died Ferris has had too much of a free hand and his hands are always looking for handouts. I think we'd better keep an eye on our Mr. Ferris. And watch out for how he treats Antonio and Enrico; he seems to have a grudge against Italians.'

Antonio and Enrico Branciaghlia had been born in 1920 and 1922 respectively near Cortina in Northeastern Italy. Antonio had grown up following in his father's trade of being a stone mason. He had become very capable with his hands in stonewalling and masonry. Enrico had become a woodworker producing furniture and doing house repairs and roofing. Although this earned him his bread and butter his delight and skill was in carving animals for children. Both Italian boys learned to shoot in the hills around Cortina. Country life was tough and the odd rabbit helped fill the dinner pot. When World War II started in

1939 both boys enlisted in the Italian army. They ended their war when captured in North Africa in 1943. They had been shipped as P.O.W.s to the U.K. and moved to be farm workers on Fotheringham Manor Estate which was desperately looking for skilled, energetic young men in 1943. Although it was usual to employ P.O.W.s the transfer of Antonio and Enrico to Fotheringham was done deliberately, and by specific request. George Lord, Desmond's father, had fought with Italians in 1914-1918 in the Dolomite Alps, and still spoke some of the language. George, and Albert Templeton, the old gamekeeper who was in the same artillery regiment were both impressed by Italians. Virginia Lord had climbed and skied in the Cortina area and she too admired the hard-working character of the local people. Everyone at Fotheringham gained with this arrangement.

As the war progressed the two Italians learnt that their parents and the rest of their family had been killed back in Italy. With a smattering of broken Italian and simple English old Albert Templeton trained Antonio and Enrico. The brothers could already do drystone walling, building repair, wagon repairs, cottage repairs, and fencing. From their days with old grinders and woodworking tools they became familiar with small motors. They also learnt basic forestry operations from Albert. In 1945 at the end of the war the two Italians asked to stay on at Fotheringham Manor. As old Albert retired they could help his son Edward Templeton who had inherited his father's position. By this time Antonio and Enrico had earned a lot of respect in the village. They made wooden and stone toys for the kids for Christmas, which they offered through the Church. Their way of life stayed simple, almost like village life back in Italy. Although they had many friends and were well liked in the village neither of the two brothers married. They kept very much to themselves.

In the 1960s and 1970s, as Anthony's children grow up, Antonio and Enrico made toys for Geoffrey, Michael, Samantha and Daniel. Geoffrey liked them but Michael spurned the toys, wanting more proactive things – things that go fast or make a loud noise. Samantha loved her doll's houses with the tiny people that Enrico had carved. Perhaps because he was the youngest child, or because he was the child who visited Antonio and Enrico most often, Daniel was their favourite. Antonio created a magnificent rock fort for Daniel and Enrico carved a whole army of soldiers. The fort came complete with crenellated walls, round corner towers, a working drawbridge, and even a moat to fill with water. Sylvia was not impressed when the moat understandably overflowed, as it was apt to do with young Daniel. However, this toy was a long-lasting favourite with Daniel, and Antonio and Enrico shared the little boy's delight.

By 1990 the lives of Antonio and Enrico were settled into the steady world of the forest and the village. Early in the year, before winter had really released its grip on the trees, the two Italians had been carefully pruning the white pines. Both eastern and western white pine grow well in southern England but the eastern species, so-called Weymouth pine does suffer from white pine weevil. This insidious pest spends part of its life on blackcurrant bushes and trying to eliminate those from southern England is a non-starter. Albert Templeton had heard about western white pine being more resistant and he had bought some seed and established some fine plantations, the oldest of which was now sixty years old.

'Remember the early work we did here Antonio?'

'It was one of our first jobs on the estate,' replied Antonio to his brother. 'We had just come here and old Mr. Albert explained what had to be done.'

'Si, in his broken Italian as we didn't know any English at that time.' Enrico slowly drew the file over the teeth of the long-handled pruning saw.

'But between us, and Mr. George coming down from the Big House to explain as well we all got it sorted out.'

'The stand was how old then, maybe thirteen and the trees six metres tall. It was a grand plantation old Mr. Templeton had started. He had high hopes for these stands.'

'He would be proud to see them now,' said Antonio. 'See the tops are up around thirty metres. Actually, this pruning may be a little too late to really help.'

'They'll need to wait another twenty or thirty years before they see the returns in clear lumber.'

'Let's get on then Enrico, these saws will reach to six metres giving one good clear log.'

Assuredly the two brothers moved along the rows of planted pines. They selected about one tree in three to high prune for lumber. The ones in between would come out in thinnings before the final clear-cut and it didn't pay to high prune them.

'Did you leave all this rubbish here?' came the loud indignant shout. The brothers looked towards the voice. 'I could have torn a fetlock with this mess all over the ride.'

'Buon giorno Mr. Michael,' said Antonio. 'How are you today?'

'Forget the pleasantry mister, just clear this pile of branches off the ride. It's too bloody dangerous for the horse.'

'We'll clear the ride Mr. Michael when we have finished the outer rows and all the material is down. That makes it......'

'No, clear it now, and keep it clear at all times. Just do as I say or I'll have Mr. Ferris on your backs.'

'Fine Mr. Michael, and how is your horse today? We saw Mr. Ferris grooming it a while back.'

'Never you bloody mind about my horse, or Mr. Ferris, just do as I say.'

Michael rode off satisfied that he had made the ride safe for his horse. The two Italians were just getting too old for the job thought Michael. Funny, that's what Ferris had said at the end of last year. Still, Ferris just wanted the brother's cottage so he could move his sons out there. The games people play thought Michael. Need to keep Ferris around though thought Michael - could be useful with his contacts. Antonio and Enrico continued carefully selecting final crop trees to prune and piled the slash inside the plantation off the ride.

'Don't expect to see Ferris out here this cold of a morning,' said Enrico.

'True brother, he'll be wrapped up somewhere making sure he isn't doing too much.'

Norton Ferris was the resident forester at Fotheringham Manor. His mother had given birth to this unwanted child in the poverty of 1925. The father, he supposes, was a merchant seaman. Who knew? Life in the unkempt streets of Liverpool was hard with so many folks on the dole. Somehow Norton had survived this rough upbringing but he grew up with a permanent resentment of people above him. As soon as the war broke out Ferris tried to join up. Even the army refused him as being too young. Tales from his mother about life on the ships deterred him from going to sea. Young Norton found that he worked well with his hands and with horses and so he worked on bread delivery with a horse and cart. That way he could thieve something to eat. He also worked with a local rag and bone man in fixing up furniture and peddling it. That way he could earn some money. Eventually he managed to lie his way into the armed forces. Once in the army he quickly found a way of being fed, being clothed and doing bugger all. This worked really well until 1943 when the army caught up with Private Ferris and he was posted to fight in Italy. In Italy he tried again to perfect his way of getting fed, clothed and keeping his head down.

Norton nearly succeeded, but his ability to get into debt proved his undoing. To try and raise some cash and pay off his debts before someone seriously hurt him Norton tried selling parts of the army. However, he wasn't smart enough to wheel and deal like some of his other squaddies. The scam Norton tried had to be relatively simple. Somewhat naively Norton thought he could fool some of the young lads of Naples. Now the youth of Naples live a life where the right hand should never know what the left hand is doing and very quickly Norton was out of his league. But, Norton did have access to something that was desperately needed. Food in Naples in wartime was in very short supply and even army rations sold well. Norton promised young Luigi.

'So compadre, you all set to collect this stuff?'

'Si amico. You bring. We pay.'

'You've got the money. I need American dollars.'

'Si, e buono. It's good.'

'You've got the van? Remember it has to be very quiet. I've told the sentry at the gate to expect you.'

'Who is this sentry amico?'

'He's a friend. He knows the score. He's part of my end of the deal. I've taken care of him. Just tell him you want Garibaldi.'

'Don't take the piss Englishman.'

'No, no amico. Just an easy name for you Eyetalians to remember, yes?'

Luigi looked at Norton. The dark eyes looked him up and down. He'd remember this one. Norton beamed back. Simple lads, he had their number. Bloody starving they were. Take anything, and he needed the dollars. This was a good chance to get ahead again. It all seemed so simple. Norton had purloined five cartons of rations and repacked them into eight cartons making up the space with packing and empty boxes. This was not too greedy and the Italians wouldn't find out until they unpacked them. They couldn't come back and complain now could they? This was money for old rope so to speak.

Luigi quietly eased the van down the alleyway. His three friends crouched in the back. At the sentry gate Luigi rolled down the window and looked at the sentry.

'Who goes there?' said the sloppy sentry as if he hadn't seen the van coming slowly down the street.

'Halt and be identified,' he shouted, and he brandished his rifle.

Luigi breathed in slowly and thought what a stupid prat he looked. Christ, with a little more forethought our group could walk in and get everything for nothing but we will play their stupid game.

'I'm looking for Garibaldi,' he said to the sentry. Because he said it in Italian his three friends in the back of the van rolled around in hysterics. Holy Mother, these people were funny.

'Who goes there?' came the more insistent demand of the sentry.

'I'm looking for Garibaldi,' said Luigi, but this time in English.

'Who?'

'I'm looking for Garibaldi,' insisted Luigi. 'I'm a friend of Norton the Scouse.'

'Blimey, why didn't you say so then you bleeding idgit. Any friend of the Scouse is a friend of mine. Enter friend and drive over to the light there.'

Luigi eased the van in through the gate and parked by the light. They sat quietly in the van and waited. Norton strolled out smoking. 'Want a fag? A ciggo?'

'No amico. Where's the stuff?'

'Half a mo', where's the money?'

'Show us the cartons?'

'And you show me the dosh mate. I wasn't born yesterday. Money up front 'ere.'

After a quick flurry of Italian a package was passed up front and Luigi opened it under the light. 'You want to count it paesano? Real professional like?'

'No, no, we have a deal here. I trust you. Here, just inside the door. Get your mates to haul it out into the van quick like. Let's move eh? We don't need the Sergeant wondering why I am talking with the enemy.'

It didn't take Luigi's friends long to move the eight cartons into the back of the van. A few words of Italian accompanied this transfer and Luigi gave Norton another long hard look.

'It's good. Eight cartons at ten dollars a carton, so eighty U.S. dollars compadre.'

'Si,' said Luigi and he carefully counted out eight ten dollar notes from the package in his hand.

Norton licked his lips as he saw the amount of money in Luigi's package but there were four of them and this wasn't the place to start anything. Luigi saw Norton's face and quickly put away his cash.

'Let's go lads,' he said to his friends and they jumped into the back of the van. Luigi carefully closed the doors and came back to the driver's side.

'We don't want anything falling out now do we? The packages might split open right here on the street.'

'No, well, as you say, off you go and drive carefully,' said Norton.

'Until next time my friend,' said Luigi and he eased out the clutch.

'Oh, I'm off posted next week,' said Norton, 'so we won't meet again. Take care eh?'

'Until we meet again, maybe,' said Luigi, and he drove back past the sentry.

'Take good care of Garibaldi for me,' said Luigi to the sentry. 'He may end up wearing a red shirt if we meet him again.'

'Op it chum. Get yourself out of here. He's okay is the Scouse.'

'He won't be okay for long,' said Luigi in Italian to his three friends and they all fell over themselves with laughter. 'Not if he knows his numbers he won't,' said Marco. 'All those U.S. notes have the same serial number. Oh, by the way Luigi, most of these boxes seem a little light to us. I think our Garibaldi friend tried to sell us short.'

It wasn't until Norton tried to payoff his debts with his newfound wealth that the shit hit the fan. Not being able to pay the debt was one thing but being a laughing stock was another. The word spread around his post quickly and Norton was furious. 'Can't even get one up on a bunch of yokels from Naples Scouse? No wonder you're such a loser mate.'

There were three other lads from Liverpool in Norton's platoon. None of them liked the fact that the Naples lads had got one up so they decided to settle the score. Norton set up another meet with Luigi to arrange a second deal, planning to ambush this smart-arse Neapolitan. The four lads from Liverpool thought they could beat some sense into Luigi and maybe lighten him of his pile of U.S. notes. Perhaps some of them would be genuine.

The military police arrived with a great fanfare of blowing whistles and searchlights. The fighters quickly broke apart and half of the combatants vanished into the alleyways. Knives dropped onto cobblestones, glistening with blood. As Luigi had warned, Garibaldi was wearing a red smeared shirt. His cuts needed stitches and he had a distinctive slash across his cheek. The other three soldiers all had knife wounds and a couple of broken arms. The squaddies' story was that they were jumped by a gang of youths and defended themselves as best they could. The duty officer didn't believe a word of this and threw all four of them in the brig for a week.

For the rest of his time in the army Norton tried to keep his nose clean and out of the reach of debt collectors. He had also tried to grow a beard to mask the scar on his cheek but the army wouldn't have any part of that. The scar continued to gnaw away at Norton's character and you would frequently see him running his fingers down the rough joint of flesh on his cheek and muttering. On demobilisation Norton had a clean nose and a distinct aversion to anything Italian. Despite his lazy and surly attitude Sergeant Norton Ferris had also earned some respect from a Colonel Travis. Colonel Quimby Travis really didn't belong in the army but it was part of the family tradition, and there was a war on at the time. Everyone had to do their bit don't you know? Travis had been attached to the office responsible for administration of occupied Italy but spent his time in Rome working on restoring gardens and replanting trees. Norton Ferris, with capable hands and a talent for finding easy posts became Colonel Travis's handyman and developed some skills with plants, especially trees.

'So, what's it going to be in civvy life Ferris?'

'Dunno sir.'

'Going back to Liverpool and the furniture business?'

This question was founded on an illusion that Ferris had spun to Colonel Travis about having been in the furniture business, as opposed to the rag and bone trade. Well, thought Norton, with a name like Quimby you can spin any old yarn. It's like having a name of Pussy.

'Quite like working with horses sir.'

'And you work well with hand tools and plants,' said Colonel Travis, gently establishing a young poplar tree. 'You ever think of forest work? I know a few people in the Forestry Commission back home. Perhaps I could put in a word for you.'

'Dunno about that sir. Never really thought about it; could do the job of course,' he added quickly. 'Piece of cake really, working with horses for chopping 'em down and such, plus all the planting work.'

'Sounds like it would be just up your street. I'll talk to a few chaps. The Forestry Commission will want all the help it can get after the ravages and neglect of the war. Should be easy to get you qualified as a Forester.'

'As a Forester? Not bloody likely. I ain't going to be no boss. I'm a worker me.'

'No Ferris. A Forester works in the forest, often alongside the men. He's the man on the spot seeing it's all done right, kind of like a Sergeant, and you've become a Sergeant. Just think of it as transferring from the Army to the Forestry Commission. You'll be dealing with trees instead of lorries, uniforms and such.'

'Well, as long as I ain't sitting in any bloody office. Would drive me nuts that, I need to be out of doors.'

'There's lots of out of doors in forestry man. That's where the trees are.'

True to his word Colonel Quimby Travis talked to the right people and Norton Ferris managed to become a Forester through the school at Gwydyr in North Wales. His capabilities with horses, hand tools and plants helped him practically and he managed to cheat through the written tests to qualify in 1948. As Colonel Travis had suggested the forests of the Forestry Commission had suffered through the war. Forester Ferris found employment in the Forest of Dean where he met and married Blodwyn Rees in 1958. Once established Norton found he could slide back into his old ways of laziness and finding a cushy billet. During the 1950s and 1960s he added drunkenness, brutality and fathered two sons. Idwal Ferris was born in 1960 and John (named after a Beatle) born in 1963. Without any real guidance the two boys grew up to be tearaways. Under rather suspicious circumstances Blodwyn died after a drunken accident in 1980 and the three men continued to live and work in the Chepstow area. Not long afterwards, in 1983 the Forestry Commission eventually decided to fire Norton Ferris for drunkenness and theft. Norton had become too fond of horses and bet too often at the Chepstow track, usually unsuccessfully.

In 1984 the estate of Fotheringham Manor was a thriving business. On the farm, they had developed an international reputation for breeding sheep. In the forest, the neglect of the forties had all been cleared away and the forest supported the farm with fencing, gates, wagon boards, cottage building materials, plus commercial sales of poles and construction lumber. Just after his marriage to Sylvia, Anthony Lord had hired Ronald O'Rourke as a professional forester. O'Rourke had been born in 1939 in Killarney and after school in Eire he had gone to the University of Oxford to study Forestry from 1958 to 1962. From there O'Rourke had been very lucky to land a job at Dartington Hall in Devon from 1962 to 1966. There, the young O'Rourke had learned a great deal about forestry as a business from the renowned W.E.Hiley. This background of running a forest estate as a business had really appealed to Anthony Lord. He hired O'Rourke as the professional forester for Fotheringham Manor Estates in 1966, the year after Geoffrey was born, when work, family, and estate proved too much for Anthony and Sylvia. The professional Irishman O'Rourke worked well with the traditional and rural Englishman Edward Templeton. O'Rourke also recognised the skills of the two Italians. With good leadership and hard-working staff O'Rourke developed the Forest Estate on a very sound commercial basis.

It seemed ironic that Norton Ferris, who hated authority, the Italians, the Irish (having been brought up in Liverpool), and the upper crust of society should be helped by the old boys' network. Colonel Travis, by now in his dotage, had heard of the plight of Norton Ferris. He had heard of Norton's loss of his wife and the struggles of bringing up two boys. In his youth Quimby Travis had been madly in love with Rosamund DeWinter and had never really forgotten her. After Desmond's death in 1968 Quimby Travis had been round to Fotheringham Manor on several occasions to take tea with Rosamund. Somehow, in a rather muddled set of incidents and based upon a glowing account from Colonel Travis, Norton Ferris ended up at Fotheringham Manor as a forester in 1984.

Norton couldn't believe his luck at first. He had been given a new job at age 61, complete with a cottage, and work for Idwal and John too. After the initial shock however, Norton found he hadn't been quite as lucky as he thought. Ronald O'Rourke was a firm taskmaster.

'Ferris, you've got those seedlings ordered from the nursery?'

'Sure Mr. O'Rourke. I ordered the forty thousand white pines and another thirty five thousand ash trees.'

'What about the hemlocks?'

'Which hemlocks?'

'The ones for underplanting the oaks in compartment seventeen. We discussed this last week at the management meeting. We need to thin out the oaks and establish the hemlocks as an understorey. This was all agreed upon on Thursday morning.'

'But I wasn't there on Thursday,' whined Ferris. 'I was sick.'

'I know that, although I'm not so sure you were really sick. Charlie Francis saw you that afternoon coming out of Dicksons, the bookies. Anyway, the decision was all recorded and you got a copy of the management meeting on Friday. You were in Friday I take it?'

'Yes, of course. I felt better.'

'And the hemlocks?'

'I'll get onto the nursery straightaway.'

'Too right you will, and don't be fobbed off with any eastern hemlock like last time. We need western hemlock here. The wood of the eastern hemlock is really poor. Get it right for once can you? Oh yes, while you're here, I heard that Idwal was giving Enrico a hard time the other day. Said he wasn't pruning the branches tight enough on the pines. First of all, Enrico's been doing that job since before Idwal was even a lustful gleam in your eye, and second, it's not Idwal's job to boss anyone about. If anyone tells Enrico what to do it is you, not your son. Hear me Ferris?'

'Yes sir, I hear you, but Enrico's a lazy Italian, like all bloody Italians. You don't know them like I know them do you? Safely tucked up in neutral Eire you was during the bloody war. I was over there in Italy fighting for king and country. I know how lazy those bloody wops are. Jesus, we tidied them up in their own country too.'

'Wasn't how I heard it Ferris. I hear the beard's to cover up a nasty knife scar you got from some kids in Naples. Seems they got the better of you there. Western hemlock man, order them! Now, get going.'

Ronald O'Rourke turned to some papers on his desk inferring that the discussion was over. Ferris turned red, clenched his fists but thought better of it and strode out of O'Rourke's office.

'Bloody bog Irish. Bloody kid too. What the fuck does he know about the war and the fighting Italians? And who the hell told him about Naples? Ah shit, how can I work a deal in the nursery for those hemlocks? Angela in the nursery and I have a good deal going with the pines what with seconds coming here and us paying for top quality. Can blame the poor survival on the planting crews and nobody will know they were rejects. Hello Larry, what can I do for you?'

'Well Norton me old mate, how about twenty big ones?'

'Strewth, you don't want much do you?'

'Norton, Mr. Dicksons is looking for some kind of settlement; some show of good faith in paying your account so to speak.'

'Well, I ain't got it. Tell him I'll pay next week.'

'Next week? Norton with you everything is next week. Manana. You should have been Spanish not a Scouse.'

'Watch it. You watch who you're slanging off. I ain't no wop.'

'Four hundred quid mate is what Mr. Dicksons is looking for, just to be even again. Clean the slate so to speak.'

'I'll clean your bloody slate. Don't let me catch you when I've got Idwal and John with me.'

Larry laughed. 'Sounds just like you Norton. Can't fight your own fights any more can you. Couldn't even fight them when you were young I hear.' Larry stroked his cheek and laughed again. 'Never seen you clean shaven Norton, wonder why?'

'None of your bloody business. Now clear out. I've work to do. You'll get your precious money. Just piss off.'

'Make sure we do Norton, make sure or else Mr. Dicksons might think about scarring the other cheek!'

Larry Thomas left a rather shaken Norton Ferris. There were too many balls in the air and some of them were in danger of falling to the ground. Norton had spent most of his life juggling balls in the air. He was always in one scrape or another, mostly through scams that never quite came off. And they never quite came off because Norton was too lazy to think it through and carry it out properly. Wherever he could he cut corners, or sometimes missed parts out completely. Through his youth, the army, through Forestry School, through marriage and now at Fotheringham Manor Norton continued to "just make do". With the job at Fotheringham Manor Norton had muddled along under the direction of Ronald O'Rourke. It had been an on again/off again battle with Norton hanging onto his job by the skin of his teeth for some weeks until a fateful day in October 1987. On that day forestry in southern England was treated to a rare display of nature's wrath when a storm roared through and broke and uprooted trees across the country. Old veterans, mature plantations, and young pole crops all felt the impact of a violent windstorm. The damage to the forests was extensive. However, for Fotheringham Manor there was an additional item of damage. A large oak tree fell on Ronald O'Rourke's Land Rover, obliterating both the Land Rover and the life of O'Rourke.

As of 1987 Norton Ferris became the Head Forester at Fotheringham Manor as Sir Anthony decided not to replace O'Rourke for a while.

Ferris's past experience with felling proved invaluable and the entire work force was engaged in clearing the wreckage from the storm. Broken and uprooted trees were bucked and hauled to the mill. Leaning trees were carefully felled to minimise future damage. Norton Ferris was in his element as he was now able to be his own boss. Anthony Lord's computer business was expanding and so he had no time for the estate. Norton found Geoffrey Lord too serious and wrapped up in his father's business and family, even though officially Geoffrey was Norton's boss as the overall Estate Manager. However, Norton found he could bypass Geoffrey Lord and find favour with Michael Lord. Norton still had a good hand with horses and he took special care of Michael's. He also introduced Michael to some other acquaintances in the horse-betting world.

By 1990 the world of Norton Ferris had settled down into a life of looking busy and doing as little as possible. As Antonio had suggested Norton Ferris didn't make any effort to go out and check on the pruning that the Italians did early in the year. However, come planting time in the Spring Norton didn't have much choice. He had to appear involved.

A little later in the year, as Spring came to the estate, Michael had another reminder that Antonio and Enrico were getting old and he watched Ferris trying to make them feel it. Planting time in forestry is mostly labour intensive, although on the flatter terrain it is possible to use planting machines. Using a machine wasn't possible at the particular site where the crew was working. At Fotheringham Manor Norton Ferris managed to organise both farm and forest estate labour for tree planting this year. The farm labour had finished with lambing and there wasn't a lot of activity for a month. Ferris decided to enlist the farm hands for the forest work and try and record their labour costs to the farm, keeping his forest costs low.

'Keep them rows straight you young tosser,' Ferris shouted at young Freddie. 'Keep your place in the team and don't go charging ahead. You're planting is a joke. Look, I can pull these plants out with two fingers. It's a bloody good job you aren't working on piecework lad. You'd be broke before you started.'

Young Freddie muttered beneath his breath but kept on planting carefully, firming in the roots with the heel of his boot.

'Heh, Antonio, get the spacing right you stupid old Eytie. They're supposed to be eight feet apart in the rows.'

'Si signore, two and a half metres.'

'Don't you give me any of that European backchat old man. This is bloody England and we deal in feet here. Eight bleeding feet between the trees. Comprende? Enrico, you're lagging behind again. We don't do siestas here you know. Keep up the pace.'

The rest of the planting crew heard the exchanges but kept their heads down. Mr. Ferris had given the easy jobs to his two sons. Idwal and John were bringing out the transplants from the nursery and heeling them in at the end of the compartment. Occasionally they might water them but for much of the time they were lying down in the shade and smoking. This new plantation was on rolling ground with a couple of sharp outcrops on one of the ridges. Norton had arranged the line of planters so that Antonio and Enrico had to clamber around these outcrops trying to find suitable sites on the line for their trees.

'Up and over old man,' cried Ferris to Antonio. 'Keep the rows straight you old bugger. You too Enrico, see there's sites for new trees on some of those shelves on the outcrop.'

Michael sat on his horse in the shade of the adjacent forest and watched the planting crew in the bright sunshine. Even for springtime it was warm in the afternoon. Norton wanted to finish planting all of his pulled trees today even though the conditions were getting stressful for the new transplants. He drove the crew despite the heat.

'I'll keep 'em going Mr. Michael,' he said. 'How's the new shoes on your horse?' Michael looked down at the old forester.

'See you're keeping your whistle wet Ferris,' he said, watching Mr. Ferris trying to hide the bottle.

'Well, it's a thirsty job in this sun. Got to keep talking to this shower or they'll slow down. Dries your throat out you know.'

'But you're not out in the sun now are you Ferris? Neither I see are Idwal and John. The work too much for them is it?'

Rather too late Idwal and John realised who was talking to their father in the shade of the trees. They scrambled to their feet and tried to look busy checking on the heeled in bundles of trees and fussing with the water supply.

'I've just come in like. Had to scramble over those outcrops to make sure Antonio and Enrico were doing things right. Give those two old buggers a chance and they will plant a dozen trees down a rabbit hole.'

'What rabbit holes? I thought this plantation had been trapped out?'

'Well, yes Mr. Michael, of course. Of course we trapped it out but there are still some holes about, especially up in those outcrops.'

'Fill them up Ferris. I don't want my horse breaking his legs in any bloody rabbit hole. Get it cleared up now.'

'Yes sir, right away. Heh Enrico, make sure you fill in any rabbit holes you find up there. That's what you're supposed to do on any planting job of mine. Keep the site nice and tidy.'

Enrico stumbled a little on the edge of the outcrop and sat down hurriedly to stop falling down the steep rocky slope. His brother scrambled down to him to see everything was fine and help him up.

'Oy, get the Eyetalian team back on the pitch. The game's not over yet until I blow the bloody whistle. You're lagging behind the rest of the team.'

Michael pressed his thighs on the flanks of his horse and slowly walked away through the shade of the trees. He might think of better uses for the Italian's cottage than letting Idwal and John Ferris have it. They could both stay in with their drunken, lazy father. That cottage might be quite useful for other purposes. He would think of something later that summer.

By now summer had come and still Michael was thinking. However, after the recent series of events Michael had a lot on his mind.

'Looks like a new pin Mr. Michael,' said Norton Ferris flicking the polish rag over the bonnet of Michael's rebuilt sports car.

'Should bloody well hope so Ferris; you spent long enough on it.'

'Well Mr. Michael, it was in a bit of a mess you know; coming in through the new plantations with the firebreaks such a dusty track this time of year.'

'I was out looking at the state of those plantations. Something I thought you were supposed to be responsible for. I saw Antonio and Enrico out there cleaning away some of the competing vegetation, some of the gorse bushes. They were growing up and smothering the young pines.'

'Yes, well, those two aren't the fastest and smartest workers now are they? Still, what do you expect from Eyetalians?'

'That's as maybe, but they were out there and where were you? I thought Mr. Jeffers, the local forest officer had expressly said that those plantations needed brashing when he was out here last week.'

'Bloody professionals,' said Ferris. 'What the hell do they know either? They should stay put in their bloody offices and write up useful management plans and let us workers get on with the job.'

'Well, get on with it will you. I can change my mind about persuading father to keep you on.'

Michael jumped into his now very clean car and sped off in a shower of gravel. Norton Ferris watched him go. He needed to keep on the right side of Michael if he was going to keep his job and he needed the job because it came with a cottage and low rent. Ferris wasn't the smartest of foresters but he was broke, actually in serious debt, and needed the job to keep a roof over his head. With the job and an impression of security he might keep the bastard debt collectors at bay.

As he walked away to his office he smiled. He hadn't done a thing to Michael's car but had had young Freddie the gardener work on it all of the morning. Ferris beat the shit out of young Freddie on a regular basis just to keep him in line. Now, thought Ferris, what the fuck were Enrico and Antonio doing up in the young pine plantations. He thought he had told them to look for some good larch thinnings for fencing material. Oh well, perhaps he hadn't. He couldn't really remember and it was definitely time for a drink. He would have to think about Antonio and Enrico, bloody Italians.

It was Daniel who had told the two Italians about the young pine plantation. Daniel had been out with Michael looking at different parts of the estate. Michael wasn't inspecting the estate but was trying out his rebuilt car. Having sideswiped it under a lorry and lost his licence Michael was anxious to drive it again. He could do this with abandon on the Estate. Daniel had gone out with Michael because Michael promised to teach him to drive in something with speed. After twenty minutes of Daniel's dawdling down the rides between the plantations Michael took over in disgust. He was showing Daniel just what the car could do around the soft dirt rides of the forest. It was when they were fishtailing in soft sand that Daniel happened to notice the abundance of the gorse bushes. He mentioned this to Antonio and Enrico.

'These young pines that Daniel mentioned got overlooked Enrico; seems nobody came out to this end of the estate for a while.'

'True Antonio. We've not been out here since we planted them two years ago and the gorse has run riot.'

'I thought Mr. Ferris patrolled all of the estate on a regular basis. Didn't Sir Anthony tell him that was part of his responsibilities?'

'Yes brother, but what Sir Anthony says and what Mr. Ferris does are often two different things.'

'It looks like we have some work for a couple of days here.'

'Your right, but it does my heart good to see how well these trees have grown. The soil is truly good here.'

'Yes, everything will grow well here, including the weeds unfortunately. Come, let's get on with the job and leave this plantation well established. After this brashing the trees should be well on their way.'

The two brothers worked slowly but surely along the rows of planted trees. Patiently they cut away all of the competing woody vegetation being careful not to cut too close to the planted pines. The brush was just piled between the rows where it would slowly break down naturally and leave its nutrients in the site. Already several of the planted pines had their leaders clear of the competing vegetation.

In July Sylvia had managed to persuade Christina to come home with little Peter. As Enrico had suggested this helped bring Daniel out of his depression. Christina had sorted through Geoffrey's clothes and other things, which had helped her come to terms with her loss. Daniel had helped Christina with this work and had turned it into a game for Peter. This August morning Daniel and Peter were exploring the attic on Home Farm where Christina and Geoffrey had lived. It was dusty and the single electric light bulb didn't give much light over the piles of boxes and furniture up there. As is usual with little boys, especially at this young age, everything is an adventure and boxes can be a treasure trove.

'Careful young fella, you'll have that lot on your head if you're not careful.'

Peter didn't heed his Uncle Daniel's warning and there was a cascade of boxes tumbling down onto Peter. The thump was followed by a loud howl.

'Daniel, Daniel, cose successo? What 'as 'appened?' called Christina from downstairs.

Daniel upended the boxes and found Peter giggling under a pile of papers. The howl had been in surprise but the resultant spill hadn't done any damage.

'It's nothing Christina. Peter's discovered an easy way to open boxes and now he's reading maps.'

Christina's head appeared over the sill of the attic floor.

'He's okay then? I thought I heard him howl.'

'Sure sure, he's fine. I think it just startled him when that pile of boxes fell on him. Well, what have you found Peter? What's so interesting in those dusty papers? You've found a picture?'

Peter was holding a piece of paper in both hands and looking at it seriously. With a solemn look on his face he turned the paper round in his hands to look at it upside down.

'Well little man, which way up is the picture? Oh, it's not a picture, it's a map. Where did that come from? Let's have a look shall we?'

Daniel sat down beside Peter and looked over his shoulder.

'Christina, come and look at what Peter's found; looks like a map or something with some old writing on it. Perhaps we should take it down into the light where we can see it more clearly.'

As Daniel started to take the paper out of Peter's fingers there was another howl, but this one was in protest. Peter hung on tightly to his treasure.

'Okay, okay, we'll take you and the paper into the light. We'll take these other papers that fell out of that box along with it. There may be some other hidden delights. Here Christina, take Peter and his precious map down into the kitchen. It's dusty up here and we could all do with a drink. Then perhaps we can look at what young Peter has found.'

Christina picked up Peter and slowly went back down the ladder into the house. Daniel packed the various papers back into the box and he too descended out of the attic. They all dusted themselves down and sat around the kitchen table.

'How about a nice cool drink Peter?' asked Daniel. 'It's pretty dry and dusty up in that attic. I think we'd all like a nice cool drink Christina.'

Once Peter had two hands around his cup Daniel felt he could remove the map and have a closer look. It was an old and faded piece of paper and as Daniel had surmised it was a very crude map.

'It really doesn't tell me a lot,' said Daniel. 'There's a long wriggly line and it has a big indent and inside the indent are a couple of something like circles. By one of the circles there is a square, but smaller than the circles. By the side of the wriggly line there is another sort of picture. It has two irregular lines and a semicircle drawn on the bottom one. Well, it sort of looks like a semicircle. Beside that is what looks like a tree with a big fork low down but it's very sketchy and smudged. Here Christina, you take a look.'

As Daniel handed the paper to Christina Peter dropped his drink, let out another loud yell, and reached out his stubby hands.

'Me, me, me,' he yelled.

'Caspita,' said Christina, 'the lungs on this one. Alright cara, you can have the paper but gently eh?'

Peter took the map and looked at it intently as if trying to understand it. After a minute he resolutely turned it over in his hands and peered at the back.

'Well Peter?' asked Daniel, 'and what do you see on the back that's so fascinating?'

Christina had mopped up the spilt drink and nudged against the pile of papers that Daniel had brought down from the attic. As they fell over across the floor another map appeared.

'Daniel, we've found another one, only this one has many more lines on it.'

The three of them spent the next hour carefully sorting through the pile of papers that had been in the box. There were only the two maps but all of the papers were very old. Some appeared to be accounts and some were just writing. Although the penmanship on the accounts was excellent the writing for the text was very hard to read. A couple of the accounts were marked with dates indicating the papers were written around the 1790s. Some of the accounting papers looked like lists of supplies or goods and opposite each item there a price. Others of the accounting papers were lists of names and these too had a price against each name.

'Christina, I'll make a copy of the map that Peter has, complete with colours and give him the copy. That'll keep him quiet and happy while I try and decipher what these papers are about. Is that okay? I mean, the papers were found in your house and so they are really yours?'

'Off course Daniel; that's a good idea to make a copy for Peter. He will be happy I'm sure with the colours as well.'

Daniel made the copy and delighted Peter with the various colours. He left Peter on the kitchen floor with the map and the crayons. Peter started adding to the picture right away.

As Christina had nothing special to do that morning she spent an hour with Daniel going over the papers that they spread all over the kitchen table. Daniel found some more papers with dates and they tried to arrange some chronological sequence of the papers. It appeared that many of the earlier papers seemed to be lists with prices and a brief explanatory text. Trouble was it was hard to decipher the text. Towards the end of the pile Christina came on a paper labeled "Map". This sheet contained some words and some numbers.

'Perhaps it explains where something is?' suggested Christina. 'Perhaps the family hid something, like when the Protestants were hunting Catholics for bibles and crosses.'

'I'd have to check back with father to see whether he knows anything about the family history back then,' said Daniel. 'I'm not sure the Lord family was ever very religious. From what I've heard they would have had to go to confession a lot if they were.'

'Daniel, you're awful,' laughed Christina, 'you're family is quite religious. It just doesn't go to church a lot.'

'Anyway, let's bundle these papers up again and put them somewhere safe. I will ask father about family history but I won't tell him why. Let's keep these papers a secret for a while Christina. I don't want everyone learning about them.'

Norton Ferris walked back to his office and eased his lazy body into a well-upholstered swivel chair. He perched his boots up on the desk and sat back. Without too much effort he could reach the cupboard and its resident bottle. 'Just a little sip will go down well,' he mused out loud.

'Any more sips and you'll go down well Ferris, down the bloody road.'

Sir Anthony strode into the mean little office and thumped his fist loudly down on the desk top. Norton Ferris tried to put down the drink, stand up, and protest but this was two tasks too many and he succeeded in falling out of the chair, dropping the drink and almost choking on the whiskey in his throat.

'I was just in looking for the plans Sir Anthony. I had been talking with young Mr. Michael about the brashing being done up in the pine plantation. I was reminding Mr. Michael that I had put Mr. Jeffers' suggestions into effect straight away. Both Antonio and Enrico have been up there for quite a while as I instructed.'

'Well it didn't look like that to me Ferris. It looked like Michael was giving you a bollocking for getting young Freddie to clean his car.'

'Oh that. Well, no, Michael wanted his car cleaned and Freddie wasn't doing anything the lazy lad, and so I had him clean it while I was going over the Management Plan.'

'So, you do know where the Management Plan is do you?'

'Sir Anthony, of course I do. It's out with me all the time, well the Operating Plan is.'

'And the Management Plan is where might I ask?'

Norton Ferris walked over to the filing cabinet and pulled it open. He thumbed through as if looking diligently.

'Find it?' barked Sir Anthony.

'Can't seem to put my hand on it this very moment sir.'

'You surprise me. Actually I would be very surprised if you could even recognise it if you fell over it. Anyway, here it is. I've been reading it after getting a phone call from Mr. Jeffers. He was telling me about some new developments in transplants and wants us to try them next spring at planting season. He thought it might come under research in the Management Plan and so could be financially paid for through the government scheme.'

Sir Anthony handed the Forest Management Plan document back to Ferris. Any forest enterprise that is partly subsidized under the government scheme needs a professionally approved Forest Management Plan. It is this document that describes a planned series of operations over the next twenty years on the forest estate to fulfil certain specified objectives. It is a comprehensive document and contains a series of four five-year Operation Plans, which include more detail of year by year activities. The actual field operations laid out in an Annual Plan are the responsibility of the local forester who is technically trained, as opposed to being a professional. Norton Ferris was a forester, but he bitterly resented any professional or officer style supervision. Since Fotheringham Manor's professional forester had died, and not been replaced, Ferris was in charge, but he needed to operate under a plan prepared by a professional. Norton Ferris didn't want to operate under anyone's plan but his own.

After a week of quiet research, and several hours trying to decipher the old papers Peter had found in the attic Daniel sat down with Christina and quietly told her what he had discovered.

'Back nearly two hundred years ago the Lord family was quite involved in shipping out of Bristol. We didn't own any ships but we put up the money for cargoes.'

'That might explain the lists Daniel,' said Christina.

'Yes, that's what I think. I think they are ship's manifests, or at least that part of the cargo that was ours. The notes with each list seem to explain the voyage, or the destinations.'

'Did you decipher what were the cargoes Daniel?'

'Some of them were ivory and some precious stones I think, but it's hard to read some of the texts,' said Daniel.

'And the lists of names?' asked Christina, 'what were they?'

'Those I'm sure are slaves. The destination in many cases was Kingston and father told me that we had plantations in Jamaica many years ago.'

'What about the map, or the maps?'

'That's where it becomes ever more confusing. I showed Dad the bigger of the two maps, the second one you found. He thought it looked a little like a picture he had seen in a book that his grandfather had. Trouble was he couldn't remember which book or where it was. The library is full of books as you know. Dad was interested though because he could remember his granddad saying that our old gamekeeper had been very interested. That would be old Albert Templeton if I remember correctly.'

'Why did it interest your gamekeeper Daniel?'

'Well, old Alfred seemed to think he could recognize what the map was about.'

'And, what was the map about?' asked Christina, who had become quite interested now.

'Alfred thought it was part of our Estate. He thought it showed an area lying up in the north where our land extends up into the cliffs and hillside of the Mendips.'

'So, we have to go through all the books in the library to find out whether Albert was right?' asked Christina. 'That could take forever Daniel with all those books.'

'No,' said Daniel slowly, thinking as he said it, 'there may be another way.'

'And, that is?'

'Well, Albert would have told his son Edward.'

'Yes, but Edward's dead too Daniel, so how does that help?'

'Let's think of the timing and who was where. Great-grandfather George didn't die until 1946. By that time Albert had just retired, but was still alive. Edward Templeton had taken over running the forestry operations. Great-grandmother Virginia was still very active 'cos she didn't die until 1966. Antonio and Enrico came here in 1943.'

'All very interesting Daniel, but so what? What has that to do with the map?'

'Albert would have told Edward and Edward would have told Antonio and Enrico. They all worked on the Estate and knew the land intimately. So, Antonio and Enrico probably know what the map describes, and, more importantly Christina, Enrico was talking only the other day about hidden treasure.'

'So, we just ask Enrico?'

'No, not quite like that. Just let me talk with Enrico a little and see whether I can find out some more about the "rumour of the Lord family treasure".'

Christina laughed. 'It sounds quite spooky when you say it like that Daniel.'

Two days later Daniel had the chance to talk with Antonio and Enrico. The two Italians were having their lunch and Daniel asked about the "Lord treasure". After some guarded conversation and questions from Daniel Enrico took him to the northern end of the Estate along a line of cliffs. Enrico stopped outside a narrow slit entrance to a cave. Suddenly Daniel became very excited. 'That could be it,' he exclaimed.

'What could?' asked Enrico.

'Look, look,' cried Daniel and he showed Enrico the second smaller map. 'See, perhaps these two wriggling lines indicate the cliff, sort of top and bottom. Then the semicircle thing could be this cave entrance. The single wriggly line perhaps is a top view and the indent could be this cave. Look, there's a very old tree there, right by the side of the cave. And, here there is a tree on the paper too. It's even got a fork in it, or would have had if one side hadn't been split off. Let's look inside Enrico and see what we can find?'

'No Master Daniel sir. I've no time as I'm supposed to be at work. We've got no torches and I don't want to go into no caves. No thanks. Let's leave it until another time.'

Somewhat reluctantly Daniel did leave it and walked back with Enrico to where Antonio had been resting after lunch. He left the two old men to carry on working in the afternoon and slowly found his way back to Christina's house.

'Ah Daniel, good, you can help me please? Peter is not feeling too well and I must take him into the doctors. You come with me and keep him happy while I drive. You know I get nervous when I drive and with Peter in the car it is too much. You will come yes?'

'Sure Christina. Just let me wash my hands and I'll be right with you. O, by the way, I've found a cave with Enrico and it looks just like the map shows. He knew just where to look but he wouldn't go in.'

'What's that Daniel? Oh where did I put Peter's shoes? Daniel, look for them please. He must have shoes on going to the doctor's.'

'Slow down Christina. There is no rush. Here are Peter's shoes and I'll put them on while you get the car ready. You're all set. Now let's take this slowly.'

Christina jerkily drove out of Home Farm with Peter safely strapped into his car seat and Daniel happily sitting back in the front seat. He turned round and said to Peter, 'well, we found what your precious map showed us young'un. Leastways, we know where to look. Wonder what we'll find?'

As the car turned out of the Estate you could look back as the summer did come and slowly pass over this pastoral part of England. The rolling hills of Somerset here support some fine woodland. The soil is fertile, the rainfall plentiful, and the climate is warm to mild. Following some of the ideas of Virginia Lord the Foresters of the estate of the house of Lord had developed these woodlands from hunting domains into a diversified commercial forestry enterprise. As well as hardwoods of oak and ash there were some mature plantations of larch for estate fencing and lumber, plus a few acres of western white pine. The pines, from Western North America were growing at their northern limit in England, but they still grew fast, tall and stately. And so by this late summer Antonio and Enrico were back in the pine plantation they had pruned earlier in the year. The dominant trees in this plantation were now thirty metres tall. The two Italians were back to thin out some of the trees they had not pruned. In this way the pruned trees, the final crop trees, would have more space to grow and put on clear valuable wood. Antonio had looked through the plantation for 'wolf" trees to fell. These were big sprawling and branching trees of low quality, which were interfering with the better crop trees. Felling these was always difficult because the big crowns of these trees tended to become tangled with the standing trees.

The chainsaw whined in the still of the late August Friday afternoon. The large pine tree swayed as Antonio continued to cut through the trunk.

'Don't let it hang,' said Enrico. 'We will be here past quitting time.'

'Have faith little brother,' answered Antonio.

Inside the woodlot it was quite dark as the pine trees were spaced closely together. A thinning was definitely needed to let the remaining trees grow with less competition. The two brothers were now well into their sixties. Neither was quite as agile as they used to be.

The saw completed its cut above the backcut and the tree started to fall. Slowly, with a swish of its many branches the stem keeled over. Although the fall appeared to be slow Antonio was slower. He failed to see the large top of the wolf tree smash against a standing tree and snap off.

'Antonio,' screamed Enrico, 'look out!'

Unfortunately Antonio looked up just as the spear-like end of the smashed off top hurtled downwards. The four-inch wide end of the heavily branched top crushed the forehead of Antonio and he fell backwards under the foliage.

All of the passion of Latin people flooded into Enrico's 'no, no, no.' The scream echoed around the quiet woodlot. Desperately Enrico dragged the fallen top off his brother. Antonio didn't move. Feverishly Enrico lifted his brother's head. Blood dripped out of Antonio's mouth. Enrico thrust his fingers between the lips and pulled the tongue forwards so his brother would not choke on his own blood. Sobbing Enrico cradled his brother in his arms.

Antonio moaned. He lived. Enrico looked at his brother in amazement. He lives. Frantically Enrico considered what to do. Enrico gently rolled his brother onto his side and made sure the tongue could not slip backwards. Quickly he rolled a small log against Antonio's back so he couldn't fall backwards. He covered his brother with his jacket. Shock would soon set in and Antonio would shiver. Checking that his brother was as safe as possible Enrico set off for help. By this time on a Friday afternoon the rest of the forestry crew had long gone. Norton Ferris would be drunk past caring, and he wouldn't care even if he were sober. As it was harvesting time all of the farm labourers would be out on the fields. The only possible place for help was the Big House.

The woodlot was over a mile from the Manor house. Enrico flew. At the farm buildings behind the Manor house there was nobody. All of the farm vehicles were out working on the harvest. Enrico called out in desperation as he ran around the various outbuildings.

Michael walked round the corner of the barn dressed in evening clothes.

'Enrico, what's all the commotion? What are you screaming about?'

In his excitement Enrico had lapsed back in Italian.

'Come, come quickly,' shouted Enrico, and he grabbed at Michael's arm. 'My brother is dying.'

'Get your filthy bloody hands off me,' shouted Michael as he thrust Enrico away. 'You're covered in dirt and sawdust, and I'm going out.'

'No, no,' protested Enrico, and he grabbed Michael again. 'My brother was smashed by a tree. He needs a doctor, now. He needs help. He needs attention. We need to get the doctor in your car.'

Enrico frantically was trying to drag Michael back to where Michael's car was standing.

'Piss off you hopeless little bugger. I told you I'm going out, now.'

'But his head is smashed. There is blood. We must get a doctor,' screamed Enrico, now frantic with the situation. 'I go. Give me the keys. I go and get the doctor. You wait.'

'Like hell. Who do you think you are? Get out of my way and bother someone else. I've an important party to go to; a pretty lady to collect, and I'm late already.'

Michael thrust Enrico aside onto the ground.

'I've a good mind to put my boot to you but you'd dirty the polish.'

'Please, please,' implored Enrico rising slowly from the ground. 'He's bleeding, he's dying.'

'Too bloody bad. Ah, good pun that,' smiled Michael and he jumped into the car and drove off.

Enrico sank to the ground exhausted and shattered. Up in the wood the blood seeped away from Antonio.

'Enrico,' Antonio whispered, 'my brother.'

Michael sped his car along the Manor's long driveway.

Enrico wept.

Antonio died.

Michael whistled on the way to his party.

10

Suicide

Sylvia took Enrico to attend the coroner's inquest and so he was there in body but Sylvia was sure he was not there in spirit. The loss of his brother Antonio was just too much to comprehend. It would be a while before Enrico remembered the whole chain of events and a gentle stirring of vendetta came into his head.

Anthony was sufficiently upset by the accident that he deferred his decision to find a new forester, but he did ponder on the Company. His software business was well established. He continuously searched for new innovative people to ensure his development and products kept at the cutting edge of an ever-changing technology. Michael had an aptitude for mathematics and was familiar with some more specialised applications called Operations Research. Some of Michael's mathematical skills could form a basis for encoding routines and security products. Perhaps Anthony should steer Michael into this aspect of the business as a foundation for the time when he might be the owner. That might give Michael some credibility with a few of the staff, which was sometimes a useful asset dealing with software prima donnas. Anthony had employed Michael for two months now and had found he could apply himself.

Despite the diving accident Michael had managed to patch over any ill feelings with Ted. That particular project was near completion and Anthony thought he might try and move Michael into another area of expertise – perhaps with his friend Nathaniel.

ꟈ

Cohen and Townsend, Security for the Security-minded stated the business card. Anthony had arranged several contracts between his company and Cohen and Townsend. Whereas Anthony Lord's company dealt exclusively with software, software locks, software security, Cohen and Townsend embraced a wider perspective on security. They handled people security, building security as well as computer systems security.

Rosalind Townsend came from a family of locksmiths. Some of the family made locks and some of the family undid them, usually illegally. Rosalind's East End brothers, sisters, uncles and aunts carefully worked with the complete spectrum of locks. It had been a family "business" for a long time. Almost all of the business ran on tradition and memory. Very little was written down and the Townsends were taught never to forget.

For many generations the men and women in the Townsend family were all short and slender. Good eyes, steady hands and sensitive fingers also characterised the various family members. The one trait that did vary in the family was volatility. Despite being in a trade where patience and perseverance was a valuable asset some of the family members could become explosive.

Uncle Sid had run a quiet and lucrative business lifting illegal pedigree books of dogs. Because of the controls in the greyhound business this was a lucrative but specialized trade. It was not really possible with horses. Good dogs would go missing, especially dogs with good pedigrees. Their offspring would surface under different names and run well. People in the know of which dog had which real parent could make money.

Pedigree books could be sold, very carefully to the right people. First of all though, you had to acquire pedigree books from within safes, from within locked cupboards, from within locked houses. Uncle Sid was good with locks. It ran in the Townsend family.

In appearance Uncle Sid was a quiet, dapper little man. He wore a cheap but tidy suit. Depending on the locale he wore a bowler, a trilby, or even a flat cap. The other thing that Uncle Sid was good at was sussing out which people he could deal with. However, just to be on the safe side Uncle Sid had his own protection. Uncle Sid's protection was Dave Cohen. Traditionally the Cohen clan had been in the jewelry trade. They bought, they reworked, and they sold. It was a small business peopled by small people until Dave came along. Dave stood six feet six in stockinged feet and built like a backyard privy.

Although Dave Cohen was primarily Sid Townsend's bodyguard he also ran other aspects of the protection business. Dave commanded respect through his brain as well as his brawn. In the jewelry trade you occasionally needed some help in 'buying' goods, and often in protecting them afterwards. Starting in this business Dave gradually built up a payroll of drivers, trailers, and heavies. His team branched out into other trades needing security. Dave's group did well. They didn't make too many waves with the Bill, and so the firm earned respect.

The trouble all started when Dave's son Nathaniel became a teenager, almost a grown-up. Nathaniel was an intelligent kid. Growing up in the East End of London Nathaniel had looked about him and thought he could do better than the rest of the family. Primarily, Nathaniel seemed ashamed of his dad's job.

'Protection, my arse,' said Nathaniel. 'You're nothing but a private army looting the honest traders; a bunch of strong-arm villains protecting your own interests.'

'Paid for your schooling though Nat. Gave yer Mum a nice house. Kept you looking smart and talking proper. Covered you going on school trips to Majorca and France rather than Leigh-on-Sea or perhaps Southend. Come to think of it you've never been to Southend.'

'That's not the point Dad. Maybe I would have liked Southend.'

'In your dreams son. The pier's too long for you to walk out on and you never were the athletic type. Just stick to working with people Nat, you're good at that.'

Nathaniel looked up at the impressive frame of his father. Although he himself was six feet tall his father was a really big man. 'Look at yourself Dad. You could be in the genuinely helpful service business. You could have gone into security for money deliveries, for jewelry companies, for something straight for God's sake.'

'Now Nat, don't you go bringing God into this. We do good business in the jewelry trade looking after legitimate traders.'

'Right, and you do even better business in the jewelry trade working with thieves.'

'We gotta' live son. We all gotta' live. You gotta' look after the family.'

This conversation went on and on in the Cohen household. Liz Cohen listened to father and son and smiled. Fathers and sons throughout history, certainly Jewish history had argued over principles. What was right? The subject rankled Nathaniel and he thought deep inside himself. What did he really think? How honest could he really be and still make a way for himself in the world? He lived in a part of London where everyone seemed to have something going on.

Something going on smacked Nathaniel in the face. 'Don't you ever try that again,' she said. Rosalind Townsend stood fully upright in front of the bent over Nathaniel. Fully upright for Rosalind was five feet, and it was a furious five feet. Nathaniel had been looking for a brush in the cupboard under the stairs in his home. He hadn't bothered to turn on the light and knowing where it was he had reached in and groped for it. Rosalind was in the dark where he groped.

'What did you think you were doing?' she hollered as she swung her right hand. 'Whoa,' said Nathaniel as he unfolded his six foot body and stopped Rosalind's hand in full swing. 'I was looking for the brush and pan.'

'Bloody unlikely with your fingers on my leg and chasing upwards.'

'I was surprised.'

'Not as bloody surprised as you will be if you don't back off. My fist is just at the right height for your goolies.'

Nathaniel stepped backwards quickly and the wall behind thrust him forwards again all over Rosalind. To stop them falling Nathaniel clasped his arms around Rosalind. She in turn exploded with arms, knees, and loud noises out of her mouth. Nathaniel in turn yelled. Liz came out into the hallway to see what was going on. When she saw Nathaniel draped all over a volcanic Rosalind she collapsed with laughter.

'I know it's not funny but you should see the pair of you. You're all arms, legs, surging bodies and wide open mouths.'

In a moment the two antagonists disentangled and glared at each other.

'Nathaniel, meet Uncle Sid's niece Rosalind. Rosalind, this long-legged gangle is my son Nathaniel. Rosalind has come over to talk to your Dad. She is in her last year at University and was looking for some advice.'

'Some advice! From Dad!' Nathaniel was stopped in his tracks. His dad was in the protection racket and what would he know from anything, especially for a young lady.

'You thinking of going into the protection racket with a lady gang?' Nathaniel asked.

Rosalind gave Nathaniel a long cool appraising look. Despite his slapped face and bruised goolies he looked all right.

'I discovered you're not eligible to join,' she said. 'You don't have the right equipment.'

'Bollocks,' said Nathaniel.

'Exactly.'

Liz laughed. 'You two will get on well together. Combine Rosalind's expertise in electrical engineering and your knowledge of people Nathaniel and you have all the makings of a great team.'

Nathaniel's mother's assessment was good. Rosalind talked to David Cohen about his ideas on future developments in the security business. From her family background in locks Rosalind had developed some ideas for the future with regards to electronics, radio controls, and computerised controls. From her Uncle Sid Rosalind knew that Dave's business clients included all sorts of people who would be looking to update their security. When she graduated Rosalind started work with one of her families lock business but she was ambitious enough to want to be her own boss. Uncle Sid always quietly told her to look out for number one, herself.

Rosalind remembered her first meeting with Nathaniel Cohen, and the comments that Liz Cohen had made. With some coaching Rosalind reckoned Nathaniel might have the right equipment after all. Within a year of graduation Rosalind had married Nathaniel and together they created Cohen and Townsend. Initially there had been a battle over the name, but Rosalind quietly realised that if Nathaniel was going to be the front man it was probably better as Cohen and Townsend. Within ten years Cohen and Townsend was a good team, a very successful team.

Contrary to their family backgrounds the two youngsters had gone straight. They had built up a legitimate business in security. Rosalind had brought in a friend from College, Ms Tina Morland. Tina had graduated in finance, and this added to the firm's expertise in money storage, transfers, and fraud. Nathaniel sort-of inherited his father's team but changed the clientele a little. This appeased Nathaniel's conscience. He felt more comfortable within himself being honest.

Cohen and Townsend established themselves as a profitable and creditable company. Several of Anthony Lord's clients had availed themselves of the services of Cohen and Townsend to install and service Lord's products. Saad Brothers, a very large Middle Eastern company in the import/export business contracted both Lord and Cohen & Townsend when they opened their new London offices and warehouses. This successful contract with Saad Brothers led to a mutual respect between the two English companies.

Sylvia and Anthony Lord were in complete agreement. Learning started at the ground floor wherever you ended up in a company. This would be good experience for Michael and that was easier in the service business than in production. Over a couple of business meetings Anthony Lord made a deal with Cohen and Townsend to employ Michael and have him work on the installation end of security devices. Michael was already quite familiar with several of his father's software products and so he could be employed usefully right from the start. Rosalind and Nathaniel would try and expand the work environment to let Michael experience other aspects of security. Michael combined working for Cohen and Townsend with his return to the University in London. That way Anthony Lord thought Michael would have more than enough to do to keep him out of mischief.

London however had other ideas. Melanie Rogers had come back from California and she soon tracked Michael down. She also had another friend in tow, complete with long blond hair in a ponytail, a very compelling smile and amazing fingers on a guitar.

'Michael, meet Sasha, and where in the hell have you been all summer? For a fiancée you have been remarkable by your absence. Daddy has been asking about you and whether you are for real. You were supposed to come over to California but you vanished off the face of the map sometime in June. There was some accident in the family wasn't there?'

'Whoa, hold on Melanie love. Let me get a word in edgeways. Hi Sasha, welcome to London.'

'Michael, my pleasure. Melanie says you're cool man. How they hanging?'

Michael shook the proffered hand and noticed the intensive eyes under the long blond hair.

'You still haven't answered my question Michael. You never contacted me, or replied to all the messages I sent. Your Mother said you were recovering from shock. In fact she said the whole family was recovering from shock. What happened?'

'It's a long story Melanie. We'll get to it some other time. Is Sasha here to party or what?'

'Sasha used to work for my Dad Michael, but Daddy got into a huff over something and fired him. Something silly happened with money and friends of Sasha's back in Russia and Daddy got all patriotic and anti-Russian all of a sudden, so I told Sasha he could come over with me. That pissed Daddy off but I don't care.'

'Actually Michael, I play guitar more than any form of work, so I thought I could come over here and check out the Club scene. You know, find some group, try some jam sessions and just hang out for a while.'

'But before that Michael I have an invitation for you for the Saturday after next. Daddy's flying over for some large Charity bash and wants me to take you. Apparently anybody who is anybody in town will be there. Daddy thought it would be good for us to be seen together with all the right people. You know how potty he is over English aristocracy and mixing with the right set. So, get set for Saturday night with your best tie and tails.'

'Am I allowed to party before that?' asked Michael with a smirk on his face. 'Can't I take you and Sasha somewhere more lively than a stuffed-shirt Charity bash? Is Sasha's guitar for Spanish people or straightforward hard rock, or maybe Ukrainian folk music? Well Sasha, what do your fingers do with the strings?'

'A little of this and a little of that Michael; the fingers can get quite deft when needed.'

'Yes, I think I understand from Melanie's comment that your fingers got too deft.'

'Michael, that's uncalled for,' shrilled Melanie. 'Let's go to some club and have a drink.'

'Hadn't you better snort first Melanie?' asked Michael. 'You rarely go out partying without a little dust up your nose, and this is gray cloudy London you know. A little colour in your life will be good for you.'

'You are a pig at times Michael. You're so uncouth. I always thought you 'Lords' had class?'

'Melanie, you're right as always, I do have class, and I have some class stuff that will set you flying. Let's go and get stoned and enjoy life. Come on Sasha, let's see whether we can find you some guitar soulmates.'

The three of them took off to London's West End and succeeded in getting stoned and enjoy themselves. True to form Michael gently interrogated Sasha as to his background and interests. Sasha had worked for Stanley Rogers at Future Graphics as a systems analyst. Something called the "web" was coming into more common usage and Stanley Rogers needed his business to keep up with the new developments. Sasha had come from Berkley where the University, along with other Universities was using this "www" or world-wide-web. Through the web it was easy to talk with other experts, share experience, share computer code, and even control other facilities from a remote location.

At the University of London Michael had also developed some expertise with the web and had in fact helped his own father's Company became familiar with this new development. In Sir Anthony's case it was a valuable tool to be able to control and secure facilities from off-site. It also enabled him to maintain and trouble-shoot problems his clients might have with his products. At this time the web was still in its infancy, primarily being used by Universities and certain industries in Defence. Gradually, as more students who had used the web and found it useful graduated into the workplace there was an expansion of its user base.

As a trade off for some more detailed knowledge from Sasha on the web Michael took Sasha round to a series of clubs to meet and jam with other musicians. Although Michael might be viewed as a computer nerd, specializing in mathematics as he did, he was also a party animal and knew a lot of the wilder artistic crowd. Michael came away from these sessions around Sasha musing on opportunities.

The Charity Gala Banquet and Ball was a lavish and opulent affair. Large sums of money were raised for various charities, mostly to do with children in Third World countries. Over and above the "good works" was the fact that it was an annual event where one had to be seen. Stanley Rogers had flown in from California with his wife and both of them were determined to be seen. Several royalty were scheduled to come and Mrs. Rogers just couldn't wait to get her and her daughter photographed with a titled personage.

Contrary to Mrs. Roger's expectations Michael Lord arrived on time at the Roger's Hotel room and looked very much the part in tie and tails. Melanie inevitably fussed around but her mother stood back and looked at the couple.

'My, but you do look fine the pair of you. Stand still a moment Melanie for heaven's sake. Just stand by Michael and try to look a little like a lady. Stanley, come here: just look at them.'

Stanley Rogers dutifully appeared from the bedroom adjusting his bow tie. 'Yes my dear,' he said, 'and you're right; they do look a most charming couple.'

Stanley Rogers shook Michael's hand. 'Good to see you again Michael. Sorry to hear about your family's loss; quite tragic. Understand completely why you couldn't come out to California this summer. Father and mother okay are they?'

'No Stanley dear, of course they're not,' said Mrs. Rogers, 'losing a son like that, and young Daniel getting hurt in the process. Of course they are not okay. I know I wouldn't be okay as you so crassly put it.'

Michael quickly interjected before the conversation got any more convoluted. 'The family is fine thank you sir. Father's business is doing well and I am working with one of his partner's companies. My mother is spending a lot of time with young Daniel to make sure he recovers quickly. You're right, it was a tragic accident and everything was done that could be done but Geoffrey got a little too ambitious. Once I had treated young Daniel and made sure he was safe I took off for the Rescue Team and got them organized as fast as possible.'

'I'm sure you did Michael,' said Mrs. Rogers, 'but let's try and put that aside tonight and have an elegant evening in the spotlight. Stanley, have we got everything – money, tickets?'

Stanley went through the charade of "spectacles, testicles, wallet and watch" and beaming at his wife he said, 'yes dear.'

'Don't be disgusting Stanley, there will be royalty there tonight. This is not some Lodge Dinner, this is real people.'

Linking her arm through Michael's Melanie whisked him away towards the door. 'Come on Michael; let's go before my mother puts us all in place. I'll go and get a cab Dad.'

The real people, in real clothes, elegantly mingled their way through the foyer and into the lavish expanse of the dining room. Tickets had enabled waiters to politely usher the various attendees to specific tables. The settings were sumptuous and everything gleamed in the discreet lighting. When the waiter pulled the chair for Mrs. Rogers to be seated Michael was quick to offer the same services for Melanie.

'Thank you my Lord,' she said, as she elegantly sat down. She turned and smiled up at Michael.

Very soon the other four people who made up their set at the table were seated and introductions ran around the table. Mrs. Rogers was impressed that Michael stood when the two new ladies were brought to the table. Mr. and Mrs. Pengenny were part of the horse set from Buckfast in Devon, on the edge of Dartmoor. It didn't take Mrs. Rogers long to be deeply involved with both of them about quarter horses, bridles, saddles and the finer points of dressage. All of the Rogers family rode in California and Mrs. Rogers was anxious to assure these English country people that she and her daughter could fit right in.

Dr. Cameron MacDonald came with his wife and he wore a splendid dress tartan. With a spotless sporran and quite elegant legs Dr. MacDonald was a sight to behold. Standing well over six feet tall he had a full head of white hair and a wild beard. His wife was also in highland dress, sporting the same plaid tartan with a beautiful classic clan brooch pinned to her white flounced blouse. Mr. Rogers was almost at a loss for words as these two large Highlanders bore down onto the table. As Stanley Rogers and Michael rose to their feet a booming voice said, 'och away with you. Dinna fret about ous. Seet yo' down. It's champion to see you all.'

After his wife was seated, spreading comfortably over the somewhat frail and spindly chair, Dr. MacDonald announced,' this is the love of my life my Mary, and I'm just plain Cameron Macdonald. Guid day to you all.'

'Is he for real?' whispered Melanie to Michael. 'I've never seen such a distinctive couple.'

The Banquet went well, especially for Mrs. Rogers as two young princesses were announced at the top table. As she looked around the room there was a plentiful array of sparkling jewelry and even a couple of tiaras. 'Such an elegant gathering Melanie,' said Mrs. Rogers, 'how wonderful of your father to bring us to this banquet.' The Chairwoman of the Charity gave a short speech, primarily of welcome to some notable patrons, thanking them for their contributions and their attendance. Apparently this year the Charity had raised a record amount of money and this was really appreciated as the number of needy had also increased. Without more ado everyone was welcomed into the ballroom next door and asked to enjoy themselves.

Michael was dutifully gliding Mrs. Pengenny around the dance floor to a strict tempo quickstep when he was soundly bumped in his back. He nearly stumbled over his partner but quickly righted himself and whirled around crossly to see who had deliberately bumped him. In the arms of a rather pretty aristocratic young man was a very aggressive-looking Vanessa Worthing angling out her elbows.

'Pardon me Mrs. Pengenny but I didn't know they let riffraff like your partner into this bunfest. I don't think Mr. Lord qualifies as a charity-giver, more like a charity case to me. Don't be fooled by the name, he's no Lord.'

Michael was quite beside himself. He had been bottling everything up all evening. It really was a bit of a charade, so many pompous people playing at being nice. 'You don't fool me Ms. Worthing, I don't think you're worth anything, or your prissy little brother.' Michael turned and started to lead Mrs. Pengenny into a reverse turn in the dance when two hands clapped hard about each ear and a ringing thump pounded through his head. Letting go of Mrs. Pengenny Michael bent forwards in pain with his hands to his head. Suddenly he was on the floor in agony. Vanessa Worthing was not going to let anyone belittle her brother Aubrey. She balanced firmly on the left foot and brought the pointed toe of her right shoe full force into Michael's crotch. 'That's only part payment for what you did to Aubrey Michael Lord,' hissed Vanessa. 'Crawl away and lick your wounds; you've messed up my shoe.'

Without another word Vanessa whirled away with her partner as if there had been no break in the dance. Michael got to his knees with a white face and excruciating pain. A rather embarrassed Mrs. Pengenny half carried, half supported Michael back to their table by the dance floor.

'Michael, what happened?' asked Melanie. She looked inquiringly at Mrs. Pengenny.

'Michael had a little argument with a rather aggressive young woman, Vanessa Worthing I believe. Anyway, Ms. Worthing was quite brutal and I think Mr. Michael is in severe pain.'

'Severe pain,' muttered Michael, 'I'll throttle her. Wait until I can stand up.'

'Michael just sit still for a moment,' said Melanie. 'Let's not make a fuss.'

'Right on,' boomed an authoritative voice, 'let's not make a fuss. In fact let's just clear off with your tail, such as it is between your legs. I think Vanessa should have disabled you even more than that. Just be thankful I didn't see you first, but I'll get my licks in later. Just you wait Mr. precious Lord. Your day will come.'

'Who was that? Who is that dragon?'

'Lady Diana Worthing,' said Michael through clenched teeth. 'That family has never had any time for us. Think we're jumped up nobodies because our family only goes back two hundred years as opposed to eight hundred. They don't like it because we made our money the old-fashioned way, by working as opposed to sponging off the backs of their serfs.'

'Well, she certainly made an impression... Oh Michael, I'm sorry. That wasn't meant to be funny or spiteful.'

'Get me home Melanie. The pain is killing me.'

Melanie found her parents. Mrs. Rogers was twirling around the floor in the arms of the impressive Dr. MacDonald and Stanley was guiding the light-footed Mary. She quickly explained that Michael was hurt and had to rush home. They should stay and enjoy the rest of the evening. Back at the table Melanie made her apologies to Mr. and Mrs. Pengenny. Supporting Michael with her arm she guided him out of the ballroom and away to a taxi.

Lady Diana watched the retreat. She turned to her daughter. 'Well Vanessa that might remind young Mr. Lord not to mess with the Worthings for a while. You did well daughter, but Aubrey is not yet completely avenged.'

Another group on the edge of the dance floor had observed the exchanges. 'About time somebody took young Michael Lord down a peg or too,' said Alan Matheson. 'That lad's become too big for his britches.'

'Yes, it's too bad because Sir Anthony is a good chap.'

'Too true Dad,' said Charles Dampier, 'I've seen him climbing in Chamonix. He's a sound fellow.'

'That's right, you did mention it Charles,' said Lord Dampier.

'Yes, I was out there too,' said Alan. 'It was a shame that the eldest son Geoffrey got killed: he was a more level-headed young man.'

'Don't I remember Michael was involved in that accident with Geoffrey? That was climbing too wasn't it?' asked Lord Dampier.

'Yes,' muttered Alan, 'Michael seems to have a dangerous affect on people resulting in accidents.'

'My solicitations to you Alan; seem to recall you had a loss earlier this year.'

'Yes Dad, poor Veronica crashed after the party at our house. I feel partly to blame for that accident.'

'No Charles,' said Alan, 'you weren't to blame at all. Veronica always had highs and lows and unfortunately that evening she had both. She was so excited about going to your party but something happened and she got hurt. It was a treacherous night with slick roads and ended in a disaster. No, it certainly wasn't your fault at all Charles.'

The three men were silent for a moment watching the swirl of dancers when another man joined the trio. 'I suppose you saw that little fracas out on the floor?' asked Foster Faxon. 'That young Vanessa sure punts well; scored a very telling goal if I'm not mistaken.'

'She takes after her mother,' observed Lord Dampier. Diana always was a woman of action. Shoots well too does Lady Diana, but then it's not the season eh?'

'I hear you shoot Mr. Faxon?' asked Charles Dampier. 'Dad should invite you up to the shoots some time, when it is the season.'

'Yes Charles, I have done a lot of small-bore competition shooting but I've never been on a genuine Scottish grouse shoot. If I get the chance I'd love to come and try. Anyway folks, I'd best be off before my good lady takes offence. If I see Stanley Rogers I'll tell him what really happened out there on the floor before young Melanie and Michael adjust the story.'

At that moment Michael wasn't doing any adjusting. Every time he moved something hurt. Melanie managed to get a taxi and eased a tense Michael into the back seat. Curled up on the seat Michael was seething with anger and seething with pain. He didn't know which to concentrate on most. To be humiliated on a dance floor was one thing but to be humiliated by a woman was something else. God he had to fight back somehow. Someone needs to pay for this. It didn't seem to matter to Michael who paid but surely to God he would be avenged on someone.

A couple of days later a rather slow-moving Michael was back in the offices of Cohen and Townsend. He still could not hear clearly in one ear and walking was rather a delicate matter.

'Michael, good to see you. How are you this morning, and why are you walking funny?'

Tina Morland was peering around the edge of her work cubicle as Michael limped into the office corridor.

'Eh?' asked Michael, 'what did you say Tina? I've got a cold and my hearing's not too clear today.'

'I said good morning Michael, and I asked how you were. I also said I was glad to see you.' Tina smiled and spun her chair around. She stood up and moved closer to Michael. 'I mean it is really good to see you. I've missed you. You're always such fun to be around, especially with what you usually have in your pockets.' Tina moved in closer to Michael and attempted to reach into his pockets.

'Not today Tina love,' Michael said, 'things are a little painful at the moment. I think I have an old rugby groin injury come back to haunt me.'

'Perhaps an old hooker caught you,' joked Tina. 'Anyway, if you can't play I'd better get back to work. I'm running behind as it is.'

'Anything special?' asked Michael, 'anything I can help with?' Michael eased himself gently into Tina's cubicle and sat down carefully on the edge of the desk.

'Heh, let me try that', said Michael, peering over Tina's shoulder.

'No Michael, that's not for you to play with. This is rather serious.'

'But guarding other people's money is cool. You could get very inventive here. Actually, talking of inventive, I have some very special product that really widens the mindset. I do have something in my pockets for you.'

Tina leant back in her chair and smiled. At thirty-four, single, and decidedly pear-shaped Tina was looking for some widening of the mindset rather than the hip set. Michael was a good source of places and potions to help her enjoy herself.

'What are you really doing?' asked Michael. 'That looks like transfers rather than locking and guarding.'

'Well, that's what it is. This is a special request from Saad Brothers to move some of their funds from A to B and lock up both A and B afterwards, plus fuzzy up the trail from A to B.'

'That sounds simple enough.'

'Yes and no. The movement and the locking is simple. The fuzzying up of the trail and still leaving it look legitimate is rather more complicated. Some of your dad's software is quite clever in masking and misleading. You should understand some of that because it is partially mathematics derived. It has a lot to do with Markhov chains, dynamic programming and probabilities.'

Michael pondered the opportunities. He thought back over the conversations he had had with Sasha and wondered what it was that Sasha had been doing? Why was he fired from Future Graphics? Exactly what was it Melanie had said? Using the web you could access these accounts from anywhere and do what Tina was doing. Maybe a little discussion with Sasha was in order thought Michael. Wonder what I can trade our friend Tina here with for her password?

'Michael, Stanley Rogers fired me because I hacked into Department of Defence files and got caught. We were testing things on the web and I wondered how far you could go. The Department was on the web and I went looking in their Personnel files. It was nothing too criminal. It certainly wasn't anything like spying.'

'You hacked into U.S. Department of Defence files?' Are you crazy? You with a Russian name.'

'They didn't know my name Michael. Someone in the Defence office discovered what I had done and traced it back to Future Graphics. They called Stanley Rogers and he knew that the only person who could have done that was me. He wasn't going to upset the Department of Defence and so he fired me.'

'But what did you do?'

'Nothing much. I got into their system and read some files at first. I could identify their personnel and if necessary I could have altered some of the records.'

'And you could do all this without leaving a trail?'

'I thought so, but obviously they had some people on board who were smarter than I realized. Without me knowing they had found what I had done and traced the link back to Future Graphics. However, what I did learn was how to be more circumspect and hide my trail better. I was working on refining this when Melanie's dad fired me.'

Michael sat and thought on this awhile, although sitting was still a careful and sometimes painful activity. Vanessa hadn't damaged his eardrums but she had sure damaged his ego and Michael was still hell bent on revenge. However, before he attacked the Worthings it might be prudent to have a test run on a less suspecting target.

Watching what Tina Morland had been doing gave Michael an idea for a test target. Saad Brothers moved large amounts of money on a daily basis. Maybe, thought Michael we can use Sasha's talents to try out a version of the shell game – now you see it and now you don't. With the software that Tina was using, with its ability to fuzzy up trails of money movement, and Sasha's ability to do this discreetly and remotely it may be possible for some of Saad's money to be used elsewhere. Sasha had also mentioned that he had some connections with a Chinese dealer in San Francisco and the information about a numbered account based in Hong Kong. Okay thought Michael, let's not get too complicated with this. We transfer the money enough times with an ever-increasing fuzzy trail until it disappears and we use those monies to buy from the numbered account. Bingo, I get some drugs at Saad's expense. Simple.

'Michael, let me understand this,' said Sasha. 'You want me to hack into these accounts and then you have some software to move the monies around in ever-decreasing circles until it appears to have disappeared.'

'Right-on.'

'But the money doesn't really disappear it quietly finds its way to this account in Hong Kong as payment for some merchandise.'

'Right again.'

'And I've convinced you that the supplier will not renege on the deal when he gets the money because trust, or face in the case of the Chinese is all important in business.'

'Absolutely right Sasha. This is simple business. If you are in business long term you do everything by the book. You are honest with all your clients. That way you build up a successful trading house. It's the way all serious business works. Ask my Dad.'

'In this case I think we'll skip that step and take it as read. This isn't that honest a business.'

'So,' said Michael, 'we can do this eh? Do you need Tina's password?'

'That'll help Michael so we can start the transactions looking legit. However, the access won't come from your offices and that should remove any come back on you if we do this through the web.'

'Just one final thought Sasha, just so this doesn't completely backfire, you can reverse all the transactions back to square one if somehow the shit hits the fan? I might be really pissed off with the Worthings and hope this works so that I can really screw them but I have no real beef with Saad Brothers. It's just that they won't miss five million pounds and it isn't really their money anyway. Their insurance will cover any loss for them so that's not an issue.

However, I don't need my Dad hearing Saad mouthing off about poor software. Know what I mean?'

'Keep cool Michael. I can unravel this very quietly. I learnt that after the run in in California.'

One week later, on a Thursday afternoon the roof fell in. The London Office Manager of Saad Brothers telephoned Nathaniel Cohen and demanded five million pounds from Cohen and Townsend, plus complete severance from their services and full re-imbursements for the payments they had made on the security systems. Monies had been used to pay for drugs from Hong Kong; Saad Brothers monies.

Nathaniel was at home when he got the call.

'Mr. Cohen, we are very surprised and very disappointed with this state of affairs. We had been given to believe that you were an exceptionally trustworthy company. Sir Anthony Lord recommended you for the installation and maintenance of our security systems. However, our own security people have discovered a disturbing fraud. Although the amount of money is insignificant we are particularly upset over its apparent use. One of our staff has some knowledge with the Far East and he had heard of this particular numbered account. On checking with our Branch Office in Hong Kong our suspicions were confirmed. The monies were used to buy drugs Mr. Cohen and that we will not tolerate. You will hear from us later.'

The telephone line clicked as Saad Brothers severed the connection. Fortunately Nathaniel was sitting down. With a very shaky hand Nathaniel very gently lowered the telephone receiver onto its cradle. He sat back in the chair and closed his eyes, trying to blot out the message and its implications. All his life he had worked legitimately. He had fought with his dad over his dad's business. He had built Cohen and Townsend up into a strong and trusted company. How had this happened?

The telephone bell startled Nathaniel out of his misery and self-pity. Automatically he picked up the receiver.

'Nathaniel, it's me. Sorry to bother you love but I've got to go over to Mum's tonight. Dad's not too well and I've promised to pop over and see what I can do. You know what Mum's like, she's all of a fluster. Are you there Nathaniel? Can you hear me? Say something.'

'Yes,,,,,,,yes, Roz I'm here, just a little shocked that's all.'

'Well, it's not for you to worry about Nathaniel. I'll look after it. It's probably nothing. My Dad does make out so. Still, I'll probably have to spend the night. I'll be back tomorrow. There's food in the fridge. Take care. Bye love.'

Rosalind rang off and it took a while for Nathaniel to realize what had happened. Once again Nathaniel slowly and quietly replaced the telephone. He moved in slow motion. Purposefully Nathaniel moved through the house arranging things. When all was set he moved into the garage.

Friday morning Rosalind Townsend was back in the office having "sorted out" her Mum and Dad.

'Tina, have you heard from Nathaniel this morning? I've tried ringing him but get no answer. I tried last night but that didn't work either.'

'No Roz, I haven't heard anything this morning but I did hear your phone ring last night after you'd left. Perhaps he left a message.'

Tina heard Rosalind's phone lift and after a short silence she heard her dial. Then all she heard was a loud crash and a stifled scream. Rushing into Rosalind's office all she could see was a pair of feet. Looking around the desk Rosalind was sitting on the floor gasping for breath.

'Roz, what's up? Who did you phone? Has something happened to Nathaniel? Michael,' Tina shouted, 'Michael come here quickly. Rosalind's had a fall. She's had a shock. Something has happened to Nathaniel.'

Michael came limping up the corridor from his own cubicle.

'Rosalind, are you all right?' asked Michael. 'Here, let me help you up. What's happened?'

Rosalind slowly stood up. Rather white-faced she braced herself against the edge of her desk and looking at both of them she said, 'shit; shit has happened and I might well have you two to blame for it.'

'Us, what do you mean Rosalind?' asked Tina. 'What have we done?'

'At the moment Tina I'm not sure exactly what you have done but I'm sure as hell going to find out. The pair of you had better listen and then start talking because I'm fuming mad and both of you know that is dangerous. So sit, and listen.'

'The message on my phone was from Nathaniel. He said Saad Brothers had phoned him late yesterday with some rather disturbing news. He asked me to phone Saad Brothers to learn the details. It appears that we have stolen five million pounds of Saad's money, and not surprisingly they want it back. Also, they will cancel all contracts over the security systems we have installed, with no payments of course and they are working on punitive damages. Any questions so far?'

Tina sat there open-mouthed. Michael kept very still but thinking furiously.

'So,' said Rosalind, 'where do you suggest we go from here?'

'But how, where, who?' asked Tina. 'How do they know we did this? They deal with all sorts of monies and they have transactions going on all the time. In fact five million pounds is nothing to them.'

'But it is,' said Rosalind, 'it represents a flaw in the security system; it represents a weakness that someone else can remove fifty five million, or five hundred and fifty five million pounds. Our flaw in our system, and, apparently, you Tina removed the paltry five million.'

Rosalind looked up at Tina and said, 'your password using our software neatly clipped the paltry five million and whisked it around until it disappeared.'

Tina was at a loss for words again, but Michael had had enough time to think what to say.

'Rosalind, so far all we have is Saad Brother's word that this has happened. Why don't we look at the system and the transactions and see whether this is true first before we do anything else, or anything foolish. Even if it is true I need to see what has happened and learn if there is a flaw and how it can be resolved. Maybe we can find where this precious five million pounds has gone and restore it to Saad Brothers. Don't you think we need to get the facts clear first of all? Find out what actually is the current status, and then check the transactions to see whether this supposed fraud ever really took place. Perhaps Saad Brothers themselves have deliberately hidden the money to test us, to see whether our system for them really is effective. Maybe this is just a test. It happens you know.'

'Yes Rosalind, Michael's right,' said Tina. 'Perhaps this is not true, or perhaps it is Saad Brothers testing us as Michael says.'

'That wasn't the impression I got down the telephone,' said Rosalind. 'The Manager sounded dead serious. He said he'd talked at length with Nathaniel and Nathaniel fully understood the situation. However, Michael does have a point. We do need to check what actually has happened and how it happened. So, top priority Tina, look into the accounts and compare balances over the past week and then try and recreate a sequence of transactions. There should be a log of all the transactions and we have backups to confirm the status at set times. Michael, look into how these transactions are controlled and monitored. Look for unusual events, unusual amounts, or even irregular destinations. See whether anyone else can gain access to the transactions. Saad Brothers knew it was us because the original set of actions started through Tina's password but I'm still old-fashioned and suspicious about this web access technology. Don't forget that the Townsend family has dealt in locks for generations and we have always been careful with new keys. This web thing is rather like a new key and I'm not sure all my locks are safe. Right, it's going to be a hectic day. Perhaps it is good that Nathaniel isn't here because this sort of crisis worries him to death. He's always been fighting to escape the stigma of his Dad's dealings with less honest folk. Me, I take on anybody and right now let's put Cohen and Townsend back on its feet. I'm not going to have anybody slag off this Company. Let's work people.'

Michael scooted out of the office as fast as he could. Tina, still somewhat dazed by the news, stood slowly and looked at Rosalind.

'Roz, I don't know. I don't know how.'

'Well darling it's your password.'

'But I wouldn't. If fact I couldn't.'

'Well somebody did. Somebody moved a lot of Saad money illegally; costing five million pounds!' shouted Rosalind.

'Yes, but Saad deal with those kind of orders all the time. They deal in millions and so it didn't appear special.'

'But you know you never made the transaction?' asked Rosalind, 'even though it's been done through your terminal. So, the sooner we find out what has really taken place the better. Pull yourself together Tina because today is the most serious Friday of your life kid.'

While Tina stumbled out of Rosalind's office Michael was already on the phone to Sasha. Good thing I made sure that Sasha can reverse everything thought Michael. Let's hope he does a better job of that than he did at the front end. Perhaps by the end of today we will have everything back to square one and the weekend will be cool.

'Heh man, how they hanging?'

'Sasha, listen up, and listen up good. We are in the shits man. Saad Brothers has rumbled the action and are demanding their five million quid.'

'So, they must have some guys as good as the old Department of Defence. Heh, there's some clever people out there in the world Michael. Some of these guys know a lot.'

'Screw that Sasha, the crux of this is whether you know enough. Like I asked at the start we need to reverse everything very quietly, and we need to reverse it even more quietly than you first did. Rosalind here is fighting mad and has got Tina going over all the balances and transaction log. You need to work fast and tidy up the bloody mess.'

'Sure man, no problem. Be cool Michael. Remember this was just a trial, a dummy run. Tina still using her old password?'

'I suppose so, although I'll recommend she change it as soon as we sort this mess out.'

'Fine, give me half an hour and all will be, how you say it, hunky dory. Hasta luego amigo.'

The phone went dead in Michael's sweaty hand. Jesus Christ, what a fuck up. Perhaps it was just as well I'd tried this out before I took on the Worthings thought Michael. Saad Brothers getting politely upset down the telephone was one thing but Lady Diana breathing real fire was something else.

Rosalind sat in her office and thought over the implications of this event. Security companies rely on trust and credibility. Lose those and you lose the client. Now the world was seeing Cohen and Townsend losing or stealing their client's money and the management not even knowing it was happening; incompetence as well as philandering. Would you trust them? Actually, in the business world, the real sin was getting caught. Saad Brothers had not gone public with accusations and demands. If this turned out to be true then with some judicial financing and payments the whole problem might be kept quiet. The markets would just learn that Saad Brothers had decided to change their security systems to ensure their competitors did not learn their existing setup. This was just another precautionary step.

From the tone of the telephone conversation and from the vibes in Nathaniel's message Rosalind thought the accusations might well be true. Tina sounded innocent, and really what would she do with five million pounds? Somehow Rosalind thought Tina had been duped. So, that left Michael: Michael and his knowledge of Sir Anthony's software, plus his knowledge of this web thing. No fool was young Michael Lord, but to try and steal five million pounds? Well, think about it said Rosalind to herself. Saad Brothers wouldn't miss it. It was nothing to them. But, Michael would disgrace his father's company, or their products anyway, and discredit Cohen and Townsend. What would Michael gain at such a price? Let's wait thought Rosalind. Let's see at the end of the day what Tina and Michael really discover.

Half an hour later Michael phoned again. 'Sasha, what's happening? I'm into the system and I can't see any great changes. Tina's still looking at balances but I haven't heard her finding anything either.'

'Michael, be patient. Some of these things need to bounce around the world a little so that they sort of disappear. I also need to close up a few little holes and access points. I'm trying to leave things tidy, the way they were.'

'What about Hong Kong?'

'Michael, that was all a dummy deal. It never was for real. The messages I sent explained that this was a test run and not to be acted upon. No transaction would have taken place.'

'You mean there never was going to be any purchase?'

'Nope, no deals, no drugs, no payments.'

'Shit man, all this hassle over nothing.'

'Well Michael, you said you wanted to try out the approach. The method works, but you need to be aware of how clever the cats are on the other side.'

'Sasha, just unravel the bloody charade. The office here is not a happy camp, and I can do without Saad Brothers dumping on my Dad from a great height.'

'Michael, you have to learn that if you play on the edge you occasionally get cut, or even fall off.'

Once again Michael was left holding a dead telephone. He went back to his computer looking through the various events since last Friday trying to see what Sasha had done and whether there were some serious flaws in the software routines. Perhaps I can learn something out of this bloody mess thought Michael. He twisted in his chair and caught his scrotum the wrong way. The bruises of a week ago hadn't yet completely gone and Michael got another reminder of living on the edge.

Rosalind called Tina and Michael into her office around lunch time for a progress update. Tina had tracked back the various accounts and balances from last week. As far as she could tell the first three days had been normal and she hadn't found anything yet out of the ordinary. Michael too had looked at these transactions, noting how the security software controlled and monitored them and all of those routines appeared to be in order and working. So, the team were halfway through the past week's events and so far everything seemed acceptable and above board. Rosalind was thoughtful.

'Good,' she said, 'maybe this was a test and I over-reacted. However, we need to finish this right up to date before I get back to Saad Brothers. Once we know our side of the story I can go to work.'

The afternoon wore on. Rosalind started to prowl around the offices. The tension was getting to her. By four o'clock Tina had finished and came back into Rosalind's office.

'I can't find any missing money. As far as I can tell all the transactions appear proper and valid. Monies have been moved but there is paperwork behind the activities. Things balance. I can't see any evidence of improper entries, nor are there any transactions under my password that I didn't make. There are some transactions in the Far East that I can't remember the exact details but they all balance out. As far as I am concerned Rosalind this appears to be much ado about nothing.'

Tina sat back in the chair opposite Rosalind and the tension seeped out of her. She sort of collapsed into the chair. 'God what a day.'

'Okay,' said Rosalind, 'that looks like good news. I wonder what Mr. Lord has to say for himself. Go and get him for me will you Tina?'

Tina forced herself upright in the chair and then stood up. She walked slowly and purposefully down the corridor to Michael's workspace. Michael was sitting looking at his monitor but Tina didn't think he was seeing anything. She thought he was looking through his monitor.

'Michael, Rosalind wants us in her office.'

'What, Oh you startled me. I was just checking on these controls.'

'Bullshit Michael, absolute utter bullshit. You were sitting pissing your pants for something you can't quite control. Somehow Michael you used my password to be too clever and Saad Brothers caught you out. Now you're pissing yourself because you don't know exactly what you have done, and all under my password. You really are a shit aren't you?'

'Tina, when this is all over change your password. The security software actually requires you to change your password every month you know. I don't remember you doing that have you?'

'Michael, don't you even try and pass this bloody mess over onto me. I'll change my password all right, and I will never give it out to you again. In fact just get out of my life.'

Tina strode back down the corridor and into Rosalind's office. 'He's on his way,' she said to Rosalind.

'Michael, what have you found?'

'Nothing, nothing at all. It's as I suspected. I said as much first thing this morning here in your office Rosalind if you remember. I thought this might be a test: just a check by Saad Brothers to see that we really can handle their accounts. The security software works well. I found several routines where I think we can make some improvements and tighten things up while still not damaging efficiency. Tina tells me the accounts all balance and no monies were lost. So, it was an exciting day, but you can phone up Saad Brothers and give them shit Rosalind, politely of course.'

'Michael, I think you are full of crap, but that is beside the point. I do believe your last point. So, thanks the pair of you. Now, clear out, go home and let me get on with putting this company back where it belongs. Out, go. This wasn't the best of days for either of you. I won't forget.'

Michael was out in a flash and Tina rose more slowly. She looked at Rosalind.

'Roz, I'm sorry. It won't happen again. I think I've learnt my lesson.'

'Well let's hope so Tina. Nathaniel and I put a lot of trust in you. We had talked about the possibility of offering you a partnership. You contribute a lot to this company. I will have to talk this over again with Nathaniel after today's events.'

'Sure Roz. I'll go. Tell Saad Brothers we are on the level and can be trusted.'

Tina left and Rosalind sat back exhausted in her chair. Now, she thought, let's talk politely to Saad Brothers and see whether we are all still friends. Before she phoned Rosalind thought slowly and carefully what she had to do. If it had been a test then Cohen and Townsend had come through with flying colours. They had identified that all was well and the original assertion was false, which they could now prove. However, if there really had been a problem, and during the course of today someone somehow had rectified the situation she had better be careful in re-assuring Saad Brothers it was just a software glitch and it had been corrected. Their monies would be perfectly safe with the systems Cohen and Townsend had installed and would maintain. Softly, softly thought Rosalind. And, she thought, before she lifted the receiver, there was a second call she had to make.

The call to Saad Brothers was very polite and civilized. Yes, Saad had noted that the balances were all correct and there were no improper transactions in the system. The five million pound discrepancy obviously was some glitch in the system and it was expected with new software there would always be some hiccups with the introduction of a new system. Saad were quite satisfied with the work being done by Cohen and Townsend but there was a strong hint down the telephone that the situation would be monitored very closely from now on. Rosalind thought she could detect something was not quite right and something was not being said down the telephone. Saad Brothers finished the call hoping Rosalind would enjoy her weekend.

'One down and one to go,' she said to her empty office, 'although the next call may not be quite so cordial.' She dialed long distance from London down to Somerset. 'Sir Anthony Lord please,' she spoke into the receiver, 'and yes, I will hold thanks.'

Tapping her pencil on her teeth Rosalind sat very pensively in her chair. 'I wonder what really happened: I wonder what Michael really did.'

'And what did Michael really do?' came the question down the telephone line.

'Oh, hello, Sir Anthony, sorry I was thinking out loud. Thanks for taking my call. We have a problem I think, although I have managed to salvage most of the pieces this end. Let me explain.'

Rosalind spoke clearly and lucidly down the telephone for some fifteen minutes without any interruption. She never raised her voice, even though the grip on the pencil tightened a few times. At the end of her explanation she said, 'so you see I think it will be for the best if Michael leaves us. I hope that you understand?'

For a moment there was silence before Sir Anthony quietly said, 'yes, I think you are right. I will try and get to the bottom of this from our end. If it is agreeable to you I will also telephone Saad Brothers and talk with both their Director and with some of their I.T. staff. I would like to know technically what has transpired as well as confirming the reputation of our products. Rosalind I do hope that Cohen and Townsend has retained its reputation over all this. I will make every effort to confirm my faith in you when I phone Saad Brothers. Thank you for the call and please give my best wishes to Nathaniel.'

So, thought Rosalind, two problems resolved. However, she had a third problem. Exactly what do I tell Nathaniel? He obviously knows part of the story from the initial call from Saad Brothers, but what do I really tell him? Being a people person and wanting to do the right things, and above all needing to appear to be doing the right things Nathaniel is very proud of his reputation. You my love, thought Rosalind are my third problem.

The third problem solved itself, although Rosalind didn't know this until she came home that night. Nathaniel was swinging from the roof truss in the garage and his body was silhouetted in the lights of Rosalind's car as she opened the garage door.

First shock, then screams, and then sobs. Rosalind's short height couldn't do anything to lift Nathaniel higher and relieve the stress on his neck. Neighbours came to Rosalind's screams and peeled her off Nathaniel's knees.

The shame, the incredible shame of an association with drugs was just too much for Nathaniel's sensibilities. He could live with theft. His family had lived on the edge of that world for ever. He could live with being caught. Several of Nathaniel's family had lived for a while at the expense and pleasure of Her Majesty's government. Nathaniel could not live with any association with drugs. This too ran in the family. The Cohen's had had a longstanding principle of not touching drugs.

11

Steal

As soon as he got off the telephone with Rosalind Sir Anthony Lord did telephone Saad Brothers as promised. The Managing Director of Saad explained the circumstances. He also told Sir Anthony what he thought had happened. When the call was forwarded to the Information Technology staff at Saad Brothers they told a slightly different and more damming tale.

'Yes Sir Anthony, the balances were changed and monies did eventually disappear but they were used to pay for an offshore transaction. We have one major concern with your software and one major concern with the use of the monies. Firstly, although we applaud the ability to move monies quickly and discreetly we think there needs to be better controls over these transactions when they are done remotely, like over the web. We agree with your philosophy that web transactions will soon be commonplace and that that ability is vital. However, it appears possible to hack into that part of the code and perform illegal operations. To ensure the integrity of our clients' money we must have tighter controls in this area.'

'And the second concern?' asked Sir Anthony, 'you said you had two concerns.'

'This concern does not appear to be one for your Company Sir Anthony,' came the very smooth reply, 'but it probably does reflect on who did the illegal hacking. As we said, the money was paid to an off-shore Hong Kong numbered account.'

'But I thought that all of the money was accounted for from today's activities? There was no payment.'

'True Sir Anthony, at the end of today all was in balance. However, we think someone went back into the accounts today and reversed the transactions of the previous week, including the payment to Hong Kong.'

'So, nothing was stolen and nothing was bought?' asked Sir Anthony.

'Correct, but, and it is a concerned but, we do know the kind of product that was to have been purchased before today's activities. When we told Nathaniel Cohen we thought that the transaction had gone through and we were very concerned. So, I might add was Mr. Cohen.'

'So, tell me, this was a numbered account in Hong Kong?'

'Yes sir, and through our colleagues in Hong Kong we were able to confirm the order was for five million pounds worth of drugs. That was our second concern.'

Back in his office in Somerset Sir Anthony slumped back in his chair and took a deep breath.

'And you're sure of this?' he asked.

'Yes sir,' came the brief reply.

Sir Anthony sat up straight in his chair and took a firmer grip on the phone.

'Right then, let me see if I have got this straight. Our software works well for Saad Brothers and their clients. It was satisfactorily installed and maintained by Cohen and Townsend. They have done a good job I hear. I have a problem to correct for you with regards to the controls and security of remote access of the accounts: so far so good?'

'Yes sir, correct.'

'But, finally, something has happened this past week and that activity was going to steal your money and purchase drugs. Did the purchase say where the delivery should be made?'

'No Sir Anthony. We would guess that there were a series of innocuous messages sent through some other medium, or through some other system telling the vendor about the transaction, including a destination address.'

'Well I thank you for this lucid explanation. I will have my staff work on solving the remote access controls as a top priority and will telephone you early next week with a progress report. As for the other matter I will resolve that in some other way. Good day to you and thanks again.'

For the next five minutes Anthony sat in his office pondering over the afternoon's telephone calls. After weighing up some alternatives he made two calls.

'Ted, how's it going for a Friday afternoon?'

'Hi Sir Anthony, just fine actually. The work's coming on well. I'm starting to get my thesis into shape although there is a bit of a lull at the moment as my supervisor has gone to Russia for three weeks.'

'That's old Doctor Kershaw isn't it? He's your supervisor?'

'Yes, you know him?'

'No Ted, but I know of him. He's a wily old bugger and has the ability to think laterally better than anyone I know.'

'And don't I know it. Still, you must have phoned for a reason given how busy you usually are. What can I do for you?'

'You're right, I do have a reason, two reasons actually. First, can you come down to Fotheringham Manor this weekend? If Lester Donald is free bring him too.'

'Well I can answer that one right away. Lester is here with me now. Hang on a sec and I'll ask. Yes, we're both free and would enjoy a weekend in the country.'

'Excellent, but come prepared to do a little work because that leads into the second request. If you have some time on your hands I would like to re-employ you for one, maybe two weeks starting immediately. Can you answer that one?'

'Lester asks whether the work applies to both of us or can he just come down for a nice relaxing soak in the sun on the Estate?'

Sir Anthony chuckled. 'Good to see postgraduate work hasn't dulled your senses of humour. There's work for both of you if you can fit it in. I have a problem related to what you were doing for me in the summer; the sooner that I can get it solved the happier my client will be.'

'We'll both be down midmorning tomorrow. Lester will have to check on his schedule but he thinks he can fit in a week if that's helpful. All of our notes from the summer are down in your offices.'

'Well the weekend was just a bribe when all I will do is explain the problem and some thoughts on its solution. The rest of the time we will enjoy the Estate. I don't expect to start working on the solutions until Monday morning in the office so come down to enjoy the weekend and some R & R away from the studies.'

'Sounds good to us,' said Ted. 'As I said, expect us mid morning.'

This second call may not be quite so friendly thought Sir Anthony as he dialed a London number.

'Hello, Michael is that you?'

'You have reached Knightsbridge 2755. I'm not able to take your call. Please leave a message and I will get back to you. Pip, pip, pip.'

'Dam,' said Sir Anthony. 'Michael, call me as soon as you can. This is important and urgent.'

Just outside London Michael circulated easily amongst the well-dressed set at Foster Faxon's house in Surrey. As promised Chuck Faxon had introduced Michael to the Faxon household and Michael managed to secure invitations as often as he dared. Several of the guests spoke with a genteel southern drawl and Michael perched on the edge of conversations listening for opportunities.

It was a large sprawling house. As soon as he arrived Michael took the time to seek out his hosts and thank them for the invitation. Foster Faxon was very much an American with hearty handshakes and exuberant charm. He delighted in Michael's quiet reserved English greeting.

'Michael, Michael, welcome to the party. Come and meet the folks. Lots of people who'll just love to hear the accent. Cute clothes too; a little somber perhaps, but come, come and meet my lady.'

Foster whisked Michael away to a beautifully gowned Southern Belle. All she needs is a parasol and a young black boy thought Michael.

'My dear, young Michael Lord has come down to see us again. See how beautifully refined and English he looks.'

Louise-Marie Faxon eyed Michael up and down, and then she graciously raised her gloved hand.

'Lawd, but don't you look the part. Foster, he looks such a gentleman.'

Michael was quick enough to step forward and take the proffered hand and raise it slowly to his lips.

'And he has the manners and charm to go with it,' she sighed.

'My pleasure Mam,' said Michael, and he almost bowed as he stepped backwards, but that would be overdoing it thought Michael.

'Michael, now you circulate now. Don't you waste your time with us folks. There are lots of beautiful people here and you'll fit right in.

Chuck says you're a good mixer, especially with the ladies.' Foster nudged Michael in the shoulder wheeled him round and pointed him at a cloud of colour giggling further down the garden.

Michael took Foster up on the offer and spent the first hour exploring. Well, checking out of the lie of the land and the nature of the clientele really. With a large house party, including several people in the media world you could find all sorts of interesting cameos. Several people sniffed a lot. They were that kind of people. Suddenly, an arm reached out and spun Michael around.

'Michael, I hear you have been working on something special? Chuck tells me you have a gift with mathematics and clever algorithms. What have you got that would interest an old-timer radio person?' Foster Faxon had found Michael wandering and couldn't have people all alone at any one of his parties.

'Heard of www?'

'Yes, something my techie types keep hyping about. What is it? Wonderful world of wankers?'

'World Wide Web actually; the name sort of hints at where it will go. Universities and some specialized industries use it to share data and information. It lets you search for answers to your questions, or similar questions.'

'You mean like a library?' asked Foster.

'Kind of. But it could be much more than that. You're in the media business. Think of having your news out there before anyone else, and, in front of everyone. Think of having your entertainment available to people when they want it, not at TV-scheduled times. And, yes, think of everyone having the Encyclopaedia Britannica or whatever you use in America in their home without having ten large outdated books sitting on a shelf.'

'How will people find what they are looking for? I find looking for a book in the library hard enough and now you want me to look for a specific subject in a book?'

'That's where a search engine comes in.'

'Michael, this sounds like something out of science fiction. What in 'tarnation is a search engine?'

Michael stepped back away from Foster's arm and thought for a moment.

'Well?' asked Foster, 'is it so complicated this old-timer won't understand?'

'No, I'm just trying to think of a familiar analogy for you. Let's try this way. You do a lot of film, advertising and even news reporting but how do you find the suitable cast for any of these productions? You must have someway, or somebody who can find who is the most suitable person for the various roles?'

'Sure Michael, we have casting specialists, and we use Agencies, everybody does.'

'And you screen, or filter the hundreds of choices in some way so you don't have to test everyone? Isn't that right Mr. Faxon?'

'Sure.'

'Well, there has to be some label on each of these people to help you screen them. For example, they are male, or black, or tall, or three-legged, or..'

'Yes, all of them have a portfolio.'

'Which lists their attributes?'

'Exactly, so we can whittle down quite quickly who is the most suitable.'

'You produce a short-list of the most suitable?'

'Yeah, kind of.'

'Well, imagine being able to do that for anything, not just for people, but about any subject. Imagine being able to ask for the latest news from

Afghanistan, or the names of chemicals preventing measles, etc., and being able to do this very quickly – I mean in minutes.'

'So you can do this for anything?'

'Well, for any data or thing that is in the digital world and soon most things will be in the digital world. For some things you obviously get lots of answers. It is up to the inquirer to sort out which references are the most useful, or perhaps refine the search, but the key is to do this quickly. In the old days of written encyclopedias you could write a question for the publisher's research team to answer and it would come back days or weeks later. With an efficient search engine the list of answers comes back in minutes or even seconds. Such a piece of software is a potential goldmine.'

'And you have a special search engine?'

Before Michael could reply Stanley Rogers clamped his hand firmly on Michael's shoulder. He whirled Michael round.

'You have a lot of nerve coming here. The bold colonial approach to strike out, irrespective of the mess you have made behind you. It's a bloody good job you never managed to come to California. It saves us having to kick you out before you ruined America.'

'Steady on Stanley; Michael's my guest.'

'You know who he is? You know what he's done?'

'Sure, he's Anthony Lord's son and smart with it. He was just telling me something that might be of interest to me back home.'

'Oh he's smart all right. Too bloody smart for his own good and it is usually for his own good that is the prime objective. You always seem to do all right, don't you Michael? While all around you disaster strikes and yet you walk away unscathed. So Foster, did you hear about Bella Turner?'

'Yes, an accident. You're daughter was there wasn't she?'

Rogers inhaled noisily and stiffened his body. He continued his harangue.

'What about Aubrey Worthing? What about his cousin Jean?'

'I had nothing to do with that,' shot back Michael. 'Aubrey was fooling about with his dad's stuff.'

'Yes, and I wonder why?' said Stanley Rogers.

Foster Faxon tried to ease the tension. 'Stanley, I hear you have a neat graphics interface for maps for service agencies. They tell me it helps the police, ambulance and fire people all talk about the same location; some digitized georeferencing system I hear. My news people could use some clear way of getting to news scenes in a hurry; most of them find it difficult to find their way out of the studio.'

Stanley Rogers relaxed his hand off Michael's shoulder and Michael wheeled away out of sight. The two Americans launched into a discussion on communications. Michael swiftly found safer ground.

ꟗ

Terry Dodds slowly released his hold on Vernon Trelawney. He unfolded his wet passionate body away from his lover.

'Christ, you're wonderful. You make me feel alive. I can't get enough of you. I don't know what I would do without you.'

Vernon listened to all this with half of his mind. Sure, Terry was very loving and endearing but sometimes a little over the top. While half of Vernon's mind was feeling its way through his love life the other half was caught up in the efficiencies of gates, stacks, logical units and other intricacies of machine language. However, it was a plus that Terry could also dovetail his software talents as well as his soft body.

Terry and Vernon both worked for Anthony Lord as systems analysts. Both men had extensive knowledge and experience in database design. They were also competent code writers in second, third and fourth generation languages. With the development of microcomputers the computer world had been turned upside down. In the "old" days a team of white-coated, be-spectacled wizards operated wonders in an air-conditioned temple. The poor lowly user waited for reams of landscape-oriented paper containing pages of hieroglyphics and the occasional answer to the question or calculation. But not today. The user was king, or queen in some cases, and "user-friendly" interfaces were a necessity. Terry and Vernon were specialists in both user-friendly interfaces and the smarts behind the interface.

Several fourth generation database languages existed at this time and most of these were fairly easy for the user to learn. What really made question and response speedy, especially for complicated or inter-related questions, was a very efficient database design and search engine. With the rapid progress in computer graphics over the last five years you also needed a search engine that could deal with "where" was something. You needed to understand not only what something was, and its characteristics, but also where it stood in the world, and perhaps what was beside it. As an example, consider where should the education authorities place a school in the town? You needed to know where were the children of such-and-such an age; where were the dangerous roads; where were the bus routes, and so on. Terry had a real flair for this kind of problem. He could see things in three dimensions and four over time if needed. But he could also take this vision into the realities of the computer world and make the software respond to the user's questions.

The emerging microcomputer environment generated the usual industry clash of approaches and technologies. Like almost any technology the early days are full of different possibilities. The pioneers come into the world with different backgrounds and different solutions and for a while there is exciting chaos. Eventually some form of standardization emerges. With microcomputers most of the user community divided itself into Apple users or Microsoft users.

As systems analysts Terry and Vernon didn't really live in either of these worlds. Their world was primarily structured by hierarchical or relational databases. Crudely put do you look for something from the top down or could you search side to side. But now a new world was peeking over the horizon. Something called the World Wide Web was starting to make itself known to the great unwashed in the early 1990s. Vernon had been exposed to this environment while he was doing postgraduate in the States and had kept himself up to date with papers in the journals.

'Just imagine the potential for being able to look at anything, anywhere, wherever it is stored.'

'Yes, you could use a general map to locate all the Universities in England, and then identify which ones had modern computer facilities.'

'Continue that into which ones did database research and inquire into the system what kind of research.'

'You could pursue that at your fingertips in a moment.'

'Finally, you telephone the one researcher who is leading the field.'

'You think British Telecom will support such an endeavour? You think you'd get through?'

Still the possibilities boggled the mind and the minds were close. Terry and Vernon had been working long hours in each other's minds. They already had a prototype search engine that could navigate through several types of databases very efficiently. They were working on the user-interface component with Terry spear-heading the charge. In their world this was a very impressive professional development. Also, there was money to be made, as well as prestige to be earned. Vernon had already briefed Anthony Lord a couple of times that this particular line of work was close to completion. However, he had also told his boss that the technology was a little in advance of the world of 1990 in England. It was an answer for tomorrow. But, he pointed out, that tomorrow wasn't far away. Although Anthony Lord was a man of action for today he also liked to be prepared for tomorrow.

Tomorrow was Saturday, and true to his word Ted Crichton brought Lester Donald down from Bristol on his motorbike to Fotheringham Manor. It was a cool morning and the October breezes just rustled the leaves starting to turn on some of the trees on the estate. The larches were already a stately sight of glorious gold and the hardwoods exhibited a range of colours from yellow, through orange, red and into brown. Before reaching the house Ted stopped on his bike just to take in the spectacle.

'Look at that Lester. I can't get colours like that back home.'

'Thought you got lots of vivid reds,' said Lester. 'I seem to remember seeing pictures of the Fall Colours, sort of tourist attraction of Canada I thought.'

'Well, you're right and wrong in that. You're right in that Eastern Canada has a beautiful array of Fall Colours, including bright red maples as you say. But, I come from the prairies and the only change in trees we see in the Fall are yellow aspens, and they tend to blend into rolling hills of golden grain. We don't get this variety, especially in such a small compact vista.'

'Well this small compact vista behind you would like to get to the house and off this bloody bike. My body wasn't designed to perch in the birthing position for any length of time. I think a reclining sofa and a long drink would go down very well now.'

'Hold on back there guy, we'll be right there. Besides, I think I see a welcoming party at the head of the drive. Looks like Sir Anthony himself is out to meet us.'

Ted drove on the remaining few hundred yards and stopped quietly alongside Sir Anthony. He pushed up his goggles and took off his gloves.

'Good to see you Sir Anthony. We were just admiring the view back there. The trees look magnificent.'

'You worried me for a moment Ted. I thought you'd changed your mind and were going to escape.'

'No, I wouldn't let him Sir Anthony,' said Lester. 'I'd already had enough bouncing on the back tyre and was urging him not to stop and get all romantic. I kept telling him it was time for a drink.'

'Lester, you're right. Ted, just put the bike in the stables over there and then join us in the house. Come on Lester; let's see whether we can find you a drink.'

For the rest of the morning Sir Anthony explained some of his conversations with Saad Brothers. Ted and Lester had both worked on much of this security piece of software and so they were quite familiar with the overall design. During the course of the conversation Ted had asked whether Sir Anthony had been in contact with Michael, who had been working on the software installation in London. Ted and Lester both thought Michael could offer some insights into the problem. Sir Anthony mentioned that he had tried to contact Michael but with no success so far.

'If you can't reach Michael have you tried talking with anyone else at Cohen and Townsend?' asked Lester.

'No Lester. I tried to phone Rosalind Cohen earlier this morning but her phone was engaged.'

'Didn't she have someone else working on this application with Michael?' asked Ted. 'I thought Cohen's had hired someone, or trained someone to work with Michael on this. Weren't they going to maintain the system for Saad Brothers when the installation and testing were complete?'

'That's right,' said Sir Anthony, 'Michael did mention he was working with someone in their offices. She was an old school friend of Rosalind's

I think, Linda something maybe? We need to talk with her when I can reach Rosalind or Michael. Anyway, enough of the problem for now. We can go into that starting on Monday, but let's get you two organized for a relaxing weekend. Is there anything special we can offer you?'

Ted and Lester looked at each other but neither was very forthcoming. Lester relaxed even further into the comfortable sofa and Ted smiled.

'Actually Sir Anthony I would like a chance to see more of the Estate. When we were here earlier in the summer we got too tied up with the diving accident and I never did get a chance to see more of the area. Michael sort of hinted at the various things you do here, over and above the Company activities, and I was interested in both the farm and the forestry. Michael said he had an Aunt, your sister I believe, who has done some active work in genetics. He also said you had some Canadian trees I should see. He was boasting that they grow better here than in Canada.'

'Well that's all easy to look after, but what about our recumbent friend here? Lester, is this as much R & R as you can take, or does Ted's intensive sightseeing programme interest you?'

Lester sat up and appeared to consider the question. 'If the truth be told,' he said, 'I'd like a chance to ride.'

'Well that can be arranged very easily too,' said Sylvia Lord as she swept into the room. 'It is a grand day out there and I will gladly ride with you young sir.' Sylvia curtsied and smiled at Lester. Lester sat bolt upright, blushed, stood and stammered, 'Mrs. Lord, what a delight to see you again.' He offered Sylvia his hand, which she took warmly.

'Relax Lester, I didn't mean to spring on you quite so suddenly but a ride is a wonderful idea. Actually Anthony, we could all ride. It would be an easy way to see parts of the Estate and give the horses an outing too. I'm sure we've got enough clothes to kit out these young men. What do you say love, and why is Ted laughing so much?'

Ted also had stood up when Sylvia came into the room but he was somewhat shaking with mirth on hearing Lester's request.

'I'm sorry Mrs. Lord, it's just remembering Lester's earlier comments about coming here on the bike. He was complaining loudly about sitting straddling the bike and now he wants to sit astride a horse. I just found the idea rather ironic.'

Lester looked at Ted but didn't deign to make any comment. Sir Anthony looked at the pair of them but realized that no further explanation was forthcoming and so he said, 'yes Sylvia, we can kit everyone out. I'll go and see whether Ferris is around and get the horses organized. Can you look after Ted and Lester's gear?'

Needless to say Ferris wasn't around but Freddie was eager enough to collect the saddles and bridles for the four horses. Sir Anthony went and changed while Sylvia managed to find appropriate breeches, boots and helmets for Lester and Ted. With a click of hooves the foursome rode out of the stable yard and down towards the buildings of the Home Farm.

Back in Surrey Michael had slipped the wrath of Stanley Rogers to find the smiles of Melanie Rogers. However, at that time Vanessa Worthing was enjoying the smiles of Melanie Rogers. The two young ladies were exchanging opinions on the merits of certain male tennis players. Melanie was waxing eloquently about subtlety and slices. Vanessa, true to family tradition, favoured the aggressive, in your face McEnroe style of play. Michael joined the group just as Lady Diana Worthing swept into view.

'There you are Vanessa. I've been looking for you everywhere.'

'Not quite Mother. I've been here all the time and this really isn't all that big of a house.'

'Don't be sarcastic Vanessa. It doesn't become you.'

Suddenly Diana noticed Michael. 'You,' she almost screeched. 'You,' and she pointed an aristocratic finger at Michael like a rapier. 'The bringer of death and destruction.' Diana stepped forwards with her finger still outstretched.

'Parry Michael, for god's sake parry or she will pierce you to the hilt,' giggled Vanessa.

Diana whirled on her daughter. 'This is family business and don't you ever forget it.'

Melanie stood somewhat bedazzled at this dramatic turn of events. She spun her head from Diana to Vanessa like a spectator at a tennis match. Michael however decided that he had had enough harassment for the day and he turned on his heel and circled away.

'Well Melanie, you said you preferred people who slice although Michael didn't show much subtlety. I would sooner have seen him brazen it out with mama. She also prefers a good stand up fight. Still, she had him going for a moment. Did you see the look on his face?'

Melanie had seen the look on Michael's face. However, she had only seen the first look. At first Michael was taken aback and looking cornered, and a little embarrassed in front of Melanie. But, after the initial attack he morphed into his second and inside face of personal gain and revenge.

The target, or targets really for Michael's personal gain and revenge were not at Foster Faxon's house but the means were. Michael hadn't gone far and was lighting up a cigarette when a foreign voice asked whether he would like something better for his nasal passages. Michael thought that coke would certainly make him feel better and so he turned to the voice and said 'yes.'

The voice belonged to Wesley Winchelow the IIIrd.

'I heard part of your conversation with Foster a while back,' said Wesley. 'Like to tell me more?'

'And you are whom?' said Michael rather pompously.

'Wesley Winchelow the IIIrd., at your service. I'm a freelance writer with access to several computer magazines back in the States. I'm sure some of my editors would like a little insight into any future wizardry from the Old World. I'm not sure that U.S. readers realise the Acorn has grown into a new heart of oak.'

Michael pondered the thin curled lips and belittling tone of the foreign voice and wondered whether Wesley Winchelow may be the IIIrd and last Winchelow. Uncurling his fingers Michael calculated he might possibly achieve personal gain and revenge on more than one person. Maybe he could make WW the IIIrd realise that the new heart of oak could still be wielded as a weapon on one member of the Colonies.

'Yes, actually I do have something negotiable. We need to discuss releasing this into some prestigious journals as well as mainstream publications. I'll need you to find some reviewers as well as approvals from the right editors. I have something that will, how do you say it, "knock your socks off".'

Wesley agreed to contact Michael as soon as he had some publication possibilities lined up back in the States. Michael in turn left the chattering crowd of Foster Faxon's house and drove quickly back home. He had a little burglary planned, plus a little revenge.

Out on the Estate the four riders gently walked their horses around Home Farm. Sir Anthony explained some of the work that Stephanie was doing with sheep. Lester thought you could model some these trials and possible results into a computer algorithm and let Stephanie predict some useful outcomes in a simulation. Ted poohed poohed this idea and wanted to see the plantations. 'Now there's a domain you can model,' said Ted, 'just imagine the fun you could have with modeling forests. It's been done for a while in America and you can build in fires, insect damage, plus improved growth rates through genetics and fertilization. Hell, I'll bet I could grow trees like a charm on the computer.'

Sir Anthony laughed. 'That's all very well Ted but I have to do it in real life and that often has a lot of uncertainty built in. Ah, but here's a part of my forest where there is always a certainty.' Sir Anthony had noticed Enrico up one of the rides in the plantations. 'Good day Enrico, I see you're out looking after our trees,' said Sir Anthony.

Enrico smiled at the group of riders. 'Si Signore. Good day Lady,' Enrico said as he lifted his cap to Sylvia.

'You said our trees?' asked Ted, 'why our trees?'

Sir Anthony smiled at Ted's question. 'That's a long story, but I'll let Enrico tell you. Enrico, can you spend some time with my young people here? I have to get back to the house and try and track down Michael.'

'I'll come with you Anthony. I have several things I have to do this afternoon too,' said Sylvia.

'I'll look after the young sirs,' said Enrico, 'they'll not come to any harm with me. I'll show them a little part of the Fotheringham Manor history, as told by the trees.'

Sylvia and Anthony turned their horses around and cantered back to the house. Enrico gently led the horses further down into the plantations.

'Let's go to the beginning,' he said, 'and it started to improve just after the First World War when Sir Anthony's grandfather and grandmother got interested in forestry. That was George and Virginia Lord and their gamekeeper Alfred Templeton. Much of the early work came from the thoughts and ideas of Virginia. She was a grand old lady. It was she who really brought up Sir Anthony and his brother and sister, at least when they were very young in the War.'

'So the first plantations date back to the 1910s?' asked Ted.

'Yes,' said Enrico, 'we had pine and larch plantations, partly for farm timber but also for commercial sales. Some of the pines came from Canada, the white pines, and they turn into good lumber.'

'It's rather a historic tree for Canada,' said Ted proudly.

'Yes, I know that,' said Lester. 'I learnt in school the English colonialists cut down all the big white pines for masts for sailing ships, so the English navy could keep the colonials in check.'

Enrico chuckled. 'That's as maybe,' he said, 'but we like them here and I grew up with them when I came here as a young man. My brother and I spent a lot of time pruning and thinning these white pines, and then the accident....' Enrico went silent for a moment and ran his hand through his hair. Replacing his cap he looked mournful for a moment and then angry.

'Heh, I'm sorry to have upset you with our wrangling,' said Ted. 'I apologise.'

'No, I lost my brother near here in an accident with the white pines but I was angry when I think of what happened after that. That Michael, he could have helped but he ran away. He's got a bad streak in him that one. I hope Sir Anthony can keep a tight rein on him because he causes damage wherever he goes.'

'Well we know all about Michael and damage don't we Lester?'

Ted recounted the story of Nicole Masters and the diving accident. 'I was there when Michael was urging Nicole to higher and harder dives.'

'Then, when there is an accident Michael adds to the damage with this "I'm in charge" attitude,' added Lester.

'Well, Michael was not so helpful when my brother was hurt. Antonio had his head split open when a broken top came down and smashed his head. I ran for help but there was no one at the Farm and so I ran on to the Manor. Michael was there but Michael wouldn't listen. Oh no, Michael had to go out to some precious party and my brother died. I will not forget, never. Sir Anthony's family has been very good to my brother and me. His Grandfather George took us both in when we were Prisoners-of-War. From him and Alfred Templeton we learnt forestry and a good life here in the village. His son Desmond helped us and we became part of the Estate. We make things for the children, toys, play things. Anthony too, and Sylvia, they have helped us feel at home here. Even with Geoffrey the life was good, although Geoffrey was not often in the forest. But, now, with that drunken old man Norton, and self-centred Michael, life is not so good. Maybe I should do something about it.'

At that moment Sir Anthony was doing something about it. Finally he had managed to reach Michael on the telephone. The conversation was not cordial.

'Michael, where the hell are you, and what, repeat what have you been doing?'

'Heh, hold on, I've just come in from a challenging meeting at Foster Faxon's drumming up some business. A couple of people there were very interested in some of the things that we do. I may have generated some offshore interests.'

'Bull-shit Michael. You've been to a party, probably not invited, and talked off your head to some people who don't know you. Anyway, enough of that; I've just got off the phone with Rosalind Cohen.'

'And how is dear old....'

'Shut up Michael and listen for once. Rosalind is both heart-broken and furious, whereas I am just furious. Do you realize what you have done you stupid bastard?'

'No, and why is Rosalind so pissed off? When I left the office Friday everything was fine. We'd worked our butts off on Friday to pass some test that Saad Brothers set us. They were trying to claim we'd lost five million pounds of their money. Well, we put that straight. I left Rosalind as she was going to phone Saad Brothers and tell them we had passed their test.'

'Michael, this is your father you are talking to not some wet-behind-the-ears neophyte. That is absolute crap. I've talked with Saad Brothers at length, both with the Managing Director and with their I.T. staff. There was no test. Somehow you screwed around with the software and tried to steal five million pounds. When you realized that you'd been caught you tried to put everything back the way it was. Trouble is you left too many trails and one of them was the purchase in Hong Kong.'

'There was no purchase in Hong Kong.'

'Just as well there wasn't Michael, or you'd be in jail. Obviously from your tone of voice you haven't heard what happened with Rosalind and Nathaniel?'

'No, Nathaniel wasn't in the office at the end of the week and Rosalind seemed fine on Friday afternoon. So what's Rosalind so wound up about?'

'Nathaniel hanged himself Michael, that's what Rosalind's so wound up about as you so crassly put it. When he heard from Saad Brothers what had taken place he couldn't stand the shame. His family has always been absolutely against anything to do with drugs. But now his Company, his own Company is caught buying drugs with client's money. Rosalind found him hanging in the garage when she drove home Friday night.'

'Christ, Jesus Christ, but I had nothing to do with that. There were no drugs. There was no purchase of anything and we didn't steal five million pounds.'

'Who's the "we" Michael?' asked Sir Anthony. 'You just said "we".'

'Hell Dad, it was just a test. I saw Tina doing something for Saad Brothers and wanted to test the software a bit further. We didn't go through with anything wrong. Saad Brothers will have told you that.'

'Michael, pack up and come down here. Rosalind doesn't want you anywhere near her office. I think it's time you quit your studies for the year and came down here. Your mother is really upset over all of this. She really liked Rosalind. So Michael, down here! We've got some sorting out to do with the software plus I need you somewhere down here out of harms way. Later today Michael, later today or else!'

Ted and Lester slowly rode into the stable yard and dismounted. Freddie led the two horses away and looked after them. 'Bit of a sad story about Enrico's brother don't you think?' asked Lester. 'It must have been a horrible way to see your brother die and not be able to do anything about it.'

'Sounds like he didn't actually see Antonio die though; that happened when Enrico was going for help.'

'Still, I can understand why Enrico is so pissed off with Michael, and now Michael's in charge of the Forest Estate.'

'Yes, apart from that weasel of a man called Ferris.'

'Wonder what Enrico will do about it? I asked him whether he shoots and he told me he and his brother grew up shooting in the mountains of Northern Italy. They had to as food was short when he was young. He still shoots crows around the Estate. Perhaps the peasants will shoot the king like William Rufus in the New Forest.'

'I hardly think Enrico will go that far.'

'Food for thought Ted, food for thought.'

'And what's food for thought?' asked Sir Anthony as he met Ted and Lester in the stable yard. Ted and Lester looked at each other and Ted quickly said, 'we were back arguing about modeling forests and whether it would be better as a simulation or an optimization solution.'

'If it was optimization what would you make the objective function, the bottom line?' asked Sir Anthony, half in jest. 'Would you be looking for profit maximization, cost minimization, or some airy-fairy environmental objective?'

'For you Sir Anthony it would be profit maximization, but if Mrs. Lord asked then I would try and find a "green" objective function.'

'Ted that's a very diplomatic answer and my wife would like the response as well, although she keeps a very close eye on the bottom line. She's the one who went to L.S.E. remember. However, did you have a good tour of the Estate? It really can be quite fascinating, especially listening to some of the history that Enrico knows.'

'Yes,' said Lester, 'he is quite a character. He and his brother have had a long association with the Estate.'

'My Grandfather George fought with the Italians in the First World War, as did the gamekeeper we had here at the time. My grandfather was very impressed with the workmanship and the pride of the people from the Dolomites. He was a good judge of men was my grandfather.'

'He was a good judge of trees too,' said Ted. 'Those Canadian pines have certainly done well here. They seem to do better than they do back home.'

'That's not all Ted,' said Sir Anthony. 'We have several species from Canada, although most of them are from the west coast. And you're right, several of the species do grow exceptionally well here. Still, let's go in. I think Sylvia has prepared some tea for us and we can relax before dinner.'

Sir Anthony hadn't told Ted and Lester that he had called Michael, and he certainly hadn't mentioned anything about the death of Nathaniel Cohen. Michael however did come quietly into the drawing room while everyone was having drinks before dinner.

'Michael, good to see you love; come and have a drink.'

'Sure Mum, it's good to see you too. Hi Dad. Say, what are you two doing here? Shouldn't you be slogging at your theses? I thought this was your last year. Shouldn't you two be sweating over personal contributions and original thoughts or something?'

'Hi Michael,' said Ted, 'Lester and I are just down for the weekend. Your Dad thought our original thoughts might benefit from some welcome R & R. Actually, seeing you are still supposed to be at Uni how come you're down here? Isn't it getting close to End-of-Term Exams as I remember?'

'You're memory is going Ted,' said Michael. 'I've only just re-registered but Dad wanted me down here to help solve some minor problem that has arisen with a client's software.'

'Let's not talk shop please,' said Sylvia, 'dinner's in fifteen minutes. We took Ted and Lester around the Estate today Michael. Ted particularly was interested in some of our "Canadian" trees and how well they grow here.'

'Seems they get a lot of TLC,' said Ted. 'We met Enrico and he explained some of the history of those particular trees. He explained that your father's grandmother had a lot to do with the original planting but he also went on to describe all the work that he and his brother had done. What was his name, Antonio, that's it?'

There was a moment of quiet in the room until Sir Anthony spoke. 'Yes, my grandmother was a remarkable lady. A couple of visits to Imperial India and she came back with a whole head full of new ideas. She really upset Alfred Templeton, the gamekeeper my grandfather had, but she had changed the Estate before he and grandfather came back from the war. Taught them all what she wanted and the plantations never looked back.'

'Dinner is served,' said Sylvia and she held Michael's arm and steered him into the dining room. The other three followed and Lester gave Ted a dig in the ribs as they went through the door. 'Stop stirring the pot old man,' he whispered, 'I think Michael is in enough shit as it is just watching his father's face. I think Sir Anthony is close to exploding at the moment. Let's just keep a lid on it eh?'

Although Sylvia had asked they not talk shop there was one brief item from Sir Anthony during dinner that Michael did pick up on. Ted had asked whether Brainware, Sir Anthony's software company had anything special in the works, anything in the research end. Perhaps because he knew that Michael had an interest in mathematics and problem solving Anthony Lord did briefly describe some of the work being done by Terry Dodds and Vernon Trelawney. Michael had noted how enthusiastic his father had sounded about this development. Even without going into any details the senior Lord hinted that this could be a major software scoop. What had really intrigued Michael was the fact that the little poofter Terry was the main architect.

After dinner Michael excused himself rather abruptly and disappeared. The other three men went back to the sitting room while Sylvia organized tea and coffee. In the quiet of the evening Sylvia spent a lot of time talking with Ted and Lester, mostly about where they came from in Canada and what they intended to do when they had finished post-graduate work. Neither of the two young men had really thought through exactly what they wanted to do and it was an interesting evening exploring possibilities. Sir Anthony was fairly quiet through all these discussions, as if thinking something else over in his mind. He was quite glad Sylvia had sensed she had better be the leading talker that evening.

English Public Schools with boys in charge of boys, with dormitories, changing rooms, and corporal punishment all make for a hot bed of homosexuality. In reality it happens but it is not prevalent. In fact it is not necessarily the norm. Some boys go through this as a phase of life and some boys find it abhorrent from day one. Michael found it gross, but he also found he could use knowledge of the lifestyle to pressure any bumboys. And finding Terry Dodds, an insipid bumboy of the limpest kind was the creative genius behind his dad's new software project was a piece of information of value.

The Annual Meeting of the shareholders of Brainware Pty Co. was scheduled for late November and Anthony Lord wanted to showboat the new product from Terry and Vernon at this meeting. It would be an innovative new step for the company. Typically the day after the shareholders' meeting Anthony Lord would host a news conference where he would release to the media the highlights of the company. Vernon Trelawney had produced a brochure outlining the capabilities of the search engine and the simplicity of the user-interface for both the meeting and that news conference.

After a weekend of keeping out of his father's way and thinking through some possibilities Michael purposefully entered Brainware's offices early Monday morning. Michael had found out that his father would be in a meeting with Ted and Lester first thing and that he would be safe visiting the research lab. With everyone in the offices now realizing that after Geoffrey's death Michael was potentially their new boss Michael felt he could dominate things. He wanted to know something but not through any direct approach. He thought a little name-dropping would impress researchers like Vernon and so Michael wandered unhurriedly into Vernon's workspace.

'Heh, I met a big wheel from Silicon Valley last weekend when I was at Foster Faxon's place,' said Michael as he ghosted into Vernon's office. Vernon with his head still thinking about linked structures sort of grunted. 'This guy's really into graphics. He heads up Future Graphics. Stanley Rogers, you know him?'

Michael's words still zoomed past the top of Vernon's head. 'He has some neat three-dimensional images combining data from satellites with ground-based map data.'

Vernon gave up trying to concentrate on his immediate problem and swiveled round in his chair to face Michael. 'Michael, who are you trying to impress? So why should I be interested? Terry and I have some really intensive work to do and I don't need the interruption. Capisce?'

'Vernon, this is important to the Company, my Company, and yeah, well, you know this guy Rogers was kind of interested in what you are doing.'

'Michael, this project is not in the public domain. It is still a secret so to speak. And I can tell you that Terry would be incensed if you go bandying it about. Actually, your Dad would be pretty pissed too if he heard you had been speaking out of school, and if I remember correctly it is his Company.'

'Okay, okay, keep your hair on. I didn't tell him anything technical.'

'Well don't, nor to anyone else. Terry wants to publish this. He thinks it might win us an award, sort of Developers Medal of the year. He is very protective of his baby and it really is neat work. Have you seen the new piece that Terry has just tested?'

Michael's mind gently focussed and he said, 'no, I haven't seen the most recent version.'

'Well, now we are up to Version 3.0 and this was a major leap from V2.3. We think this Version 3.0 will be the production Version 1.0 Release software package. It really hums along. I've just finished the media release notes with some examples for your father.'

Michael watched as Vernon quickly launched into Version 3.0 of "SearchLord". Vernon talked as he demonstrated some simple searches and then gradually made the questions more complex. The data had to come from numerous databases scattered throughout the U.K. and the answers could be compiled into tables, written text, or even simple map formats if needed. The response times were fast and for a couple of questions Vernon demonstrated that the data could be fed into other more complex mathematical analyses in spreadsheet format, or regression analyses and even linear programming if needed.

'How does that grab you?' said Vernon enthusiastically.

'And you've written all this up in a simple form for the media?' asked Michael.

'Yes. Terry and I quite like what we've written and your father has approved the first draught. We've bounced it off a couple of other systems analysts in the company and they thought it was good.'

'Yes, that's okay for techies,' said Michael. 'What about lay readers? What about the great unwashed who we want to use this product? Will they understand all the techie-talk?'

'We covered that,' said Vernon. 'We let Sally Peters in the marketing department write up a lay description of what she saw and what she understood SearchLord could do. She wrote it up for marketing, in simple English. I checked that Sally had seen and understood what was really happening.'

'And did SearchLord's mother like the description of her baby?' asked Michael sarcastically.

'Heh, mothers are possessive. They are rarely happy with other people's description of their offspring. In fact Terry wants to write up his own version of SearchLord's capabilities. He keeps trying to do this but every time I ask to see what he has written he goes coy.'

'Hell, if he won't share it with you then who will ever see this other love of his life? I thought you were the love of his life Vernon? Leastways, the cock for the mother hen' said Michael crudely.

Vernon's face went red, and just as quickly went black.

'Tread carefully Michael. One of these days your mouth will say too much. Your past may well come back to haunt you when you least expect it.'

'Piss off Vernon. Everyone knows Terry takes great delight in being reamed by you; front, back and sideways. There's a cartoon going round of you with a keyboard strapped to your knees.'

'And what's that supposed to mean?'

'It's so Terry can kneel down and suck your cock at the same time as keying instructions. It's entitled "Entry work and play" but no-one is sure which is work and which is play.'

'Get out Michael. Take your twisted mind elsewhere.'

Down in the village Michael knocked softly on Tom Daley's door.

'Tom, you home? Can I come in?'

'Sure Michael. Got something for me?'

'You bet. Good stuff. Should help you fantasize for hours.'

'Come in then. Nobody's home. I was just chasing down some new porno sites. Some guy up in South Wales has some stuff from Thailand. Well, what have you got?'

Michael handed over a bag of high-grade grass. Tom smiled as he opened the bag and let some of the aroma waft into the room. He unfolded a couple of papers and expertly rolled two joints. A quick match and the aroma intensified as Tom inhaled deeply and the smoke seemed to issue out of his mouth, his nose, his ears, and from most of the rest of his body.

Before Tom got too far out Michael broached the real reason for his visit. Tom was a very tidy and skillful hacker. He found places few people were supposed to find and he did it without leaving many traces. Michael needed Tom's skills to get a copy of SearchLord, or rather the writeup. Packaged the right way Michael was going to get his revenge on the arrogant Vernon and castrate the wimpy Terry. Although, come to think of it you can't really castrate a queen, so perhaps it was rape the queen. Can a Lord rape a queen mused Michael? Just watch.

'Tom, I have a challenge for you; just something in return for the grass.'

'Sure man. Whatever. Lead me there.'

'Somewhere in our company database is a simple little essay by Sally Peters. She has a neat ass by the way. I need a copy without our systems logging the request.'

'Got any title this essay? Got any date? Never mind. That shouldn't be an issue. I was in your company's records the other day. Did you know that Trevor Moss was fiddling his expense accounts? Did you also know that the pig-faced Harry Robertson, the prim and proper accountant who sits on the Town Council and vetoes any Youth Centre in town is quietly siphoning money to Doris Tellman? He also visits her every Friday night.'

Normally Michael would have paid attention as all of this could be good to know, but his mind was already on the next phase of "SearchLord" by Michael Lord, the new way to do business.

Tom meanwhile was smoking contentedly while his fingers skipped constructively over the keyboard. Various jargon flashed across the monitor and Tom rambled on. 'Delia Chambers has over-extended herself in the Prisonware project,' he said. 'She has gone way over budget and she still hasn't got all of the bugs out. She's working on radio signals from prisoners patches, like a shackle, but she can't always be certain where the prisoner is.'

'That's the best way,' said Michael suddenly.

'What is?' asked Tom.

'What? No, sorry. I was thinking of something else. What were you saying about Trevor Moss?'

'Here you are,' said Tom as the laser printer quietly generated three crisp sheets. He handed them to Michael. Tom quickly returned to the keyboard to close up his hacking and leave no trace.

As Tom deftly returned to his original investigations of the delights of Thailand Michael read through the three sheets. 'Looks good. Looks really good,' muttered Michael.

'Yeah, some of them do look good,' agreed Tom. 'See number twelve. Now that's some....'

'Sure Tom. Got to go. People to see you know.'

'Whatever man. Stay cool.'

Opening the door of the cottage Michael walked out into the clean sunlight still dragging an aroma of grass in his clothes and hair. Well, I'm off to see the wizard, the wonderful wizard of WW the precious IIIrd. thought Michael as he steered his car back up to the Manor House. However, before we see the wizard we must do a little personal wizardry on this script.

To Michael's delight he found WW had sent him an email when he logged in at home. Contacts had been made in the U.S. and WW was awaiting the next move from Michael. Michael in fact made several moves but it was a month before the effect of these moves reached the local scene.

'You shit,' screamed Terry. 'You absolutely, despicable, fucking bastard. You thieving whore.'

'You cock-sucker?' queried Michael. 'No, can't be. You're the cock-sucker.'

Terry flung his meagre one hundred and twenty pounds at Michael with fingers hooked. 'Scratch my eyes out would you? Having a hissy fit! You'll wet your knickers.'

Michael didn't hear Vernon quietly come into the office. The first he knew of it was a ringing in the ears and he was picking himself up off the floor. Terry lashed out with his foot but Michael was quicker and twisted the slender ankle until Terry went sprawling.

Vernon grabbed the scruff of Michael's shirt and pulled mightily. 'Shirt-lifter, that's what you are,' gasped Michael as the collar tightened round his neck. 'That's as maybe, but I don't go round plagiarizing. I don't steal other people's work. I don't broadcast trade secrets.'

'Rapist, fucking rapist,' squealed Terry. 'Rape and pillage, that's all you know.'

'Get lost Michael. Get lost fast. I'm surprised your dad hasn't already seen the article.'

Vernon turned away from Michael and tried to console the sobbing, shuddering Terry. Dusting himself off Michael defiantly walked out of the room. That'll bloody teach 'em.

One month later the U.S. computer magazine published a letter of apology to their readers over a mis-representation of last month's article on SearchLord. It seems that Michael Lord was not the creator of this software product but merely the son of the Company's owner. The editor was sorry if this error created any misunderstandings. Unbeknownst to their readers the editor sent "end of contract" letters to WW the IIIrd. to tell him that his services were no longer required. The article had cost the magazine a lot of money and it had been an embarrassment, not the scoop promised by WW. Michael turned the fee for the article over in his hands and concluded that the day at Foster Faxon's house hadn't been so disastrous after all.

12

Exposure

Christina put Peter in his bed and lovingly tucked the covers around him. He was still awake and smiled gently up into his mother's face. 'Sleep sweetly little one,' she whispered and slowly backed out of the bedroom. She tiptoed softly downstairs and sat down in the kitchen. A gentle knock came on the back door. Christina rose and walked across the kitchen, wondering who was visiting this evening.

'Enrico, what a surprise, do come in.'

Enrico smiled and slowly walked into the warm kitchen.

'Come and sit yourself down. Can I get you something, a glass of wine perhaps?'

'No thank you Christina dear. I've just come for a brief moment, a question perhaps about Peter.'

'Surely Enrico, what can I tell you. We haven't seen you for a while and Peter has asked for you.'

'It has been hard Christina. I miss Antonio and I am somewhat at a loss. Still, as I said to Sylvia earlier in the year with Daniel, perhaps I should do something special, something different and so I had an idea.'

‘That sounds more like you Enrico. I understand it has been hard. I miss Geoffrey just like you with your brother, but as Sylvia told me we should look forwards and not backwards. How did she say it, “life is for the living” I think.’

‘So like Sylvia,’ said Enrico, ‘she dealt with her own son’s death, with Daniel’s loss and now with more strife in the family. Still, enough, let me ask about Peter. I would like to build something for him, like I did for his father, some toy or other. I wanted to know whether there was anything special that Peter liked? I know he is still young but is there something he is very attached to?’

Christina sat and thought for a while. This was so typical of Enrico. Geoffrey had told her of all the various toys that Antonio and Enrico had made for the Lord children, and for other children in the village. A smile came over her face and Enrico said, ‘you have thought of something?’

‘Yes,’ said Christina, ‘I believe I have. At the moment Peter is very excited about a paper, a map that he and Daniel found in the attic here.’

‘Ah si,’ said Enrico, ‘Daniel was showing me this map. We went and found where it might be on the Estate. It was up at the north end under the cliffs. There was a cave up there.’

‘Yes, Daniel came back very excited after the trip with you. He told me about the cave and believes the map shows where something is hidden. He said he was going to discreetly ask you about the old legend of “Lord Treasure”. He mentioned that his Great-Grandfather George had been excited about this with old Albert Templeton, the gamekeeper.’

‘Yes, yes,’ said Enrico, ‘I know the story too. Albert shared the story with his son Edward and with us. There was supposed to be old money that the Lord family hid way back in time. They had done something, probably illegal knowing a little bit about the family, leastways that’s what Albert said and his family had been gamekeepers here forever. Anyway, the money was hidden somewhere on the Estate but Albert didn't know where. George Lord did have a picture, in a book somewhere that showed part of the Estate and indicated approximately where this might be, but it was very vague.'

'Yes, we know about the big map. We found that too, along with this smaller map. The smaller map appears to show a specific cave, marked with a tree or something.'

'And, when I was out with Daniel looking at the bigger map we found a cave which really excited Daniel.'

'He didn't show you the smaller map?' asked Christina.

'No, he just got excited using the bigger map. He muttered something about a forked tree and wanted to explore the cave we found. I didn't see any other map.'

'Well we did find another map,' explained Christina, 'and that is why Daniel got so excited. The smaller map shows a cave and a forked tree outside it. Actually, it is this smaller map that has Peter excited. He found it really when exploring with Daniel in the attic; ever since he won't let go of it. In the end Daniel wisely made a coloured copy for Peter to play with and we kept the original safe from gummy teeth and grubby hands. This is why I smiled. I wondered if you could make a model of a cliff with a cave in it and a tree outside. The cave could have animals and people and perhaps some treasures. I'm sure Peter would love to play with a model version of his cave picture.'

As Sir Anthony had asked, Ted Crichton and Lester Donald had come down from Bristol University in early October to work on some corrections and enhancements to the software for Saad Brothers. The work was very successful and Sir Anthony was able to persuade Saad Brothers that this would take care of any concerns they might have about security. With some diplomatic telephoning and a personal visit up to London Sir Anthony also managed to re-establish good business relations with both Rosalind Townsend and between her and Saad Brothers. It had been a rather trying month but Sir Anthony worked hard to win back some confidence in his products and his clients. To ensure some technical re-assurances Sir Anthony even took Ted and Lester up to London to talk to the I.T. people at Saad Brothers and over to see Rosalind. By way of a show of thanks Sir Anthony invited Ted and Lester back down again to Fotheringham Manor. Lester begged off with pressure of post-graduate work. He said that he was stalling with his thesis and he needed some quiet thoughts but Ted accepted the offer gladly.

Daniel had managed to get a weekend at home, away from Bristol House School. Now he was in the Sixth form this was a little easier. Despite all of the nightmares of June and his brother's death Daniel had done well in his 'O' levels of GCSE. He had passed in eight subjects and had moved on into the Sixth form looking forward to some really useful schoolwork. However, he still wasn't too sure what he really wanted to do. Geography interested him in many ways, especially parts of it and so he carried that on into the Sixth. He still had an interest in animals but wasn't sure he was cut out to be a vet like his Aunt Stephanie. Just to hedge his bets he decided to do Botany and Zoology. Finally, Daniel had decided to do Geology in the Sixth Form. He argued to himself, and to his dad that this really was a special part of Geography. However, part of the reason he didn't explain was because Bristol House School had just hired a new master, Dr. Fergus MacRae, and Dr. MacRae was a very interesting character. Geology was going to be a very hands-on, out in the field sort of learning and that appealed to Daniel. He liked the outdoors but shied away from the competitive aspects of climbing and sailing. He'd had too much of brother Michael for that thank you very much.

So it was Daniel who took Ted out on horseback around the Estate that Saturday in early November. Ted was still interested in the trees and Daniel took him to see some other Canadian trees on the Estate.

'We have western hemlocks, western red cedar, and some Douglas firs as well as the white pines you saw last time.'

'How come they grow so well here?' asked Ted. Daniel laughed, and then coughed with embarrassment over what he was going to say and then laughed again. 'Well, 'he said, smiling into his hand, 'we look after them. Think of it this way. We have so few of them and the area is so small that we almost know each of them by name. Whereas in Canada, if I understand my geography correctly Ted, you have square kilometers of them, farther than the eye can see. We can ride through our Estate in an hour whereas it would take you over an hour in a plane to cover some of the forests in Canada. It's all a matter of scale, plus of course you don't have the TLC that comes from someone like Enrico. He cares for them like they are his children, and in some ways they are.'

'How is Enrico by the way?' asked Ted. 'I know about the accident and how torn up he was over the loss of his brother but has he recovered?'

'Yes, a little,' answered Daniel. 'Actually we have found a rather exciting new project together and this has helped lift his spirits. If truth be told it was little Peter who found the project when we were tidying up some papers in the attic. I was helping clean out some of the papers of Geoffrey's and I had turned it into a game for Peter. Peter tried to upend some boxes and succeeded in spilling the contents out all over the floor, and low and behold we found some treasure.'

'Fine, I understand all that but where does Enrico fit into this discovery?'

'Okay, bear with me a moment as this is somewhat involved. Let's see if I can get it right. Peter found a map, actually two maps in this pile of papers. When we sorted the papers out Christina and I think they describe some sailing ship's cargoes of long ago and the money that came from the cargoes. Back when we had this money, sometime in 1790 or so, something happened to the family and they decided to bury the money.

The rumour was that the money was buried somewhere on the Estate. Now the maps might show us where.'

'I'm with you so far Daniel. Help me with the connection to Enrico.'

'I'm coming to that. Just be patient. I said it was involved. Back around 1920 Great Grandfather George found a map in one of the books in the library. He thought it described somewhere in the Estate. He showed it to Albert Templeton our gamekeeper but neither of them did anything about it. Albert told his son Edward and he in turn told Antonio and Enrico about the map and the rumour. Now Enrico knows the Estate very well and so when I showed him one of the maps he thought he could recognize where this was. He and I went there a couple of weeks ago now. I hadn't shown Enrico the little map at this time.'

'There were two maps then?' asked Ted, 'two maps that Peter found?'

'Yes. To start with Christina and I didn't want to share this information until we had got all the facts right. I mean the whole thing might be a hoax or a dead-end, or absolutely nothing. So, we kept the second little map secret. But when Enrico took me to where he thought the map showed at the northern end of the Estate I got very excited because it matched the little map. I came home and told Christina what we had found. We'd found the cave of the little map.'

'And you went into this cave?'

'No, Enrico was working and we didn't have torches or anything so we left it. I came home and told Christina. Anyway, to continue, Enrico came round to Christina's and wanted to do something for Peter. He wanted to make him some special toy and he asked Christina what particularly interested Peter. Christina told Enrico about the little map and showed him. I had made Peter a coloured copy as Peter wouldn't let go of the map and I thought the original would get damaged. So, Christina asked Enrico to make a model of the cave, and the forked tree, and a special treasure chest with lots of animals and people. Enrico loves working with wood and he learnt a little how to work with stone from Antonio, and so he is making a model.'

'So you haven't been to the cave yet, or even inside?'

'No, I haven't had time being away at school and I still want to keep it a secret. Michael's back home now and if he heard about it he'd have someone up there right away digging everything up. I want to check quietly to see if it's real before brother Michael invades the scene. Anyway, to come back to your original question, Enrico is now all excited about making this model for Peter and this is helping him forget the sorrow over his brother.'

Ted filed the story away and the conversation changed to other areas about the Estate. Daniel was very familiar with most of the forestry work and Ted thought he would make a better manager than his older brother, even though Daniel was only sixteen. That Sunday Ted drove back to Bristol University mulling over some of the things he had learnt that weekend at Fotheringham; some interesting thoughts. Back in Bristol Ted had a long discussion with Lester.

The same weekend that Ted Crichton was going round the Forest Estate Melanie Rogers had driven down to Fotheringham Manor from London. With Michael having no legal driving licence and his father banning him from being up in town Michael was grounded down in Somerset. Melanie wanted to have a long talk with Michael about their future. She was getting a little frustrated with Michael's somewhat cavalier attitude and the rumours about other women.

'Michael, can we set a date or something? Daddy and Mummy are going to want plenty of warning about a big wedding, and I will want to have many of my friends over from California. This is my special day Michael, you know that?'

'Sure Melanie, in fact, yes Melanie darling. How about sometime next spring? Let's make a big announcement just after New Years, at a big party up in London. I've arranged for us to go to a terrific New Year's Eve bash in the West End. We'll need a couple of days to recover from that and then we can have your parents host a formal party with the announcement.'

'That's wonderful Michael.' Melanie danced around Michael, 'a spring wedding, a spring wedding, how truly heavenly. Oo, I've just remembered something Michael. I knew there was another important thought somewhere in my little head.'

'And very delightful it is too,' said Michael gently stroking Melanie's cheeks. 'You give the most delightful head,' whispered Michael. 'Hush Michael, don't be so crude. Now I've forgotten what I was going to say.'

'That doesn't matter,' said Michael, 'now that you have the right thought in your head. Let's go upstairs for some head to tail talk.'

'Michael, forget it for the moment. I'm trying to remember.'

'I'm sure my cock can stimulate your tongue cells to remember what to say,' Michael said as he ran his hands up and down Melanie's body.

'Shit, cut it out for a second. Heh, I've remembered. You promised me something ages ago Michael and I want you to do it.'

'But that's what I want to do. I want to do it. I keep trying to persuade you that's what you want too.'

Melanie stepped back and looked at Michael. 'For one second hold your horses or something and listen up. Back in the summer you promised me you would take Rodney hiking in the mountains when he came over from California. Well he's over here now at school just outside London. He's having a great time and he has found rugby a lot more exciting than football was back home. Anyway, that's not the point. He's been out walking around the Downs with Chuck Faxon and the two of them are thinking of going up to the mountains somewhere at the end of the month. I told Rodney you would go as you know the area and where's best. So Michael, can I get you to talk with Rodney this weekend and sort out some details? I told him I would call him on Sunday morning. You promised Michael.'

'It's a thought,' said Michael, 'in fact anything to get out of this place for a while. I feel like a school kid who's been grounded stuck down here. Look, I'll tell Dad that I'm not going up to London but going on to Snowdonia. I still can't drive you know so I'll have to come up by train. Of course, you could always come down here and collect me.'

'Christ Michael, you never put yourself out do you? Okay, sure I'll come down and get you and take you up to Rodney but you find your own way home you lazy devil.'

'That's me gorgeous, a devil, now come and give us a kiss.' Michael stepped forwards to grab hold of Melanie but she twirled quicker than Michael.

Sylvia Lord didn't really approve, but then it was the 1990s and so she didn't say anything. Letting Melanie sleep in Michael's room and Michael's bed wasn't the end of the world and Melanie was a nice girl, for an American that is. Anthony had explained to Sylvia that girls from California were not like any other girls, especially when he was at Berkley in the 1960s. Sylvia gave Anthony a hard time asking him how Anthony knew this as he always said he was working too hard on his PhD to "turn on and tune out". Just trust me love Anthony had said.

After an intimate night and a languid sensual lie-in Michael was in a friendly frame of mind on Sunday morning. Melanie was also pretty dreamy as she stirred her coffee and played with a piece of toast. Meredith the butler broke her reverie by stating that there was a call for Miss Rogers and would she like to take it in the hall? Rodney hadn't waited for his elder sister to call, knowing what she was like early in the morning and so he had called to check on progress. Melanie came back from the hall and after a kiss and a cuddle gently led Michael back to the telephone.

'Friday the 28th we can leave in the early afternoon and be up in Snowdonia around late evening. I'll book us to stay at a pub in Bangor and we can play the weekend from there. Melanie's going to drive me up to your place on Friday. I'll bring my own gear and I'll assume that both of you are kitted out okay. I don't know exactly what we'll do as it will depend on the weather. What's that? You've already got an idea of what you want to do? Walking over the Carneddau. Yes, that's fine. You want to go in from Aber and do a loop over all of them? Oh, you've looked at the map and worked out a route already. That's great. Seems you have this all set up. Chuck's hiked before I understand? He has, shit that's a long way to go, the whole length of the Appalachians. Anyway Rodney, I promised Melanie I would look after the pair of you. You know, be the guide like as I know the area. Just a sec., Melanie wants a word.'

Melanie took the phone from Michael and chatted about family things with Rodney. She told him that Michael was looking forward to the trip and that the three of them should have a blast. A real guy thing she said, not my kind of trip at all. She hung up and stood there in the hall thinking. No, she thought, not my kind of trip at all. Wonder whether Michael will really enjoy it after what Rodney has told me.

That next week Ted and Lester arranged to go into Brainware's offices and talk with Vernon and Terry. The Annual Meeting of the shareholders of the Company was scheduled for the end of the month and some of the work of all these four men was part of the agenda. Ted and Lester led the discussions on the security transaction work that they had worked upon. They also explained the events at Saad Brothers and Vernon and Terry understood a little more why Michael was unceremoniously hauled down from London.

'So that's why the little shit suddenly arrived in our offices,' said Vernon. 'He came in throwing his weight about saying he had been touting for business with some high flyers.'

'High flyers bollocks,' said Terry viciously, 'he's nothing but a bloody parasite. He stole my project. Tried to grab all the glory as if it was his own idea. We worked on that, didn't we Vernon love?'

'That's as maybe Terry,' said Lester 'but no one really got hurt did they?'

'Not hurt,' screamed Terry, 'all my lovely work broadcast to the world as a brilliant idea of Michael bloody Lord. Christ, it was professional rape.'

'Yes, okay Terry, but just think what happened with poor Rosalind Cohen with Nathaniel hanging himself,' said Ted.

'Not to mention Michael's earlier bloody mess with poor Nicole Masters. She's even worse off.'

'So, are we going to sit around here listing Michael's efforts at living?'

'No Vernon. I learnt something this past weekend when I was down at Fotheringham Manor with young Daniel.'

'Now he's a Lord I can live with,' said Vernon. 'He's a thoughtful lad.'

Terry looked at Vernon rather jealousy and said rather spitefully, 'pretty too isn't he?'

'Terry, just cut it out and listen. We all need to think about the possibilities of cutting Michael off at the knees somehow. Daniel explained that Geoffrey's son Peter had found an old map and that Daniel had subsequently found where this is on the Estate.'

'So, is this precious map worth money or something?' asked Terry, 'cos if it isn't worth anything Michael won't be interested.'

'Well, it maybe,' said Ted, 'but let me explain further and you might get some ideas. The map shows a cave, which Daniel has found by the way and the cave seems to be the site where the Lord family buried some money a long time ago.'

'Shit, I can't see bloody lazy Michael digging up supposed treasure in an old cave. That's too much like hard work.'

'Agreed, but suppose the money actually is there, and, just suppose Michael is really in desperate need of money.'

'So Ted, how do we engineer both these suppositions?' asked Vernon.

'Well, Lester and I discussed this yesterday evening and Lester had one idea that would help. Tell them Lester.'

'We all work with software, don't we? Plus, we're all pretty good at it. Can't we rig some scam operation to suck Michael into debt? As an example, can't we gamble under Michael's name and suck him into deep shit with the bookies? They come on heavy and Michael is looking for instant money. If we do it cleverly Michael can't go running to Sir Anthony. We can probably lean on Michael's friend in the village not to play silly buggers with the Company's money.'

'You mean Tom Daley?'

'Yes, that's who. I think we know enough about Tom Daley to keep his mouth shut, or his hands off the keyboard at least.'

'So, we suck Michael into debt. Yeah, that shouldn't be too hard for us but won't Michael find out quickly?'

'Not if we set it up with the bookies as a secret thing that Michael doesn't want to hear about for a couple of weeks as if he knows it is a sure thing. Anyway, I think Sir Anthony is sort of banishing Michael somewhere for a couple of weeks so he won't be anywhere near the Annual Meeting.'

'What about the other half of the supposition? How do we let Michael know about this apparent treasure and why would he bother to go and get it?'

'Well, another thought Lester and I had was to secretly leak it that it should belong to little Peter, or Christina, or perhaps Daniel who found the cave. Michael thinks he is the heir apparent to the Lord fortune and couldn't stand the idea that anyone else in the family should get this money. He'll want to lay his hands on it first. Anyway, these were some ideas to share with you. Lester and I have got to get back to Bristol but we can come down again next Thursday. We have to come down anyway to finalise the presentations for the Annual Meeting. We'll leave you with those thoughts.'

Ted and Lester left and Vernon and Terry looked at each other. There was an air of positive excitement in the room. 'Ted's right you know. Perhaps we could actually do something to upset our precious Lord.'

'Yes Vernon,' said Terry, 'and without doing the Company any more damage. Sir Anthony has been good to us.'

'And we've been good for him too,' said Vernon. 'So, let's get the Company presentations fixed first. We have something really good to explain to the shareholders. Most of them won't have read any U.S. computer magazines and so they won't know about the premature leak. It will be ours to show off.'

Terry leant over and kissed Vernon, 'sure,' he said, 'ours.'

That same Monday morning a different kind of presentation was taking place in London's West End. Foster Faxon was back in London and promoting some of his company's capabilities with a view to getting a foot in the European market. Some of his media people were graphic artists and in the digital world a new form of "art" was emerging. Foster had been talking over this kind of promotion for some time with Stanley

Rogers and the two Americans had combined the talents of some of their staff. Using graphic terminals there were a series of presentations of generating both abstract art with three-dimensional shapes through fractals and then some more life-like art with free-hand graphic drawing of people, animals, and still life. Some of the creations were frozen on the screen and spun off to a large printer to produce hard copy. It was a sort of visual art creation workshop using today's technology.

The setting for this presentation was a large West End Gallery that Mr. Faxon had hired for the week. It was well lit with high ceilings and pale coloured walls. The computer graphic screens were linked to large display panels so the various attendees did not have to crowd around a workstation. The atmosphere was airy, light, and somewhat surreal. Likewise the people circulating around the gallery, gently holding their flutes of champagne were an eclectic crowd. There were young people in an array of bright colours. Clothing ranged from chic to bohemian. One or two older more conservative people also circulated, although calling Lady Diana Worthing conservative was perhaps misleading.

'Now what in hell do you call that Vanessa?' came the strident voice of Lady Diana. 'Looks like my dead hound's guts when he got caught up on the fence.'

'Mummy, hush, it's art. Think of it as an abstract pattern of colours rather than some precious life form. Try and see the bigger picture.'

'Tosh, bunch of bloody faeries; should take 'em out and let them see real life.'

'Lady Worthing, so good to see you. How are you enjoying this rather modern form of art, or rather media presentation?'

'Foster, good to see you too. Just saying to Vanessa here that some of your employees could do with a good dose of real life don't you know. Do any of them ever get out into the real world, or do you tie them down to these robots all the time?'

'Lady Worthing, Vanessa will tell you that some of the operators are not only artists but do have outside lives. In fact Celia over there rides as often as she can and Carl, the blond giant doing the still life, spends all of his spare time rowing on the Thames. So, I do let my guys out into the big wide world.'

'Huh, perhaps they've got split personalities because you'd never think so looking at some of the daubs hanging on the walls. Vanessa what are you looking at now?'

'Actually Mummy I was looking at Carl; quite a hunk isn't he?'

'Wash your mouth out daughter. Please remember to speak English, at least when you are in England. Hunk is slang, common, not even appropriate for a piece of cheese. Still, as you say, Carl is good to look at. Say he's a rower Foster? Isn't that what your son does? What's his name Vanessa?'

'His name's Chuck Mummy, as well you know.'

'Yes, Charles.'

'No Mummy, it is Chuck. It isn't short for Charles it's straightforward Chuck.'

'Yes Lady Worthington, Chuck is a rower; plays rugby too, a wing three-quarter.'

'Excellent, excellent. Good hard working position with lots of action, hard tackles, plenty of drive eh?'

'He certainly enjoys it. It keeps him fit.'

'He'll need to be fit later, at the end of the month,' came a fourth voice. Stanley Rogers joined the group. 'I hear he's going hiking with Rodney eventually.'

'Yes, the two of them have been planning this for some time and eventually they've got themselves organised to go later this month. I heard they were going somewhere up in Wales, somewhere near Aber something. When Chuck showed me the map I couldn't read half the place names let alone pronounce them. They were planning to walk over the Carneggies or some such mountains. Whatever they are they are a lot lower than the Appalachians back home.'

'Don't let the altitude fool you,' said Lady Worthing, 'this time of year you could get snow in Snowdonia. It'll look a little different from the Appalachians too; not many trees up on the tops.'

'Well Rodney has hiked up high above the tree line in Colorado, as well as the top end of Yosemite. He's seen bare tops, and snow too even in the summer.'

'Good to hear them both getting out wherever,' said Lady Worthing.

'Wherever they are going they had better be extra careful,' added Vanessa.

'Why's that?' asked Stanley Rogers.

'Well,' said Vanessa, 'perhaps you don't know but Melanie has persuaded Rodney to take Michael Lord along. Apparently Anthony Lord wants Michael out of the office this month, and not up in London, and so Melanie asked Rodney to let him join them. Michael knows the area well and so he can show them the highlights.'

'I'd like to show Michael Lord some highlights,' said Lady Worthing, 'in fact I'd like him to see lights, stars in front of his eyes if I get hold of him.'

Vanessa smiled at her mother. 'Actually Mummy, I believe Rodney and Chuck have a few surprises for Master Lord. Both of them are quite capable of looking after themselves and keeping away from any of Michael's mad ideas. Oo, there's another thing I learnt last week about Master Lord's mad ideas; he has a black mistress and child.'

'And child?' said Lady Worthington imperiously, 'tell all.'

'Did you know that Michael has a son?'

'What,' exclaimed Stanley Rogers, 'he's not married, never been married?'

'Yes, but I don't expect such trivialities have ever been any concern of Master Lord,' said Lady Worthing.

'But he's engaged to my daughter,' said Stanley Rogers.

'You might want to think about talking to Melanie on that subject,' said Vanessa. 'When we learnt about little Anthony Lord and his precious black mother Danielle Made, Melanie wasn't overjoyed.'

'Anthony Lord, the cheeky bugger,' said Stanley Rogers, 'to name his son after his father.'

'Now I don't think that was Michael's idea,' said Vanessa, 'in fact I don't think Michael knew much about it until the baby was born and Danielle tried to blackmail Michael into marriage.'

'How do you find out about such things Vanessa? With whom have you been talking? Where did you find this little black bimbo?'

'Okay. Question one: I was at a party with Melanie a week ago and who should be there but David Frinton.'

'He's the artist from Zimbabwe isn't he? Does sculpting, very impressive and powerful.'

'Yes, he does, but he's also a singer and he was at this party really to sing. Anyway, Melanie knows him.'

'Yes, that's right,' said Stanley Rogers, 'Melanie was with David Frinton in a car accident earlier this year. Fortunately she and David weren't badly hurt.'

'Yes, yes,' tut tutted Lady Worthing, 'but go on about the baby.'

'Well, question two: I was talking with David Frinton and he had been talking with Danielle Made.'

'Funny sort of name,' said Lady Worthington, 'but then we don't know any black people.'

'Danielle is from Mozambique: came over with her mother about three years ago. Apparently she has known Michael for some time. Anyway, she wanted to get Michael to marry her and so she got pregnant.'

'But Michael wouldn't have any of it?' asked Stanley Rogers.

'No, but Danielle isn't a person who takes no for an answer. I think she's just waiting for the right moment to spring some trap. Her child's turned one now and she's still seeing Michael. In fact, David Frinton mentioned that Danielle is living somewhere down in Somerset close to Michael.'

'Well, I think I need to find my daughter and have a serious heart to heart with her,' said Stanley Rogers. 'Precious Michael Lord has some explaining to do.'

'Well gentlemen, I might not have found the art very stimulating but the conversation has been quite illuminating. At times Vanessa you really amaze me. You do seem to meet the most bizarre people.'

'Just like to keep you on your toes Mummy,' said Vanessa, and the two women wheeled away arm in arm.

'Dangerous couple of women there Foster,' said Stanley Rogers.

'Yes, and let's trust that our two sons are an equally dangerous couple,' added Foster Faxon.

Back at Fotheringham Manor Michael was surprised to find Christina in the library poring over several large old and dusty tomes. She was very purposefully flicking through pages and tap-tapping her foot with impatience.

'Can I help?' asked Michael. 'Don't think I've ever seen you in the library Christina. Is there something special you are looking for?'

'Oh Michael, you startled me coming in quietly like that; almost like a cat prowling about.'

'Yes, little sister-in-law, I'm a very possessive Tiger and always making sure I get what's mine, and so, as I so politely asked before, what are you looking for amongst the Lord archives?'

'Nothing Michael, I was just interested in something Daniel had said.'

'And what, specifically, had young Daniel said?' asked Michael, still sounding very polite.

'Nothing to do with you Michael,' said Christina adamantly, stamping her foot and looking Michael right in the eyes. 'It was a private matter between Daniel and me.' She slammed the book shut and placed it carefully back on the shelves. Very deliberately she collected the other books off the table and similarly relocated them in their correct places. Almost in slow motion she moved graciously out of the library without another glance at Michael.

Michael let his eyes slowly traverse the beautifully paneled and comfortable room of the library. 'I could fit in here very nicely,' said Michael to the room, 'but I wonder what Daniel has found? Christina was certainly looking for something.'

'Looking for what Michael?' asked Sir Anthony as he strode into the library. 'Talking to yourself is not a good sign Michael and I was looking for you anyway. In fact, what are you doing here as opposed to work? Tuesday today isn't it? I thought we'd agreed that you would do a tour of the forest Estate every Tuesday morning. In fact I thought we'd agreed that you would see Ferris off at seven thirty with the work crews and then follow up with an inspection. What happened to the agreement Michael? This place doesn't run itself you know and Norton Ferris doesn't run anything. In fact I'm very close to firing him and his two useless sons. Not sure why....'

'Hold on Dad. Stop a minute and draw a breath. First, I did see Norton Ferris and the men off this morning but after that I got sidetracked and came looking for something I thought I had left in the library. When I came in here Christina rudely rebuffed me. That lady gets up my nose sometimes Dad. She acts as if she's the lady of the Manor.'

'Okay Michael, that's enough. Christina had asked me whether she could come and look for something in the library. She had been talking with Daniel about some papers of your Great Grandfather George. Daniel said that Peter had found something when they were going through Geoffrey's old papers and Daniel discussed it with Christina.'

'Whatever could Peter have found that is interesting? He's only one year old for God's sake.'

'Christina didn't tell me all the details. Daniel had come to show me something earlier and I mentioned that grandfather had a picture in a book that looked very similar.'

'Similar to what? Anyway, anything found in Home Farm belongs to us. I should know about it.'

'Michael, leave it. I came to tell you that I want you out of the House and away from here over the last week of the month. The shareholders' Annual Meeting is being held then and I want you out of sight, especially after that fracas at Saad Brothers, and then the leak over SearchLord. Hopefully none of the shareholders will know about that leak anyway, but if you're not around there will be fewer questions. So, not up to London and not around here, understood?'

'Shit Dad, you can't do this. I belong here. In fact it will all be mine someday. Remember what I expect on my twenty-first birthday; Geoffrey's shares of the Company and a rewrite of your will. And just to remind you, it's next month that I turn twenty-one.'

'Michael, I'm getting very pissed off. In fact I'm about to get bloody angry. You know the rules. Inheritance in the Lord family passes from eldest son to eldest son. Translated that means me to Geoffrey to Peter.'

'Christ Dad, move into the twentieth century at least. You pride yourself that our Company looks to the twenty-first century and you still have your feet back one hundred years.'

'Enough Michael enough; out now and go and check on the forest. For once in your bloody life do as you are told. And I mean it about the end of the month. I'll talk to your mother about your birthday but for now go!'

Just to make sure he had the last word Michael spun on his heel and shouted back over his shoulder, 'I'm off to Snowdonia anyway at the end of the month. I'm taking precious Rodney Rogers and Chuck Faxon hiking in the hills, so I won't be embarrassing you by cluttering up the bloody shareholders' meeting.'

Michael stormed out of the library. Sir Anthony stood calmly in the middle of the room and looked around him. The trials and tribulations of the Lord family he thought. Some of it is written in the books all around me. Wonder what it was that Christina was looking for? That map that Daniel had I do seem to remember when I was a boy; in this room too. Granddad was quite excited for a while and what was it he said, "but we don't need the money now anyway; let it lie." Edward was here too if I remember. He kept apologizing for the mud off his boots on the carpet but granddad didn't care. The two of them were looking at a map. Granddad called me over and showed me something. "See here son, another hidden part of your inheritance." Something like that, but I can't remember. Still, mustn't stand here all day, work to do. Sir Anthony turned and briskly left the library to its normal quiet and secrets.

In the village, Enrico pushed open the door of the general store. The bell jangled as always as the door closed behind him.

'Morning Enrico, and how are we today?' Mrs. Larkin pushed a lock of hair away from her glasses and smiled warmly at Enrico. 'It's a fine morning for November; touch of frost to loosen the last of the leaves off the trees. Things'll be pretty quiet up in the forest now this time of year I expect?'

'That's true Mrs. Larkin,' replied Enrico. 'There is nothing much on this morning and so I have come in for a little shopping. I just need a few things and I'll place an order for delivery on Friday if that's all right.'

'To be sure Enrico. I'll make sure young Tommy brings the order up on Friday. Actually he likes coming up to your cottage. You're always doing something special there he says; making toys and such for the kids.'

'It passes the time Mrs. Larkin, and keeps my hands from hurting too much with the arthritis. Keeping the fingers active helps the joints from seizing up.'

'Tommy tells me you're making something special for young Master Peter, with lots of model people and animals.'

'Young Tommy talks too much, but yes, something Mrs. Christina told me. She said Peter was interested in a special treasure he found with Daniel, but I'm supposed to keep it secret.'

'Safe with me it is Enrico. By the way, talking of secrets, did you hear who was living in the old caravan up above the quarry?'

'No Mrs. Larkin, I'm not much for gossip. It won't concern me.'

'Aw, that's where you're wrong Enrico, 'cos it does concern you, or at least it should.'

'Why so?'

'Well, I've been told, and I've also seen it with my own eyes, there's a young girl living in the caravan, with a baby no less.'

'There's nothing special in that.'

'But there is,' whispered Mrs. Larkin, 'here's the interesting part, she's black.'

'Black?' said Enrico, 'what's a young black girl doing living down here? There's nobody black here. There's no black men, leastways not that I know of.'

'Well, I told you it should concern you because the man in this case is Master Michael. I'm told that the baby is his.'

'Get away.'

'True as I'm standing here. Old Dora Telford who runs the Post Office told Mrs. Bibcott. The girl was in there the other day getting stamps and asking about child support forms or something. Anyway, her name is Danielle Made; at least I think that's what she said. Dora was chatting up the baby making coochy-coochy noises and such, and this Danielle said the baby's name is Anthony. Bold as brass she told Dora; Michael Lord was the father and that they were going to get married soon.'

'I don't believe it.'

'Well, that's what I heard. So, the other morning I happened to pass by the caravan on my way here like.'

'Mrs. Larkin you live here!'

'So, I had to see for myself you know. Opens the door herself as I pass by. Says "Good Morning" as bright as a blackbird. Holding the little one by the hand she was. I'd say he was about one. Walking like but not too steady on his feet yet. So, as I told you, young Michael's son is sitting on the front steps of his dad's house. Come to think of it, wasn't Michael supposed to be engaged to some American girl? They were down here earlier in the year, last winter with that sad accident up at the House. Somebody said then that she was Michael's fiancée. Not the one that got killed like, but the other girl. Her dad came in the shop I remember. He had a funny voice and told me he was from California. Said my shop was quaint. Smart man he was and well spoken.'

Enrico stood silently listening to Mrs. Larkin go on. Quietly he let himself out of the store and it was only the jangling bell that brought Mrs. Larkin out of her monologue. Suddenly she realized that Enrico had left.

Well, there's a thing she said to herself, just when I was telling him something interesting. Funny old man he is to be sure. Forgotten to leave me his order too he has. The death of his brother has made him a little senile too soon. Perhaps he needs a good woman to take care of him she thought.

Back in London, away from the slow pace of the village, Rosalind Cohen was trying to organize some security procedures for a special art exhibition. When she saw the pictures of much of the art she wasn't quite sure why anybody would need security. The sculpted pieces were big enough to look after themselves she thought. Still, the client said there were some smaller pieces, which had religious and political significance and they needed to be protected.

After two relatively successful five year plans in the newly created, or perhaps reborn country of Zimbabwe, Robert Mugabe still had a problem. Every five years, with or without any plan, there was a drought, and sometimes the drought stayed for two or even three years. People went hungry and people died. Despite help from Red China with money for hospitals and clinics people died. China also purchased most of the main tobacco export, because everyone smokes in China, and yet still Zimbabwe was not going forward as planned.

David Frinton, like his President Robert Mugabe was Shona, and passionate about the future of his country. David's mother and her people came from Mutare in the eastern part of Zimbabwe. David's maternal grandfather had fought against the control wielded by the English, and he had also fought against the old tribal enemy, the Ndbele. In his own way as an artist David's grandfather had created strong symbols defending his culture and way of life. David had inherited this talent. Through his white father, who had been a tobacco farmer, and the strong personality of his mother, David's talent had further developed until he became recognized internationally. Now David was trying to give something back to his country. He had put together an exhibition to raise money to help offset famine and starvation. It wasn't a very big exhibition and David had gone to a small firm to provide security.

'We'll provide overall security for the exhibition room itself and the surrounding building. We'll also have some staff patrolling the area, complete with radio communications. We'll install a metal detector if you think that is necessary, although we'll make it look like something else. You've seen our brochure and so you know what we can provide. Shall I draw up a Proposal complete with prices?'

Rosalind sat back in her chair and regarded this large black man opposite. He was a force to be reckoned with she thought. Not a man to mess with. David was reading through the brochure again and thinking about the various aspects he might need.

'How come you came to us?' Rosalind asked. 'We're a very small company and usually work in the digital and financial world. I'm surprised in a way you didn't go to one of the companies who usually handle exhibitions like yours.'

David smiled. 'It's a long story but in a way it's a meeting of two people who have lost someone recently.'

Rosalind looked puzzled. 'I'm sorry,' said David, 'I'm not being very clear. Earlier this year I was out to a charity concert where I was singing for children.'

'I didn't know you sang as well as sculpted,' said Rosalind.

'Yes, well, I was lucky and inherited some wonderful talents from my parents. I just want to share them with people, and where I can give something back.'

'That's a noble and beautiful gesture,' said Rosalind.

'At this concert I lost a good friend. She died. As a result I found out a little more about the man who caused the accident. I didn't know him before and don't really want to know him again, but I did learn, through a mutual friend, a Melanie Rogers, that you too had been an acquaintance of Mister Michael Lord, and that you too had suffered a loss at his hand.'

'Don't you mention that name in this office,' said Rosalind, 'he's a nobody, or he should be a nobody.'

'True,' said David, 'anyway it struck me that you would be more sympathetic and understanding about my cause than anyone else.'

'Mr. Frinton I'm not sure about this. I'll have to think about it. As you can understand I'm still a little sensitive about anything to do with that man. God I could …., I don't know what. It makes me so mad.'

'Well I'll share something else with you that may give you an edge in any battle with our mutual acquaintance Michael. I found out the other day that Michael has a son. Without being too racist he is like myself, a baby of mixed blood. The mother is a young escapee from the ravages of Mozambique, although she didn't appear to have suffered much when I last saw her; in fact anything but as she was living with a young Earl of something or other, or so I was told.'

'What was the name of this black girl?' Rosalind ground out through her teeth.

'Her name is Danielle Made,' answered David, 'and more recently I had heard she had been ejected from the bed and life of her friendly Earl. If truth be told I think the Earl's mummy found out and didn't approve. Anyway, young Danielle and child have decamped down to Somerset to find Michael.'

'That'll really make for an interesting meeting if this Danielle turns up at Fotheringham. I'm sure that Lady Sylvia will have something to say about that, not to mention Sir Anthony. I'd like to be a fly on the wall at that confrontation.'

'Anyway, food for thought,' said David. 'I'll hear from you with regards to the estimates then?'

'Certainly Mr. Frinton. I think we might be able to do business after all.'

After leaving the library Michael went down to the Forest Office. Not surprisingly Ferris wasn't there. Where did they say they were working this morning Michael asked himself? I know there isn't much going on right now because Enrico asked for time off to go shopping and Ferris even said yes: seemed to want Enrico out of the way for some reason. With a suspicious mind Michael got into his Landrover and drove down to Enrico's cottage. Most of the leaves had fallen off the hardwoods by now and lay scattered on the forest floor. There were touches of colour still remaining and most of the conifers still held their green needles. The larches had turned a deep golden yellow. Doves cooed and rooks cawed as Michael quietly eased the Landrover down the forest track. It was peaceful, even splendid thought Michael as the sunlight splashed through the bare ash trunks in an array of stripes. It really is a lovely place to live.

As Michael suspected Norton Ferris's pickup was parked outside Enrico's cottage. The front door was shut and no smoke came out of the chimney. Michael coasted to a stop alongside the pickup and quietly opened his door. Leaving it ajar Michael walked very softly around to the garden at the back of the cottage. Most of the vegetables had been picked by now and Enrico had already started to turn the soil over. Knows the early frosts will help break down the clods thought Michael. Enrico might be old and slowing down but he still has his marbles.

Pushing open the back door Michael entered the flagstone kitchen. 'Looking for something Ferris?' Michael quietly asked. Norton Ferris jumped a mile into the air and dropped the box he held in his hands. The box came down hard on the stone floor and scattered its contents. Ferris managed to stay upright but staggering, and he put out his hand to the table to steady himself. The table slid on the stones and Ferris fell full length on the cold floor. 'Well, anyone would think you were a little upset by my question,' added Michael, still keeping his voice low key.

'Christ Mr. Michael, you put the living fear of God into me.'

'I'll put more than that into you you useless piece of shit. You really are the laziest scheming son of a bitch I've met. Not only do you not do your job but you come snooping around in places you don't belong.'

'No, you've got it wrong Mr. Michael. Enrico told me he wanted me to check the hot-water heater. Said it was making some funny noises lately. I said I knew a bit about them and I'd take a look see.'

'Crap.'

'It's true.'

'Absolutely bloody crap,' said Michael, 'and even if for a moment I thought it was true the water heater doesn't live inside that smashed box, now does it? The hot-water heater won't fit into that box, will it Ferris?' Michael's voice had hardened by this time and the decibel level had started to escalate.

'No, well, I was just moving it see when you came in and frightened the life out of me.'

'Ferris, get out, now! You can't work worth a shit and your lying is fucking useless. First thing tomorrow morning I'm going to get you to publicly apologise to Enrico in front of all of the work crew. Now fuck off.'

Ferris backed out of the kitchen and Michael heard him shuffle off to his pickup. The starter whined and the truck took off in a cloud of exhaust. Michael stooped down to pick up the various papers that had fallen out of the box. He straightened them out to put them back but one folded over paper got stuck. Putting the box on the table Michael pulled out the folded paper. "For Enrico from Daniel – our secret", were the words on top of the paper. Underneath the words were a wriggly line with an indentation and then two wriggly lines with a semicircle on the lower one. There was another couple of vertical lines by the semicircle. Michael folded it over and placed it with the other papers. He bundled the whole lot into the box and placed it carefully on a ledge by the firenook. With a pensive look on his face Michael closed the kitchen door gently behind him and walked across to his Landrover. Still thinking Michael got in and started the engine. 'Now I wonder,' he said, 'I wonder what my little brother has found? I think it is time to pay dear sister-in-law a visit. She'll tell me what I want to know.'

It wasn't very far to drive from Enrico's cottage to Home Farm and during the drive Michael thought over how he would play this. The confrontation in the library hadn't been very productive but at that stage Michael didn't know what he knew now. Perhaps we'll try the "Happy Families" approach. If my little nephew Peter found it perhaps he will tell dear Uncle Michael all the useful details.

Christina was working in the kitchen at Home Farm. After the early morning confrontation she was a little upset at seeing Michael back so soon.

'What is it now Michael? I'm up to my arms in flour as you can see, in the middle of baking. I've no time for arguments. Now please go.'

'Peace sister,' said Michael holding up both his arms, 'I surrender. I just came here to apologise about this morning. I'm sorry I was a little abrupt. I was just so surprised to see you going through all those old books. I suppose I get a little too possessive on occasions. Anyway, I've just come from Enrico's and he wanted me to pass on his regards. I told him I was coming here to say sorry and he asked me to say hi. He also asked whether Peter was enjoying his new toy. Is Peter about? I haven't seen him for a while. I can hear him laughing to himself in the living room. Okay if I go in? I'll just take my boots off.'

'All right Michael, if you must. I'm too busy at the moment but don't you upset him now. He sounds quite happy in there at the moment.'

'No, sure Christina, I'll just go in and say hello, thanks. Peter, and how are you this bright morning little fella? Hey, neat, did Enrico make this? It looks like his work with all the wooden animals. Do you know what this one is Peter? It's a cow. Can you say cow?'

'Peter looked up at Michael and smiled. 'Caaw,' he said, 'Caaw.'

'No not quite Peter. It's cow, cow, it's an ow sound. Cow, bow, sow, meeaouw.'

'Peter laughed at his uncle's voice. Michael knelt down on the carpet, more at Peter's level and looked over the other parts of the toy. It looked rather like Daniel's fort that Enrico had made long ago, although not so regular. Inside the sort of courtyard were some boxes. As Michael picked one up Peter said, 'trezor, trezor,' and he reached out his stubby little hands, 'mi trezor, mi trezor,' he repeated.

'Mmm,' said Michael, 'mi trezor eh?' Michael's eyes flicked over the "fort" and mused back over the paper in Enrico's box. The inside courtyard of the fort was semicircular, a little like the indentation on the paper. 'Perhaps Daniel has found himself a cave,' said Michael very quietly, 'perhaps he has found a possible Lord family treasure. Very useful I think.' Looking at Peter Michael said, 'thank you little nephew, you may have made my day. Mi trezor indeed, well not if I have anything to do with it.'

Michael gently handed the box back to Peter who tried to place it back in the courtyard of the fort. He picked up two of the animals and made them charge at each other, clashing their heads together. 'Pow, pow,' said Peter. 'Too true,' said Michael, 'pow, pow.'

Michael rose and quietly went back into the kitchen. 'He's fine Christina, happy as a lark. He loves Enrico's fort and the animals are perfect. Still, I must away. Dad wants me to check over the forest. We think that Norton Ferris is going to have to go. See you later Christina, bye.'

Michael slipped on his boots and quickly left the warmth of the kitchen. The sharp tang in the air felt bracing as Michael strode purposefully to his Landrover. So he thought, Daniel and Peter found some maps and smarty-pants Daniel has found out where on the Estate, and precious little Peter thinks it is "trezor". Well, fancy that. Now I wonder where brother Daniel would have kept the maps he found? I doubt he would have taken them back to Bristol House. Things go walkabout too easily at school so Daniel must have left them somewhere at home. Methinks a little searching would be useful right now.

'Crack'. The sharp explosion rent the air and all three men peered down the laneway to the target. Foster expertly slid another shell into the rifle, braced, sighted, squeezed and the bullet sped away. He continued with four more shells and then pushed the mufflers off his ears. He laid the rifle down on the counter and the other two men turned to him.

'Let's see how you did then Foster? You said you were good, so let's see how good?' Stanley Rogers activated the target return mechanism and the human outline whirred back to them from the end of the alleyway. 'Well, I'm impressed,' said Alan Matheson. 'I thought I could shoot but six in the chest looks good to me.'

'Still, you told us you shot competitively so what should we expect? Let me have a go and see whether I can still shoot. Haven't done this for a while mark you.'

'Come on Stanley, let's have no excuses before you start. Was Melanie telling me tales when she said you shot for UCLA for a couple of years? Actually, come to think of it you must have been in Nam. Did you see any action or were you in Intelligence? I was a Radio Op. for a Tour but got invalided out quite early.'

'We were lucky to be out of that one,' said Alan. 'I suppose we had our fill of that part of the world in the fifties with the commies in Malaya.'

'I was a sniper for a while,' said Stanley, putting the mufflers back on his ears. 'Suit up you two while I see whether I can remember how to do this.' All three men covered their ears and their eyes while Stanley lifted the rifle. It was lighter than the sniper rifle he had used. Six quick shots rang out on the range and when the target came back to them there were six neat holes in the head.

'So Alan, what is it that you have for us that is so special?'

'Well, it's amazing what you can do with freezing things nowadays. If you put your mind to it and with a little engineering you can freeze most anything. So try these.'

The three men came out of the Range into the sunlight. Alan carried an insulated container and packed it carefully away in the boot of his car. Foster and Stanley had left the rifles in the Range and as Foster opened his car door he turned, 'so we'll meet on the 15th. next month for another trial Alan. It's coming along though. See you.' Stanley got in with Foster and they drove away. Alan held his car door open and muttered, 'yes, on the 15th. and I'll get it right, don't you worry. It's someone else who needs to be worrying, not me.' Quietly Alan Matheson slid into his car and slowly drove back to his factory.

Michael quietly and diligently searched Daniel's room at Fotheringham. 'Where would the silly little bugger hide something like a map?' said Michael to the room. 'I can't quite pull all these bloody books out because my saintly little brother is such a clean and tidy chap. Any great disturbance and young Master Daniel will know that I've tumbled his precious secret. His precious secret – balls Daniel – it's mine you cheap little bugger.' Keeping half an ear to the door Michael continued looking and poking about. He opened one of Daniel's cupboards and searched the pockets of the various jackets and coats hanging there. 'No,' said Michael, 'he's too emotional, it'll be somewhere with a special significance.' Michael poked further into the cupboard. 'Shit,' he said, 'I almost broke my toe on that bloody fort he's kept. Ah, fort's he's kept, just the place to store a treasure, safe in the fort. How about that idea young Daniel? Just the sort of thing you would think of, and, behold hidden treasure.'

Carefully Michael reached inside the fort and released the catch that Enrico had made to let you take the walls of the keep off the interior. Inside the keep the model had floors, a great hall, and several chambers just like a real fort. Neatly folded in the great hall was a square of paper. Michael stepped back out of the cupboard and into the light as he unfolded the paper. He held the two sheets in his hands. 'So these are the keys to the secret,' he said, 'and the keys to my fortune if I play my cards right. Okay young Daniel, you keep your little secret for now and I will wait my time.' Michael was so intent on reading the maps in the light by the window he didn't notice the shadow as a form with watchful eyes glided quietly away from the door. Folding up the papers Michael replaced them in the keep, put the walls back on and reset the latch, and backed out of the cupboard once more. Taking a quick look around the room to make sure nothing was out of place Michael smiled and walked quietly back downstairs. The shadow stood at the top of the stairs and watched.

Friday the 28th. of November dawned clear. Melanie had come down the night before and drove Michael off early up to London to meet up with Rodney and Chuck. For some sixty other people however, this was a special day in Somerset. The Annual Meeting of Brainware was an important event and Sir Anthony took special care with the shareholders of his Company. As the Company offices were too small to host such a gathering he had contracted with the Community Hall Authorities in the local town. This really wasn't just a Hall as such but a complex, which included two theatre auditoriums, a gymnasium and several small meeting rooms. The meeting typically had four distinct parts and these included a description of the Company and its achievements to date; a financial accounting; a description of research activities and things to come; and a discussion session for ideas for the future. The Session ran over two days and finished with a Banquet on the Saturday evening. Sir Anthony hosted a news conference on the following Monday morning.

During the Friday morning session Ted Crichton and Lester Donald briefly outlined the project and product covering financial transactions and security. They described how these routines could be operated away from the office of the client and the various controls. Rosalind Cohen and Tina Morland had come down from London and they explained and demonstrated some of the practices. The concept and operation of off-site transactions created considerable interest with the audience. A representative from Saad Brothers spoke briefly about the satisfaction by the client. At lunchtime Ted Crichton managed to speak to Rosalind privately and the pair of them shared some information of mutual benefit.

In the afternoon session a small bevy of suits explained the financial health of the Company. For some of the shareholders this was the most important part of the meeting. ROIs for some people are their bread and butter but Ted and Lester were more interested in other financial matters. They took some time out with Terry and Vernon to assess a different kind of investment.

'I've sorted Tom Daley out,' said Ted, 'so he won't give us any grief. I managed to get some proof about his porno distributions that will keep him very quiet for a while.'

'It wasn't easy,' said Lester, 'but I've found a way into Michael's main source of finances. He didn't know it but his dad helped me really. We don't all need to know this but I can move money out to other places.'

'Mr. Dicksons is the bookie that Michael uses most of all. Actually, it is the same bookie that Norton Ferris uses, and loses to,' said Terry. 'Now Michael has an account there. I think Ferris told Michael that having an account makes you look like a serious gambler. I also managed to find Larry Thomas.'

'Who's he?' asked Lester. 'We don't need too many people involved in this or it will go tits up.'

'He's gorgeous. He's ..'

'Cut it out Terry, who the hell is Larry Thomas?'

'He's Mr. Dicksons regular heavy. He's the hunk sent round to collect payment when you're sort of late.'

'And, what did you find out from this Mr. Thomas?'

'Well, Mr. Dicksons will let things slide a little but when you're over five thousand behind you get a little note and when you're ten thousand behind you get a visit. Twenty thousand is likely to cause a minor earthquake. I wanted some idea of the scale we should be looking at.'

'Vernon, what have you found?'

'Heh I'm sorry guys. I've been so engrossed in SearchLord that I haven't really done anything, other than give Terry some support like. Once tomorrow's out of the way I may be able to get more involved, but I'm in, I'm in okay.'

The four of them discussed some more strategy and how the timing could unfold. They agreed that applying pressure in January would be most productive. People are always somewhat groggy after New Years.

On the Saturday morning Vernon and Terry did put on a dog and pony show about SearchLord. This was one of the two highlights Sir Anthony had in the Research session. Terry did some of the computer analyses live with the activities projected onto a big screen facing the audience while Vernon annotated the kinds of questions and results you could expect. They explained that with the power of the web, and as more information is put into digital format, the importance of this kind of searchengine would expand exponentially. It was a very professional presentation and well received by the audience. At the back of the Hall Terry had laid out copies of the SearchLord brochure that Vernon and

Sally Peters had compiled. The various shareholders snapped these up enthusiastically at the end of the presentation.

'Well my love, and how did we do?' asked Sylvia in a low voice while sitting at the Banquet Table. 'Will we still have jam for tea?'

Anthony looked at his wife beside him and gently smiled. 'I've quite forgotten where that quote comes from,' he said, 'but yes my dear, I think there will be jam for tea. In fact, we may have cream as well.'

'Then our little baby is still flourishing. Seems we've come a long way from 1964 and our impetuous launch.'

'Yes we have, and with a lot of help from various family members. We had some great advice from Uncle Matthew, some very useful contracts through Aunt Veronica, and even some useful thoughts from my Mum before she went gaga.'

'Not to mention some useful financial input from Veronica.'

'Yes, but she wanted her pound of flesh for her money. She might be my aunt but she's one of the most demanding shareholders we've got.'

'Please reassure your aunt Anthony that I've got her precious money well and truly invested and brilliantly managed. I may not have her money but LSE did help groom my brain. I still look after some of the financial parts of this Company you know. We're a good team.'

'Too true. Actually, the team is better than you think. You should have heard some of the technical presentations over the last two days. We've got some smart kids on board and the future looks really good. Anyway, I'll have my usual short news conference on Monday and that should help share prices. Let's eat before we don't have any jam left.'

Like Foster Faxon, Stanley Rogers had wanted his eldest son to experience schooling in England. So, when Rodney turned eighteen and was set to move into his final year of High School, Stanley arranged for Rodney to spend it at a school near London. His dad told him in no uncertain terms that whereas Melanie had come across from California primarily to party, Rodney was supposed to learn. His dad also wanted him to experience sports as the attitude is a little different. Rodney had grown up as a fullback on the gridiron in California and was built to run through tackles. He found rugby fascinating. There were no pads, no helmets, no bandaged hands. It was fantastic all this freedom. He was fast, solid, and agile on his feet swerving right and left with ease. His school groomed him into a very mean and dangerous fly half. Rodney would go for anything.

As directed by his father, on the day of the Annual Meeting Michael found himself hustled out of the house. On the way up to London in Melanie's car Michael mused on the differences and similarities between himself and Rodney Rogers. With Michael planning to marry Melanie it could prove useful if he became a little buddy-buddy with young Rodney. Listening to Melanie describe her brother Michael wondered what might be some possible mutual interests. At Bristol House Michael was athletic, and could run, but he had decided that being bounced on the rugby ground wasn't for him. Even as a wing three-quarter you had to carry the ball occasionally and that meant you were a target. What else is there thought Michael? Well, there are the mountains. I've hiked and climbed from a very young age. Dad has had all of us out on the local Mendip hills as soon as we could walk. From there I had graduated to the mountains of North Wales, the Lake District and even the Cairngorms in Scotland one year. So, what was it Melanie said about Rodney? The Rogers family lived just south of San Francisco but they also had a cabin just outside Yosemite National Park. She said that their dad had taken them hiking up at Tuolumne Meadows, wherever that was and around parts of Mt.Whitney. When Michael had asked about these areas Melanie was a little vague. 'Hell Michael, I didn't even want to go but Rodney was always out in front. Dad took him climbing a little in the Valley too, and that's some serious rock climbing. I didn't go there

Michael, that's freaky, nothing but vertical rock. After he got the bug dad sent him out to the Tetons for three summers. Believe me, with his solid frame and strong legs this teenager can hike your legs off.' We'll see about that Michael muttered to himself.

Melanie drove to Rodney's school and Michael transferred his gear to Rodney's car. Chuck Faxon was already there. 'Well I'm off, 'Melanie said. 'I'll leave you three men to enjoy yourselves. I think I'll find some better things to do up in the West End rather than scrambling over dirty peat bogs. The weather forecast said snow so I hope you've got your snuggies.'

'Melanie, we're all set. The weather forecast said clear and fine so don't go giving us this bluff about snow. Anyway, Chuck's dad gave him this special secret weapon. It's a communications beacon and when you set it off spacemen come and transport you back to home base.'

'Rodney, you're full of it, but for a little brother you'll do.' Melanie had the final say as she stepped up quickly and kissed her brother on the cheek. With his face going red Rodney bolted into the car.

'Michael, I've got a better kiss for you my love.' Melanie wrapped her arms around Michael and slipped her tongue into his mouth. She wriggled against him seductively and then slipped easily out of his arms and into her car. 'And I didn't even get a hug,' said Chuck.

Michael hadn't been out on the hills seriously since the accident with Geoffrey in June. This trip might help shed any ghostly memories of that climbing accident with his brothers earlier in the year. For Chuck it was a new experience to be in mountains where there really were no trees anywhere. This was quite different from the mountains in the Eastern U.S. For Rodney too it was different. He looked about him. They were certainly smaller and more rounded hills up here than the Tetons, but still wild he thought. You still needed to keep your wits about you.

'So where was the accident Michael?' asked Rodney very quietly.

'Just two cwms over,' said Michael. 'In Cwm Llafar under Carnedd Dafydd.

'How did you get out?'

'I went north down Afon Llafar to the village of Bethesda to find the Mountain Rescue Team.'

'And you found them?'

'Yes, they went out straight away once they had contacted all the Team Members.'

'Didn't you have to register where you were climbing?' asked Rodney. "That's a necessity in some of our National Parks. They make you sign in with an estimated time of return.'

'Sound like Russia,' said Michael. 'I thought America was the land of the free?'

'Yes, well, it helps in some ways. The areas are so much bigger there. You need to know where to start looking.'

The third member of the party, who fortunately had not heard the earlier part of the conversation joined them and said, 'talking of looking did you see the goats?'

'Goats Chuck? What are you talking about? Those are probably sheep.'

'No Michael,' said Chuck. 'There are goats up here. I read about them in geography class. You know Michael we did quite a lot of research on this area before deciding to come here. Pass me your map and show us where we are.'

Having come up from Aber the three young men were standing on Foel Fras looking over the rolling expanse of the Carneddau. This part of the Snowdonia National Park was less populated than the area around Snowdon itself. You could hike up here and not see a soul all day, especially at this time of year in November. Young Chuck had a school project to write about the wildlife of North Wales. He had persuaded his father that doing this live in the field was much better than doing it from books. Foster Faxon agreed with the idea and persuaded the school's headmaster that a long weekend would help Chuck develop a hands-on feel for the subject. Foster tried to convince the headmaster that the Americans set great store from practical hands-on approaches to anything. The headmaster didn't agree with a word of it but Foster was paying the school fees and so Chuck was hands-on.

It was a grand day. The sky was a clear light blue and you could see out to sea to the north and way over Snowdon towards Portmadoc to the south. There was only the zephyr of a breeze and the hiking was easy over the occasional rocks with its ground-hugging vegetation.

'It's amazing to think we're only three thousand feet above the sea,' said Rodney. 'Yet we're well above the tree line. They had left the trees behind when climbing up beside the waterfall above Aber.

'One thousand metres,' explained Chuck.

'Not in the States guy. We don't have that metric nonsense there.'

'No, and you don't have proper gallons, or proper tons,' added Michael.

'Well right now Michael I could do with part of whatever gallon. I'm getting dehydrated and that's not wise in the hills. How about a five minute break and a drink? The view's good, the rocks are dry and it'll lighten the load.'

'Good cliffs down that side,' said Michael pointing to the left.

'Got a name?' asked Rodney.

'Craig Yr Ysfa,' said Michael. 'Some good routes on the walls. One of the original guidebook authors, Tony Moulam put up some routes that were ahead of his day.'

'Sort of isolated isn't it?' said Rodney, thinking of the more crowded floor of the Yosemite Valley.

'Yes. One of the splendours of the climbing is the fact that it is sort of shut off away from the crowds. You've got to make an effort to get here and once you're on the cliff it is either up or down, and only up or down.'

'We'll go past the top of the cliff won't we?' asked Chuck, holding the map.

'Yes, we go across the top on the way past Carnedd Llywelyn.

'And then onto Carnedd Dafydd,' said Chuck.

'What names,' said Rodney.

'Yes, but you know you were mentioning Tuolumne, and what was it? Nez Percy or something?'

'Nez Perce. They were a tribe of Indians who lived in the area.'

'Well Dafydd and Llywelyn were David and Lou who lived here or hereabouts a long time ago too.'

The threesome continued on over Foel Grach following the broad ridge leading to Carnedd Llywelyn and the junction with the ridge to Yr Elen. As they passed over the top of Craig Yr Ysfa they looked down Central Gully to the foot of the cliffs.

'That's an easy scramble down,' said Michael. 'Like the Easy Way Down on any climbing cliff.'

'You don't have to rappel?' asked Rodney.

'No, not often here. Nearly all of the cliffs are small and compact with a way of scrambling down to the bottom. And all of the climbs end up on top of the cliff. Not like some of your climbs in Yosemite.'

'Are we going down there?' asked Chuck. 'It would be a good place for goats.'

'You and your goats,' laughed Rodney.

'Well, they are special. There are not many of them left and it would be a highlight of the project to see one.'

'We might go this afternoon,' said Michael, 'depends on the weather. It can be a nasty place to get caught if any weather blows up, especially as we are staying in Bangor away to the north. Have to come up this gully and then down besides Yr Elen and all the way down Afon Caseg to the Bethesda and on again to Bangor.'

'What about going the other way?'

'Lot of broken country below the cliff; easy to get lost with no really clear topography: if it was bad weather and misty you could wander round in circles.'

'But not with my compass Michael,' exclaimed Chuck. 'Look, I carry it everywhere. I wouldn't wander round in circles.'

The three were making good time and briefly stopped for a quick bite and a drink on the top of Carnedd Llywelyn. It was still clear and from this high point you could see in a complete circle.

'If we look far enough Rodney we can see America,' said Chuck. 'Look, out there to the west. Look further.'

'You'll bump into Ireland first Chuck,' laughed Rodney. 'You're just too optimistic by half.'

Away to the west, but closer than Ireland, sprigs of cirrus curling up like long thin skeins of white wool started to appear. A slight breeze stirred the three hikers and they resumed their way along the ridge connecting the two Carnedds. Michael shuddered a little as he passed over the top of Western Gully, the scene of this summer's earlier fatal accident. He didn't say anything to Rodney but their eyes met and both young men kept quiet. They easily reached the top of Carnedd Dafydd around eleven o'clock.

'Seeing as how we've left the car at Aber we won't bother to go down to Ogwen,' said Michael. 'It's an easy descent but a bitch of a slog coming back up. So we'll skip that and go back and do a route on Craig Yr Ysfa. That's if you two lads are up for it?'

'Sure Michael. We didn't bring all this climbing gear up just for a hike. It's a grand day, especially seeing as it's November. As you said, it looks like a good cliff and I might still see my goats.'

'Okay. Let's scoot back to the top of the cliff and have lunch. Go down Easy Way Down and do a climb back to the ridge. We'll need to be sharpish though.'

Having decided on the plan the three of them turned round on Carnedd Dafydd and retraced their steps. Overhead the skeins of cirrus had filled in a little and the breeze freshened. Michael set off at a brisk pace without looking back. The two Americans followed on behind and Rodney glanced at Chuck. Looks like typical Michael he thought.

At the top of the cliff the wind had picked up quite considerably and the temperature had dropped. It had turned chilly.

'Let's skip lunch,' said Michael. 'It's too parky up here and I don't want to lug everything down to the bottom and then have to climb with it on my back. We can just grab some snacks, a drink and leave the rest of the spare gear up here. All we need to take down is the climbing gear. Let's sort that out now.'

The three of them emptied their rucsacks and sorted out two ropes, helmets, a set of slings, some nuts, and several karabiners. 'We won't need those,' said Michael, looking at the bundle of pitons Rodney had laid out. 'We just use nuts here.'

'What about chalk Michael?'

'No, don't use that much, certainly not here. Just leave it. You both got your harnesses? Actually, we may as well put them on, easier than carrying them.'

"I'm going to go down in my boots and change into my climbing shoes at the foot of the climb Michael. I can carry my boots up in my sack.'

'I think I'll do the same,' said Chuck. 'I get more support scrambling about in boots than in my "cheaters".'

'Okay you two, but you'll regret having to lug your boots about behind you on the climb.'

The two Americans looked at one another and decided that safety overcame shortcuts and packed their climbing shoes in their rucsacks, along with the other climbing gear. The three of them quickly stuffed some power bars in their mouths and slipped water bottles in the sacks. A sudden gust of wind rushed in from the west and north.

'Let's just pack all the surplus gear in my sack and stow it somewhere safe,' Michael said, 'somewhere where it won't blow away. You two look after that while I finish tying up my shoes.'

As the three of them were about to descend another wild gust of wind chased in and without much warning the clouds blotted out the sun.

Rodney and Chuck did a quick check that they had everything they needed. They had divided up the climbing gear and they each carried one of the ropes. They had given Michael the slings and the rack with the nuts to carry. Chuck put on his helmet and cinched up the strap. Rodney slung the climbing sack onto his shoulders and adjusted the balance. He too was wearing a helmet.

'So what do you recommend we climb Michael?' asked Rodney. 'What's a distinctive route on this cliff?'

'Pinnacle Face,' said Michael decisively, 'it's a classic and quite dramatic.'

'What's the grade?'

'Originally it was VS,' said Michael, 'or, what, 5.7 or 5.8 in America. Now it's only 4b I think. That okay with you two? Not too hard or anything?'

'Should be fine Michael. I was leading 5.9s and 5.10s in the Valley when I left so that should be fine.'

'Let's go before we change our minds then,' Michael said, and he turned to descend the cliff.

'You're not taking a helmet?' asked Chuck.

'Naw, shan't bother. The climb is fairly short and there's a couple of traverses so we won't be above each other. Besides, this cliff has been climbed on for years so there's no loose rock.'

'I was thinking more of protecting your head if you come off Michael actually,' said Chuck.

'In your dreams.'

'Well, I heard last time you tried to lead you were lucky not to have been killed.'

'When was that?' said Michael. 'I don't remember falling off.'

'A little sea cliff climb down in Cornwall, when you were with Geoffrey: didn't he have to lower you down or something. Rather bruised I heard.'

'O that, well it was greasy and I wasn't quite myself that day. I had climbed the route a couple of weeks beforehand and walked up it. I suppose I just wasn't paying attention on some move or other. No problem though.'

Michael shot off down the gully in a flurry of loose rock. 'See you at the bottom,' he shouted.

Rodney looked over at Chuck. 'Glad I'm not beneath him, the amount of shit he's knocking off down there. Just hope there's no poor bastard at the bottom in the way. Anyway, we'd better follow or God knows where he'll go.'

As Rodney and Chuck left the ridge and started down the gully the clouds dropped completely into a thick mist all around them. Suddenly the air crackled and an electric charge ran along the narrow ridge. The crash of thunder took everyone by surprise and the heavens opened in a deluge of rain. Chuck and Rodney called down to Michael but there was no response.

'Shit, I suppose we'd better go and find him. Glad I've got my boots on as the rocks will get pretty slippery in this rain.'

The two Americans carefully descended the gully. There were a couple of chimneys to downclimb and some loose open scree patches. Through the mist they could see the slabby walls rise up above them as they descended.

'Looks like a pinnacle up there,' said Chuck, peering through the mist. 'Wonder if that's where Michael intended us to go?'

'Well right now we need to find Michael before we go anywhere. Michael, Michael,' rang the shouts down the gully. The white cloying mist swirled down around them in the gully but no answer came up. The gully started to flatten out and then narrowed into another narrow slot between steep wet slabs.

'Must go down that chimney,' said Chuck. 'Those slabs are too slippery to solo down now.'

'True,' Rodney said, 'but go carefully. There's some lichen on some of these rocks and that's like grease when it's wet. Look, I'll go first if you like so I can watch your feet coming down that chimney.'

'Good idea Rodney, you've been climbing longer than I have. I appreciate that.'

The two lads slowly reached the top of the chimney. It wasn't very long, about thirty feet, but it was vertical and the walls were now running with water.

'I'll straddle down at the top,' said Rodney, 'but lower down, where it narrows, I'll just foot and back it; should be safe with my feet flat on the wall. You okay with that?'

'Yes, I understand. I'll come down slowly, but you're right, it is slippery.'

Slowly Rodney straddled down the top of the chimney, using the various footholds to maintain balance. Lower he put his back on one wall and his feet on the wall opposite and slowly backed down. When he was near the bottom he called up to Chuck to start.

'I'm down Chuck. Just don't kick too much crap over the edge when you start. It's pretty loose on top of the chimney. It's not so bad in boots.'

And that was true. Chuck successfully stood beside Rodney at the foot of the chimney and the pair of them looked down. As the mist lifted a little they could see what must have happened. Michael's body was fifty feet below them and not moving. Carefully, so as not to kick any more loose rock down Rodney and Chuck clambered down to Michael's body.

'He's alive for starters,' said Rodney, and he started to gently inspect Michael's body from top to bottom. 'He's got a bloody great bruise on his forehead, but the skin isn't broken and there's no blood off his scalp. Looks like he must have slipped in his climbing shoes on the wet chimney and just fell down the gully and knocked himself out. I'll carry on looking though to see if there's any more damage.'

True enough thought Chuck. His climbing shoes like ours are smooth soled, which is great for climbing, edging and smearing but act like short skis on wet greasy rock. Not wearing a helmet didn't help either.

'I can't find any other injuries,' said Rodney. 'Actually I am surprised he didn't bite his tongue or something when he knocked himself out. Sometimes happens. He's probably got some nasty scrapes and bruises but there are no strange swellings on arms and legs so I don't think anything's broken.'

'Jesus, and what would you know if it was,' grunted Michael. He tried to sit up but as he wasn't stable to start with he just rolled another six feet down the slippery wet gully. 'Shit, Christ I hurt.'

'Michael, for God's sake stay still a moment until we can get you stable. You've had a nasty bang on the head. You're probably still in shock.'

Rodney scrambled down to help Michael sit up straight on the scree slope with his feet safely downhill. 'Here, Chuck, come down here and make sure he doesn't move about while I look for some spare clothes.'

'Piss off, you're like two old women. I bumped my head sliding down that bloody chimney. I'm fine, just a bit bruised. Couple of moments and we'll go and find that climb.'

'Michael, I'm not sure whether you have noticed but the mist has socked in solid, it's pouring with rain, and up on the ridge lightning was running around like a mad thing. If you hadn't had your hearing upset with the fall you might also have noticed that there is thunder every so often. I think you're in shock. Let me look at your eyes to see whether you have any concussion?'

'I'm fine!' Michael stood up swiftly, swayed, and promptly collapsed in a heap. He tried to sit up but couldn't manage that. He lay there grunting with frustration, and then he fainted.

'Chuck, here's what we do. We can't get Michael back up the way we came so we've got to walk out down the valley. I think he will be mobile enough to try that. Michael said it was complicated terrain down the valley and so we need the map and compass, which we left with the rest of the gear on top of the ridge. So, first of all we wrap up Michael as best we can to minimize shock. Then I'll go back and collect the rest of the gear and come back down here. After that we'll look at the map and use the compass to find our way out of here. Any suggestions?'

'Why don't we make Michael safe here and both of us climb up to the ridge and walk back the way we came to the car. Then we can drive and find the Mountain Rescue to get Michael out. It won't be easy to walk him anywhere and he may be more concussed than we think.'

'It's a good idea, especially as it would take us back to the car straightaway. But, and it's a big but, remember this morning the plateau terrain for much of the early morning was flat with cliffs off the edge. Also, it was a narrow and steep valley entrance up past the waterfall from Aber. To walk out the way we came we would have to be very accurate with the compass and could get into more trouble. What do you think?'

'Either way we need the map and compass, and they are up on top. Yes, I'll try and make Michael safe while you go and get the rest of the gear. I think you're right overall though. Keeping the three of us together will be safer for Michael in the long run. Just be careful with those chimneys and try not to kick too much crap down on top of us partner.'

Rodney smiled at Chuck's last comment. 'Here's my anorak. Wrap it over his shoulders. I won't be long, and I'll be as careful as one of your precious goats.'

'Fat chance of seeing them in this mist,' said Chuck.

Chuck made Michael comfortable; made sure he was breathing freely and draped the anorak over his shoulders to keep off some of the rain. True to his word Rodney was quick and was up and down without moving a pebble. He dumped the rest of the gear beside them. 'Okay, let's get some spare clothes on before we catch cold and see where we go from here. Any change in Michael?'

'Yes, Michael's wondering why you two buggers are taking so long to get my spare gear. I'm bloody freezing, and sitting in a puddle's not doing my piles any good either.'

Chuck looked at Rodney. The slurring in Michael's speech was quite distinctive but obviously his brain was more or less working. Rodney sorted out Michael's gear, not that he had much. The two Americans had brought spare sweaters, toques and even gloves. They all had windproof jackets. After the three of them gradually got themselves better dressed for the weather Rodney suggested they look at the map and work out an escape route.

'Escape route, escape route!' shouted Michael, followed by a gasp as he held his head in his hands.

'Hold him Chuck, he's going to collapse again.'

Chuck's solid bulk held Michael from falling further down the slope and gradually eased him back into a sitting position. 'Christ my head hurts.'

'Michael, we need to walk out of here. There's no way we can climb back up that gully and so we decided to stay together and walk out eastwards. You said it was complicated but it is downhill and we should be able to manage that.'

'No, no, no!' said Michael. 'We scramble back up this stupid little gully and go back the way we came. It's easy. Come on, follow me.' Michael turned and tried to walk up the loose bed of the gully back to the first chimney. Two steps and he swayed, three and he stumbled. Chuck caught him again before he pitched face forward.

'Sit down Michael while we look at the map, just sit!' Rodney said emphatically. 'You're in no state to walk uphill let alone try and climb those chimneys so we walk out downhill, together. Prop him up again Chuck while I get the map orientated and sort out some sensible cross country jaunt.'

It was Chuck who became the leading light for the next four hours. He had had extensive experience in hiking with map and compass in the hills, gullies and ravines of Georgia and the Carolinas. This countryside was rolling with convoluted topography and Chuck had learnt well. Between them the two Americans half supported half carried the now rambling Michael, but they gradually got him down the hill. The thunder rolled away and the rain eased. Unfortunately the mist stayed with them which made the route finding more difficult than it should have been.

'What's he on about now Chuck?' asked Rodney, 'some cave or something. Tell him we're not doing any more climbing but we're going home. There are no more caves Michael. We're down in the fields, or thereabouts. Wherever we are we're surrounded by these bloody stone walls. Getting you over them is proving to be a pain. Don't they believe in roads in this place?'

'I think we're nearly at a road Rodney if I know where we are on the map. No, Michael's somewhere in a cave with Lordly treasure. That's what he is ranting about. Listening to him he's also very possessive about it. "It's mine, all mine" seems to be repeated at frequent coherent intervals.'

'Thank God, a gate, and heaven be praised, a road.'

The three young men emerged from the mist onto a surfaced road. Holding Michael between them they staggered ever more down the hill. At the first farm they came to they knocked on the front door. Michael suddenly became more aware and muttered, 'round the back, the back.'

'Oh yes Rodney, in English farmhouses you always go in through the kitchen from the yard,' said Chuck and they staggered around the side of the house and into the farmyard. Instantly they were set on by a gaggle of geese. The two border collie sheep dogs just looked at them with quiet but alert eyes.

'They'll not hurt you lads, there just good security like. Still, looks like you've come to some harm up on the hills? Just sit him down on the sacks there.'

'Bring them all in here Owen. Bring them in out of the rain man. There not like sheep with big wooly coats you lummox, they're tired lads.'

Mrs. Williams promptly took charge and had the three of them inside the kitchen in nothing flat. With no more ado they were sitting at the table with steaming mugs of tea in front of them and large wedges of seed cake. Only when they had eaten and drunk did she ask them any questions. While they were eating and drinking however, there was a rapid and fluid exchange between Mrs. Williams and Owen in what Rodney assumed was Welsh. Rodney had checked that Michael was still coherent when he sat him down at the table but Michael had now gone very quiet.

'We were climbing on Craggyisfer,' said Chuck, 'and Michael here slipped on wet rock and banged his head. We couldn't go back up to the top of the cliff and so we hiked out this way.'

'Americans by the sound of you son; don't find many of your people up here. Still, we do get an occasional Yank through who's been training at RAF Valley on Anglesey.' Another rapid exchange in Welsh took place during which time "Craig Yr Ysfa" got mentioned. 'Yes, that's right,' said Rodney, 'that's where we were.'

'And you brought him out from there bach? Aye, that's a fair walk, in the mist too.'

'We think Michael here has concussion and we'd like to get him to hospital. Our car is over at Aber. Is it possible to get us there and we'll take him down into Bangor?'

Mr. Williams didn't have a car big enough for all of them but he telephoned a neighbour who had a station wagon. Within a few minutes the car pulled up in the yard. With much thanks for the hospitality the two Americans helped Michael into the back of the car along with their gear. They could lay him down relatively flat but making sure that his head was still above his feet. Michael was conscious, but just. Rodney and Chuck squeezed into the front seat with young Gareth Rees and they were off. Within minutes the front seat was abuzz with rugby stories. When Gareth learnt that both Chuck and Rodney played rugby, and loved it they were all in their element. To keep the conversation going as long as possible Gareth stopped at Aber to let Rodney pick up the car and then continued with Chuck and a comatose Michael on into Bangor, talking non-stop rugby moves and tactics the whole time. Chuck said afterwards that it was a nightmare as Gareth talked a lot with his hands and they were rarely on the steering wheel.

The hospital wanted to keep Michael in for observations. Rodney telephoned home, Chuck's dad and Sir Anthony to tell them all what had happened. After some telephone discussion Chuck and Rodney drove back to London that night. Sir Anthony spoke to the hospital and made arrangements to be notified on Michael's progress. Apparently he was badly bruised and scraped and had a slight concussion. The hospital told Sir Anthony they would keep him in for a couple of days and Sir Anthony arranged to come up and collect Michael when he was to be released.

Chuck and Rodney spent some time with their fathers going over the events of the weekend. 'Seems you were rather wise to be so well prepared; boots, spare clothes, map and compass. Obviously some of the things you learnt back home Chuck have served you well. Good show son. You too Rodney; you made some tough decisions and carried them through. I like the stories about rugby in the car to Bangor though. This Gareth sounds quite a character. You say Michael was quiet at this time?'

'Yes Dad. He'd been burbling much of the time coming down the hill but right at the end he was silent. Actually, we were worried something more serious had happened.'

'And he was burbling about treasure in caves?'

'He was talking nonsense much of the time. He started off quite coherent but the further we went the more he sounded out of it. He was looking in some cave for his precious treasure, which he insisted very emphatically was all his, but it wandered off by the time we reached the road. Sounded like a lot of fantasy to us.'

'Well maybe I'll ask your sister what she knows about it,' said Stanley Rogers. 'She may know what young Michael is so excited about. Still, good job the pair of you didn't get too excited or the result may not have been so successful. Looks like we all learnt a little this weekend.'

13

Smokescreen

Stephen felt happy for the first time that he could remember in his life. It was his twelfth birthday and he had presents, a party and friends to tea. He felt loved.

'Happy birthday Stephen,' said Mrs. Davidson. 'Here's your first guest, young Trevor.'

'Hi Stephen. Happy birthday. Here's a present for you.'

'Ta Trev. What's?'

'Open it and see donkey.'

'Cor, a video game. Gee thanks Trev.'

Other guests arrived and Stephen was the centre of attention. Mr. Davidson came home from work and he too was friendly and wished Stephen all the best and formally shook his hand. They had cake, and ice cream, and lemonade. As it was late winter and dark already, Mr. Davidson had organised the use of the village hall for an evening of party games as the house was too small for ten rambunctious twelve-year olds. Mr. Davidson had even coerced the local scoutmaster to supervise the noisy ragamuffins, as looking after little boys was not part of Mr. Davidson's expertise. Under the experienced direction of the scoutmaster they played British Bulldog, Capture the Flag and ended up with a soccer match. It was a day to remember that day in February.

Mr. and Mrs. Davidson had been married for ten years and had been trying for a baby for most of that time. After several years of frustration, embarrassment, tests and frank discussions between themselves they decided to adopt. They had been foster parents for a couple of years and that experience helped them decide that they would sooner adopt a young boy and not a baby. They had fostered Stephen for six months and were slowly working with the authorities towards full adoption.

Stephen Dodds was an orphan. Left on the steps of a medical centre he had become a ward of the State. Stephen had struggled as a baby. He had asthma as a young child. He had had bronchitis and double pneumonia at two that had nearly killed him. Stephen had rotated through several foster homes and unfortunately these early experiences had nurtured an ill-mannered and surly child. By the time he reached eleven Stephen was "a problem". Apart from a spiteful and malicious temper, which he had developed from being the outsider in foster homes with other children, he had acquired a record of petty theft, arson, and knifing. With this kind of character Stephen had been in and out of several foster homes in his short life. His move into the Davidson's household had been a kind of godsend. It had been a godsend for both Stephen and Mrs. Davidson.

Anne Davidson was kind-hearted, motherly, and childless. Now nearly forty she wanted so much to be a mother and have someone to look after. Reginald Davidson didn't need looking after. He worked as a self-employed accountant. He was neat, organised, and very self-contained. He needed no motherly attention. It was partly his decision that if they adopted it should be a grown-up youth and not a baby.

Mr. Reginald Davidson had been a single child. He had grown up rather lonely with aged old-fashioned parents. Sent off to boarding school at a young age he had had a miserable childhood. Reginald did very well at 'O' levels and wanted to stay on in the Sixth Form and take 'A' levels. He explained to his parents that he wanted to go to University. He thought this would be a chance to make something of himself. However, fate intervened and his father was injured at work. His aged mother was poorly herself so Reginald was the only breadwinner in the family. He had to leave school and start work immediately in a large accounting office. Going to night school he had soon passed his exams to be a CPA and by the time he was twenty two he had left the big office, moved to the country, and started his own free-lance practice. He was a very successful sought-after accountant. Reginald was a man who also felt everyone should work for his or her rewards. He thought he had had a challenging time, having to adjust to circumstances of sick parents, but with hard work he had made a man of himself. As part of his "plan for life" he acquired a wife and presumed on having a family. Unfortunately life had other plans for Reginald as the family didn't arrive on schedule; hence ten years of trying but to no avail. At thirty-five Reginald had decided that a child would be good for his wife. She needed something to occupy her time and an "instant" family was just the answer. Stephen seemed to fit the bill very well. As Mr. Davidson was not at home for much of the time he did not see some of the trauma that came with Stephen.

Anne Davidson had loved the party. She enjoyed the excitement of the preparations: all those things to do with a cake to make, decorations to buy and fun for everyone. It had been a really nice surprise when Reginald told her he had taken care of the evening's games. So much the sensible and right thing to do she thought; a careful family planner was her Reginald.

The family planning was moving smoothly along on track until April. Easter had come and Reginald and Anne had taken Stephen for a short week's treat to Torquay. Stephen had been on his school holidays and Reginald had specially taken time off work. The moves towards adoption had reached the final phases and Stephen was quite excited. His behaviour had improved under Anne's tender care and even his attitude at school had become more sociable. In April something happened to potentially derail this happy scene. In April Anne was told she was pregnant.

'Doctor, are you sure? I don't feel any different and we'd thought it would never happen. I don't have any sickness or feel at all queasy.'

'Rest assured Mrs. Davidson, later this year I will be delivering twins to your household.'

'Twins, oh my goodness. What ever will Reginald say? I can't imagine the shock for him.'

'Well, it's a nice shock I'm sure. I know you have been trying and hoping for so long now. All your wishes and prayers have been answered. You will be able to have the family you always wanted.'

Anne Davidson went home with her mind in a whirl. Back in the house she tried to settle herself with a nice cup of tea but even that didn't really calm her down. Still on an emotional rollercoaster she telephoned Reginald at work, something she was told not to do.

'Reginald, you'll never guess what the doctor said, that I'm pregnant, I'm going to have twins, we're going to have babies, we're going to....' The words gushed out down the telephone in a full flood and Reginald held the phone away from his ear for a moment.

'Anne, Anne, slow down. Is everything all right? I'm rather busy with a client. Please call back later.'

'But Reginald, I've got to tell you.' The click registered and Anne stopped talking to the dead line. She slowly put down the receiver and sat in her armchair. Leaning backwards and relaxing at last she let her mind wander over the pictures and images of twins. Her own babies: holding, feeding, changing, dressing, and bathing; all those wonderful motherly actions. She was going to have her own babies to love and cherish.

Anne's reverie was shattered when the front door opened and crashed shut as Stephen came home from school. She heard him drop his things on the floor in the hall.

'Stephen, oh Stephen,' exclaimed Anne to the empty room. 'What will we do about Stephen?'

'What's for tea Mum?' asked a disheveled Stephen.

'Go upstairs and wash dear. I'll get something for you right away. When you come down please set the table for me and I'll bring you something in.'

There was the usual crash upstairs and the sound of running water. School clothes were dropped en route to the bedroom and Anne heard the toilet flush. Stephen, what shall we do about Stephen?

In an automatic series of actions Anne prepared Stephen's tea and carried it in to him. She sat down at the table with him and shared a cup of tea. She chatted about school and what had he been up to today? She barely heard Stephen's replies as her mind whirled around her question. She cleared away the tea things and bustled Stephen out to play cricket with his friends down on the playing fields.

'You know how Reginald likes to come home to a quiet dinner dear. You go and play till sundown. That way yer Dad can come home and relax after a hard day at the office.'

'Sure Mum. I'll be off. Be 'ome before dark. Something good on tele tonight, 'bout nine.'

'That's right luv. You go and have a good time with your friends. Mind the door.'

Stephen didn't hear the last suggestion and the door crashed behind him. What to do thought Anne? Still in automatic mode she cleared away the table and set about preparing her husband's dinner. Promptly at six o'clock Reginald's key turned in the lock and he set down his briefcase by the hallstand. Hanging up his coat he unlaced his shoes and put his feet into his slippers by the door. The routine continued with a quick move across to the downstairs closet and Anne heard the hand basin's squeaky tap turn as Reginald washed his hands.

Anne knew better than to try and talk to her husband before he had eaten and so half an hour passed while she picked at her dinner. Her husband solidly chomped his way through a lamb chop, occasionally garnished with mint sauce, potatoes, peas and two slender carrots. A piece of apple pie followed and the whole ensemble was washed down with a cup of strong tea. When Reginald pushed his chair back from the table and started to light his pipe Anne began.

'Reginald, Reginald. I had the most startling and wonderful news today.'

'Yes dear. You were trying to tell me something earlier but I was very busy. Now, what is so special?'

'Well, as I was saying, I went to the doctor today. Mrs. Vincent was there too with such a sad case of arthritis. She really is in such pain.'

'Anne, I'm sure your news is not about Mrs. Vincent.'

'Oh no dear, it's about me. Well, about us really. It's so exciting I don't know where to begin.'

Reginald pulled strongly on his pipe and looked expectantly at his wife. 'Continue dear, tell me all about it.'

'Well you know, it's funny. We've been trying all these years and nothing has happened. We wanted it to happen and it never has. It seems it was never going to happen.'

'What Anne? Please, I'm having trouble mind reading. What is all the excitement?'

'Reginald, I told you earlier. I'm pregnant. I'm going to have a baby. In fact I'm going to have two babies.'

'Two babies?'

'Yes, two babies. I'm expecting twins Dr. Evans says. Everything is fine. I'm healthy and the babies are healthy. They should be delivered in November. Isn't it exciting? It's what we always wanted.'

Anne's enthusiasm enveloped Reginald so much that he forgot his pipe which he knocked on the floor as he jumped from his chair to embrace his wife. The hug and the kiss were cut short by the smell of burning thread.

'Dam,' said Reginald as he retrieved the pipe and scuffed out the smoldering hole in the carpet.

'Doesn't matter, doesn't matter darling. Nothing really matters now. We've everything you always said you wanted.'

The excitement of the news held them both for a moment and then Anne remembered her question; the one that had been troubling her all afternoon.

'Reginald, what about Stephen?'

'Yes, good question; what about Stephen?'

'He's okay, but now that we will have our own family does it seem right? How would we explain him to the twins? I mean, he would be all grown up when they are old enough to understand. Would they resent him?'

'I think we should seriously reconsider about the adoption. It was a good idea at the time but now this news changes everything.'

The conversation carried on for a while but without conclusion. Stephen came in around dusk dragging a large amount of the cricket pitch with him. He switched the TV on to his programme and didn't notice any changes in the atmosphere around him. Once the show was over he announced he was off to his room and Anne and Reginald heard the bedroom door crash shut. Rock music reverberated through the ceiling as Mr. and Mrs. Davidson looked at each other. Later that night, in the quietness of their bedroom they made their decision.

Six years passed and it was a bright sunny December morning when Bert came out of his office to do his early morning floor check. Bert Rawlings was a tall, well-built man, wearing a white coat and white cap, and he came slowly and purposely down the staircase to the factory floor.

'Morning Seaun. Going well this morning? Moving on those schedules okay?'

'To be sure Bert, to be sure. Everything's going a treat.' The soft singsong brogue of Seaun Kevin O'Reilly flowed back to Bert. 'Are you going to the pub tonight? But of course you are. Aren't you the one with the steady hand and the sure eye?'

Bert smiled. 'Yes Seaun. I'll be there for the dart's match. Never you worry. You're bets are safe. We'll beat the Wheatsheaf Team.'

'That's a relief then Bert. Like to make sure of my bets I do. Weren't you in the army then?' asked Seaun. 'With hands like that were you a doctor, patching up the lads like? Dangerous to make mistakes in that business.'

'No Seaun. If I made mistakes there wouldn't be much patching up to do. But, yes, I was in the army.'

In his youth Bert Rawlings had needed a good eye and steady hands. Early on in his career in the army Bert had been at the front line of bomb disposal. He was the man on the sharp end when it came to defusing shells and bombs that had landed in the wrong place and stayed quiet. It had been Bert's task to make sure they stayed quiet.

As he continued his inspection of the factory floor of Carters Colourworld Bert mused on those days. His very early wild youth and bouts of drunken fights had landed him in the army in the first place. A drunken bet had resulted in volunteering and the world changed for Bert Rawlings. Through a fortunate set of circumstances the army managed to regiment Bert away from the drink and into a position of self-respect. Funny old life Bert thought to himself. Still, he thought, it did teach me one other thing as well as having steady hands. Bert had seen several boys come into the army the same way as he did, and had seen that the army could turn them into men. The discipline, the routine, the insistence on detail and eventually the camaraderie gave some people self-respect. In this environment Bert learnt to care for people.

Having checked that all was well on the factory floor Bert continued his tour of the factory. He looked in to see Harry quietly checking inventory in the paint store and passed the time of day. From there Bert continued into the packing area. Stephen was listlessly sweeping with a large broom.

'Damp it down a bit Stephen before you sweep. We don't want the dust spread all over the factory.'

'Thought that's what the fucking fans were for,' said Stephen swiping viciously at a snagged piece of strapping.

'No Stephen,' said Bert patiently. 'The fans keep the fumes away from the factory floor but they won't pull all the bigger dust particles away.'

'So get bigger fucking fans. What a dozy lot. I thought management was supposed to be smart. White coats don't do bugger all but walk around and harass the workers.'

'Stephen, just keep the area clean and tidy. No great hassle, just steady graft. Turn the job into a simple routine and it becomes easy.'

Stephen muttered away and Bert continued his inspection. Well, I hope he makes out okay thought Bert. In the army Bert had developed a skill that had surprised even himself. He had done well individually with both bomb disposal and later in electronics and weaponry design. Seeing things and thinking things through to their conclusion had come easily. What had been a new experience was the ability to lead, mentor and gain respect from his other squaddies. Even some of the officers had seen this capability and Bert had risen through the ranks. In the army Bert Rawlings was doing very well for a grammar school kid from a working class background. Unfortunately, it was this rise through the ranks that had also caused Bert's downfall.

'Bloody Major Rupert Stanfield-Brown,' muttered Bert to nobody in particular. 'He's an arch-prick with a titled father, a Sandhurst education, and too much time on his hands; plus being jealous of anyone who could command respect.' Major Standfield-Brown had been the officer in charge of the weaponry design section where Bert worked. Several of Bert's ideas had come up the line and had sat immovably on the Major's desk. The Major was waiting until the right time to pass these onwards and upwards as his own ideas and was getting the scheme organised when a chance visit by a technically-minded Colonel upset all that. Coming into Major Standfield-Brown's office unannounced Colonel Gittings had found it empty. He glanced over the desk and his eye caught some of the technical designs. Impressive, ingenious, some ideas with potential thought Gittings.

'These yours Major? Some ideas of yours? One or two good ideas here. Why haven't you passed these on to me?'

Major Standfield-Brown was caught flat-footed, or more relevantly open-mouthed.

'Yes sir. Good sir. I'll package them up right away. Just some ideas sir.'

'Good show Standfield-Brown; now let's see the design floor shall we eh? Let's see some of your chaps' work. Heard some good things going on here don't you know.'

The impromptu inspection went swiftly and without incident. By chance Bert Rawlings was out of the design office at the time but he heard about it when he returned. The Colonel had stopped by his workstation and was knowledgeable enough to tap a couple of keys to see his latest designs.

'I see you have this officer working on your designs Major. Doing a little refinement eh?'

'Yes sir. This officer is quite good at detail work. Doesn't quite grasp the big picture so to speak. Can't see the whole range. I put him to work on the graphical and annotation parts. Sort of tidies the concept up. Can't expect a man from the ranks to have vision sir. They don't have the background, do they sir?'

'Quite Standfield-Brown. Lead on. Lots to do.'

The whole story, including a line by line account of the conversation got back to Bert on his return. Bert had been in the army long enough to keep his head down. Line authority ruled. Let the precious Major strut his stuff. However, the Major wasn't so thoughtful. Officers coming up through the ranks were an anathema. Smart officers coming up through the ranks were not to be tolerated.

Bert's court-martial was engineered by two of the Major's cronies and presided over by a General who was a good friend of the Standfield-Brown family. Before he knew it Bert was out on civvy street with a good education in electronics and explosives, a praiseworthy ability to mentor and lead, and a warning that drunkenness and fraud would not be tolerated in the Queen's army.

The owner of Carters Colourworld was willing to overlook the drunkenness and fraud, wasn't really interested in the explosives, but did need someone who could oversee men and knew electronics. His paint plant was fully automated with a small staff of operators. For the most part the plant ran itself and the shop floor work was tedious. The plant foreman needed to be able to run the place and make sure that the staff was on its toes despite the boredom. If and when things did go wrong they went wrong quickly and so action was needed immediately. The environmental authorities could come down hard and fast these days if there were any spills.

'Double top, no problem. Piece of cake for our Bert here.' Seaun's voice sang assuredly across the noisy bar. 'Take your time big guy. Hit 'em where it hurts.'

Bert smiled. Seaun was always positive. Seaun was always pushing at the opposition. Mark you, Seaun probably had his week's wages riding on the match.

The weekly darts match between the Crown and the Wheatsheaf was always a lively event. With members from both teams and several supporters there wasn't a lot of room in the crowded bar. There wasn't much light either with the clouds of smoke wafting about. The teams were well matched with some excellent players on both sides. Bert's good eyes and steady hand helped as the anchor of the team.

'Slow and steady,' he muttered to himself. 'See the flight in the mind. Let the arrow flow on the arc to the target.' The hand and the eye combined to propel the dart straight between the wires at the top of the board. 'Double twenty,' said Bert. 'Right where it is supposed to be.'

'Way to go boyo. Here Bert, have a pint on me and me winnings.' Seaun lined up the pints and toasted the success of the Crown team. It had been another successful match, and bet of course.

'So how's young Stephen making out?' asked Bert.

'He's a pain in the rear end,' said Tom. 'All full of mouth and bugger all effort. Not sure why you took him on Bert. You'd better watch him if you're standing surety for him.'

'He's had a rough life,' said Bert. 'He was an orphan dropped off at the local Medical Centre and has lived in foster homes on and off all his life. Some of the early ones were a real fight. You come into a family who have already got kids, and the parents are just in it for the money and you have to fight for everything.'

'Yeah, well, young Dave who works in the packaging department never had it good either. Look at him Bert. He lost his dad out at sea when he was three and then his mum was killed in a bus accident two years later. His old gran brought him up and she lived like a witch. She's enough to scare anyone and yet Dave does his job. He listens when you ask him to do something. Stephen doesn't even listen but opens his gob right away.'

'Why did you bring him on anyway Bert? We all think he's a bloody liability.'

'He's on parole for a stupid robbery but I think the lad needs a chance. He needs someone to talk to: someone who will listen to what he wants to do and where he wants to go.'

'So, what did he do? Maybe we had all better mind our wallets?'

'No, no. He got into an argument in the pub with the barman. The landlord asked for his I.D. and the kid is already eighteen so he can drink. Anyway, Stephen got narked about being asked in front of his mates. Sort of felt it made him look a bit stupid. So, he opened his mouth and told the barman to piss off and that he was old enough to drink in any pub. Well, one thing led to another and next thing Stephen's out on his ear and barred.'

'So, teach him to open his mouth. Maybe he should learn to listen for a change. Anyway, how did that turn into robbery? Did he pinch the pub sign or something daft?'

'No, he decided the pub owed him a drink so he went into the off licence next door and pinched a crate of bottles. He had drunk three and smashed three by the time the police arrived.'

'Cheeky sod. So they let him cool his heels in the cells overnight?'

'Yes, but the sergeant at the station knows I volunteer to help with kids in trouble. The sergeant also thinks Stephen needs help. He's seen the kid work before and thought there was a possibility so he called me. Anyway, I went down and put up the bail and signed off on Stephen to come and work at Colourworld until his day in court. Old Frank

Carter said it was okay as long as I kept an eye on him. Said he was my responsibility.'

'Frank was right there Bert. You had better keep young Stephen on a short leash.'

'I'll look out for the lad. Just let him get some work done without too much hassle. Let's see if we can get him to court with some good news behind him.'

The pub emptied around ten and the patrons made their ways home to their comfortable beds. Stephen re-arranged the sleeping bag on the old office floor and tried to sleep. Bloody hell he thought. What a life? Earlier in the day his landlady had thrown him out. Stephen hadn't paid his rent and having his room reek of marijuana didn't help. Silly old bag thought Stephen. Just couldn't wait another couple of days for the bloody rent could she? Anyway, I seemed to have found a cozy deal here. If I keep my head down and my eyes open I might be able to pick up a quid or two.

Reginald Davidson looked back over his shoulder. 'All buckled up?' he said. 'Yes Daddy,' came back the twins in unison. 'Have a nice day at school you two,' said Anne leaning into the car. 'I'll come and get you at lunch time. You wait at the school gate. No going out onto the road remember.'

'No Mummy,' said Susan.

'Or you either miss,' said Anne.

'No Mummy, I promise,' said Sally.

'Got everything?'

'Yes dear. Don't fuss. The girls have everything and so do I. Remember, I will be home around five thirty as we are going out to the Chamber of Commerce Dinner tonight. It will be all formal bib and tucker.'

'Oh Reginald, I am so looking forward to it. We haven't been out for ages.'

'Can we go Daddy? We'll be late and Miss Edwards gets very cross if we miss the bell.'

'We're off then. Bye love.'

The car eased out of the driveway and took the Davidson twins to school. They arrived before the bell. Reginald continued on to his office and smoothly started another exciting day at his accounting office. Back home Anne flustered around the house trying to think of all the things she had forgotten. Life with the twins was a round of activities and she never seemed to be able to get organised. Phone Danielle said the note on the fridge. Danielle, Danielle thought Anne. Who was Danielle? Oh, yes, Danielle and she picked up the telephone and dialed.

'Hello, hello. Is Danielle there?'

'Who, what? Who is this?' A rather sleepy voice on the other end of the telephone perplexed Anne.

'Is that Danielle?' she repeated in a slow and punctuated voice.

'Yes, yes, yes. Christ, do you know what time it is?'

'Well, yes, it's, it's just gone nine o'clock,' said Anne glancing at the kitchen clock.

'Nine o'clock! Jesus! Who is it at this ungodly hour?'

'Danielle, it's Anne Davidson. You promised to babysit for us tonight. Do you remember we talked about it a week ago when I bumped into you in the chemists? You said you could do it. Do you remember?'

'A week ago? I have difficulty remembering an hour ago. Who did you say?'

Anne started to become even more concerned at this stage. She needed someone to look after her two darlings. She needed someone responsible. Reginald had been quite clear that she should find someone adult and qualified. He didn't want any teenager in the house getting up to who knows what.

The telephone conversation continued in a rather disjointed fashion but eventually both parties agreed on time and place. Danielle would be round by six and Reginald would run her home about eleven when they came back from the dinner. Anne put down the phone and sat down wearily. She hoped that she had got that right but it really was kind of trying.

Unfortunately for Anne that was only the first upset of the day. As she promised she went out before lunch to pick up the twins from school. They were waiting at the school gate as they promised. Just as Anne turned with the girls in tow she saw a face she hadn't seen for a long time.

'Hello Mum, Anne.'

'Stephen. My you've grown. I hardly recognised you.'

'Sure. Been away but it's good to see you. Didn't think I would ever see you.'

'No, well, Stephen,' Anne stuttered as her face crimsoned. 'We moved to a bigger house just before the twins were born. This is Susan and Sally. Girls, this is Stephen, a.... friend.'

'Why did he call you Mum?'

'Well, when he was younger he was like a son to me and so he got used to calling me Mum.'

'But is he still your son? Don't want a brother, do you Susan?' said Sally glaring at Stephen.

'No, certainly not,' said Susan. 'We live in an all girls house,' said Susan loudly.

'Well Stephen. It's nice to see you again. You look well. We're off home for lunch. Maybe we'll see you again. Come on girls.' Anne whirled away holding onto the hands of Susan and Sally and set off down the street. Sally peered back over her shoulder and poked out her tongue.

Stephen felt all mixed up inside. He balled his fists and glared back at Sally. He thought back to the happiness he once knew with his Mum, Anne. Then he flashed angry again when he remembered the disappointment when the adoption never went through and he was back in the orphanage with never a goodbye. His happiness had been snatched away with no explanations. His beautiful happy world had suddenly ended; the parties, the holidays, a mother and father and then nothing.

Without really thinking what he was doing Stephen started to follow them. He trailed some distance behind and kept out of sight. Anne and the two girls turned into a leafy avenue that ran down beside a tree-lined stream. Stephen saw them go through the gate of one of the large houses and up the driveway. He heard the door open and close. Noting which house he doubled back to the end of the street and found a path alongside the stream that led down behind the houses. Keeping hidden in the trees he walked down along the row of houses until he thought he was behind Anne's house.

'Push me, push me,' called Sally.

'As long as it's my turn afterwards,' said Susan.

'Higher, higher, push Susan.'

Stephen could hear the voices of the twins and found that he had the wrong house. He struggled through the bushes down a little further until he could see into the back garden where the girls were playing on a swing set. Stephen broke through the bushes at the end of the garden and strode purposely up to the French doors at the back of the house. He walked inside and looked around the room. Nice he thought.

'Mommy, Mommy that man is back. He came into the garden and now he's in the house.'

'What did you say dear?' asked Anne. 'I can't hear you through the kitchen window,' she said as she opened the casement.

'He's here. He's here in the house,' shrieked Sally. 'He just barged right in.'

'Who Sally? Who's here?'

'The man from the school,' said Susan. 'He's in the lounge.'

Anne rushed from the kitchen and into the lounge and stopped abruptly. 'Stephen, what are you doing here? Whatever do you want?'

'Well I thought I'd come home,' said Stephen.

'What do you mean?' said Anne.

'Nice place,' said Stephen as he eyes slowly traversed the room, 'very nice. Be a nice place to live compared to where I am now. What do you say Mum?'

'Stephen, all that's over. You know that. We've got the twins now. I'm sorry things didn't work out but you see how it is.'

'Can't see it at all myself. Nice big house with lots of room; just needs a bigger family.'

'Stephen please. This isn't going to happen. I'll just call Reginald to have him explain it to you. I'm sure he can make you understand the situation.'

'Just give us a hug like old times,' said Stephen, advancing on Anne.

'No Stephen please. It's not like old times. You are a dear but it's all changed now.'

Suddenly the room seemed too small for Anne and she turned back into the kitchen and lifted the telephone. Stephen followed watching her carefully. Anne shrank a little as Stephen entered the kitchen.

'Mommy, what's he want? Why is he here? Go away.' Sally's vibrant voice rang through the kitchen.

'Do you hear me? You're frightening my Mommy.'

'Yes, go away,' chimed in Susan as both the twins stood side by side in the doorway.

'Stephen, please go,' said Anne in a low voice. 'Please.'

He turned and strode up the hallway. He pulled open the door and walked out down the driveway. Without saying a word Stephen marched back up the leafy street and away to Colourworld. Inside he was saying a lot. He repeatedly clenched and unclenched his fists. My home he muttered, taken away by those two noisy brats. Anne loved me first. I was her son before those two monsters came on the scene. This turmoil of emotions stayed with him all the way into the packing room of Colourworld.

'And where have you been? Lunchtime's long over mate. You thinking of doing any work here? Bert's sticking his neck out for you you know.'

'Sod him, and sod you you noisy git. Just get out of my face.'

'Well pull your weight then. There's a mess of packaging to clear up in here and its got your name on it.'

'You be careful old man or I'll package you up in it and dump it over a cliff.'

'Hey, just remember who's looking out for you. Bert said you need a break and a chance to work. We all heard you'd had a rough time. Just give it a go eh?'

Stephen had calmed down by this time and the emotions drained out of him. He sat down on a packing case and came close to tears. 'Sod it, sod it, sod it. Why can't I go home?'

'You all right kid?' asked Bert as he came round the corner from the factory floor. Colin reckoned you were pretty worked up about something and was sort of worried like. I'm here to help Stephen, if I can.'

'I've seen them again,' said Stephen. 'After all this time with not a word, I've seen them again, complete with the cuddly twins. All cosy and wrapped up in themselves. Living in a rich house with all the creature comforts. Should have been mine: should be my home, my mum. Oh shit.'

'Who, what Stephen? What's this all about? What brought this on all of a sudden?'

'Where I used to live, or rather who I used to live with. Anne bloody Davidson and lord Reginald that's who. They were going to adopt me. I lived with them for a year and it was all set up. Christ, I was part of the bloody family: a real mum and dad for a change. We had presents, parties, and we even went on holidays and then, out of the blue it stopped. There was no warning, no word, no nothing. Suddenly I was back at the orphanage and precious mum and dad disappeared. Can you imagine how that felt: after all those years of being in and out of foster homes to be with a real mum and dad and then poof!'

'Pretty rough I'd think,' said Bert. 'It would have torn me up, especially at your age.'

'You'd better bloody believe it. Shit, I went on a rampage for a while, but now I've found them.'

'But it's over kid you said. They've got their own family.'

Bert was a little aware of Stephen's background and had heard this story before from the social workers. It had been a rough deal to be sure but life was a bitch. Anyway, Stephen seemed to have survived and showing some potential. Kid needs a chance.

'So, can we get this show on the road Stephen? There's some packaging to clear up in storage and Colin was looking for a helping hand too. Past is past lad. Put it behind you. You've other things to worry about now. Don't forget we are trying to look like we are doing well for the court.'

'Sure, sure,' muttered Stephen. He picked up his broom and set off to the packing shed.

Bert wiped his brow and hoped the afternoon might progress constructively. Colin had worried him for a moment and he rushed round in case Stephen blew his stack. That would really not look good at court and not do Bert's credibility any good either.

The rest of the afternoon passed peacefully enough and Bert was fully occupied in his office with paperwork. Stephen actually got into a friendly game of footie at tea break and the day ended quietly. Bert went round his usual final inspection to check on the automatic mode for some of the machines. Coming round the corner into the packing shed Bert noticed a shadow flit across the wall. No one should be around here now. Everyone should have gone home.

'Who's there? Anyone there?' he shouted. Listening, he heard nothing. He walked on through the packing shed towards the older part of the factory. There had been two offices and another storage shed over this side in the early days. With the modernization the area was no longer used. Bert hadn't been through this part of the factory for a couple of days and was surprised to find the office door open. Looking inside he couldn't see anybody but he could see that the dust on the floor had been disturbed recently.

'Anybody there? Come out who ever you are.' Bert continued on to the second office. Through the doorway he stopped and saw the sleeping bag, the crisp packets and the old rucsack. 'Who's there?' he said again.

Stephen came slowly out of the old shed into the second office. 'Got kicked out of my digs didn't I? Had no fucking place to go. Seemed a good place to doss down. Not doing any harm. What's the problem?'

This flood of sound filled the little office and Bert almost had to step backwards with the barrage of words.

'Whoa, slow down kid. Don't get your knickers in a knot.'

'Didn't think anyone would mind. Old bag threw me out 'cos I didn't pay all me rent. Silly old cow. But I've done no harm. Kept it neat.'

Another flow of words filled up the room again. Bert scratched his head. 'Come on kid. Let's find somewhere better than this, at least for tonight. Maybe we can sort something better out tomorrow but come on over to my place tonight. That'll be better than dossing down here. Just grab your gear and let's go and have a burger somewhere.'

'No, I've got to go somewhere tonight. Got something to do.'

'Well can't it wait until we've sorted out somewhere to sleep? Grab your gear anyway. We can go back to my place after you've sorted out whatever it is you have to do. Anyway, I'm getting hungry and a burger would go down well now.'

The burger did go down well. Stephen was starving and so Bert ended up buying him another one. Bert sat back and watched Stephen's young face. Bit of an uphill battle for the youth he thought. Perhaps a good night's kip would help.

'So, where is it that you've got to go to tonight? What's so important?'

'I've got to go and see Anne and Reginald. I've got to sort it out with them, see when I can come back.'

'Stephen, we've talked about that lad. Let it be.'

No, no, you don't understand. They've got to understand. I should be there with them, in the new house like.'

'Hell Stephen, look here, it's over.'

'Well, I've got to go and tell them. Tell them I know where they are. Tell them I'm looking out for them.'

'Stephen, now don't go and do anything stupid.'

'No, I won't, but I've got to tell them both, not just Anne but Reginald too. Actually, I think Anne wants me back. She always liked me. She always thought I was someone special. She looked after me real good. She was really kind to me, she was...'

'Stephen, snap out of it. We'll go and see them. Okay? Just go and see them and tell them you understand that they have their own family now. You're glad to see them and maybe visit now and again. So, that's what we'll do. Just to go round there and explain you understand how it is?'

Stephen nodded but his head was somewhere else. He slurped the end of his drink and stood up quickly. 'Let's go now,' he said. 'Let's go and tell them we know where they are. We know where they all are.'

Bert caught the tone and the words and stood up quickly before Stephen could take off solo. He grabbed Stephen's arm and steered him out of the door. Not really letting go of Stephen Bert walked the pair of them over to his car and made sure Stephen was inside before he went round to the driver's side.

'Well Stephen, where are we headed? Tell me the way, but remember let's keep this cool. No bloody outbursts, just a visit.'

'Left at the lights and then straight on for a couple of blocks. You'll turn right at the chemists and down towards the Valley Primary School.'

Bert let out the clutch and his Ford Escort slid out of the burger house parking lot into the flow of traffic. The lights were green as he turned around the corner. He kept his eyes on the road for there was a lot of traffic in the narrow street. However, he also kept glancing at Stephen who was hip hopping up and down in the passenger seat.

'Stephen, where next?' asked Bert, trying to relieve some of the tension building up in the car. 'Two blocks down you said?'

'Yes, yes,' said an exasperated Stephen. 'Didn't you listen? Didn't you hear what I said? Two blocks down mate and then turn right at the chemists. See it, see it down there. Turn, turn.'

'Okay, but there's oncoming traffic Stephen. I can't just cut across them. Slow it down for God's sake. There's no bloody fire.'

The car drove down the road passed the Primary School and Stephen bounced up and down again.

'Where now?'

'Over the bridge and turn right down that leafy avenue. See where the trees meet up over the road: posh looking houses with big gardens going down to the stream. Stop, stop, stop! Christ, you passed it. Back up.'

Stephen had the door open and was out of the car before Bert could even put the gear into reverse. In the crash of events he stalled the motor. It took Bert a moment to sort things out but as fast as he could he was out of the car after Stephen. Without looking at any traffic Stephen was across the road, up the gravel driveway and pounding on the door. Bert was just coming through the gate when he saw the stream of light as the door opened and Stephen barge inside.

'Where are they? Where are they?' Bert could hear Stephen's strident voice and then another voice scream back. 'Get out of here you madman. Who the hell do you think you are barging in here?'

'Where are they? Where's Anne and fucking lord Reginald? Come on you black little tart, where are they?'

Bert had reached the front porch by this time and was greeted by the sound of two shrieking little girls. Susan and Sally were standing at the top of the stairs screaming as loud as they could. Before Bert could even take in this part of the scene he saw Stephen push Danielle out of the way as he rushed through to the kitchen. 'Out of the way bitch. I'll find them.' Not finding anyone in the kitchen Stephen was hot foot upstairs before Bert could move. This rush of Stephen upstairs caused the pitch of the screaming to go up several decibels. Close behind Stephen went a raging Danielle with hair and clothes flying like a black panther. Stephen was in and out of the bedroom by the time Danielle reached the landing. There was a crash of bodies, more screams, and a lamp went flying which caused instant darkness upstairs.

Bert fumbled around looking for a light switch for the staircase or the upper landing. Suddenly a body came tumbling down the semicircular staircase in a cascade of arms, legs, and flying clothing. Danielle landed at Bert's feet with a loud thump and a crack. Screams upstairs had risen again and Bert saw Stephen's legs come in to the light as he came downstairs.

'They're not here,' he said quietly and wistfully. 'Anne's not here.' Stephen slumped at the foot of the stairs shattered. 'They need to know,' he whispered.

Bert bent down to see what had happened to Danielle. 'Stephen, move. I can't see how she is. Move yourself.' Stephen seemed to have closed down and just sat there. Bert pulled Danielle away from the foot of the stairs and started checking how she was. Fortunately he found nothing broken but she was dazed. Just as he turned away her eyes opened and a pair of hands with claws came streaking towards him. 'Bastard,' came the cry. The claws missed but the eyes were full of malice. Finding Danielle was not seriously hurt was a relief. Bert started up the stairs to find the screams and try and sort out that situation.

About ten minutes later the household was quiet again. The twins were safely tucked up and pacified. A very bruised and disheveled Danielle was spitting fire but sitting down with a drink. Stephen seemed to have gone into a coma, just muttering to himself. Bert put the furniture back to rights and made sure that the visit wasn't too obvious.

Bert started to take out some money from his wallet. 'Keep your poxy money mate and keep your mad monkey on a leash. Christ, if I catch him alone I'll have his guts for garters. I'll scratch his bloody eyes out. Who the fuck does he think he is anyway?'

There didn't seem any point in trying to explain so Bert pulled Stephen up by the arm and led him out of the house. Hopefully Stephen had got all of that out of his system for the night. He folded Stephen into the front seat and went round to the driver's side. Slowly Bert pulled away from the kerb and drove back into town. He quietly pulled up on his street and collected Stephen's bits and pieces from the back seat. Stephen followed docilely as Bert unlocked the front door and led Stephen upstairs to his flat. A nice quiet evening Bert thought. That's all I wanted tonight after last night's dart match, just a nice quiet evening.

The following morning went by without incident. Stephen seemed quiet enough in the morning and Bert took him to work in the car. At the factory Bert did his usual rounds of the shop floor, passing the time of day with each of the employees. Colin told Bert that Stephen seemed fine this morning. Said he was actually doing a bit of work for a change. Bert mentally filed this bit of good news and returned to his office. There he did some paperwork and assumed that life was back to normal.

It was about two o'clock that Colin came to Bert's office with a worried look on his face.

'It's Stephen,' he said. 'You need to come and see him.'

'What's up Colin? Everything seemed fine this morning. You even said Stephen was fine.'

'Well he's not fine now Bert. He's a mess. Somebody's really given him a going over.'

'What'd you mean a going over?'

'You come and see for yourself. You try and talk to him. He's spitting blood and flames at the moment. Won't listen to anyone.'

Bert followed Colin through the factory and everyone watched. Seemed the word had got out about the recent turn of events. Work went on but you could see everyone watching Bert. Outside the packing shed, sitting on a pile of old crates was a mess of torn clothing hanging off a bloody mess.

'Christ, what the hell happened? You run into a threshing machine or something?' Stephen turned his head which revealed a closed eye, a very bloody nose, and three parallel slash marks across his cheek. The rest of the body didn't look much better.

'I'm surprised he managed to walk here,' said Colin. 'All of this happened a way away.' Stephen swayed and Bert thought he was going to fall off the crates.

'Here, help me,' said Bert to Colin. 'Let's get him over to my office and organise some first aid. Maybe when we get him cleaned up it won't look quite so bad.'

Together they supported Stephen's battered body. They passed all the floor workers up to Bert's office. Stephen didn't say anything but winced when they banged his arm against the staircase railing. It took a while as Bert cleaned up the blood, checked for breaks and made sure the pupils weren't dilated. Stephen appeared pretty stunned and Bert wasn't sure whether he was concussed at all. Eventually Bert reached a stage where he felt he could ask questions.

'Well, are you going to tell me what this is all about? You obviously wound someone up for this to happen. Colin said it happened away from the factory. Where the hell were you?'

Stephen slowly held up his hand. 'A moment for fucks sake. Jesus I hurt all over. Those two bastards really did me over.'

'What two bastards may I ask?'

'The two bastards after last night, or the one black bastard and her toffy-nosed friend.'

'Who are you talking about? Where did you go?'

"I went back to Anne's house to see her. I had to tell her about seeing her again.'

'You did what?'

"I went to Anne's house. I told you I had to tell her. Well, surprise, surprise lord Reginald is there too. So, I told the both of them didn't I? Had to tell them I knew where they were.'

'And what did they say?'

'Told me to piss off like. Told me never to come round there again. Told me to leave off pestering Anne. Told me that if I ever go round there again he'll send the police after me, so I hit him.'

'You did what?'

'I hit him, silly sod. Bloodied his nose too. Serves him right. Toffy-nosed git never did really like me. Just wanted a proper family or something to go with his proper lifestyle.'

'And what happened?'

'Well he got mad like you know. Said I was scum. Tried to throw me out of the house.'

'And, what next?'

'Anne screamed, and of course the twins screamed. Bloody bedlam it was. So I hit lord Reginald again and scarpered.'

Bert drew a breath trying to imagine the scene. Christ, what a mess. 'But you didn't get into this state just from that?'

'No, bumped into the black tart didn't I? Silly cow was driving down the road with her poncy boyfriend. She sees me and screams blue murder. Anyway, the car stops and out jumps lover boy. God, I didn't have a fucking chance. Next thing I knew he's hit me and the black bitch is trying to scratch my eyes out.'

'Couldn't you run or something?'

'Run, with those two falling all over me. The bloke caught me with his fist in the guts and I'm doubled over see. I end up with all last night's dinner flooding over my shoes. A right mess I was. And then that little lady with the claws has hold of my hair and I end up with nail marks down my face.'

'How did it stop then?'

'Two blokes were coming down the street and shouting so lover boy and his black tart took off. Not before a last kick though that nearly broke my nose. I could still see through one eye and waved the two blokes away. They came on though and ended up bringing me back here.'

'So it was the fight after going to Anne's that caused all this trouble?'

'How was I to know she was going to go crazy? What's her problem anyway? I didn't do anything to her, just pushed her out of the bloody way. Silly bitch fell down the stairs because she was probably drunk or high. Seen her around town and she is usually floating around somewhere.'

'Who was the bloke?'

'Some toffy-nosed bugger with a flash motor: one of those sports cars with chrome and headlamps. Bright red it was.'

'That sound like young Michael Lord,' said Bert. 'He's a rough character to be sure. And you're right, he does go out with Danielle. Seems you have a score to settle with young Michael.'

'Yeah, well next time we'll get the odds right. No more two of them on one of me. Maybe you and me should teach young Michael a lesson. He needs to learn not to kick someone when they're down.'

'Young Michael doesn't play by the Marquess of Queensberry's rules.'

'Who the fuck cares whose rules he uses. He wasn't playing by any rules this afternoon, and that bitch has got sharp claws.'

'Anyway, we'd better get you some new clothes as the ones you've got on look like rags.' True enough as the shirt was partly shredded and Stephen's trousers have a big rent down one leg. Bert decided there and then to take Stephen to the shops and buy some new clothes. He told Seaun where he was going and to act as foreman while he was out.

The shopping expedition was partly a success. Stephen came to life and paraded around the dressing room of the clothing store with an array of bright shirts. Bert had found a couple of pairs of trousers suitable for work but Stephen would have none of those. 'Christ mate, I ain't an old man. I need jeans to wear, preferably Levis.' Stephen insisted on wearing one of his new bright shirts out of the store and was really chuffed up as he told Bert, 'got two for the price one there. See, got this other one on underneath. They never saw it and now I've got it.'

Bert saw no point in trying to argue against this theft. That would only complicate matters and put everyone's nose out of joint; a definite lose/lose situation but he was worried about the flighty moods of Stephen. As they left the store Stephen tore the key out of Bert's hand and jumped into the driver's seat.

'Let's go, let's go before the silly old sod finds out.' Stephen had the car in gear and rolling forwards before Bert had the door open. He managed to just fall into the passenger seat as Stephen accelerated away.

'Stephen, for heavens sake just slow down. What's got into you? One moment you were crawling around all beat up and now you're flying around like a mad man.'

'Well I got beat up didn't I? Kicked the shit out of me they did and I feel like getting my own back. There are two of us now and you've been in the army and all. You must know how to fight. We can kick the shit out of them for a change.'

Stephen drove erratically around the streets and Bert didn't think it was a good time to try and take over. He let Stephen unwind himself, trying to make sure no one got hurt in the process. Unfortunately this didn't happen. Quite by chance Stephen saw Michael's bright red sports car.

'It's him. It's the poxy boyfriend himself. He must be in the pub.' Stephen swung Bert's car into the pub car park and jumped out. 'Just you wait here for him. I'll go in and lure him out and you be waiting for him. I'll make the bugger chase me and when he comes out of the door just flatten him. Then we can kick his precious goolies in. Bastard kicked me hard enough.' Stephen took off through the pub door and Bert looked for a suitable place to teach Michael a lesson. There really had been no need to give young Stephen such a beating.

It was a set up and for once in his life Michael never saw it coming. Stephen came flying out of the pub and the first moment Michael knew that something was wrong was when he realized his feet weren't on the floor. The crash that followed as he landed on the gravel knocked some of the wind out of him.

'Bastard, bastard,' screamed the voice above his head as a boot thumped into his ribs.

'Pick on someone your own size,' said another older voice as a fist grabbed the collar of his shirt and lifted him bodily off the ground. A solid punch thumped hard into his chest and Michael winced with the pain. Another sharp pain raced up from his ankles as a boot lashed out at his feet. Michael rolled away as fast as he could to be able to stand up and see who his attackers were.

'You,' he said as he caught sight of Stephen out of the corner of his right eye. He never saw the fist that promptly smacked into his left eye and knocked him flat again.

'Leave it now. That's done.'

'No, let me teach the bastard a lesson. Let me kick the shit out of his toffy nose.'

'No! That's enough. We're out of here.'

The fight had taken less than twenty seconds and no one had come out of the pub. There hadn't been anyone coming down the road in that time and so Bert and Stephen drove away with no one the wiser. No one except Michael for he remembered Stephen and he recognised Bert's car through his one good eye. Michael gingerly felt his ribs. Nothing seemed to be broken but his left eye was closing fast. Slowly he limped over to his car and drove sedately home, musing on future events.

Stephen's high crashed down right after the fight. He too was quiet in the car as Bert drove back to the factory. Everything there was working smoothly and Stephen went back to the packing shed and his cleaning up while Bert checked everyone on the factory floor. Bert decided against telling Seaun about the afternoon's turn of events. There seemed no point in telling anyone about the incident with Michael.

Knock-off time came and Bert walked round for his last inspection. He turned off the air-conditioners in the offices; he checked the controls on the various machines and switched the fume-remover fans on and off to make sure they were working properly. At the end of the tour Bert collected Stephen and said they'd better do the same as last night as Bert hadn't had time to try and find alternative accommodation for Stephen. With his new clothes Stephen wasn't really thinking about anything but how he looked at the moment. He just nodded and jumped into Bert's car.

The following day passed without incident, although a little snow fell which was unusual even though it was December. Bert had been out most of the day involved with a special client for Mr. Carter. Seaun had been in charge of the factory floor and everything had worked smoothly. Even Stephen did his job, such as it was. Things quieted down until Thursday morning.

There was a loud knock on the door, followed by an insistent ringing of the bell.

'Holy Moses, who's that at this hour?' asked Bert to the room at large. He staggered into some clothes and walked down the hall to his flat door. He opened it to a large, cross and overdressed middle-aged woman. 'Rent! You know rent? You're a week late.'

'Yes, I know Mrs. Reaper. I've been busy and haven't got to the bank.'

'Bank is it? Since when have you had to worry about the bank? Paid in cash you are at Carters. Rent, now!' She moved the support for her large amount of flesh from the left leg to the right leg and everything quivered.

'What's that noise?' she suddenly said loudly as she caught the sound of the shower. 'Who you got staying here? You got someone in here? You know the rules; single lodgings these are.'

'There's no one Mrs. R. I just left the shower running.'

'Then how come you're dry and.......' Mrs. R. stopped talking for a moment as she caught sight of a young male naked body waltzing down the hallway. Her hand went up to her fleshy mouth but not before a shriek sprang out and reverberated round the corridor.

'Who's that?'

'Oh that's Stephen, my son,' said Bert. 'Come, come to stay for a couple of days. I was going to tell you but I was out all day yesterday.'

'Son, in your dreams you pervert. You don't 'ave no son. He's a..... a rent boy, a toy boy. Out, out, out,' she screamed as she charged down the hallway towards Stephen. Stephen stepped sideways quickly into the kitchen and Mrs. Reaper's bodily mass collapsed over Stephen's stuck out foot and she sprawled the full length of the hall.

'Who's this old bag then?' he asked Bert.

'Mrs. Reaper is my landlady,' answered a reluctant Bert.

'Well, she shouldn't have such a dirty mind. Should you you dirty old cow?' Stephen rolled Mrs. Reaper over with his foot. She lay there gasping like a stranded whale. 'You, you, you...' she struggled for words.

Bert extended his hand to help her up. Mrs. Reaper spurned the hand and struggled to a sitting position and finally a standing position. She drew herself up to her full five feet and said,' out, out now. I'll not have any perverts in my lodgings. Half an hour and what's not gone will be thrown out. I'll have the cops down after that.'

Stephen giggled. 'You silly old fart. Think we'd want to stay any longer in this fleapit? We were just going anyway, weren't we Dad?' Bert looked sort of shell-shocked. Everything was going tits up too fast. He brushed past Mrs. Reaper and Stephen into the bedroom and started to throw clothes into a suitcase. The door slammed and Stephen came back into the room. 'Well, we took care of her real quick, didn't we?'

'Sure youth, and she's taken care of us. We're out of here and now neither of us has a place to stay.'

'No problem, you were going to have to look for a bigger place anyway with me staying now weren't you?'

'Stephen that was never the arrangement. I took you in because you had no place to go. Given time I was going to sort something out for you with the social.'

'Well now you won't have to worry will you? Let's find somewhere where we both can stay. It's easy.'

Bert was too bewildered to think this through at this point in time. He would need a moment to try and organise his thoughts and then some proper solution. There was a pressing item right now though.

'Stephen, grab your gear and pack it all up. I've got to sort out what's mine here and get it into suitcases. Finally, let's not forget it's Thursday and we've got work to go to.'

They arrived at Carters Colourworld a little late and Mr. Carter's car stood by the front entrance. As Bert parked Mr. Carter got out of his car and stood beside it waiting for Bert to come to him. 'Running a little late Rawlings? Everything going okay?' Mr. Carter watched young Stephen exit from Bert's car and stand there.

'Go and clock in Stephen,' said Bert. 'Tell Colin you got held up. Work a bit over lunchtime.'

'What's he doing in your car Rawlings?'

'He had a spot of bother with his landlady and I helped him out. Remember Mr. Carter, Sergeant Lewis reckoned the kid had something going for him and I agreed to mentor him. We talked about it and you agreed.'

'Yes Rawlings, I remember. How's he making out at work? No trouble I hope?'

'He's doing what we ask. He's still a teenager with problems. They never quite know where they're going next.'

'Fine, but that's not why I'm here. Seems Makens over in Bristol want a consultation over this new contract. Their order is pretty important to me and so I said we would go over and talk delivery dates and colour options. I need you to come to Bristol now.'

'Sure Mr. Carter. I'll just tell my office where I'll be and make sure that someone checks on the factory floor.'

'I've done all that. I've seen your girl in the office. We need to go now.'

It was very late in the afternoon when Frank Carter dropped Bert off at the front door of the factory to collect his car. Carter sped away having had a successful day in Bristol and thought no more about Bert Rawlings. Bert looked around the factory yard but there was no sign of Stephen. He went inside. All was quiet except for the low background hum of the exhaust fans, and then he heard another noise, a noise that shouldn't be there. Up in his office Stephen had arranged his sleeping bag and brought up Bert's suitcases. Stephen looked up as Bert came into the room.

'This seems as good as anywhere for the night. Worked for me.' Bert was too exhausted to protest. It had been a long tiring day trying to stay in tune with his boss. Unfortunately Mr. Carter didn't keep himself up to date on the factory and its schedules and so Bert had to do a lot of double talking to the representatives from Makens before Mr. Carter promised things that were impossible.

'Stephen, the air-conditioners get turned off in the offices at night.'

'What the hell for?'

'It'll get too cold in here if they are left on.'

'Who gives a toss?'

'I do,' and Bert went outside the offices to the control panel to turn them off. They went out for another burger and then Bert took Stephen in to the pub. 'Now behave or I'll throw you out. This is my local.' Bert had a couple of practice games at darts and impressed Stephen. 'You try. Just see your target and push the dart.' Stephen's coordination was very limited compared to Bert's. 'Remind me not to bet when you're on the team,' joshed Seaun.

'Shut yer mouth you Irish soak.'

'Hold up young fella. No harm meant. Just takes a steady hand to throw a dart.'

'Let's see you then. You're all mouth.'

'Actually Stephen, he's all hands,' said Bert, coming across to make the peace. 'Used to be a top rate jockey with hands to hold any reins. Soft of hand and strong of arm with the whip when needed, eh Seaun?'

'To be sure. I used to love the horses. Be as one with them I was.'

'So what happened? Why are you pushing knobs and twirling wheels in Colourworld? Lost your bottle?'

'No Stephen, not quite. Seaun here has all the bottle you can imagine but the trouble is keeping him sober and the right weight for any big event.'

'Aye, that's my downfall young lad. I like a pint and I like me's food. When I'm like that it's not fair on the horses, or the punters,' he added. 'Bert, remember tomorrow night's the match against Dewleys.'

'I remember Seaun, that's why I'm in here taking a little practice.'

'Well remember that their floors sloped like. Makes the board look like it's tilted. Try standing on one leg to practice.'

'Get away with you Seaun. You're like an old woman. I line them up and throw.'

After closing time Bert and Stephen drove back quietly to the factory. Bert had to persuade Stephen again that the air-conditioners stayed off. They settled down for the night. Bert told Stephen he would try and get something organised tomorrow. Also, he reminded Stephen that he would be out in the evening at Dewleys Pub in the next town for the darts match. Stephen told him 'so what', but Bert was already asleep.

Not far away Danielle was inspecting Michael's body for improvements from her first aid. Michael had gone home after that second encounter with Stephen and licked his wounds. There was nothing seriously wrong but his left eye had closed up a little more and the surrounding eye socket now fluoresced in a startling array of colour. Michael put in a token show of work for his dad at the office on Thursday and managed to keep out of everyone's sight. He really didn't feel like a long interrogation about his face colour. Most of the afternoon Michael spent on a quiet investigation and then included an evening visit to Colourworld. While there he noticed that Bert's car was still in the parking lot. Somewhat satisfied with his sleuthing Michael went on to Danielle's on the Thursday night looking for some more TLC. The town was quiet.

Friday should have been a quiet day too but different people were up to different things. Bert awoke and quickly stirred Stephen. They packed away their belongings and had a quick wash and brush up in the men's room. Bert decided they would drive away in the car and then come back around clock-on time as part of a normal routine. Stephen couldn't see what all the bloody fuss was about but Bert didn't need the aggro and told him to shut up and get in the car.

About the time that Bert drove back to Colourworld Michael stirred himself and started on his day's plan. Still peering out of one good eye he drove sedately to Bristol to talk with Hammond Brothers, a company who had previously done a contract for his father. Bert meantime walked into his office to find Sheila his secretary had a message for him from Mr. Carter already. 'Seems you're back out on the road again today Mr. Rawlings,' she said. 'The telephone was ringing itself off the hook when I came in. Mr. Carter was really worried about a break in. Said someone had seen lights on in the factory late at night. He was checking to see everything was in order.'

'Well the silly bugger should hire a night watchman like any other owner. Tight-fisted old buzzard won't pay out the cash for that though will he?'

'Don't know I'm sure Mr. Rawlings,' Sheila said as she looked at her new nail polish. 'Do you like the colour?'

'What colour? Oh, your nails. I was still thinking about Mr. Carter's message.'

'Oo, and he had another one, another message too,' said Sheila suddenly remembering, 'something about Chomleys. Now what was it?'

'Come on Sheila, I've haven't got all day. What did he say?'

'After he wanted you to speak to the police he wanted you to go and see Chomleys, something about locks or bolts. He was quite rude about it. Said it should have been done long ago. Said you should have seen to it.'

'What was it he wanted?'

'Safety, that was it. It's Chomleys Safety Company isn't it? They have a hardware shop in the High Street, next to Boots. That's where I got this nail polish. Thought it looked a nice colour in the shop but I'm not so sure now.'

'Sheila!' Bert said in exasperation.

'O yes. He said you were to go and visit their offices and get them to install locks.'

'Sheila, this is all a little confusing. Perhaps I'd better phone Mr. Carter.'

'No, I'm sure I've got it right. Anyway, wouldn't do any good because he's off.'

'Off, what do you mean off?'

'Well, you know, he's gone for the day hasn't he? Said he was off to play golf or something. Real rushed he was about it too. Some special medal thing.' Sheila paused, looked at her nails again, and then suddenly piped up with another but completely different remark. 'The air-conditioners were on when I came in this morning. Never had that happen before. That's something you or I do when we first come in. I noticed they were switched on but couldn't find you already here in the office. Gave me a bit of a spooky turn, that and the telephone ringing its head off.'

Bert scratched his head which was going round in circles. Fine, one thing at a time. He made sure that Sheila was organised for a while with a pile of paperwork. Then he did a quick tour of the factory floor. Everything seemed to be going fine there at least. Back in his office he telephoned the police but the day-shift supervisor didn't know anything about any reported lights and said to call back later.

Chomley's main office was the other side of town. Bert had telephoned before he left Colourworld to make sure that someone at Chomleys could talk to him at short notice. The meeting was set up for later in the morning and Bert had time to check on a couple of things on the shop floor before setting off.

'Remember Dewleys?' said Seaun.

'Of course.'

'We're all banking on you special tonight Bert. I heard they've got some ringer down from London. A fella who's been on the tele like.'

'I'll be there. In fact I'll pick you up from the Crown around six. I'll take you myself.'

There was quiet laughter from the several co-workers who had overheard this conversation. 'Hedging your bets again Seaun?'

'It's better to be wise than just friendly. You need to bet with your head not your heart. 'Tisn't always the favourite who comes in the winner.'

'And you're making sure your winner will be there to overwhelm the favourite?'

Bert smiled as he left the floor hearing this conversation going on behind him. The general feeling was that Bert was a good boss. He cared for people. He talked with people, and he listened.

As Bert left Colourworld to meet with Mr. Friston Smythe of Chomleys, Michael Lord was sitting down with Kevin Hammond. Spread out on the table before them was a large-scale plan of Colourworld. Kevin was explaining what they had found when their company had done an inspection of the factory for Michael's father.

It didn't take Bert long to drive through town and into Chomley's Head Office parking lot. The smart and keen Mr. Friston Smythe was in the foyer to meet him and take Bert upstairs to a spacious well-lit conference room. There, on a large table Bert unfurled a sheath of diagrams and drawings of Colourworld's factory and property. Mr. Smythe was very young and very industrious and he listened carefully to Bert Rawlings. He looked at the plans of the perimeter fence and gates. He followed this up with a more detailed inspection of the various walls, exterior doors and windows, and then looked carefully at the interior controls and the various systems. During this study Mr. Smythe asked numerous questions and took copious notes. All of this took a lot of time and Bert was already fretting about things that had to be done. However, he was also mindful of Mr. Carter's insistent instructions.

The meeting at Chomleys took up the rest of the morning. Seeking to ensure a contract and wanting to appear older than his years Mr. Friston Smythe then insisted that he take Mr. Rawlings to lunch. To make a favourable impression Mr. Friston Smythe took Bert to the local golf club, where he was a member and a recent medal winner. Luncheon was a slow formal affair in the quiet and refined clubhouse with drinks before and during. Bert, however, was chomping at the bit. He had work to do and time was awasting. As soon as he could he took his leave of the keen Mr. Friston Smythe and set off back to Colourworld.

He drove his out-of-place Ford Escort from the golf club's upper-class parking lot into the real world. Bert set off back to Colourworld to try and get something done today. With his mind on factory floor production, Mr. Carter, yesterday's promises to Maken's about schedules, Stephen and the darts match Bert didn't see the lorry failing to give him the right of way on the roundabout. The first he knew about it was a loud crunch as the lorry ploughed into his left front wing and his car being pushed sideways. The two vehicles locked together skidded across the two lanes of the roundabout and Bert's right side caught the inside kerb and his car tipped up on two wheels. Fortunately the momentum was spent and the car stayed tipped on two wheels with Bert lying on his right side on a smashed pane of glass.

Slowly, so very slowly, the lorry backed up with another loud screeching of metal and Bert's car slammed back onto four wheels. Bert was bounced off his seat up towards his car roof but the seat belt snatched him back hard before he came too far off the seat. The two vehicles sat there stalled in the two lanes of the roundabout.

'You hurt mate?' Bert asked. He had extricated himself from the passenger side of his car and was calling up to the lorry driver. 'Can you hear me mate? Are you okay?'

The lorry driver was slumped forward with his head resting on his arms. Both hands were still clasped tightly on the large steering wheel. Bert clambered up onto the bent and twisted running board and looked in through the cab window. He gently reached out his hand to the driver. 'Mate, I said are you hurt?'

The driver slowly lifted his head from his arms and looked rather dazedly at Bert. 'Jesus, I'm so tired. I'm absolutely knackered.'

'Yes, but are you hurt?' asked Bert again.

'No mister, I'm not hurt. I'm just asleep,' and his head fell forwards again onto his arms.

The car and the lorry completely blocked the roundabout and so the traffic had quickly backed up in all directions. Within seconds there was the inevitable array of rude questions, abusive suggestions, horns blaring as drivers tried to get round the mess. It didn't take long for a police siren to rise above all the hubbub and a police car drew up to the accident. Two young uniforms emerged to be greeted with another series of rude suggestions. However, one of the constables proceeded to unravel the chaos. He put up some traffic cones and took no nonsense. With a very piercing whistle and energetic waving of arms he managed to get traffic back into a semblance of normality for a Friday afternoon.

His companion first checked that neither driver was badly hurt. Once that was done he called for backup to write up the accident scene. Following this he spoke to both drivers and took statements. It was all very routine with no serious damage and no one hurt. Bert was a little apprehensive when the constable asked for a breathalyzer. There had been a drink before lunch and some wine with lunch but Bert was under the limit, just. The constable asked what he had been drinking, and where, and with whom? He said he would check all this out for his report. The lorry driver wasn't drunk but absolutely done in. He nearly fainted while answering the constable's questions.

'He should be taken to hospital,' said Bert. 'He looks like he'll collapse at any minute.'

'You're right sir. We'll try and look after him after we get the vehicles out of the way. My partner will find it easier if we drive the two vehicles off the roundabout and along the road there.'

'Have they finished with their measurements?' Bert asked, watching the backup team out with tape measures, chalk and distance wheels.

'Yes. Will your car start sir?'

Bert slid into the passenger seat of the car and over to the driver's side. The car started without any problem but the left front wheel rubbed on the bent bumper and wing. The officer came over and fairly easily pulled the offending metal off the wheel.

'Now try,' he said.

'Step back then,' said Bert and he eased the car forwards, testing twisting the wheels both ways. 'Seems okay,' he said, and drove off the roundabout down the approach road a way.

'Can you move the lorry for us too?' asked the constable, who was making sure that the lorry driver stayed upright. Bert climbed up into the cab and started the engine. The front of the lorry wasn't really damaged at all and Bert easily moved it further down the road.

'Is that all then?' asked Bert. 'If you've finished I really need to be on my way.' The words were no sooner out of his mouth when one of the backup constables came racing over. 'Fred, Fred,' he said, 'there's been a huge pile-up on the main road by the Hay Whain pub and a grand scale fight has broken out in the parking lot. We've all been called over there to sort it out. I've told your partner and he's collected up all his cones. It's off, off, off mate.'

The constable closed his book and started back to the police car.

'What about the lorry driver?' asked Bert? 'Who's going to take care of him?'

'Do us a favour can you? The hospital's on your way back to Colourworld. Just drop him in at Emergency. They'll handle him from there.'

Bert looked resigned to the chore. The police cars were already off and away with sirens blaring. The lorry driver swayed and Bert put out a protective arm to steady him.

'All right mate; let's see if we can get you some help. I'll drop you off at the hospital.'

With some difficulty Bert half-lifted and half-supported the lorry driver back to his car. He carefully folded him into the passenger seat and went round to the driver's side. The door opened that side but the glass had completely gone out of the window. Making sure that his passenger was belted in, and that he was still conscious, Bert let out the clutch and slowly drove away to the hospital. The array of concerns going round in his head hadn't gone away. In fact he had thought of a couple more. He still had to try and find some place to stay and make contact with the Social authorities about Stephen.

The hospital took the lorry driver in with lots of speed and efficiency. He was whisked into Emergency and placed in the waiting room, waiting. Bert unfortunately was not so lucky. The Administration had a massive set of questions about admittance. It was nearly six o'clock by the time Bert escaped from the hospital.

'Christ, I've got to pick up Seaun,' muttered Bert to himself. 'Just look at the time. I'll have to drive pretty fast to get to the match at Dewleys. Why does everything have to happen on Fridays?'

When Bert got to the Crown Seaun was hopping up and down on the pavement.

'Be-Jesus, you took your time. Had a nice lunch did you? Laddie from Chomleys treat you well? What happened to the car boyo?'

'Seaun, shut up and get in the car.'

'Well, what's the answer then? Thought you'd forgotten me. Left me standing like a prick in a nunnery.'

'Seaun, wash your mouth out. A sleepy lorry driver hit me. Nobody was hurt and it's all sorted out. End of story.'

'Well I was only asking. You were cutting it fine to be sure. I'm always anxious that you're in good form. No damage to the eyes then? Nothing wrong with the hands and the arm? Can still see fine?'

'Seaun, for pity's sake man put a sock in it.'

The fast drive to Dewleys was accompanied by a similar conversation the whole way and Bert was exhausted when he stopped the car in the pub's parking lot.

'Now Seaun, listen up for a moment. No talk about accidents, or adventures, or any other distortion of the odds. This is a straightforward darts match. Let me look after my side of the game. Give me a moment's peace to get my head in place. I need to concentrate on the darts, not on any tedious explanation of the day's events.'

'Sure Bert, no problem. You know me, mountain of discretion.'

Bert smiled at this assertion and bundled Seaun out of the car. He did need to get his head straightened and a chance to concentrate. He knew what he could do but he needed to get his head in the right place to do it.

The evening went well. It had been a tightly contested darts match. There was a packed house at Dewleys and everyone knew about the ringer from London. There was quiet when it was needed and cheers and claps when warranted. The crowd was well pleased with the scoring and the pace was brisk. Between games the landlord was doing a roaring trade and he also was well pleased. The final match with Bert came down to the last three darts. Bert needed sixty. His first dart glanced off the double ring and landed in the twenty; down to forty. A more pronounced hush fell over the crowded room. Bert breathed in and concentrated. However, with his second dart Bert's aim was just a little off and the dart flicked against the wire of the double ring. It landed in the rubber floor and was followed by a loud groan around the room.

'Double top or nothing mate.' The room tittered again into silence. Even the smoke seemed to stand still in the air. Bert drew a breath and closed his eyes. It had been a hectic day, but what the hell it was only a dart's match. He muttered the last comment under his breath but Seaun had heard. Pulling on some inner resolve he threw and the room filled with cheers.

'Only a dart's match,' bellowed Seaun above the din of the crowd. 'That's all you know young fella. I had most of our mates' wages riding on this match. It would have been a sore gang of fellas come Monday if you hadn't hit that double top.'

'Seaun, when will you remember that this is just a game man? This is for fun. This is relaxation.'

'Yes, well if you relaxed a little more it wouldn't be fun for any of us from the Crown, now would it? For us Bert this is serious, fun indeed.'

Bert had to turn away with a smile on his face. He supposed that working on the factory floor all week was bloody boring and this did make the week worthwhile, just a little excitement. The evening finished in some good-natured rivalry and suggestions for a return match. The big fella from London came up and shook Bert's hand.

'You stayed in the game bleedin' well mate. 'Fought you was goin' to collapse at the end like, but you stay'd the course. The other blokes in the team said you was a class act. Good on you squire. Pleasure to play against yer.'

'It's a team thing down here,' said Bert. 'We all play together and try not to let it get too serious, except for Seaun here. Trouble is you can't keep a Paddy from wanting to bet.'

'Same up in London: we've got a crowd of players and a crowd of punters. Like to play meself. You look like you've a steady 'and and eye.'

'Well, I needed it where I came from.'

'In the army I was told. Taking apart things that go bang in the night. Sooner you than me mate. That would really give me the shakes. Still, turned out useful for you ten minutes ago?'

'Yes, it comes in handy when the pressure is on,' said Bert with a smile on his face.

A couple of pints later the landlord called for last orders and the crowd in the barroom slowly started to disperse. Outside a gentle fluttering of white filled the sky as an early touch of snow fell on the countryside. The light from the pub door flooded across parts of the parking lot and the roadway as folks called goodnights and set off home. Bert collected Seaun having one last drink for the road and still chattering about bets and odds for future matches.

'Seaun, will you come on man. It's late and I've had a long day. It's going to be a slippery trip home and we need to be going.'

'I'm coming Bert, I'm coming. I've just got to sort this deal out with Patrick here.'

'Seaun, no more deals. It can wait until tomorrow or whenever.'

'No Bert, I have him on the ropes. He's gasping for a chance to lose his money.'

'He'll lose it just as fast next week.'

'Oh Bert, it seems such a shame when I had it there in me 'and.'

'You'll have it from my hand if you don't get in the car.'

Reluctantly Seaun was pulled away by Bert and propelled firmly towards the parked car. For the first time Seaun suddenly noticed the front of Bert's car.

'Jesus and Mary, who did that to you? Did someone sideswipe you here in the parking lot?'

'No Seaun, it happened this afternoon. That's partly why I was so late.'

'Did you have a crash then?'

'No man, a lorry crashed into the side of me on the roundabout in town. Fortunately he was nearly stopped when he hit me.'

'He still caused quite a dent and sure realigned your front bumper.'

'Yes, well, the police officer straightened it out so the bumper didn't rub on the front wheel. Seems to be going okay. We got here in one piece, didn't we, and in a rush?'

'Aye, 'twas a tight run. I nearly missed the opening bets.'

'Anyway, let's off home before this snow gets any worse.'

Buckling themselves up Bert eased the car out of the parking lot onto the road home. Home? Well not really home but back into town and drop Seaun off and then up to the factory.

Back in town a strident alarm rang through the building and for a moment there was ordered chaos. People put on clothing, collected equipment and assembled in their traditional places. With the bell clanging loudly overhead Malcolm steered the fully equipped fire-engine out through the open doors. He swung left onto the road leading into the centre of town. The articulated ladder truck quickly followed his fire-engine. The two machines left distinct marks down the snow-covered road.

'Storage Facility on Birch Road in the industrial park. No inhabited houses within five hundred metres. Exact contents unknown but our files show it did contain industrial machinery.' The quiet voice of the dispatcher sounded above Malcolm's head as he drove towards the fire.

'Good work Malcolm,' said Harry, the Fire Chief sitting next to Malcolm in the cab. 'We were out within the scheduled time and should be at the fire within ten minutes. You lads all set back there?' Harry turned to three other members of the crew. 'This sounds like a straightforward fire and may not need any special equipment.'

'Just as well Chief after the last one.'

'Yes lads, that was a bit of a bitch wasn't it? But you all did really well. The Regional Director was right pleased.'

'Too right Chief. We don't want a repeat of that one, but it's good to hear that the brass recognises what we do.'

'Well lads, he thinks this unit works really well.'

'What about Unit 6 Chief? How come they've gone to South Wales?'

'The Director told me we were asked to send that new pumper over for a special demonstration, along with its crew. That's why Unit 6 is over in South Wales.'

As usual on the way to a fire the Chief had the men maintain a light conversation. The crew all knew where they were going. They all knew what they had to do. To keep their minds from wandering too far the Chief liked to keep everyone awake and ready to go with just a light reminder of how well they did things. A little praise can go a long way to keep morale up in a potentially dangerous occupation.

The snow was not heavy enough to disturb the fire-engine and Malcolm made good speed to the fire. By the time they arrived though the fire was well established and the ladder truck was going to be needed. The Chief did a quick survey of the scene and deployed his forces. He explained that the fire seemed straightforward but it would take some time to control and put out. The two crews settled into an organised routine for the long haul.

The long Friday was rapidly catching up with Bert Rawlings. Out on the open road from Dewleys the snow had built up in places. The wind had lifted drifts over the open moor to settle on the road between the hedgerows. All of the various events of the day were collapsing into a stressful drive. There had been the change of routine, the jumbled messages, the long luncheon, the roundabout accident and the euphoria of the darts match, and it was all coming together in a slippery drive home through the dark night. It didn't help that Seaun had decided to go to sleep and snore loudly!

'Hey, wake up you sleepy git.'

'What, eh, what was that? I'm not a sleep, just thinking.'

'You were snoring your bloody head off.'

'Never, just some heavy breathing while I was thinking about a bet.'

'Seaun, you were long gone in the land of nod; had been for the last ten minutes.'

'Well, maybe I had me eyes closed, just for a wee bit. Watch out Bert! Look out man!'

The car seemed to ignore the bend completely and continued in a straight line through the hedgerow, clattering through the wall behind it and bounced itself into a stall.

'Christ, didn't you see the bend? Are you all right?'

Slowly Bert raised his head from the steering wheel where he had smashed it on going into the wall.

'Are you hurt Bert?' Seaun was now quite wide-awake. His voiced registered concern, and Bert despite hurting smiled as he heard the tone in Seaun's voice.

'I'm fine, or foine as you would say you old bugger. I'll live. I'm just going to have a bump on my head for a couple of days.'

'Jesus, but you worried me then.'

'Yes, I'll bet I did. The car developed a mind of its own and went straight through the wall.'

'You sure everything's fine then?'

'Well, I'm okay Seaun. How about yourself?'

'Oh, I'm right. Me seatbelt kept me in place but I might have to change me pants. Gave me a hell of a scare that did going through the wall.'

'Aye, you now sound quite sober. It must have been quite a scare.'

'How do we get out of here then?'

'We'd better have a look at the car and see what new damage I've sustained. I guess something broke or sheared off. The steering just quit and the car went straight. Can you get out your side?'

Seaun pushed open his door and stepped out. 'Shit,' he exclaimed loudly to the world.

'What's up?'

'Shit, that's what's up,' said Seaun. 'Shit up to my ankles.'

'How's the front of the car look?'

One of the headlights was still on and Seaun splashed round to the front of the car exclaiming all the while.

'You've lost a light.'

'I can see that Seaun.'

'The front end is smashed in on both sides now. Both fenders are bent back onto the wheels. The radiator doesn't seem to have been touched and the bonnet isn't buckled.'

Bert turned the ignition key and the motor fired.

'Step back a bit and I'll see what happens.' Bert eased out the clutch and the back wheels turned but the car didn't move. He revved a little more and the back wheels churned up mud and splashed it forwards over Seaun.

'Christ man, turn it up. I'll be covered in the stuff.'

'Seems the car's stuck here for the night Seaun. Looks like shank's pony for us I guess.'

'Bert, I saw a call box back aways. Let's phone for Colin? He'll be in tonight. His missus never lets him go out on a Friday night. He can come out and gives us a ride home.'

'How far back? Remember you were asleep for quite a while.'

'Don't remember exactly but that'll be better than trying to walk towards town, that's bloody miles.'

Bert turned off the engine and cut the lights. The night was dark with a slow flutter of white flakes still descending. Seaun continued to mutter as he floundered back to the car and grabbed his bag. Bert checked everything was safe in the car and picked up his own gear, including his darts case. The pair of them clambered over the broken wall and through the gap in the hedge. After sorting themselves out on the road they set off for Seaun's supposed call box.

Meanwhile, in town, a strident alarm rang through the fire station but this time there was no ordered chaos because all the crews were out. The resident duty officer had answered the phone and on instinct pressed the alarm. A phone call reporting a fire had come in about smoke and fumes coming from Colourworld's factory. The duty officer took the details, killed the alarm and radioed the Fire Chief. After listening to the situation at the Birch Road fire the duty officer rang the ambulance station and the police station with a report on the telephone call and the Fire Chief's instructions.

The police dispatched a police car and it was joined by an ambulance. At the Colourworld factory there was a lot of smoke but no sign of any fire. Wearing masks provided by the ambulance crew the two constables cautiously entered the factory. There was a lot of smoke that made it hard for them to see. Eventually one of the constables found a light switch and this helped. Using torches and the factory floor lights the two officers quickly found several piles of smoldering material. They picked the fire appliances off the walls of the factory and quickly extinguished that part of the problem.

Along with the smoke were wreaths of strong toxic paint fumes. The police explored the entire factory floor and out into the packing area but found nothing else suspicious. They just found several scattered piles of smoldering heaps. It took a while before one of the constables noticed the hum of the air conditioners.

'We've missed something Tony. Why are the fumes here?'

'Where are the offices Al?'

'Yes, that's good. Perhaps there is some control panel there?'

'We should look a bit more. Seems we've killed most of the smoke.'

'I'll just go and tell the blood wagon crew that all is under control.'

'Fine, but don't let them go just yet. Not until we have sorted out this fumes thing.'

'I'll call in to the station and let them know what we are doing.'

'Sure, the serge will be delighted to hear we have everything under control.'

Tony went out to the police car and radio-ed in to the station. He was told to carry on. Over at the ambulance he thanked them for the masks and explained they were still searching for the cause of the fumes.

'Get your station to call the factory foreman, or even Mr. Carter, the owner.'

"That's smart. Never thought of that,' said Tony.

"That's why we're doing the thinking job and you're plodding around Tony,' joshed one of the ambulance crew.

'Get off it mate. We've got the fire out but I'll call the station.'

Tony did all of this and went back to find Al.

'Where have you been?' Christ, I could have died in here the time it's taken.'

'Hold your horses Al. It took a while convincing them at the station we had everything under control.'

'Yes, well, we don't you know.'

'I know that. You know that, but they don't know that. Anyway, I've got the station to call Bert Rawlings out here, and even Mr. Carter. What do think of that smartie-pants?'

'Now that's bright. Why didn't I think of that?'

"Cos I'm the brains in this team Al, that's why. Anyway, you found the offices yet?'

'Was waiting for you wasn't I? Was checking that you were okay.'

'Come on then, let's go round the floor again. I didn't see any offices the first time around but there was lots of smoke then.'

'Where's the stairs go?'

'Up.'

'Yes, but up where you daft berk?'

'Let's go see. We're still looking for some kind of control panel remember.'

Tony and Al climbed the stairs and around the corner they found the first office door. 'Looks like we found the offices partner. Look for a light switch.'

'Found it – Christ, who's that?'

'Check him out while I go and get the ambulance crew. 'Bout time they did something for a living.'

Al set off downstairs to roust out the ambulance crew while Tony went over to the sprawled and very still body of Stephen. Kneeling beside the body he checked for Stephen's pulse. Finding it he shouted, 'get a move on you lazy gits. He's still breathing.' There was no response so Tony went back to the top of the stairs and shouted again. 'Hey, you out there? Al, the boy's still alive but looks like he needs help, and fast.' Across the factory floor came Al and the ambulance crew at a jog.

'Up here lads. He looks pretty far gone, real pale and choking like. He's going to need your help.'

'Let's at him then Tony. Let the dogs see the rabbit chum.'

'How is he then Tony?' asked an anxious Al.

'He's breathing but it is irregular and his pulse is racing away like he's struggling.'

'He's going to live?'

'Beats me Al but we've got the right help to him.' Tony turned to the ambulance crew and asked 'anything we can do to help or have you got it under control?'

'No, we're fine Tony. We've got him stabilized but it was a close call. We need to move him to the hospital ASAP. Good job you found him when you did.'

'Oy. Who's there? Where is everybody?'

'Up here, we're in the office section.'

Mr. Carter's feet rang on the metal steps as he climbed up to the office. 'Who the hell is he?' he asked, pointing to the wrapped up body on the floor.

'Buggered if we know,' said one of the ambulance crew, making sure Stephen's body was firmly lashed to the stretcher. 'Here lads, give us a hand with getting him down to the wagon.'

'Hold up,' said Mr. Carter. 'Let's have a look then. Good God, it's young Stephen. What the hell was he doing up here?'

'Beats us Mr. Carter, but we need to get him to hospital fast. He's been breathing in toxic fumes and his lungs are struggling. Don't know where they came from but they're still coming. Don't you turn them off or something overnight?'

'Hell, yes; that's the problem. The fans aren't running. And,...... Christ, and the air-conditioners are running. They're sucking in all the fumes through into this office. Quick, let me get to the panel and put things right.'

As Tony and Al helped the ambulance crew manoeuvre the stretcher bearing Stephen down the stairs and across the factory floor Mr. Carter rushed into the control room next door. He flipped several switches and then checked again that he had done it right. He wondered where Rawlings was. He knew that the police had telephoned Rawlings but got no answer the first time. After the police had phoned him he had told them to try Rawlings again. Strange that, Rawlings was so reliable. Not like him not to respond. And what the hell was Stephen doing in the factory at nighttime? Seems several things need to be explained, especially as the lad nearly died.

The police started their investigations. They were very interested where Mr. Rawlings had been, especially when they couldn't contact him at his last address. Gone he has, his landlady had said, and good riddance. I won't have his kind in my house. The police asked what kind and that started a whole raft of sidetrack queries and investigation. There was also the question of why Stephen's body was black and blue. Obviously someone had given him a real beating not so long ago. There was the question of Anne and Reginald and the recent meeting with his old foster parents. Witnesses had seen and heard the shouting match in Reginald's house. The police remembered there had been a report of lights in the factory the Thursday night. Had that been Stephen or was there someone else wandering around?

Bert Rawlings visited Stephen in hospital. The youngster had severely damaged lungs and throat as a result of the fumes. It is a wonder that he had not died. The doctor reckoned that another hour or so would have killed him. Bert mused over something that Mr. Carter had said. The air-conditioner was on and he'd told Stephen absolutely explicitly not to turn the air-conditioner on at night. If the factory fume exhaust fans did fail then the air-conditioner just sucked the fumes in through the office section. So, to prevent any such accidents the factory exhaust fans remained on all night and the air-conditioner was turned off. In the daytime, with any problem the air-conditioners were turned off as the factory was evacuated.

What if he had been there thought Bert. The police had arrived about three o'clock and Stephen and he would have been asleep. They wouldn't have noticed the fans being off and the air-conditioner on. Both of them could have been killed. Too many things didn't quite make sense to Bert. Was it just unlucky circumstances that the fire at Birch Road had pulled away the fire crews to the other side of town? The Fire Chief had mentioned that that fire was very suspicious. He thought it was arson.

'Strange business that fire at Colourworld,' said Anthony Lord at breakfast a week later. He had been reading a report on the whole matter in the weekly regional newspaper. 'Seems there's more to that than meets the eye. You were out that night weren't you Michael?'

'Yes Dad, and the night before. I was over at Danielle's.'

'Oh yes, the black as night Danielle.'

'Dad, she's fine. She's a good friend.'

'I thought you were supposed to be a good, or perhaps better friend with that young American?'

'Well yes, but you know how it is? You have to keep them all guessing. Melanie will be down later this month for my birthday by the way. You haven't forgotten have you?'

'No Michael, but to come back to the previous subject and talking of guessing, can I guess why you were over at Hammond's the other day?'

'I was checking over the work they did for you last year. You remember I spent some time watching them when they had the contract. I told you I wasn't sure that Kevin and his brother weren't trying to pull a fast one. They charged you a lot for that assessment. I went over to their office unannounced to see whether they had forgotten anything they should have told us.'

'And, what did you find?'

'All seems kosher, although the recent events with the electronics would have been dangerous if you had taken over that building.'

'Unlikely, because I would have rewired it for our business, as well you know. Part of the Hammond contract was to see whether that was possible and how costly it might be.'

Sunday December 21st. arrived at Fotheringham Manor with a fanfare, or maybe a farce depending how you looked at it. Samantha had come over from Switzerland the day before but she had arrived home very late at night. 'I wasn't to know,' she said, 'nobody told me he was sleeping with her. Gosh though, it was funny, the look on their faces when I pranced in.'

'Really Samantha, I'm not sure that school of yours has taught you anything about being a lady. I think your father and I will demand our money back.'

'Tosh Mum. I'll do lady Samantha this evening, just you see, but for this morning I just played little sister on my twenty-one year-old brother, and bloody funny it was too.'

'What did you do Sam?' asked Daniel, coming late into the dining room. 'What have I missed? I heard such a commotion from Michael's bedroom. He usually sleeps in late when Melanie's here.'

'Well Daniel, your sister decided to wake her older brother up with a birthday dance and a bucket of cold water. The plan as I understand it was to wake his lordship up and then dance around so he couldn't catch her. You know how Samantha used to tease Michael about getting up late. It seems that no one told Samantha about Melanie being in bed with Michael, and so Samantha doused both of them before she fled.'

'Hell fire Sam, you'll cop it when Michael comes down. He'll be as mad as hell. He's already been beaten up this month and you flinging water at him won't cool him down.'

'Who's Michael been fighting with? Some girl I'll bet, and who is the girl in his bed anyway?'

The girl in question came quietly into the breakfast room.

'Hi, I'm Melanie Rogers, you must be Samantha. I'm pleased to meet you, again!'

'Hi, yes,' stammered Samantha, 'sorry about that, silly old family prank and I hadn't seen Michael for yonks; pleased to meet you too.'

'Mum I'm starving, can I eat?'

Anthony came into the breakfast room and looked at everybody. 'Can someone please tell me what all that commotion was a moment ago? It sounded as if the hounds of hell had been released.'

'That my love,' said Sylvia, 'was your dearly beloved daughter greeting her brother on his birthday. She did it rather unconventionally with a bucket of cold water.'

'But Melanie was in there too.'

'Exactly, and that explains more of the commotion and why Melanie still has dripping hair.'

'Dad it was so funny, I couldn't stop laughing. You should have seen Michael's face. Actually the rest of him was pretty funny too but he was dressed.'

'Dressed, in bed?' asked Daniel, between mouthfuls.

'Yes silly, in his birthday suit,' and Samantha burst into another fit of laughter and doubled over.

Even Sylvia smiled. She turned to Melanie. 'As you can see Melanie we do have some rather eccentric members in this family.'

During the day many of the rest of the extended Lord family came to Fotheringham. Fortunately this continuous stream of people wanting to greet Michael, wish him well, and hear all about his future prevented him from cornering his wild sister. However, the bottled up annoyance did not sit too well with Michael. Daniel rather unwittingly stirred the pot by recounting to any visitor who would listen the unusual awakening of Michael that morning. The listener was either amused by the event or shocked that Melanie was in Michael's bed. By the time dinner was served the atmosphere had become a little tense.

Anthony and Sylvia had organized a full formal dinner for Michael's special twenty-first birthday. Sylvia had thought for some time how best to arrange everyone; she had even thought whether it would be better to have a round table rather than a conventional rectangular one. In the end she had Anthony at one end and herself at the other with Michael at a position of honour halfway down the side. Melanie was the only non-family person at the table, and Sylvia placed her beside Michael.

Great Aunt Veronica sat on Anthony's right and Sylvia had Great Uncle Matthew on her right. Sylvia wanted Aunt Stephanie on Michael's left with Henri next between Stephanie and Veronica. That should keep Henri from being a pain with the younger ladies thought Sylvia. Between Melanie and herself Sylvia had placed young Philippe. Across from the "head" side of the table Sylvia had arranged Samantha, Peter, Christina, Daniel, Giselle, and Marie. Only Cousin Marcel was away, and he was racing somewhere in the Pacific. Despite Sylvia's best efforts, and the excellent dinner provided by cook, the atmosphere around the dinner table continued to build.

Anthony pushed back his chair and stood. 'Ladies and Gentlemen, I would ask you to raise your glasses and toast our son Michael on reaching his twenty-first birthday. Michael'

'Michael, Michael, Michael,' came the voices from around the table, with a touching of glasses.

Anthony came from one end and Sylvia from the other. 'Stand my son. We want to wish you a really happy birthday.' When Michael had stood Anthony embraced his son and gave him a fancy envelope. 'Yes Michael,' said Sylvia, 'happy birthday son, and many more of them.' Sylvia gave her son a heartfelt hug. She really wanted Michael to do well and be able to enjoy life. He always seemed to do things the hard way.

'Michael, I too have something for you, but at my age you will have to come to me dear,' said Great Aunt Veronica. 'Now help me with my chair and give your very very old Great Aunt a kiss.' Michael laughed and warmly embraced his Great Aunt. 'You're only as old as you feel Auntie,' he said, 'and you still manage to get out on the river from your cottage so let's have less of this old old stuff.' Veronica also gave Michael a fancy envelope.

'Well young man, I will meet you half way,' said Matthew as he rose from his chair. 'Obviously I can't be old as I'm a year younger than my sister, although you won't find me messing about in boats like Veronica.' Matthew walked up from his foot of the table and gave Michael a big and obviously unexpected hug. 'Take care young man and use your life wisely. Bye the way, this might help.' He too gave Michael a fancy envelope.

'Speech, speech,' cried Samantha as Michael walked back to his place at the table, 'let's hear some words of wisdom from this young man with an old head on his shoulders.'

Glancing inside the three envelopes Michael's expression changed from interest to annoyance very quickly but there was a smile on his face when he stood behind his chair and looked up and down the table. In the candlelight of the room Michael took some time looking at each face in turn before he finally looked down at Melanie. Like everyone else she too wondered what Michael would say. Melanie had also felt the atmosphere running around the room and something has just happened to intensify it.

'Mum, Dad, family and dearly beloved Melanie, I would like to thank you all for coming as it is a special day for me. In more ways than one you have made it a most memorable day.' Here, Michael looked rather pointedly at Samantha who stared straight back. 'Memorable,' Michael mused, 'and just to share with you all I have just received a full 10% ownership in the Company. Now that's memorable as Geoffrey received 25% on his twenty-first birthday.' There was a stifled intake of breath around the table. 'But that's fine because obviously as the eldest son the Company will all come to me anyway. Then just think what I have contributed to the Company and the Estate in this past year. At the end of last month at the Annual Meeting Dad was describing the Security Contract with Saad Brothers, well it was yours truly who worked with Cohen and Townsend to successfully install that software. As Dad explained that brought a lot of money into the Company, whereby increasing the value of my 10%. On the Forest Estate, well since July I was responsible for the overall management and the shaking up of our inefficient forester. By the way Dad I think we should fire him as soon as possible.'

Anthony thought this was neither the time nor the place but kept quiet. Let Michael get things off his chest.

'But, let's end on a positive, forward-looking note. Samantha wanted words from a wise head. So, I will look forward to a bright future and I am starting it early in the New Year when Melanie and I will announce the date for our wedding. So, I will ask you to raise your glasses for another toast and that is "health, wealth and happiness in the future".'

The company rose and raised their glasses to Michael's toast. As they sat down Samantha sprung up again, 'I for one would like to propose a toast for our guest of honour and his lovely lady Melanie. So, to Michael and Melanie, every best wishes.' Samantha raised her glass and was delighted that the guests rose again to toast 'Michael and Melanie.' This action of Samantha's rather eased the strain after Michael's speech. Young Peter Lord squirmed and let out a shout. 'I think the youngest guest has had enough,' said Christina, 'please excuse me mother if I put this young Lord to bed.'

'Yes, certainly Christina. It's been a long and tiring day for Peter with so many faces wanting to see him. Take him off to bed dear. Do you want Daniel to drive you down to Home Farm?'

'I'll gladly look after Christina,' offered Henri, standing up so quickly that his chair fell backwards behind him.

'Thank you Henri but Daniel knows where everything is. I'll let him see me home thanks. Michael, Happy Birthday brother, and the best of wishes to you and Melanie.' Christina rose and carried Peter out of the room. Daniel held the door open and closed it after he too left the room.

'Let's move to the drawing room,' said Sylvia, 'and I will organize coffee, or is it tea for you Veronica?'

'Sylvia, rest up. I'll get all that taken care of,' said Stephanie. 'You've been on the go all day. Take your son into the drawing room and let him learn something from Veronica and Matthew about wise heads. Meanwhile, I'm going to borrow Melanie here and introduce her to the intricacies of looking after Lords. Come on Melanie my dear, it's time for us to earn our supper.'

Stephanie plucked a somewhat surprised Melanie from her chair and the pair wheeled off to the kitchen. Sylvia laughed but she took Stephanie's suggestion and tucked her arm into Michael's and led the rest of the guests into the drawing room. 'Trust your Aunt Stephanie to be practical Michael. Melanie could learn a thing or two from her son. Come on, let's go and tap inside that font of knowledge in Great Uncle Matthew's head. Anyone with that halo of white hair and craggy eyebrows has got to be a boffin.'

'Disgusting word Sylvia, disgusting,' said Matthew. The party gradually drifted into the drawing room and the tense atmosphere dissipated. Sylvia glanced across the room to Anthony. They exchanged glances. There was never a dull moment with Michael, even on his birthday.

Stephen was released from hospital within one week. The social authorities took him under their control. The police investigation wound down with no obvious conclusions. The Regional Fire Director blamed the local Fire Chief for not having enough resources on hand. Bert Rawlings found some new digs. Mr. Carter went back to his golf tournaments. The environmental control people had some recommendations for Colourworld's factory that Mr. Carter grudgingly implemented. After two weeks Stephen suddenly collapsed and died. Bert Rawlings sat in his new digs and thought over the events of the past three to four weeks. He gradually pieced things together, or so he thought.

Lord's Legacy

14

Charles Dampier had very well managed parents, or perhaps they just had short memories being old and that. Far far away in the West Indies Lord and Lady Dampier enjoyed their rum punches while their son turned their London house into party city.

'Michael, we were here this time last year.'

'Close, but no cigar.'

'Michael, it's New Year's Eve so forget the fucking clichés and let's get sloshed. Actually, do you have anything better than booze? I'd sooner get high, the colours are better and the next morning is slow and fuzzy rather than splitting my head.'

'I've got some stuff from Sasha before he went back to the States. This should help. Open wide little princess.'

'Michael, Sasha went back to the States in a hell of a hurry. He didn't even say goodbye. He wasn't in any kind of trouble was he?'

'Melanie, swallow, have a drink and let's see who's who at this party. Hell, duck, there's someone I didn't really need to see. Shit, he's coming over. Be cool Melanie. Hi David, how them mombes brother?'

'Melanie, it's good to see you again. You're looking your usual colourful self. It must be the Californian upbringing. Michael, I trust you left Mighty Mouse somewhere safe. We don't need any more catapult tricks.'

'David, for God's sake leave it man – it was an accident. Mighty Mouse was virtually totalled anyway. I lost my licence out of all that. Heh Melanie, don't go love.'

'I'll be back Michael. I've just got to go and powder my nose, if you know what I mean.' Melanie swirled away in her colourful dress. David straightened up his powerful black six feet of frame and looked at Michael.

'But you didn't lose your bloody life did you, not like some friends I could mention?'

'Lighten up; it's New Year's Eve. Get Charles to fix you up with some gorgeous young thing while we all enjoy ourselves.'

'Heard you'd found some gorgeous young black thing.'

'Cut it out. Danielle's not here anyway.'

David looked at Michael and swirled the drink round in his glass. 'No, you're right, she's not here but camped down on your doorstep in Somerset I hear. Do Daddy and Mummy know about her?' David slowly turned away and mingled back into the host of young people. Michael stood and pondered. The party went downhill for Michael from that point in time.

Five days later, on Saturday January 4th, Shirley and Stanley Rogers organised a wonderful splashy affair for their daughter Melanie and her Michael. They had hired a private dining room and ballroom at a West End Hotel and invited eighty guests. The evening was structured with a dance evening first followed by a supper buffet. Mrs. Rogers thought the old folk would then likely go home while the younger set would go on to a Club. She knew that her Stanley had planned to make the wedding announcement near the end of the dancing. Sir Anthony and Sylvia Lord were up from Somerset; there were several of Stanley's business friends and their wives, and a bevy of young people that Melanie had invited. It should be a lovely evening for her daughter and Shirley Rogers smiled with envy. What it must be like to be a young girl again. Still, Melanie and her father were spending a lot of time talking together, but they were smiling she noticed. All was well.

Michael had bounced back from his uninspiring New Year's Eve bash having spent a couple of days somewhat permanently in bed with Melanie. Night times they had gone to Clubs and parties and Michael was feeling on top of the world on this Saturday night. Melanie had been away shopping most of Saturday afternoon and so Michael had amused himself with a long and sensual telephone conversation with Danielle. However, towards the end Danielle started getting a little sharpish and demanding. Michael hung up, rolled over on the bed and lit up a joint.

'This will bring me some piece of mind,' he muttered, 'and get me in the mood for this evening.' Thinking back on his previous years New Year's resolution Michael thought he had come close. 'I said it would be all mine, well, we have certainly made some progress. I may only own 10% at the moment but there is no more Geoffrey and little Master Peter has many years of growing up to do before he can make any claims. In the meantime we will soon have some of the Roger's fortune and we can put that to good use in the Company. Dad will be pleased and he is scheduled to retire soon, so his control will come to me. All in all it was rather a successful year. 'I will make this year even better' he told the room.

'Make what better?' asked Melanie quietly coming into the room.

'Life,' shouted Michael to the ceiling, 'my life, all will be mine.'

'Well get your skates on buster as this evening is Mummy and Daddy's and I don't want us to be late and spoil it for them. So best bib and tucker Michael and look sharp about it.'

'Jesus, who put you in charge?'

'My Dad Michael and don't you forget it.'

Melanie marched off briskly to the bathroom and proceeded to put on war paint suitable for the occasion. Michael drew heavily on his joint and let the aroma roll around his head. 'Such a passionate woman,' he mused, 'tonight should be a gas: stealing such a beautiful lady from precious Mummy and Daddy. Wonder if they really know what their daughter is like; the kaleidoscope kookie with chemicals for blood? Suppose I will get to see California this year as Daddy was ranting on about a wedding in some Spanish-sounding burg. Should be cool – perhaps a wedding in some magic garden, or a yellow submarine, or ....'

'Michael, the bathroom's all yours.'

Melanie's clarion call jolted Michael out of his reverie. He slowly rolled off the bed and very nearly landed on the floor. A last minute sudden twist prevented an undignified fall. Still, what the heck, it's just another party. As long as I look clean and polished lovely Shirley won't mind.

'Michael you know Louise-Marie Faxon and Foster don't you? You went sailing or something with their son Chuck, or was it hiking? I really can't remember, you do manage to do so many energetic things.'

'Yes Mrs. Rogers, I've met the Faxons before. Good evening Mr. and Mrs. Faxon, good to see you again.'

Michael stood in the receiving line alongside Melanie and her parents to formally greet the guests.

'Mrs. Revere and Mr. Revere, it is good to see you could make it. You've just flown in from L.A. Well I do hope you won't be too tired to enjoy the party. And this is your son Randall the IInd. Well hello Randall, welcome to little old England. You know Melanie of course and this is Michael Lord. Michael, this is the Reveres and their son Randall.'

'Hi, did you have trouble parking the horses?'

'What horses?'

'You're not Paul Revere and the Raiders?'

'Michael,' said Melanie tapping her foot, 'behave. Hi Randall, good to see you.' Melanie gave Randall a big hug and a kiss on the cheek. Randall turned a delicate shade of pink.

'Good to see you too Melanie,' he whispered.

'Well it's good to see that everyone's happy to see one another,' said Michael, 'it'll make for a good party if everyone's so happy to see each other. Can't stand it when there's people at a party who can't stand one another; things can get quite tetchy as we say here in little old England.'

'Michael, can it,' snarled Melanie, 'people don't understand you're trying to be funny. Americans don't understand English humour.'

Shirley Rogers quickly turned to the next guest. 'Colonel Sanders, what a delight. My, but you do look smart. That is such an original suit design. Look Stanley dear, don't you think those lapels look so outré?'

'Michael, if you say anything about chicken, or flap your arms, or anything at all I shall take you outside and give you a piece of my mind.'

'I never said a word, not a murmur. I didn't cluck, cluck, cluck.'

'Michael!! Oh good evening Colonel Sanders, we are pleased to have you here tonight.'

'Chicken's not on the menu,' whispered Michael.

'I'd like you to meet my aristocratic but ill-mannered young man here beside me. He's never had the benefits of West Point training and so he is a little rusty on the finer points of battleground etiquette.'

'Charmingly put my dear. Well sir, and what do you have to say for yourself? Seems you're a little shell-shocked with all these colonial allies dropping in on you. So, stand up straight, shoulders back and take it on the chin. Good evening to you sir, a very good evening.'

Melanie caught herself before she doubled over with laughter. Colonel Sanders walked away into the throng on the ballroom floor. Fortunately for Michael the next dozen or so guests were people he knew and so there was no great strain. Before long the band assembled and the floor started to vibrate with the smooth step and glide of quicksteps interspersed with the disjointed wriggles of rock and roll. The eclectic repertoire of the band kept most people up on the floor at least every other dance. Unlike many such dances the MC was quite successful in having ladies invitationals, snowball dances and cut-ins: everyone became involved in the evening's activities. Just before eleven Anthony and Sylvia slipped out, and soon afterwards the band performed a drum-roll to gain everyone's attention.

'Ladies and Gentlemen, I would like to thank you all so much for coming here tonight. As you know there is a light supper laid on in the adjacent dining room and we'll come to that in a moment. We think that you've all had a good time on the dance floor and earned your supper. However, I'd just like to say a few words about why we are gathered here tonight. As you know, my daughter Melanie up here beside me came over to England just over a year ago now. Soon after arriving she met a young man whom she really liked and she wrote long letters to us in California. She was having a delightful time with her wonderful man Michael. Come up here Michael so everyone can see you.'

Michael stepped up onto the tiny stage alongside Stanley Rogers. 'Anyway, during the course of last year Melanie became more and more attached to Michael. Shirley and I as parents, always the last to know aren't we, realised that this was real. This was the real thing for Melanie. So, as supportive parents we flew over and met Michael and the Lord family. Many of you will have seen Anthony and Sylvia Lord tonight, Michael's parents, and delightful people they are too. Melanie came back to California a couple of times last year and it was obvious that her mind was made up. Therefore, here we are tonight, poised for the announcement of a wedding date early in the spring.'

Ripples of delight and anticipation ran around the room amongst the attentive guests on the dance floor. Stanley Rogers paused and looked around the room. He looked sideways at Michael and smiled. 'But before we let you know what's happening when I thought I'd like to mention a few things about young Michael here. Over the last twelve months I've found out quite a lot about the man who wants to marry my daughter.' Again Stanley Rogers paused. The anticipation in the room heightened and tensed up.

'Michael is the most self-centred young man I've yet to meet.' There was a gasp in the room. Michael's face blanched. Stanley continued, 'he is arrogant, selfish, and entirely lacking in any thoughts or actions except those that benefit him. This past year he has left a scene of death and destruction behind him wherever he has been.' The gasps in the room became louder mutterings. Michael opened his mouth to speak but no words came out. 'You're two timing and despicable too Michael,' said Melanie, leaning across her father. 'Why don't you run away back to your little black whore?'

Michael jumped off the bandstand and pushed his way through the crowd. They parted easily. Shirley Rogers swooned. She hadn't known what her husband and daughter had planned to say. The doors to the dining room stood open and some of the guests filtered in. Conversations ran rampart around the room. It certainly had been an unexpected turn of events.

Somehow Michael drove down to Somerset. By the time he drew up outside Danielle's caravan the shock had worn off but the rage hadn't started. All Michael wanted to do right now was get so drunk it would all become a nightmare and that's exactly what he did. Sunday extended into Monday and Michael continued to drink, to vomit and drink again. Danielle and little Anthony just sat and watched and waited.

By Monday evening Michael had almost come down to earth. Danielle quietly heated up some chicken soup and persuaded Michael this might help. Somewhat surprisingly Michael accepted the soup and even asked for some more please. 'Thanks,' he whispered, 'that was good, just what I needed. I think we need to do a little talking.' Michael slept that night a little easier in the body and a lot more determined in the mind. There were some things he had sorted out with Danielle and some things he needed to sort out with his family.

Early Tuesday morning Michael was at the Forest Office to see Norton Ferris detail the work crew to the various activities about the forest. When all the crew had gone Michael turned to Ferris. 'I shall be out early on this morning but will be around the forest so let's not think the boss is away and we can play. I've already told Sir Anthony to fire you but I see he hasn't handled that yet. Well, I'm off to see him now. In the meantime you carry on with whatever you had planned for this morning and I'll see you later.' Michael got back in his car and drove up to the Big House. Slamming his car door shut with a crash he stormed in through the front door and strode loudly to the dining room. His parents were there are the table.

'Didn't have the decency to warn me?' he shouted at his father. 'I'm even surprised at you too Mum. What kind of family loyalty is there any more? Really set me up in front of all my friends didn't you? Planned it all with Mr. precious Stanley Rogers no doubt? Did you coerce poor Melanie when she was down here for my birthday? Well, everyone is very quiet all of a sudden!'

'Michael, if you can't behave leave now. We are having breakfast.'

'Well sorrrrry sir. Don't mind me if I just have a quick cuppa before I ask again what was all that about last Saturday night?'

'Michael,' said Sylvia, 'sit down and listen for once in your life.'

'No Mum, I won't sit down and be talked to like a child. This is my life.'

'Michael,' thundered his father as he stood up, 'this is my house. Here, whether you like it or not I call the shots. Now, sit down and behave or leave. Make up your mind son!'

'Sod the lot of you then,' shouted Michael. 'I'll find my own fortune and then this house will end up being mine. Just wait and see.' He spun round and purposefully marched out of the dining room. The silence around the table fell like a cloak and Michael's footsteps echoed down the hall and out of the front door.

Norton Ferris slumped down into a chair in the Forest Office after Michael had driven away. Christ, he thought, now what the hell do I do? Old Sir Anthony never said anything when he came back from London, although I did hear there had been a falling out over the weekend. Today's Tuesday and I said I'd get those fence posts to Larry Whelks yesterday. Shit, I'd better do it now while I still have the chance. The money will come in useful if I do get fired.

Ferris slid into the Landrover and drove through the forest to a recent cutover. This had been a fine stand of European Larch growing on a sheltered hillside. There was a stream at the bottom of the slope and with the good drainage the larch trees had grown really well. There had been three or four good sawlogs in every tree with the butt log bigger than sixty centimetres diameter. The heavy sap-filled logs were piled up in skidways, propped up by vertical posts ready to skid out to the road. Already there were several bundles of posts placed along the road ready to fence the area prior to replanting. They would need to fence the area and trap out all the rabbits before any of the seedlings would survive the rodents' sharp incisors.

At the first pile of fence posts Norton stopped the Landrover and opened the back. Having Michael's Landrover would make it seem normal to be carrying posts to somewhere off the Estate. Larry Whelks had offered to buy the posts at a discounted price if they came on Monday. Let's hope Larry's still got the money thought Norton as he piled the posts into the back of the Landrover. Jesus, this is hard way to get any money, Norton muttered to himself. If I thought they'd keep their gobs shut I would have had Idwal and John do this for me. Finishing one pile Norton moved the rover down to the next pile. The sun shone brightly over the cleared hillside. There had been a good frost the night before and the cleared ground sparkled with a frozen sheen. Norton looked up the slope and thought that the planting here would be a bit strenuous. This'll slow old Enrico down he thought. Teach the old eyetie that he's past it. Maybe I can get Idwal, John and me into his cottage if I'm thrown out of mine. Still muttering and wiping the sweat out of his eyes Norton started loading the posts from the new pile into the rover. When it was full Norton went round to the cab and opened the driver's door. He slumped into the driver's seat and drew his dirty handkerchief across his forehead. I'm too old for this he gasped. He closed his eyes for a moment.

Up on the hillside one of the skidways creaked. The retaining post collapsed and pile of logs started to slide downhill. With the hard frosty surface the large heavy logs took no time at all to crash into the passenger side of the Landrover. Norton screamed. The Landrover slid off the downhill side of the road, tipped and started to somersault further down the slope. Norton continued screaming. There was a splash as the overturned truck fell into the stream and quickly sank. Norton's scream rose higher, louder, gurgled, and died. Peace and quiet filled the valley. The sun shone and sparkled on the frozen slopes.

'Wonder where Dad is?' asked Idwal. 'It's gone five and there's no sign of him.'

'You hear the bollocking he got this morning from Michael. Shit, let's 'ope we've still got a roof over our 'eads. Anyway, knowing Dad he's probably off doing some poxy deal. He was talking to Larry Whelks in the pub last week. You know, sort of quiet like so I expect there's something going on. Let's go down the boozer and see if he's there? I'm thirsty anyway.'

'Yea, right John, that's probably where he'll be. His trucks not here anyway. Come on, let's go for a pint.'

The two lads drove down into the village to the local pub.

'Dad's truck's not 'ere either,' said John, 'but isn't that Larry's old bus over there in the corner?'

'True, well away from the light so no one can see what he's got stashed away in the back. Crafty old sod is Larry, but don't you ever try and cross 'im. Like as not you'd end up being planted somewhere in one of his fields, without your top showing. Know what I mean?'

'Stop winding me up you silly bugger and let's get a pint in. We can ask Larry where Dad is inside.'

Pushing open the door the warmth and fug of the room rolled over Idwal and John. As they jostled their way to the bar someone grabbed both of them by the scruff of their necks. 'Just the two gits I wanted to see. Now where's that no-good shit of a father of yours? I've just lost two hundred quid thanks to him and I need to sort him out.'

'Jesus Larry, give over. Let us go you dense prat. We can't talk with our collars cutting into our throats. Thanks.' Idwal shook himself and adjusted the back of his shirt and jacket. 'Give us a chance to get a pint in at least, then we'll come and talk with you.'

'I'm right behind you sunshine. You get your pint and you'll talk all right.'

'Larry, hold up mate,' said John, 'we were going to ask you the same question.'

'Don't give me that crap,' growled Larry. 'I've been waiting since yesterday for your dad and I 'aint seen hair or hide of him, but I'll bet you two have. Now where is he?'

'Larry let's take these glasses over to the corner and sit down for Christ's sake.'

When Idwal and John sat down with their pints Larry loomed over them. 'Has the old bugger done a runner then? Don't you two fuck me about. I'll find him, don't you worry.'

'Well that's good then,' said Idwal, ''cos we don't know where he is. He was at work at half seven this morning and then we all went off to work like. We never see him all day. He wasn't at the cottage when we came home and we came down here to find him. When we saw your truck in the yard we thought he'd be here or you'd know. Straight up Larry, that's the truth, ain't it John?'

'Fucking right,' said John, sipping on his pint, 'we're looking for him too Larry. Anyway, why are you so uptight? What's the silly bugger done to you, and what's this about two hundred quid?'

'Never you mind about the money, just where is the old bugger? Shit, he really let me down with an easy deal. Now I'll have to go and find some other source.'

'What was he trying to sell?' asked Idwal, 'bloody bet it wasn't his in the first place. It never is with Dad.'

'He had some fence posts. Said they were surplus to requirements and Sir Anthony had told him to sell them off.'

'In his dreams,' said John, 'he probably did some careful mis-counting.'

'Shut up you fool,' said Idwal, 'you want the whole pub to know? Christ, you and your big mouth sometimes. Still, that gives me an idea.'

'Well you go and find the silly old sod for me then. When you find him tell him I'm coming to sort him out. I need some compensation and I'll get it too.' Larry pushed his way out of the pub.

'What idea Idwal? Where do you think he is?'

'Come on, let's go and see whether I'm right. He's probably tried too hard and hurt himself. He's getting beyond it you know. Loading fence posts will be too much for him.'

'Loading what fence posts, where?' asked John.

'You'll see. Just go and get the car started. I bet I know where he is. Maybe it's just the truck that's broken down, although he would have walked out in that case. No, the silly old bugger's tried one job too many.'

A loud pounding on the front door startled the household. 'Who's that at the front door in such a state?' said Anthony, looking across the fireplace to Sylvia.

'Anthony if it's Michael let him in. I think he may have had time to calm down since this morning.'

'Sylvia, Michael wouldn't knock, he'd just come barging in, even if his tail was between his legs. Yes Meredith, who is it at the door?'

'It's Mr. Ferris's two sons sir, and very agitated they are.'

'Well show them into the hall Meredith and I'll be right out.'

'Certainly sir.'

'Whatever do Idwal and John want at this hour, and in such a commotion?'

'I don't know dear,' said Sylvia, 'but hadn't you better go and find out?'

'Sir Anthony, Sir Anthony, it's Mr. Michael's Landrover sir, it's upside down in the stream below the larch plantation.'

'And he's still inside it sir.'

'What, what are you saying? Hold up a moment, let's slow down and take it step by step. You say Michael's Landrover is in the stream below the new cutover.'

'Yes sir.'

'And Michael's still inside it?'

'Yes sir.'

'How do you know this?'

'Sir that doesn't matter. We need help to get Mr. Michael out. He might be alive and trapped inside the vehicle. It's too dark without torches and we need rope and another lorry to roll it over.'

'Fine, I understand. I'm coming at once. Go and call on Freddie, Peter Buckley, Harry Thomas, they're close by, and call at Enrico's on your way out. Enrico can come up here and get the five-ton lorry. The others can go in the minivan. Tell Enrico where to go. I'll call the garage for a tow truck. That'll help right the Landrover. I'll follow as soon as the tow truck arrives. Now go.'

The two lads took off to their car and sped away. Anthony went to the telephone in the hall and called the garage. Taffy Williams said he'd be up at the Manor as fast as he could. Sylvia came out into the hall. 'What was all the commotion?' she asked. 'It obviously wasn't Michael come begging for forgiveness?'

'Sylvia, brace yourself love.'

'What is it Anthony? What's happened? Is it Michael?'

'The Ferris boys found Michael's Landrover down in the stream below the old larch plantation. We've just finished cutting there.'

'Yes I know where Anthony but what's Michael's Landrover doing in the stream? Is he hurt? Why didn't they just help him out up to the road and bring him back here?'

'The Landrover was upside down Sylvia, and Idwal thinks Michael is still inside.'

'No, no, not Michael,' gasped Sylvia.

'Look love, I've got to go. Taffy's here with the tow truck and I've got to show him where to go. With the tow truck we will be able to winch the Landrover out of the stream.'

'I'm coming too Anthony. He's my son. I'm coming.'

Sylvia rushed to the hall cupboard and grabbed a coat and boots. She thrust a hat on her head and pulled gloves out of the box. The box tumbled to the floor.

'Shit,' she said uncharacteristically.

'Sylvia, let them stay there. We've got to go.'

On the road through the larch cutover the crew had fixed two spotlights and turned the minivan to point down towards the stream. Idwal and John were already down by the Landrover along with Freddie and Peter Buckley. Taffy backed the tow truck across the track. With Enrico Taffy tied a cable from the front of the truck up around one of the cut stumps. A couple of metal wedges held the cable from slipping off. Taffy reversed the tow truck to tighten this cable. Once he was happy that the truck was secure he released the cable from the winch at the back of the truck and walked it down the slope towards the stream.

'He's still in there,' shouted Idwal.

'But is he moving?' whispered Sylvia, 'Michael, Michael, what have you done?'

Enrico stood by the winch on the tow truck waiting to hear from Taffy. Carefully Taffy secured the cable to the Landrover with the help of the other lads. Freddie slipped and nearly fell under the Landrover but Peter grabbed him by the collar. 'Easy does it lad. Don't go too fast. We'll get him out.'

The winch started and the tension in the cable increased. The tow truck slipped a little and the restraining cable at the front went dead taut. Everyone paused. At Taffy's signal Enrico re-engaged the clutch and the Landrover moved. Slowly the cable pulled the Landrover's nose onto the bank of the stream and eased it uphill. A pile of fence posts fell out of the back and trundled away downstream. As soon as the truck was clear of the streambed Idwal rushed to the side to open the doors and tried to yank it open.

'Careful lad. It's not safe yet. It might slip and swing against you.' Water streamed out of the vehicle. When it was completely clear of the stream and up on the bank Taffy walked to the driver's side. Upside down it was hard to open the door but eventually Taffy succeeded. More water spilled out across his feet.

Sylvia rushed down the slope as fast as she could, partly sliding and partly jumping. 'Let me see,' she cried, 'let me see.'

'It's Norton Ferris marm, not Michael. It's not your son.'

Anthony Lord came quickly down the slope to be beside his wife.

'But what was Ferris doing in Michael's Landrover? Ferris knows that that is Michael's vehicle. He's got his own truck. And what were those fence posts doing sitting in the back?' Anthony asked. 'Idwal, can you explain what your dad is doing here?'

'He's dead, he's dead for Christ sake and all you can worry about is why he's in Michael's bloody Landrover. Let the dead lie in peace. John cover his face, the poor old bugger. Give him some dignity.'

'There'll have to be an inquiry,' said Sylvia practically. 'I'll go back to the house and call the police. Somebody did check that he was dead?' she asked.

'Aye marm, I did,' said Taffy quietly. 'Mr. Ferris is dead.'

'I'll stay here at the scene Sylvia while you go and telephone for the police. They won't want us to move anything. Okay lads. Thanks for all you've done. Idwal, John, I'm sorry and I apologise for speaking like I did. I'm sorry for your loss and we'll sort this out as soon as possible. Why don't the rest of you go back up to the road and take yourselves home. I'll be at the office first thing in the morning to tell you what happens next.'

'I'm staying,' said Idwal, 'and you too John. I want to find out what happened. Something's not right here.'

'That's fine,' said Anthony, 'but don't touch anything or move anything. In fact, why don't we all go back up to the road and wait there. Taffy, we'll have to keep your truck here until the police let us move the Landrover. Sorry about that but you know what forensics experts are like.'

'Too true Sir Anthony,' said Taffy, 'let's hope there are no other accidents anywhere tonight then. I'll go back with your wife if that's all right?'

'Fine Taffy. I'll be along later Sylvia, after the police have come and taken over the site.'

Slowly the group climbed back up to the forest road. The forest lorry and the minivan drove away and Anthony and the two Ferris sons sat on the side of the tow truck. A starry quiet returned to the valley as the three men pondered what would happen next.

Michael had left the house that Tuesday morning after storming out on his parents and gone to the Company offices but he couldn't settle into anything constructive. Most of the staff there was deeply engrossed in whatever work they were doing and Michael couldn't get any longterm response from any of them. It seemed as if the word had already got there about Saturday night's debacle. Michael decided that keeping a low profile might be better for a while but he had to win some greater control of the Company somehow.

With nothing really better to do Michael spent the afternoon at the races. Steeplechase races were exciting to watch as a rule and Michael had better than average luck with the jockeys. He placed his bets as usual with Dicksons. 'Trying to get some of your money back eh Mr. Lord? Doing a bit of New Year recouping?'

'Well the punters have got to win some of the time Larry, otherwise you'd get exhausted trying to get Mr. Dicksons money back. I'll bet some of your regulars don't always pay on time?'

'True Mr. Lord. Why, that little rat of yours Ferris is due a visit soon. He's pushing his luck as usual but I'll find him, never you worry.'

Michael didn't say anything, especially as Ferris might be down the road soon and harder to find than Larry Thomas thinks.

A couple of pints and some useful wins eased Michael's frame of mind and he decided that going to Danielle's would be a much better idea than another fight at Fotheringham Manor. Michael drove slowly to the caravan after a final couple of pints when the races were over.

'Ssh, he's asleep Michael. He's just gone down. Do you want a bite to eat?'

'Mmm,' said Michael, 'that's the best offer I've had all day. Which part would you like me to start on first?'

'Well why don't you start at the top and work your way down,' murmured Danielle as she rubbed her slinky body up against Michael. 'I've had a boring day and I could do with some R&R.'

'And what form of R&R is on the menu tonight?' asked Michael as he slipped off his shoes.

'How does Randy and Raunchy grab you?'

'I'll have lots of the first and smotherings of seconds.'

Through all the chitter chatter Michael had succeeded in slowly peeling Danielle's clothes off her body. Danielle helped with wriggling and twisting under Michael's hands. He held her away from him and looked.

'You're right,' he said, 'randy and raunchy, but o so very delectable, truly good enough to eat.' He pulled her closer and slid his tongue between her lips. Slowly, so slowly he rolled his tongue gently around the inside of her mouth and gradually sucked on her tongue. Danielle's fingers unbuttoned Michael's shirt and she rubbed her sensitive breasts against the smoothness of his chest. She stabbed her own tongue two or three times into Michael's mouth and he pursed his lips so it was more difficult to penetrate. He felt his pants being pushed down over his thighs and suddenly tensed up straight as Danielle dug her sharp nails into his buttocks. She rubbed against him, thrust her tongue into his mouth and clung to him with her claws.

'Christ, you get vicious lady.'

'But I can tell you like it,' she whispered in his ear, and slowly ran her tongue around the outside rim and at the same time her fingers pulled the skin hard backwards on his responding penis. In a swift but sensuous movement she slipped down until she could gently slide her pursed mouth over the swollen purple head. Both hands now held the shaft pulling the skin backwards and letting the head throb. She slid it back almost out of her mouth and ran her white teeth sharply over the sensitive skin. Using her thumbs to push it up she let her tongue slide along the complete underside whilst rubbing the head against her cheek. Without any apparent change in pace the fingers gripped tighter, the nails turned inwards and her teeth were back on the swollen head. Hard, sharp, demanding.

Michael gasped. He pushed his hands into her short curly hair, down over her head and lifted her up by her ears. His lips found hers and he slid his arms around her back, down and under her buttocks. Lifting her she slid her legs around his waist and let Michael support her with her arms around his neck. Parting her thighs widely she pressed her pelvis against his stomach and rode up and down. 'Fuck me Michael, fuck me. Randy and raunchy.' Danielle let her pelvis drop and she engulfed Michael's penis. With her arms around his neck she continued her wild ride. Michael dug his fingers firmly into Danielle's buttocks and drove as wildly as she did. The rutting continued for a moment before both of them exploded and mutually slid to the floor.

'That was only the first course,' she whispered. 'We'll have dessert later, after some relaxation.' Danielle slipped away and was back a moment later with a couple of joints. 'I scored these off some jerk in the village over New Years.'

'Off Tom Daley?' asked Michael.

'Shit I don't know. I didn't ask any names. I just wanted some good grass. Draw deeply Michael, it's going to be a long night. You said you were hungry.'

Michael lay back and enjoyed the sensation of the grass. 'Yerba Buena,' he muttered.

'What's that Michael?'

'Mexican for good grass, and the name of a West Coast band some time back in the sixties. Cool name really as it does mean good grass, whatever you think grass is.'

'You been with that Californian bitch again with all that west coast shit?'

'All done and dusted princess. Now, what was there for dessert?'

'I'd better make sure your spoon is strong enough to dip into the pudding before you go looking for your dessert.' Danielle slithered down Michael's body and found a creamy half limp appendage. 'This might take a while,' she said up the length of Michael's body.

'Well I'll just have to have a drop of milk to strengthen me up then,' smiled Michael, 'and I know just the place.' Quickly he spun himself around and let his tongue glide up Danielle's warm silky inner thigh. 'I've found some juices already,' he murmured, and he slid his hands up under Danielle's buttocks and half lifted her on top of him. He ran his hands up her back and rubbed his thumb firmly down her vertebrae. As Danielle slid his responding penis into her mouth tasting her own juices she felt Michael's tongue licking between her labia. Michael responded quicker than she thought and Danielle felt her buttocks being parted and Michael's tongue flicking over her clitoris. His penis pushed further up into her mouth as Michael eased himself further up her body and his tongue now was reaming the slit between her labia and finally sliding slickly up inside her. She could feel him sucking and slithering his tongue inside her at the same time. She moved quickly and was kneeling over Michael's head with her thighs against his ears. Flattening her thighs out she could let Michael's tongue go as deep into her as possible. Aggressively she seized Michael's penis and pulled the skin back hard. The head looked up at her purple and throbbing. She slid her nail down the narrow slit on the top and felt Michael react. Grinding her pelvis harder over Michael's face she slid her hands down to the base of his penis and gently rolled his testes round in the scrotum. Using the sweat off Michael's thighs she slid her fingers further back and gently pushed a finger inside him. Michael bucked and his hands pulled harder on her buttocks as he tried to get his tongue even further inside her. Danielle quickly moved her self into an upright position while still keeping one hand on Michael's stiff penis and the other finger inside him. Two three four five quick movements and she came all over his tongue, his lips, and his mouth. Her juices ran all over Michael's face as she rolled her thighs and slid and slipped all over him. Leaning forward again she engulfed his rampant penis in her mouth and pushed her fingers deep into his rectum. Hot creamy juices dripped from her body onto Michael.

Pulling out her fingers Danielle found herself suddenly spun round on her knees with Michael behind her. He pushed her head down onto the floor of the caravan and pulled her thighs wide apart. His excited penis slid down her back and between the cleft in her buttocks. Knowing what was going to happen Danielle slid one of her hands behind and grabbed Michael's cock. She guided it into her rectum and felt the passion as it pressed up inside her. With one hand on her hard buttock Michael's other hand came smoothly across her belly and reached for Danielle's hand. He grasped the fingers and pushed them down between her legs. Folding his hand over hers he pushed her fingers deep inside her wet vagina. Once he had held her hand there for a moment and had her start to masturbate he moved his hand back so both of them were hard on her buttocks. Danielle felt him bend up straight and hold more firmly onto her. Demandingly, possessively he drove his penis deep inside her and watched as she masturbated at the same time.

Danielle knew that men take longer to come the second time and so she relaxed into a full body rhythm and worked with Michael. At this time he seemed to be oblivious to all things except a demanding urge to dominate, to possess, to have. Michael's breath grew louder and his thrusts more forceful. Danielle reached her hand back to Michael's and pulled his fingers around her front. She thrust them deep inside herself and worked his fingers in and out of her vagina. They slid and rubbed. Pushing her face deeper into the pillow on the floor she reached her other hand under her crotch and Michaels. With some sensual thrusts she jammed two fingers hard up Michael's anus and the pair of them exploded in an expulsion of juices.

Danielle gently eased herself from under Michael and laid his body quietly down on the floor. She got up and found a couple of rugs and laid them over him. Lifting his head slowly she managed to slide a pillow underneath. Silently she padded back down the length of the caravan and checked that all was well with little Anthony. Once the caravan was quiet Danielle sluiced some soap and water over her hands and between her legs. As quietly as she could she cleaned her teeth and smiled as she licked some of the juices off her mouth. Sometimes randy and raunchy can be good for you she thought. After one last check that Michael was sleeping soundly Danielle climbed up into her bed and eased the covers over her body. Sleep tight little men she thought. Danielle will look after you.

Michael woke up early on Wednesday morning feeling a new man. After a quick coffee he told Danielle he would be in the Forest Office of the Estate all morning, catching up on some paperwork and seeing how he could fire Norton Ferris. Soon after seven o'clock Michael drove off to the Forest Estate office and was surprised to see Sergeant Penross sitting in the office with his dad. 'Come in Michael and sit down. The sergeant here has some questions for you.'

'What's going on? Where is everybody? Why hasn't Ferris got the crew organised? It's gone seven thirty already. Dad I told you to fire him, the lazy bugger.'

'Mr. Lord, can you describe your whereabouts yesterday please, starting at this time yesterday morning?'

'Whatever for? Won't someone tell me what is going on?'

'Michael, just answer the sergeant's questions. It's perfectly straightforward so let's keep it simple shall we?'

'Well Mr. Lord, at seven thirty you were here I believe? Carry on from there sir.'

'Yes, sure, I was here around half past seven. I saw Ferris send off the crew and then I had a quick word with him.'

'Saying what sir?'

'That I had something else to do that morning but that I would be about the forest later so he needn't think he could skive off for the day. I also told him that I had told my Dad to fire him. After that I drove up to the House and had a blazing row with my parents.'

'Leaving Fotheringham when sir?'

'I suppose soon after eight. It was a short and blunt shouting match sergeant and I drove off to the Company offices in town. I was there most of the morning and several of the staff saw me. Ask any of them if it's important.'

'We will Mr. Lord.'

'There was nothing much for me to do at the offices and so I went to the steeplechase races around noon. I had a couple of pints, a few bets and another couple of pints because I had a good winner. Oh, yes, I talked with that fat git Larry Thomas if you must know. He'll remember me 'cos I won some money and did him out of his playing the heavy act.'

'That takes us to when sir?'

'Well, the last race was at four o'clock. I had a winner there too so I had one for road and drove back to a friend's caravan in the village here. Must have been there about six I suppose. Spent the night in the caravan and came here this morning.'

'This friend sir, the one with the caravan; has a name sir?'

'Yes sergeant, but do you really need to know that?'

'Michael, stop messing about and tell the sergeant who. Actually, I'd be interested to know where you spent last night too, and the previous couple of nights.'

'Her name is Danielle Made. She's a friend of mine from London.'

'Yes sir. Yes, we know Miss Made. Thank you sir, you've been most helpful.'

The sergeant closed his notebook and rose slowly out of the chair. 'By the way sir, the reason I'm here is that Mr. Ferris died yesterday, here on the Forest.'

'How, how did this happen? What was he doing?'

'Michael we're not sure yet exactly what happened but Ferris was in your Landrover when a pile of logs crashed down and pushed him into the stream. The Landrover overturned and Ferris drowned inside. His sons found the Landrover and thought it was you inside. They came up to the House and we organised a rescue but we were too late. We were all very surprised, and your mother was very relieved when it turned out it wasn't you in the Landrover. That didn't lessen the shock and the pain for Idwal and John though. So, now you're more or less up to date.'

'Don't leave the area sir,' said Sergeant Penross as he left the office. 'We'll be in touch later Sir Anthony when we have some more information and some more questions. My officers are already taking statements from your employees sir but we should be finished around lunch time.'

'When can we retrieve the Landrover in the stream, and Mr. Ferris's body sergeant? I know Idwal and John will be anxious to get the funeral arrangements started.'

'The SOCO boys and the doctor have both been out to the site sir and the body has already been moved to the morgue for a post-mortem. They have kept the area taped off as a crime scene and the detectives from Bristol will tell me when the Landrover can be retrieved.'

'Thank you sergeant, just keep me posted.'

'Very good sir.' The sergeant drove away and Michael slumped back in his chair. 'Christ Dad, I thought we should fire him not get him killed.'

'Michael, don't be so stupid. It was a weird accident to be sure but the pile of logs was obviously unstable and the slopes yesterday morning were like glass so everything slid into the stream very easily. The strange thing is why was Norton Ferris in your Landrover?'

'What happened when you tried to pull it out?'

'Yes, the Bristol CID was bloody annoyed about that. Screaming and shouting that we shouldn't have moved it. I tried to explain that we had to try and get the body out. At that time we all thought it was you in the stream. Don't know how they think we could have got anyone out without pulling the Landrover out of the stream. Actually, that was quite tough, especially as there was a whole pile of fence posts in the back weighing it down. What were you doing moving fence posts in the Landrover anyway? I thought Enrico had brought out the posts for that cutover on the truck a couple of days ago.'

'There you might have found an answer,' said Michael, thinking over the scene. 'I'll bet you that precious Mr. Ferris was taking them somewhere else, for a bob or two in his pocket.'

'Possibly,' mused Sir Anthony, 'anyway I've got to go. I've got to go into the office today. You're staying here and sort out some work schedule for me for the forest crew. Ferris probably had some kind of workplan but God's knows where he would have put it. Find it Michael and sort something out.'

Anthony left and Michael sat back in the chair and thought. Normally on Tuesday I would have done that site inspection. The picky-minded Fisheries Habitat clown from the government was over before Christmas looking at that larch plantation before we cut it. Spun us that great cock and bull story about possible damage to the fish environment in the stream at the bottom. Then he insisted we inspect the culverts on the road: worried that if they got blocked up we could have a flash flood washing all the soil down into his precious fishey fishey habitat. So, everyone knew that I would be inspecting those culverts yesterday. And, thought Michael, no one but Ferris knew I wouldn't be in the forest all that morning and would be in my car. After that row with dad and mum I clean forget about the forest in my urge to put distance between us. So, people thought it was me in my Landrover. Interesting, but a rather insignificant attempt at mayhem muttered Michael. The chances of doing any serious damage were very small – the logs could have missed; could have just bumped the Landrover; could have pushed it down into the stream right way up: all very hit and miss but interesting nonetheless.

The telephone's loud ringing caused Michael to leap up out of his reverie. He snatched at the receiver, 'hello, hello, Michael Lord speaking,' he gasped into the mouthpiece while his brain was still going over the past machinations.

'Michael, Michael help me. They've got Anthony. You must come to the caravan now. Now Michael, now!'

'What, Danielle is that you? What's the matter? Where are you? Where are you ringing from? Who's got Anthony?'

After ten seconds Michael realised that he was talking into a dead phone. Danielle had rung off.

Quietly feet walked up to the caravan's door and took a look. The feet moved around the whole outside of the caravan tightening and locking a few things. Back at the door they clicked it open and stepped inside. All was very quiet. Quickly moving around the inside a similar check was made. At the door there was a fluid series of motions and a couple of quick tests. All seemed to be in order. The feet moved outside and down the little steps. Carefully the door was closed and just as quietly the feet walked away.

Danielle drove into the village around nine o'clock with Anthony sitting on the front seat beside her. He was cheerful and laughing this morning all dressed up in coat, scarf and knitted hat. He and his mother played a game as Danielle drove up to the village general shop and parked.

'Now I won't be long sweet. Just you play with teddy while I get us some food.' Danielle got out and closed her door. She waved as she stepped around onto the pavement and crossed to the front door of the shop. The bell rang as she went in and the door closed.

A non-descript grey car drove slowly down into the village and parked in front of Danielle's, just out of sight of the shop windows. People in the car came over to see Anthony and waved. They opened the door and said 'hello Anthony. Look what we've got for you.' They lifted him out and he smiled up at them. They all laughed together. Back in the grey car they quietly drove away, leaving a note on Danielle's steering wheel.

'Danielle, this is a pleasure to see you this morning,' said Mrs. Larkin, 'and how is that lovely little lad of yours?'

'He's fine thanks Mrs. Larkin, and so am I. But, how are you today? Does the cold hurt your hands with the arthritis?'

'Not as much as the damp does dear, thanks for asking though. I've been looking through your order and I've got some questions because I don't have some of the things you're asking for but I may have some alternatives. Is that okay dear if we take a minute or two?'

'Yes that's fine. I do need to get most of those things if I can. I'm trying to do something special for Michael, as a surprise.'

'And how is Mr. Michael?' asked Mrs. Larkin. 'Actually, talking about Mr. Michael did you hear what happened to his Landrover yesterday up at the Manor? It was a dreadful accident. Well, shocking really and that awful man Mr. Ferris ended up dead. Never did like the man, or his two sons. Surly people with no manners if you know what I mean. Always demanding this and demanding that. Did my best to be friendly like. You know running a shop you have to be friendly with all sorts. You feel all right love? You look awful shaky.'

'What accident Mrs. Larkin?'

'Oh I'm sorry dear, I do go on so once I've got started. Well, as I heard it Mr. Ferris was driving Mr. Michael's Landrover, doing something dodgy I heard. Anyway, somehow a great pile of logs comes smashing down and knocks the Landrover, complete with Mr. precious Ferris into the stream. As luck would have it the Landrover overturns and Mr. Ferris ends up drowning. The police are all over Fotheringham this morning I hear.'

'I've got to go Mrs. Larkin. I'll come back another time.' Danielle rushed out of the shop and jumped into her car. 'We've got to go and see Michael Anthony. We've got to.....Anthony, Anthony, where are you?'

Frantically Danielle turned round in her car seat and looked into the back seat. Turning round with her hand on the wheel she accidentally sounded the horn and that made her jump. Looking at her hand Danielle suddenly noticed the note. She almost ripped it in half as she opened it.

WE HAVE ANTHONY. WE WILL DO HIM NO HARM
DO EXACTLY AS WE SAY. WE ARE WATCHING YOU
TELEPHONE MICHAEL IMMEDIATELY FROM THE BOOTH
TELL HIM TO GO TO THE CARAVAN NOW
STAY BY THE PHONE WE ARE WATCHING YOU NOW!!

'Bastards, bastards,' cried Danielle thumping the steering wheel, 'my baby, my precious baby. Michael help me, help me please.' Sobbing Danielle got out of the car and went to the telephone booth just by the shop. Money was sitting obvious on the shelf by the phone. Still shaking Danielle lifted the receiver, pushed in the coins and started to dial.

'Michael, Michael help me. They've got Anthony. You must come to the caravan now. Now Michael, now!' She hung up and slowly slid down to the floor of the booth. People in the car up the road watched to see what would happen next.

Michael rushed out of the forest office and wrenched his car door open. Jumping into the seat he rammed the key into the ignition nearly snapping it off in the process. Violently Michael slammed the stick into first and a shower of gravel sprayed everywhere as Michael spun the car away to the village. He raced down the Fotheringham Manor driveway, something he knew would make his dad furious but what the fuck thought Michael. Someone is trying to bugger me about. Taking the back roads Michael made quick time to the lane leading to the caravan site. The caravan was parked in an open field up against a hedge and fence line. Michael raced the car up the hill to the caravan's door. There was no sign of Danielle or her car. Without thinking much about it Michael scrambled up the steps and wrenched open the door. All was very quiet.

Michael slowly poked his head in the door but couldn't see anything or anybody. Bunching up his legs Michael exploded into the narrow entranceway of the caravan slamming the door behind him. 'Got you,' he shouted, 'where are you you bastard? Show your face.' He stormed up the length of the caravan through the kitchen area and up to the bedroom. Silence greeted him. 'What the fuck's going on?' said Michael to himself. 'Danielle, you'd better not be taking the piss girl.'

In his acrobatic leaping and shouting Michael didn't notice the quiet noise of an engine or feel the slight bump as something nudged against the caravan. However, Michael did hear the engine noise as it revved up a little. Come to see me have you muttered Michael? Well we'll see just who you are shall we? He chased back to the door to greet the new arrival. The motor revved a little more and the caravan lurched forwards. 'Shit, what's going on?' said Michael as he twisted the door handle. It came off in his hands and the caravan moved some more. Michael kicked at the door but nothing happened. The caravan gathered speed. Michael ran back down the length of the caravan but all the windows were shut tight. The caravan was bouncing about quite a lot by this time. Back at the door Michael tried to push the door open with his legs but there wasn't room in the narrow hallway to get any purchase for his back. The little toilet cubicle cut down on the width of the hallway. The caravan was moving quite quickly at this time and bouncing around on the uneven field. 'The toilet,' said Michael, 'the toilet!' He pulled open the toilet stall door and looked up. 'Thank God for small mercies' he said. Standing on the throne Michael could prise open the sort of skylight for aerating the space. He thrust up an arm and wriggled a shoulder through the gap. It was tight and his clothing got stuck. The caravan did a major lurch up on two wheels and then crashed back down again and continued rolling downhill. Frantically Michael climbed down off the throne and started stripping as fast as he could. Jacket, shirt, trousers, pants, even shoes all fell onto the floor and Michael scrambled back onto the throne and pushed his arm through again. One shoulder through, twist, dip, other shoulder, then arm and push, push for Christ's sake. His hips scraped cruelly at the plastic coaming and stuck. Michael could see the speed the caravan was going now and fear spurred him on to a greater effort. Pushing upwards as hard as he could he dragged his hips through the gap leaving smears of blood in the process. With one final kick and push he was out and despite the speed Michael leapt off the top of the caravan. He hit the ground with a crash that partly knocked the wind out of him and he gashed his leg on a sharp slab of rock. Turning round Michael watched the caravan suddenly tip up on end and then disappear. Seconds later there was the sound of smashing matchwood and then silence. 'The quarry,' Michael whispered, 'over the edge into the quarry.'

Danielle jumped up and banged her head on the telephone booth ledge as the receiver jangled loudly above her. Holding a hand to her bruised head she lifted the phone off the hook and said 'yes.'

'Listen, listen very carefully. Get in your car NOW. Drive to London. Anthony will be under the clock at Victoria Station at ten o'clock tomorrow morning, unharmed. Leave now! Do not return here ever again. Repeat where and when.'

'Under the clock at Victoria Station at, at, oh yes, at ten o'clock tomorrow morning. But what about Michael? What about my things?'

'Danielle, ten o'clock Victoria Station. Michael is no longer any concern of yours.' The receiver clicked as the line was cut off. Still dazed Danielle staggered out of the telephone booth and over to her car. 'Ten o'clock Victoria Station, under the clock, Anthony.'

She closed the car door and fumbled for the keys. Without looking she drove into the village street, narrowly missing a cyclist and two kids crossing the road. She drove slowly up the hill towards the crossroads where she had to turn left to reach the London Road. Driving on instinct she slowed near the junction and stopped at the Stop sign, looking to her right to check for oncoming traffic. The door on the passenger side of her car opened and Anthony was there. 'Go,' said a voice, 'now go.' The door closed and Danielle turned left and drove away towards London.

Wearing only socks and scowl on his face Michael slowly stumbled up the sloping field to where he had left his car. The clear blue sky held a sun that shone down on Michael's nudity but it was still frosty. 'Christ it's cold,' muttered Michael. Still in shock and somewhat bruised and battered Michael reached his car. 'Shit, shit, shit,' he shouted to the world from near the top of the hill, 'my car keys are in my jacket pocket. Shit, shit, shit!' Suddenly Michael convulsed with laughter. He almost fell over as spasms of laughter and choking racked his body. 'Be prepared, that's the Boy Scouts marching song, be prepared as through life you march whatever,' sang Michael. 'The precious little spare my lovely, always be prepared.' Michael pulled the spare key from its taped place under the dashboard and started the car. Half laughing and half shaking Michael drove back to Fotheringham Manor.

Halfway across the hall on her way to the staircase Sylvia stopped and peered at her son. Michael was partway up the stairs wearing his socks; just his socks.

'Is this some new office attire Michael, or is there a more logical explanation?'

Somewhat abashed Michael covered his genitalia with his hands.

'Michael, you've nothing I haven't seen before,' laughed Sylvia. 'Remember I did feed you and change you you know.'

'Somebody tried to kill me Mum,' mumbled Michael, leaving his hands where they were.

'But they left you your socks I see,' said Sylvia.

'It's not a joke Mum, somebody tried to kill me. I was locked in a caravan and it went over the edge into the quarry and smashed to pieces.' Michael was waving his hands and arms about by this time and suddenly realised what he was doing and quickly shot his hands back over his crotch.

'How about you add a little to your wardrobe and come down and tell me. You're not making a lot of sense Michael. Dressed like that it's hard to take you seriously.'

Sylvia turned and went back to the drawing room. Michael continued up to his room and crashed on his bed.

Back downstairs a clothed Michael sat and told his mother what had happened. Sylvia didn't say anything the whole time. At the end she merely said, 'you need to talk this over with your father tonight. In fact the three of us will talk this over. I'll say nothing now. By the way, you had a letter today marked URGENT. It's on the hall table. I've got some things to do Michael. I suggest you collect the letter and we'll talk this evening.' She got up and walked out of the room.

Michael picked up the letter from the hall table and slit it open with his thumb. Reading it he let the envelope drop from his fingers. 'Impossible, that's fucking impossible. It's got to be some kind of joke.' Quickly and somewhat furtively Michael looked around but there was nobody in sight. Picking up the envelope Michael quietly raced up to his room to reread this impossible letter.

> Dear Sir,
>
> Your Account now stands at 21,360 pounds, in arrears.
>
> We expect payment to balance this account by Monday, January 13th.
>
> Yours sincerely,
>
> S. Dicksons
>
> Turf Accountant

Attached to the letter were two closely spaced sheets of computer printout. They listed the dates of the various bets that Michael had placed and the resultant debit or credit. Net result he owed 21,630 pounds. But I've never made all those bets. Shit, they go back to the beginning of December. It's impossible.

There was a knock on his door. 'Come in,' cried Michael and Meredith entered the room. 'There's a telephone call for you Mr. Michael. Shall I say you're coming or are you unavailable?'

'I'll be right down Meredith. I'll take it.'

'Michael Lord here.'

'Got Mr. Dicksons letter then my Lord?' asked Larry Thomas smugly. 'Not doing as well as you thought you were just yesterday?'

'Not my mistake you fat turd,' spluttered Michael. 'I didn't make those bets and you know it.'

'All placed from your account; everything kosher our end. You bet, you lose, you pay; very simple procedure. Now Mr.Dicksons wants you to pay. You know the drill. Anything over five thousand pounds and we send a letter, anything over ten thousand and I come knocking. Seeing as how you are a regular customer, and a Lord to boot, we've only sent the letter. Perhaps you want me to come knocking?'

'I can't find 20,000 quid in four days.'

'21,630 pounds my Lord, by the end of Monday if you please.' The line went dead.

Sitting up on his bed Michael went through a necessary series of activities in his mind. After lunch he set his plan in motion. Top priority was retrieving his car keys, wallet and other vital stuff from the quarry. Thank god it was disused and there was no pool. Michael found this easier than expected and that was one plus. Then he called the bank about the state of his account.

'Mr. Lord you are two hundred and thirteen pounds overdrawn sir, but that is no real problem as you have an overdraft policy of five hundred pounds and it is only the eighth of the month. As long as it balances by the end of January there is no issue at all sir. Is there anything else we can do for you today sir?'

'Uh., no, no thanks, two hundred and thirteen pounds you say?'

'Yes sir, overdrawn that is.'

Michael rang off. Shit, he thought, there is good news and bad news. Now I wonder where Danielle and Anthony are? Who's really playing silly buggers here? Where did she phone from because there was no telephone at the caravan so it had to be the village?

Michael drove down into the village and stopped outside the Post Office. He sat in the car and held his head in his hands. 'Who's the biggest gossip and busybody in the village?' he asked the world. 'It's got to be Dora Telford or Mrs. Larkin. We'll try the Post Office first.'

'No Mr. Michael sir, I've not seen Danielle for a couple of days. She comes in on Fridays usually as she gets some money from London every week. Don't know who it's from of course but it comes regular as clockwork. I'll look out for her though. Tell her you're looking for her if I see her.'

Striking out there Michael walked down to the village shop and pushed open the door. The bell jangled and Mrs. Larkin came bustling out from her back room. 'Just had my feet up for a quick cup of tea Mr. Michael; pretty quiet in the early afternoons it is so I thought I'd have a cuppa. Would you like one too dear, there's plenty more in the pot? Won't take a...'

'No thanks Mrs. Larkin. Have you seen Danielle today?'

'Yes dear, she was in earlier this morning. Bright as a lark she was when she came in; all cheerful and happy about something. She was muttering about last night I thought but she got really upset when I told her about the accident up at the Manor. You know Mr. Michael where your Landrover ended up in the stream and that Mr. Ferris drowned and all. Such a shock that was with poor Idwal and John having to find their dad that way. Of course, everyone thought it was you in the Landrover, seeing as it was yours like. Anyway Danielle..'

'Danielle what Mrs. Larkin? What did Danielle do when she heard about the accident?'

'Well she rushed out didn't she? She forgot all about her order and there were several things I had to talk to her about her order. She had some special things on there that I don't have. I needed....'

'Mrs. Larkin, where did Danielle go?'

'I was saying, I don't know Mr. Michael. She rushed out of the shop and jumped into her car. I heard the door slam.'

'And she drove away where?'

'That's the funny thing. I didn't hear her drive anywhere, not for a while anyway.'

'Could she have phoned, the booth's just there next door?'

'Er, maybe, I don't know like, but I didn't hear her drive away.'

'Because she telephoned me Mrs. Larkin and she was awfully upset. She was sobbing and crying.'

'Well she was pretty upset when she rushed out of here, what with your accident and all.'

'Was Anthony with her?' asked Michael, suddenly having another thought. 'Did she have him with her in the shop?'

'No, not as I remember. No, that's right, she didn't have him in the shop. I would have remembered because he always gets a sweet when they come in. Very partial to lemon drops is young master Anthony. He and his mum both like lemon drops.'

'Mrs. Larkin, please think for me, was Anthony in the car outside while Danielle was in here?'

'I couldn't say. I suppose so as she came in the car and she never went anywhere without him did she? So, he must have been in the car outside.'

'But she did eventually drive off you say. Which way did she go? Did she turn round and go back towards the caravan or did she go on through the village?'

'I don't know that Mr. Michael. I wasn't looking. I had other things to do in the shop, what with her order and the likes. I had other orders to make up too.'

'You're sure you didn't see which way she went?'

'Well, I did sort of peep out later on and I think she went up the hill towards the cross roads. Funny thing that her stopping to talk to the people at the top.'

'What people? Who did she talk to?'

'Couldn't see who they were from here could I? Was a couple of people though. Just as she stopped up at the Stop sign they opened her car door and spoke to her. Gave her something but I couldn't see what. Anyway, they were gone by the time I looked back.'

'And which way did Danielle turn at the Stop sign?'

'Well left of course.'

Michael left Mrs. Larkin pondering over the past conversation as he drove his car up the hill through the village to the Stop sign. He too stopped and glanced to the right. Slowly he turned left and followed the road and soon reached the junction with the London Road. 'So maybe, maybe she's left for the bright lights again. Just have to wait and see whether she calls, won't I?' said Michael to himself and turned to drive home.

Money, money, money, where are you when I need you? Who to tap next? Maybe a better question is where to tap next? Perhaps it is time to unearth Daniel's precious secret? Michael opened the drawer to his desk and gently prised up the little false bottom. He took out the copies he had made of Daniel's maps. Somewhere up on the north end of the Estate Daniel had said he went with Enrico. This shouldn't be too hard to find.

First of all Michael drove down to the Forest Estate office. There was no one home. This was expected as he was supposed to be drawing up a work schedule for his dad, and his dad had gone to the Company offices for the day. Michael went to the map cabinet and extracted a map covering the plantations at the northern end of the forest. Unfortunately the forest stand maps were only planimetric, with no contours, but Michael thought he could try and marry his crude map outline with the forest stands. Obviously if it was a cliff with a cave then there would be either a break in the forest or more likely it would be a plantation boundary. Tricky planting straight up a cliff thought Michael to himself with a smile. There were a couple of possibilities in matching the maps but Michael realised that he would have to check on the ground.

Driving the car up the slippery half-frozen forest tracks was a lot more difficult than Michael envisaged. He had to backtrack a couple of times when the rise was just too steep for the car. After another careful look at the map Michael found a compartment boundary that proved easier than the others. He reached a boundary fence and stopped the car. The ground rose steeply in front of him but there was no cliff. Michael turned east and carefully followed the fence line. Twice he slipped on the frozen ground and this further aggravated his already bruised body. A little more gingerly Michael descended and the ground to his left gradually became steeper and steeper until he was walking alongside a cliff. Stopping, he took another look at the crude diagram. 'The angles don't look right,' he said to himself. He went on a little further and the cliff started to get quite abrupt above him. 'No sign of any cave either.' After another fifty metres the cliff started to tumble down and looking ahead Michael could see the cliff peter out into a stone wall. 'Shit, obviously not here. Okay, back to square one and try further east. Maybe

I should have asked Enrico. Probably should have just told him to tell me where it is, seeing as it's mine anyway; part of the Lord estate.'

The sky clouded over a little and the shadows lengthened as Michael climbed back up to his car. His mood also turned cloudier as the rough frozen ground was difficult to walk over and now he stumbled more often, adding to his list of bruises and scrapes. 'Sod it,' said Michael, 'life's a bitch.' Fortunately the car started and Michael carefully turned round and slithered back down the rutted forest road. Back at the next possible junction he turned east and drove past two compartments before turning back north again. This track hadn't been used for some time and twice Michael bottomed out, almost leaving all four wheels in the air on the second time. Just as it started to turn to dusk Michael revved up a last rise. Two hundred metres further on the trees ended and Michael could see the ground rise up steeply in front.

Before he got out of the car he checked on the map to make sure he knew where he was. Michael knew his trees well enough to know exactly which plantation was beside him. Out of the car he turned and followed the northern edge of the trees along the rising land. Again the hillside steepened only this time much more quickly. Within one hundred metres the cliff was ten to fifteen metres high and curving left. Michael passed an old tree and before he realised it he had passed an opening in the cliff. Suddenly the cliff shape looked familiar and Michael looked again at the old crude map.

'Maybe baby, you're the one for me,' chanted Michael and he turned round to have another closer look at the cliff. The tree, of course the tree. The map shows a forked tree but the map's two hundred years old or more and the fork has long gone. It's now an old tree but you can see where the fork used to be, just where the tree bends sharply away from straight. So, if that's the tree where's the bloody cave? Don't tell me that it has disappeared after all this time? No, Daniel inferred that Enrico showed him but they didn't go in or something. So where the hell is the cave?

Walking around the tree Michael suddenly realised that the cave entrance was much smaller than he had imagined. The map had shown a large archway but that wasn't what was on the ground. There was a narrow slot just behind the tree and Michael wriggled into this immediately filling his face with dirt, dust and cobwebs. 'Shit and corruption. Nobody has been in here for a while.' Michael had had the good sense to bring a torch and he flicked it on and swung the beam about. Once inside the initial slot the space did open out to a larger chamber. Letting the beam delve into the depths the cave appeared to extend some way into the mass of the cliff. Up in the roof there were a few incipient stalactites and the floor was quite rough. Michael carefully eased himself more into the cave. There were two or three mounds, not really stalagmites on the cave floor. 'Step one,' said Michael to the cave, 'but where the hell is the Dragon's pile of stolen gold and jewels? In fact where is a jewel-finding Hobbit when you need one? What else did that precious map say about the cave?'

Flashing his torch on the map Michael noticed that there was a cross besides one of the mounds. 'So, "X" marks the spot my hearties. All we need now is an implement for digging, or a fucking spade. Definitely time for Step two, but not today. We shall return.' Michael turned and realised that the exit slit was not obvious. 'Jesus, it would make my day if I get stuck in a cave as well as a caravan. Ah, there it is. Out out.' With a quick wriggle Michael twisted his way out of the cave and stood beside the old tree again. Turning off the torch and not having night eyes Michael didn't see the movement further along the cliff. It took Michael a moment to be able to see now that the dusk had turned to night. He turned his torch back on and carefully picked his way alongside the cliff and back to his car. The shadow quietly followed him.

Sitting in his car Michael thought over what he had to do. 'Well first of all I need to clean up before I see mum and dad or they will ask all sorts of questions of where I have been. Then dad will want to know where the work schedule is. Maybe we can bluff that out with the events of this morning. Tomorrow we shall return for a little searching and maybe home free. Still, one step at a time.' Clear in his mind Michael drove home. Cleaned up and fed Michael felt he was in good form to talk with his parents.

Out in the forest Michael's shadow quietly walked out and into the village. The shadow placed several long distance phone calls and people on the other end of the phones started getting organised. Events were moving and action would soon be needed.

'Dad, I'm telling you, someone tried to kill me this morning. In fact, the more I think about it perhaps it was supposed to be me in my Landrover that ended up upside down in the stream.'

'Michael whatever are you talking about?' asked Sylvia.

'Mum, it was my Landrover; it was my schedule to stop and check the culverts on the road in the cutover. From the top of the cutover no one could see who was the driver. The driver's side would have been on the downhill side. My Landrover, crash, rollover, tip in the stream and drown – goodbye Michael!'

'Michael all that was an accident. The logs broke free from the retaining posts and with such a slippery surface they crashed the Landrover down to the bottom of the hill.'

'Very convenient accident I think.'

'Michael you're getting paranoid.'

'Maybe Mum but I wasn't paranoid this morning, I was bloody terrified. If I hadn't got out of the skylight I would have gone over the edge of the cliff and been matchwood.'

'Michael the police are looking at the caravan now. They haven't found anything suspicious.'

'Well it didn't start rolling of its own accord Dad. I heard an engine and felt a bump. Someone pushed me.'

'Michael all this is supposition, although you'd better go down to the Police Station tomorrow and make a statement, just the way you are describing it to us. The police are still investigating and until something positive comes up we'd better wait and see. By the way, your mother said you had an official looking letter marked URGENT come for you in the post this morning. What was that all about?'

'Nothing Urgent about it Dad: it was a practical joke from some friends in London.'

'Michael, the post mark wasn't London,' said Sylvia sharply, 'so try again.'

'Okay Mum, I'd promised someone at Bristol Uni I'd help with some programming project. I think they had a term paper to finish or something but I forgot with all the excitement of my birthday, New Years and everything else. The student was getting a little antsy.'

'Michael a student would have phoned, not written a letter.'

'Jesus, what is this, the bloody inquisition? Stuff this, I think I'm going to bed. It's been a bloody painful and exhausting day and a lot of sympathy I get. I'll take care of everything without relying on anyone as usual. Good night!'

Michael stormed out of the room and they heard his feet pound up the stairs. 'Do you know what was in the letter Sylvia?'

'I'm not sure Anthony. All I heard was Michael's first reaction and then he took it upstairs to his room I presume.'

'And his first reaction?'

'Impossible, that's fucking impossible,' was all I heard him say, but I thought I heard the telephone go soon afterwards. I don't know whom he was talking to but it didn't take very long. He went out very soon afterwards.'

'Yes, and not to the Forest Office to organise a work schedule as I requested, that I do know.'

'Anthony, you're going to have to hire a forester. This is all getting too much: neither you nor I are getting any younger and the work is becoming overwhelming.'

'Samantha will be home later in the summer my dear.'

'Anthony, if you think Samantha is going to help run the Estate think again. All she'll want to think about running will be boys, or knowing her, men! Now get real. We need an Estate Manager, now! And with that executive decision I think I too will go to bed.'

After a restless night pondering on his future options Michael decided that appearing to be doing some work might be a good idea. So he was down at the Forest Office by seven thirty to check that the forest crew knew what they had to do and see them off. Once that was done he sat down in the office and thought about a work schedule. Norton must have left some records behind and somewhere Michael thought there was an Annual Plan. The filing cabinets didn't appear to show any particular order and Michael resorted to a logical but painstaking process of starting at the front and working backwards. Halfway through the first drawer Michael found a plan of the forest with dates and notes on several of the compartments. He was trying to decipher this when the shrill note of the telephone made him jump and spill the files contents all over the floor.

'Shit, shit,' said Michael as he picked up the phone.

'Now that's not very polite I must say. Here I was about to tell you what an industrious lad you must be slaving away in the office already and all you can say is shit.'

'What do you want Mr. bloody Thomas. I'm in the middle of something important and you've just screwed it all up.'

'Not as much as I will screw you up Mr. Michael if you don't raise the dosh.'

'Hey, I'm working at it aren't I? Thought I heard you say Monday. Today's Thursday if you're dumb brain can handle more than one day at a time you thick prick.'

'Name-calling won't win you any friends, but this is just a gentle reminder that we'll be waiting. As they say in the movies "Have a good day".'

'Fuck off,' said Michael, but the line was already dead.

Over the next hour Michael scrambled together something resembling a schedule for the work crew over the next three months. There was enough work to cover the months until March when they would be starting to plant. Although Michael was no forester he was mathematically and logically minded and so scheduling was an easy matter for him and the pieces of the previous Annual Plan helped. Buried at the back of the file drawer was even a copy of the five-year Operating Plan and that contained a schedule of operations Compartment by Compartment. It wasn't very difficult to pull out the items for the next short time.

As soon as he had entered this into a spreadsheet on the computer Michael logged off and sat back for a moment's thought. Although there were several people Michael thought he could tap for funds there was no way he was going to raise twenty thousand pounds by Monday. Moreover, Michael didn't really want to rely solely on finding whatever was in the cave. It might not be a cashable item.

What was it that Tom Daley said thought Michael? Somebody was fiddling accounts? Tom can get into some useful systems, maybe he can find me some readies? The question was what did Michael have to trade? Michael mulled over what he had to hand. There was still some stuff left over from Sasha's visit, and Michael had some of Freddie's pills from last February. They had really done something to Bella's head he remembered. Still, Tom's not really into anything other than grass, but he can always trade. Michael eventually convinced himself that he could persuade Tom to find some cash, at least to tide him over the Monday deadline if all else failed. With that as a fall-back Michael took off on his own personal treasure hunt.

Back in the forest Michael retraced his tracks of yesterday afternoon. He quickly found his way back to the northern boundary and the edge of the cliff. Turning eastwards again Michael followed the cliff and there was the old tree. Sliding inside the slit in the cliff face Michael found himself back inside the cave again. He turned the torch onto the more detailed map and looked again at the few markings.

So the wriggly line is the line of the cliff and the indent is the cave perhaps? Inside the indent are two circles, well they look like circles and if this is supposed to be a plan then the circles could be the two mounds inside the cave. And if that is the case surmised Michael the box could be the "holy grail". I suppose it's worth a try anyway.

Michael had brought a pickaxe and a spade with him and he set these down on the rough floor of the cave and looked at the two mounds. Kicking the floor of the cave with his foot Michael thought he might be in for some serious labour. Not my style at all he thought to himself. He arranged the torch as best he could to see what he was doing and scratched out a likely area according to the map.

"Thunk" as the pickaxe chopped into the mixture of earth and rock on the cave's floor. The next hour saw Michael chipping away at the floor, scraping away the loose material with the spade, and generating a serious sweat. After two hours Michael had blistered hands, a torn shirt, and a very short temper. The hole was perhaps two feet deep and the work didn't look like it was going to get any easier. Tomorrow thought

Michael, tomorrow I'll come prepared and dig the bloody thing up. Disgusted with himself and his progress Michael wearily retreated back to his car on the forest track. He decided to clean up at the Forest Office before going back up to the Big House. As he pulled up in front of the office he could hear the telephone ringing.

If that's Larry Thomas again I'll throttle him Michael thought. He and I will have another little debt to settle after this is all over. 'Hello, Michael Lord here, who's calling?' There was a click, a muffled thud, and a very quiet voice said, 'Michael, we have it. We'll trade tonight at the cave at eleven o'clock.' The phone went dead in Michael's hands before he had a chance to think let alone talk. Michael sat down heavily in the office chair and slowly replaced the phone onto its receiver. Now who in the hell was that? Obviously something to do with the contents of the cave but what did they want to trade? The voice on the telephone was quick, quiet and not identifiable. Michael sat in the chair for a while and considered the options. Well he thought, nothing ventured nothing gained, but going prepared would be wise.

Back in the forest various parties were also getting prepared. There had been a meeting of the minds on several issues and now all were resolved on a simple course of action. A full moon rose in the east and started to bathe the forest in a lunar glow.

Armed with a shotgun Michael left the Big House at nine planning to be at the cave well before the scheduled eleven. Methinks I will have a look see who is planning to come tonight before I officially arrive. Quietly Michael drove back again to the northern edge of the forest and walked ten rows into the plantation. Walking very slowly and softly Michael moved parallel to the cliff's edge the one hundred or so metres to where he could just see parts of the large old tree outside the cave's entrance. Nothing stirred. Suddenly a nightjar glided over Michael's head and he started as if the bird was aiming for him and then there was another silence. Looking at his watch Michael noted it was just after nine thirty but there was no apparent movement in the forest. Very slowly Michael eased his way down the row of planted trees towards the cave's entrance. He gently pushed the branches away from him as he inched forwards. Still nothing broke the silence.

Standing at the slit of the cave's entrance Michael turned and scanned right and left. He couldn't see anything nor hear anything. He slipped inside the cave. Quiet. Darkness. He turned on his torch and played it over the cave's interior. Nobody. Over by his pile of earth and rock there had been fresh digging, more digging. In fact considerably more digging since he had left this afternoon. Moving cautiously forward Michael shone the torch over the broken earth and rock towards the hole. The hole was now much deeper. Down at the bottom of the hole was nothing: no box, no chest, no sack, no nothing. But, at the bottom of the hole was a rectangular outline that was deeper than Michael had dug, but it too was empty. Michael glanced at his watch. It was about ten. Time to retreat outside again and wait for his company. Noting the location of the exit Michael turned off his torch and inched his way over the rough floor to the slit in the wall. He stepped outside and almost fell over a chest placed just outside. Immediately Michael looked around but there was no one there. He crouched down beside the chest and slowly lifted the lid. The moonlight glittered on the contents and they silvered in the light as Michael ran his fingers through the coins. He stood up.

'Mine' was all he said as the bullet went though his head.

About the Author

John Osborn was born in 1939 in Ipswich England but grew up in the East End of London where he learnt to sail. In North Wales he graduated as a professional forester and rock climbed three days a week. After working as a field forester for three years in Australia John went to the University of British Columbia in Vancouver, BC for postgraduate studies and the Flower Power movement of the sixties. While working for thirty years for the Ontario Ministry of Natural Resources, both as a forester and as a systems analyst and authoring several technical papers John sailed competitively, climbed mountains and taught survival and winter camping. He finished his professional career with three years consulting in Zimbabwe, walking with the lions. Now retired, although working part-time at the local Golf Club, John lives with his wife in Kelowna BC where he hikes and x-c skis from his doorstep.

Printed in the United States
130899LV00001B/46/P

9 781434 395788